Robert Brown Borthwick

History of the Princess de Condé

Vol. 1

Robert Brown Borthwick

History of the Princess de Condé
Vol. 1

Reprint of the original, first published in 1872.

1st Edition 2023 | ISBN: 978-3-36815-925-2

Verlag (Publisher): Outlook Verlag GmbH, Zeilweg 44, 60439 Frankfurt, Deutschland
Vertretungsberechtigt (Authorized to represent): E. Roepke, Zeilweg 44, 60439 Frankfurt, Deutschland
Druck (Print): Books on Demand GmbH, In de Tarpen 42, 22848 Norderstedt, Deutschland

HISTORY

OF THE

PRINCES DE CONDÉ

IN THE

XVITH AND XVIITH CENTURIES,

TRANSLATED FROM THE FRENCH

OF

M. LE DUC D'AUMALE

BY

ROBERT BROWN BORTHWICK.

VOL. I.

LONDON:

RICHARD BENTLEY AND SON,

Publishers in Ordinary to Her Majesty.

1872.

LOUIS Ier DE BOURBON PRINCE DE CONDE NE EN 1530 TUE A JARNAC EN 1569.

Gravé par I. François, sous la direction de Henriquel Dupont,
d'après un dessin original de Janet.

PREFACE.

In submitting to the judgment of the public pages which are perhaps already yellowed by time, and which I have not even at hand as I write these lines, I might be tempted to offer some explanations; for seven years intervene between me and the day on which the printing of these two volumes began, and it is painful for an author to appear before the public *désheuré*,[1]—to use an expression of Cardinal de Retz.

But the circumstances which have caused this long delay are sufficiently well known; I will not recur to them.

I have not written, nor do I intend to write, an Introduction, because I have neither a new system to propound, nor have I the right, or wish, to put myself prominently before the reader. I was not influenced by party spirit when it occurred to me to profit by the numerous documents of which, through the kindness of the last of the Condés, I had become possessed, and to relate the lives of some of his most illustrious ancestors. I have endeavoured to remain faithful to the motto of

[1] 'Out of date.'

Montaigne, and I think I can say, in his words, ' Cecy est un livre de bonne foy.'

It only remains for me to discharge a single debt of gratitude. In resuming a work which was interrupted by a kind of discouragement, I seize the only opportunity in my power of publicly thanking the illustrious Advocates through whose offices I was enabled to resume the pen. Faithful to the glorious traditions of the French Bar, MM. Hébert and Dufaure have, by their talents no less than by their perseverance, achieved one more triumph of the old cause—the Right.

HENRI D'ORLÉANS.

PALERMO:
20th March, 1869.

CONTENTS

OF

THE FIRST VOLUME.

BOOK I.

LOUIS DE BOURBON.

CHAPTER I.

(1530—1559.)

CHAPTER II.

(1560.)

CHAPTER III.

(1561—1563.)

CHAPTER IV.

(1563—1568.)

BOOK I.

LOUIS DE BOURBON,

FIRST PRINCE OF THAT NAME, AND FIRST PRINCE DE CONDÉ.

BORN MAY 7, 1530.   KILLED MARCH 13, 1569.

CHAPTER I.

1530—1559.

Origin of the Capétiens and of the Bourbons; position of the Bourbons in the Middle Ages; their services in the wars with the English.—Their conduct in the Italian wars; the virtues and crimes of Charles, third Connétable de Bourbon, killed 1527.—The Connétable's kinsmen, notwithstanding his example, remain faithful to the King.—Reserve and submission of the Duc de Vendôme.—Louis de Bourbon, founder of the House of Condé, was the last of the thirteen children of the Duc de Vendôme (1530); obscurity of his early youth.—His modest début at the Court of Henri II., 1549; position of his family.—By his marriage with Éléonore de Roye, Condé becomes allied to the families of Montmorency and Châtillon (1551).—His first campaign as a volunteer, in Italy (1551).—He takes part in the conquest of Les Trois Évêchés and the defence of Metz (1552).—The campaign in Picardie (1553).—Well-fought engagement near Doulens.—The King confers upon him a *Compagnie d'ordonnance.*—Campaign in Hainaut and Artois (1554).—Fight on the Escaillon; battle of Renty.—Campaign in Italy (1555).—Notwithstanding his services, he is refused the Lieutenant-Generalship of Picardie, which his father and his brother had successively held.—Truce of Vaucelles (1556), broken by Guise and Coligny.—The Duc de Savoie invades Champagne and Picardie with forty-seven thousand men (1557).—Condé repairs to the army.—Commencement of hostilities.—Battle of Saint-Quentin (Aug. 10).—Condé, cut off on the right, is unable to hold the causeway of Rouvroy—Death of the Comte d'Enghien; capture of the Connétable, and rout of the French army.—Condé retires with Nevers; he continues the campaign throughout the autumn at the head of the Light cavalry, and performs important services.—Guise, appointed the King's Lieutenant-Governor, takes Calais and Thionville.—Condé, left in the lurch, and disappointed of obtaining the post of Colonel-Général of the Light cavalry, is appointed to that of Colonel of the Transalpine Infantry.—Discreditable peace of Cateau-Cambrésis (1559).

THE sixteenth century is the century of moral greatness, just as the succeeding one is that of intellectual lustre and purity. History, indeed, is seldom capable of being formulated thus, and we do not pretend that this classifi-

cation, which is not a new one, is strictly accurate. At
the same time, if without confining ourselves within
periods too contracted, we compare that which elapsed
from the accession of François Iᵉʳ and Charles V. to
the end of the Thirty Years' War, with the reign of
Louis XIV., we cannot fail to be struck with the very
marked contrast between the characteristics of the eminent men of those epochs. In the one we find a spirit
of independence, originality of conception, prompt and
daring execution of desperate resolves, audacity in vice,
or heroism in virtue. In the other, we see the manly
and noble but disciplined and self-controlled spirit of
the contemporaries of the ' Grand Roi.' The historical
characters of the first period present to us an appearance
of individuality; those of the second have, as it were,
a family likeness, and we might almost say that they
seem cast in the same mould.

The most illustrious of the princes whose history we
are about to retrace, the Great Condé, marks the transition period between those two epochs. If at first he
aimed high ; if he tried to play the part of a captain of
the former age, in which the individual was everything ;
yet he ended his days in the midst of that organised and
homogeneous social system, which, while it opened a
path for honourable ambition, and fostered the greatness
of a Turenne or a Colbert, forbad any future dreams of
the career of a Wallenstein or a Richelieu.

His grandfather, Louis de Bourbon, the first of the
Condés, deserves a place among the great characters of
the sixteenth century. With him we will commence
our story. But in order to a just appreciation of that
short, troubled, and brilliant life, we must first call to

mind the situation of his House when he came into the world.

The real head of the *Dynastie Capétienne* was Robert le Fort,[1] a soldier who, like forty-two of his descendants, died on the field of battle. Genealogists have endeavoured to pierce the obscurity which envelopes his origin. Some trace his descent from Witikind, others from St. Arnoul. None have succeeded in clearing up the mystery of his birth. But whether his father was a Carlovingian, or one of the chiefs who were transplanted by Charlemagne from the banks of the Elbe to the interior of Normandie, or even, as Dante would have us believe, a Paris butcher; in short, whether he was of Gallic, Frank, or Saxon blood, he owed his fame and the honours with which he was invested to the energy which amid general languor he displayed, and to the activity which he evinced in opposing the incursions of the Northern pirates.

Popular tradition, which the great Italian poet followed, assigned him a plebeian origin, and certainly the accession of his grandson to the throne was the substitution of a national Royal House for a government founded by conquest.[2]

His tenth successor was St. Louis, and under his reign new-born France (for the empire of Charlemagne was not France), France of the Middle Ages, reached the climax of her glory. Never has the name of our fatherland shone with a brighter or a purer lustre; never has a sovereign been the object, whether among his own subjects or abroad, of higher reverence or of a better deserved admiration. Several European nations solicited

---

[1] Robert the Strong.
[2] See M. Augustin Thierry's admirable letter on the expulsion of the second Frankish dynasty.

their leaders from among his kinsmen. The King and the barons of England selected him as the arbiter of their quarrels, and the Saracen emirs, even when he was their captive, wished to liberate him from prison to place him at their head. Philosophers and lawyers alike have eulogised his 'Établissements;' and the tradition of the Oak of Vincennes long reminded the nations that to the 'bon Roy Loys' they owed the first attempt at an organised system of law, the first experiment in the suppression of feudal tyranny. No form of glory was wanting to his reign—even of that kind which the backward state of society could but little appreciate. The Sainte Chapelle may be looked upon as the *chef-d'œuvre* of Gothic architecture; and the tutor of Dante, setting aside alike the Latin and the beautiful Tuscan tongue, made use of our language, rough and undeveloped as it then was, to write a book for which he desired a world-wide circulation.[1] The errors with which we charge St. Louis were those of his age; and even his misfortunes shed the halo of a martyr around his illustrious name. Before that splendid and truly national figure patriotism and good sense compel even a Voltaire to refrain from his bantering scepticism. The '*Essai sur les Mœurs*' contains the noblest panegyric that has yet been written on that great saint and great king.

Origin of the Bourbons (1256): their position in the Middle Ages; their services in the great

From him, through his last male child, Robert de France, Comte de Clermont, sprang the House of Bourbon. An ancient barony, the inheritance of Béatrix, wife of this prince, was erected into a dukedom in favour of Louis, his son, and gave to his descendants the name which they have retained, that of France being reserved

---

[1] 'Le Trésor de la Connaissance des Choses.' By Brunetto Latino.

for the Royal branch.[1] In thus following, however, the

rule imposed upon the cadets of the House, the Comte de Clermont's descendants retained the *fleurs-de-lis* on their shields. In that age of mysticism, an heraldic device would not improbably have been sufficient to ensure them that *prestige* which the Courtenays and others had lost by changing their armorial bearings. But it was not the blazon of heraldry that saved the Bourbons from obscurity and oblivion. It was their many services and their brilliant exploits. Their war-cry—'Bourbon, Notre Dame!'—had sounded in every important engagement in our wars with the English, and their blood had flowed on every battle-field. Jacques, first Comte de la Marche and Connétable of France, ancestor of all the Bourbons now living, saved the King's life at Crécy, was taken prisoner at Poitiers, covered with wounds, and fell, together with his son, at the battle of Brignais.[2] One Duc de Bourbon, Pierre Ier, had been killed at Poitiers;

---

[1] The descendants of Robert le Fort occupied the throne of France long before the custom had been resumed of designating by a common name, as at Rome, the members of one House. It was at the time of the Crusades that, owing to the immense mass of men drawn together, it was found necessary to distinguish families from each other by adopting this usage. The House which had the honour of supplying sovereigns to our country was called *France.* But our kings, jealous of that great name, reserved it for their own sons and grandsons. Hence the designation *fils* and *petit-fils de France.* The posterity of each *fils de France* formed a cadet branch which took its name from the title borne by its head, *Valois, Artois, Bourbon,* &c. At the time of the accession of Henri IV. the name of Bourbon remained with those younger branches of Condé and Montpensier, which had sprung from the main branch before the death of Henri III. But Henri IV.'s children, those of Louis XIII., and those of their successors in the throne, were surnamed *de France*; whilst in conformity with the law the descendants of Louis XIII.'s second son received the surname *d'Orléans,* from the title borne by their grandfather.

[2] Fought with the Tard-venus (Late-comers), 1361. 'The first title of the Capets is the death of Robert

another, Louis III., was taken prisoner at Agincourt, as he was turning upon the enemy in the midst of the rout, together with his cousins, the Comte de Vendôme—who, like him, was taken prisoner—and the Sire de Preaulx, who was killed. Louis II., Duc de Bourbon, surnamed 'la Fleur des Chevaliers,'[1] the pupil and companion of Duguesclin, was one of the greatest princes of his day. His renown was such that the Genoese, seeing their commerce ruined by the corsairs of Barbary, applied to him to deliver them from these pirates. In a brilliant expedition, equipped at his own private cost, the Duke landed at Carthage, a spot made memorable by the death of his saintly ancestor, defeated the kings of Tunis and Bougiah, imposed on them a humiliating peace, and set all their prisoners free. On his return thence he seized Cagliari, and destroyed the Arabian fleet (1390). Six years later, his cousin Jacques, third Comte de la Marche, fell at Nicopolis fighting against the Turks. Thus during times of peace at home, the Bourbons exercised their activity and valour in fighting against the infidel.

To the lustre which their prowess obtained for them they added that which is derived from the liberal expenditure of great revenues. Possessors of vast territories which they owed more to family alliances than to the generosity of kings, they had known how to win the affection of their vassals. Their magnificent hospitality drew around them a numerous and brilliant nobility. Thus the 'hôtel' of those brave and august princes, the

le Fort, at Brisserte; that of the Bourbons, the death of Jacques, at Brignais; both killed in defence of the kingdom against the brigands.'

Michelet's 'Histoire de France,' vol. iii. p. 438.
[1] 'The Flower of Chivalry.'

'*gracieux ducs de Bourbon*,' as our ancient poet called them,[1] was considered the best school in which a young nobleman could learn the profession of arms. The order of the Écu, instituted by one of them, had been coveted and worn by the bravest warriors of France. Sufficiently powerful to outshine the rank and file of the nobility, they had at the same time neither the large estates nor the immense power which enabled the Dukes of Bourgogne, of Bretagne, and other great vassals, to become the rivals or the enemies of the royal authority. Though not free from the corruptions of feudal life and the turbulent habits of the French noblesse, they never allied themselves to the enemies of their country during that long struggle which so often approached to a civil war. Mixed up with the deplorable and sanguinary rivalries of Bourgogne and Armagnac, they were always to be found on the national side. If at a later period Duc Jean II. took an active part in 'la Praguerie' and in 'la guerre du bien public,' it had been he who more than any other contributed to the deliverance of France from the yoke of the foreigner. He had shared with Richemont the honour of our last victory at Formigny, and deservedly won the Connétable's sword and the then glorious surname 'Fléau des Anglais.'[2]

But a fresh field had been laid open to French ardour. Charles VIII. had invaded Italy. The Bourbons figured brilliantly in the expedition. Mathieu, surnamed the Great Bourbon Bastard, was the first of the 'neuf preux' whom the King had chosen to fight by his side at

1495.

Their conduct in the Italian wars. The virtues and crimes of Charles,

[1] Villon's 'Ballade des Seigneurs du temps jadis.'
[2] 'Scourge of the English.'

CHAP.
I.

1495–1515
third Con-
nétable de
Bourbon ;
killed
1527.

Fornoue. Gilbert, Comte de Montpensier, led the advanced guard at the expedition against Naples, and was entrusted with the government, as Viceroy, of that magnificent but precarious and imprudent conquest. If he did not show himself equal to so difficult a task, he redeemed his errors by his courage and by his misfortunes. He died at Pozzuoli after he had signed the capitulation of Atella. His eldest son in like manner was carried off by sickness, after he had borne an honourable part in the second conquest of Naples (1501). The second, Charles, having married Suzanne, only daughter of Pierre, last Duke of the first Bourbon branch, inherited both the title and the property of that prince, who died in 1503. He became thus the head of his House, and seemed destined to eclipse the glory of his ancestors. Dubbed a knight on the battle-field of Aignadel by Louis XII., he rapidly acquired such renown that François Iᵉʳ, even before his coronation, conferred on him the Connétable's sword. This was the third time that a prince of his family had received this signal honour. The post of Connétable was no sinecure. It comprehended the permanent command of all the mercenary cavalry, then called the 'gendarmerie,' and in time of war of the advanced guard, that is, of half the army, when the King in person commanded the principal corps, or, as it was called, the 'bataille.' If the King was not at the head of the army, the Connétable took his place. From the first campaign of François Iᵉʳ (1515) Bourbon showed himself worthy of his high office. It was owing to his skilfully conceived and executed manœuvres that the army was enabled to cross the Alps and descend into

the Milanese territory.   At Melegnano his troops held
out for the first day almost unaided against all the
efforts of the Swiss.   The next day, he decided the
fortune of the field.   Six princes of his House accompanied him to the field of battle.   Two of them—the
Comte de Châtelleraut his brother, and the Sire de
Carency—fell by his side.   After the King's departure
he completed the conquest of the Milanese, which he
subsequently held, at his own cost and with entire success, against a great army led by the Emperor Maximilian.
But here his good fortune deserted him.   François Iᵉʳ was
growing impatient of the services of this able general, so
passionately beloved by his fellow-soldiers; of this vassal,
who was rich and bold enough to assist his sovereign out
of his own coffers.   Had not Henry VIII. said: 'My
brother of France has in that fellow a subject of whom
I would rather not be the master'?   Everything in
Bourbon offended the King; even that imperial air
which seemed a part of his nature, and that proud and
noble mien, of which the beautiful Italian type[1] has
been so admirably transferred to canvass by the pencil
of Titian.   He was therefore recalled from Italy, fettered
in the execution of his office, and deprived of the command even of the advanced guard in the campaign of
1521; he found himself superseded in the conduct of
the army by inefficient courtiers.   At length, on the
death of his wife (1521), his right of succession to
her property was contested both by the Crown and by
the King's mother, Louise de Savoie, who claimed the
greater part of it in her own right.   This double claim
was most iniquitous.   Despite the efforts of the Chan-

---

[1] His mother was a Gonzaga.

cellor Duprat, the Parliament could not admit it. But it had not the courage to decide in favour of the Connétable, and, under pretext that 'the King could not plead without holding what he claimed,'[1] the patrimony of the Dukes de Bourbon was provisionally sequestrated. Plundered, wronged beyond endurance, the Connétable burned for revenge. He forgot his duty. He quitted France, and offered his services to the Emperor. From that time his King and his country had no deadlier foe. But on the very day that he crossed the frontier his punishment began, and his criminal eagerness was no better rewarded by Charles V. than his loyal services had been by François Ier. Obtaining none of the favours which had been promised him ; scarcely tolerated by the generals who had been associated in command with him, Bourbon, weary of complaining and incapable of humbling himself, took the course of conducting war on his own account, as the ally rather than as the lieutenant of the Emperor. On his first appeal, an army of adventurers from every nation pressed to his standard. Reduced to poverty, for he had sold the last of his jewels, he could offer them no pay but the hope of pillage. His genius, however, and his wild energy inspired his soldiers with an enthusiasm which survived himself. Long after his death, the bands which overran the devastated plains of Italy used still to repeat their favourite refrain,

Calla, calla, Julio César, Annibal, Scipion:
Viva la fama de Borbon !

The Connétable was killed by a shot received at the assault of Rome on the sixth of May, 1527. A great

---

[1] 'Plaider dessaisi.'

artist and a notorious swash-buckler, Benvenuto Cellini, claimed the unenviable distinction of having put an end to that tempestuous career.

CHAP.
I.

1527–38

The Con-
nétable's
family,
notwith-
standing
his ex-
ample, re-
main faith-
ful to their
King. Re-
serve and
submis-
sion of
Vendôme.

The hateful example thus set by the head of the Bourbons was not followed by any of the princes of his House. They all remained faithful to France and to their King. Hector, Sire de Lavedan, was killed at Pavia, and in the same battle the Comte de Saint-Pol was severely wounded, and by a miracle escaped death or imprisonment. His brother Charles, Duc de Vendôme, who had remained behind in order to defend the frontier of Picardie, was urged to accept the regency during the captivity of François Iᵉʳ. He refused, however, to do so, in deference to the wishes of that monarch. But though he had become first prince of the blood, through the death of all his seniors, Vendôme never acquired either the authority or influence that so high a position ought to have given him. Whether it were natural modesty or indifference to public life which influenced him, or more patriotic motives, he seemed anxious to remain in obscurity, and was content to serve in the army with credit but without great distinction. However, neither his reserve nor his submissiveness could overcome the mistrust of the King. The property of the Connétable was definitively alienated from his House,[1] and Vendôme did not receive the hereditary possessions of the Dukes d'Alençon, to which his wife was entitled. He died on the twenty-fifth of March, 1538, leaving but a scanty patrimony to

[1] Very scanty restitutions, obtained after protracted law-suits at the end of François Iᵉʳ's reign and the commencement of François II.'s, restored to the Princesse de la Roche-sur-Yon, the Connétable's sister, and to her son (ancestor of the great Mademoiselle), some of his property. The House of Orléans was still in possession of it on the 22nd of January, 1852.

his numerous descendants. By Françoise d'Alençon he was the father of seven sons and six daughters.

Of the six princesses four became nuns. One died young. Only one was married; Marguerite, born on the fifteenth of November, 1516, became the wife of François de Clèves, Duc de Nevers, on the nineteenth of January, 1538, and died on the twentieth of October, 1589.

Five only of his sons obtained their majority.

Antoine, Duc de Vendôme and afterwards King of Navarre through his marriage with Jeanne d'Albret, was born on the twenty-second of April, 1518, and died on the seventeenth of November, 1562, from the effects of a wound received at the siege of Rouen.

François, Comte d'Enghien, the victor of Cérisoles, was born on the twenty-third of September, 1519, and died on the twenty-third of February, 1546, the victim of an accident, according to some, and of foul play, according to others.

Charles, Cardinal de Bourbon, Archbishop of Rouen, &c. (and who after the death of Henri III. became ' roi de la Ligue '), was born on the twenty-second of December, 1523, and died on the ninth of May, 1590.

Jean, Comte de Soissons, and, after the death of his brother François, Comte d'Enghien, was born on the sixth of July, 1526, and was killed at the battle of Saint-Quentin on the tenth of August, 1557.

Louis, Prince de Condé, was born at the Château de Vendôme on the seventh of May, 1530, and was killed on the thirteenth of March, 1569, at the battle of Jarnac. Thus of these five brothers, three fell on the field of battle; another, as is alleged, was assassinated; and the only one who died a natural death was in holy orders.

Even he died in prison. This resemblance in the character of their respective fortunes is a picture of the age in which they lived.

Two of these princes founded families: Antoine, father of Henri IV., who was the ancestor of all the Bourbons now living, and Louis, who was the root of the House of Condé and all its branches.

Louis was the youngest, and was scarcely eight years old when his father died. What became of him then? let us ask. How did he spend the years which mark the passage from childhood to youth? There is no sign to show what his life was at this period, upon which his contemporaries doubtless cared but little to throw light. His mother, Françoise d'Alençon, was a princess of strict and virtuous character, renowned for the good order which she maintained at home. But the 'discipline' which she exercised among the young ladies in attendance upon her—a discipline which excited the admiration of her panegyrist—was not exactly suited to sons approaching manhood. A widow living in retirement was scarcely the person best fitted to perfect that chivalrous education which was then indispensable, and which the young nobility had vied in seeking of old at the 'hôtel de Bourbon.' The ties, however, of blood, as well as those of sponsorship (closer in those days than in ours), united the Duc de Vendôme's children to more than one nobleman who could fill the place of a father to them. Already had the Comte d'Enghien, and probably also the Comte de Soissons,[1] become the wards of their uncle the

CHAP. I.

1538–49

Louis de Bourbon, founder of the House of Condé, was the last of the thirteen children of the Duc de Vendôme (1530). Obscurity of his childhood.

[1] It is maintained that the conqueror of Cérisoles was brought up by his uncle, who was also his godfather. We are of opinion that his brother Jean also passed his youth in the hôtel de Saint-Pol; for we

Comte de Saint-Pol, whose marriage allowed of his

taining a handsome establishment. Now their b.

Louis was the godson of Marguerite, Queen of Na

the generous sister of François Ier, and of Charles

léans, the King's third son, who died unmarried at

age of twenty-three, and had been represented at .he

christening of his second-cousin by the head of an illus-

trious House, whose history was destined often to blend

with that of the House of Condé, René, Vicomte de

Rohan. Are we to believe that the young prince was

brought up by one of those who, in presenting him at

the altar, had vowed to watch over him? Are we to

seek in the first impressions made upon him in youth for

the key to his subsequent career, for the origin of that

secret tendency which should hereafter draw him on to

espouse the cause of the Reformation?

At the Court of Nérac, he might have found in Henri

d'Albret, King of Navarre, the very type of the gallant

and adventurous gentleman of the age, and he might

have heard in the interval between two stories of the

Heptaméron, the voices—not yet outspoken—of the ear-

liest Reformers. The Vicomte de Rohan, indeed, was but

a brave soldier; who died, like his father, a hero on the

field of battle. Notwithstanding his embarrassed means,

he kept up a princely court on his estates in Bretagne;

and his château at Blain would have been a fitting home

for the royal orphan whom he had held at the font.

have in our possession three letters addressed by the latter to his aunt, the Duchesse d'Estouteville (widow of the Comte de Saint-Pol), in which the language is throughout that of filial obedience. These letters were written in 1554 and 1556, when Jean de Bourbon, then Comte d'Enghien, had long been out of pupillage, but before he had married the daughter of the Duchesse.

There, as at Nérac, the new religious ideas had found their way. The Vicomtesse, Isabelle d'Albret, had adopted them even more openly than her sister-in-law, Queen Marguerite; and the two sons whom she was educating were destined one day to be reckoned among the most determined adherents of the Protestant cause.[1] Lastly, not to omit any of those who might naturally have been the guardians of Louis de Bourbon, we must mention one more—the Duc de Nevers, who, as far back as 1538, had married the Duc de Vendôme's eldest daughter. We possess written testimony[2] to the intimacy which subsequently subsisted between this nobleman and his young brother-in-law; the respectful deference which characterised these relations on the part of the latter may have found its origin in grateful recollections of the past. François de Clèves was rich and powerful, and had already achieved celebrity as a warrior. In his case too faith was wavering. After some years of hesitation he died a Calvinist, according to Beza. His children, of whom we shall have occasion to speak hereafter, ' continued the profession of the [Reformed] religion '[3] with varying degrees of consistency and perseverance.

The events which subsequently happened, the part which some of these persons played, and the relations

CHAP.
I.
1538–49

His modest
début at
the Court

---

[1] Henri and René, successively Vicomte de Rohan. The first was almost always kept at home by ill health. The second took an active share in all the campaigns of the Protestant army. We shall come across him by and by. (See D. Morice's ' Histoire de Bretagne.')

[2] The Prince de Condé to the Duc de Nevers, September 3, 1559; to the Duchesse de Nevers, n. d.

Original letter, Bibl. imp., ' Mémoires du roi Henri II,' 8643. One of those letters was printed among the ' Négociations, etc., relatives au règne de François II,' published by Mr Le Pâris (' Collection de Documents inédits ').

[3] Beza's ' Histoire ecclésiastique des Églises réformées de France,' liv. v.

CHAP.
I.

1549

of Henri
II. (1549).
Situation
of his
House.

which subsisted between them, give some show of probability to the various conjectures which it is possible to
found upon the basis of the concurrence of their names.
At all events, if we must believe that Louis de Bourbon
was initiated into the profession of arms by some veteran
warrior—if we are left to suppose that his mind at an
early age passed under the influence of that mysterious
propaganda, that movement of ideas, which towards the
close of François Ier's reign was agitating the bosom of so
many families, both of the nobility and commonalty—
there is nothing whatever to show us decidedly which of
his kindred or friends took charge of his education; and
in the light-hearted companion whose early course we
are about to trace, there is no foreshadowing of the
champion of an austere religious party, the future chief
of the Huguenots. No detail, no record supplements the
gap left by the silence of contemporary chroniclers, who
seem to have ignored the very existence of this obscure
younger brother; and the earliest document in which
mention is made of the first of the Condés is the Domestic Roll of Henri II. in 1549. He appears there
under the name of 'Louis, Mr de Vendôme, gentilhomme
de la chambre du Roi, aux gages de 1200 livres.'[1] Truly
a more modest début could not well be imagined. Lost
in the crowd of courtiers, this youth of nineteen was
not even, like his ancestors, remarkable for height and
imposing presence. He was of very short stature, and
doubtless somewhat bent; for some collections of anec-

---

[1] 'Gentleman of the Bedchamber
to the King, at a salary of 1,200
livres.'—P. Anselme's 'Histoire généalogique de France.'

Under this title the Prince is designated in several accounts of state
ceremonies of the years 1547, 1548,
and 1549. (See Godefroy's 'Cérémo-
nial français,' and the numerous MS.
registers of ceremonies preserved in
the 'Archives de Condé.')

dotes represent him as hunchbacked and deformed. But
this tradition, of which it is difficult to trace the origin,
does not agree with the well-known popular song upon
him—

> Ce petit homme tant jolly
> Qui toujours cause et toujours ry,
> Et toujours baise sa mignonne,
> Dieu gard' de mal le petit homme.

At any rate there was nothing mean about him. Nimble
and vigorous, he excelled in all athletic exercises. No one
played better at tennis ; no one managed his arms better
in a tilting-match, or displayed more gracefully the paces
of a restive horse. Authentic portraits show us that his
eyes were bright and piercing ; his features, which were
agreeable without being regular, were in later life framed
in one of those beards, of a warm golden tint, which we
see so often in portraits of the sixteenth century. Brilliant and well-informed, his conversation was easy and
fascinating, with a touch of sarcasm in it, from which his
good humour took away the sting ; there was certainly
nothing of the Puritan about him ; abundance of cheerfulness and eagerness ; the wish and the power to please ;
a resolute will, a high spirit, and a great and generous
heart.

But happy gifts and the highest birth were not in
themselves enough to command distinction at the Louvre.
For this either wealth or court favour was necessary ;
and the Bourbons, well-nigh ruined by confiscations,
possessed neither. François Iᵉʳ, by a happy inspiration,
had indeed for a moment forgotten his prejudice against
the family of the Connétable, and had entrusted the
army of Italy to the command of him who was destined
to avenge the disgrace of Pavia on the glorious day of

1525.

Cérisoles; but envious tongues had not spared the young general, and the King's satisfaction in his success had been alloyed by secret jealousy. Nor had the Comte d'Enghien long survived his victory; stricken down by death in 1546, he did not live to watch over the initiation of his brother into the life of Court or camp. His royal guardian was no more, and the 'Sires des fleurs de Lys' found themselves farther than ever from Royal favour; so much so that the most direct expression of the wish of Henri II. was needed to overcome the reluctance of his aunt Marguerite to what she seemed to think a mésalliance—the marriage of her daughter Jeanne d'Albret with Antoine, eldest son of the House of Bourbon. The latter, an easy-tempered and light-hearted man, always lived in Béarn with his father-in-law, or in the province he governed, Picardie; and the favour of the feeble Henri II. was divided between his aged mistress, the Duchesse de Valentinois, and his aged friend, Montmorency. With one or other of these two, everybody at Court sided; Condé's choice was soon made.

Among the partisans of the Duchess, the most prominent were those younger members of the House of Lorraine, of whom François Ier had said that 'they would one day strip his children to their doublets, and his poor subjects to their shirts.' One of them, the Marquis de Mayenne,[1] had just married the favourite's daughter; and the new Duc de Guise[2] had become, as much through the influence of Diane as through his great personal abilities and his already brilliant services, one of the King's most trusted advisers. But notwithstanding their

---

[1] Afterwards Duc d'Aumale, third son of Claude, Duc de Guise.

[2] François de Lorraine. His father died April 12, 1550.

alliances,[1] the Guises were on the most distant terms with the Bourbons. In camp and at Court their paths crossed, as though by some adverse fate; points of etiquette had become occasions for the most annoying altercations between them, and one dark suspicion gave to their rivalry a yet deeper bitterness. We have already spoken of the death of the Comte d'Enghien, who in the prime of his life and his glory had fallen a victim to a melancholy accident.[2] Vague, but widespread rumours had attributed his death to foul play. But François Ier had forbidden all enquiry, and it was whispered that the murder had been committed at the instigation of the Dauphin and of the Duc de Guise, then Comte d'Aumale.

Condé was thus naturally thrown into intercourse with the opposition, or Montmorency faction. Anne de Montmorency, a man destitute of great military talents, but very brave and determined, had won, by his splendid defence of Provence in 1536, the Connétable's sword and the surname of 'the Fabius of France.' He was already Grand Maître of the King's Household, and had recently been created 'duc et pair' (1551). Though almost sixty

---

[1] Antoinette de Bourbon, mother of the Duc François de Guise, was sister to the Duc de Vendôme, father of Condé.

[2] In the winter of 1546, when the King was at La Rocheguyon, the princes and lords in attendance were amusing themselves with the attack and defence, by snow-balls, of an extemporised fortress. The Comte d'Enghien was at the head of one party, the Dauphin and the Comte d'Aumale of the other. In the midst of the game a violent dispute arose; it almost came to drawing daggers; and there was a good deal of difficulty in appeasing the quarrel. Before going indoors, the Comte d'Enghien was sitting on a bench beneath the castle wall, when a chest fell from one of the windows and injured him severely. He died from the effects of this a few days afterwards. Bentivoglio, an Italian, a great partisan of his enemies, was suspected of having purposely dropped the chest upon the Prince's head.

years of age, a veteran courtier, concealing deep craft beneath a rough and blunt address, he yet exercised less influence upon those at Court than upon the military nobility of the provinces. His official position as well as his large private fortune enabled him to dispense extensive patronage. He was surrounded by young and gallant sons, and reckoned among his principal followers his nephews the Châtillons, already remarkable for their ambition, bravery, and independence of character. One of them, Coligny, was admiral; and the other, D'Andelot, colonel of the Cisalpine infantry. Condé was before long closely united by marriage with the two great Houses of Montmorency and Châtillon. He became the husband of their near relation, Éléonore de Roye,[1] heiress of a house more noble than wealthy. The marriage was solemnised (June 1551) at the Château du Plessier-lès-Roye by Cardinal de Bourbon, uncle and guardian to the Prince. The latter did not yet bear the title by which he is subsequently known in history.[2]

This alliance, although it added very little to his fortune, was destined to exercise a great influence upon his future prospects; but it in no wise subdued his taste for gallantry.[3] While, however, he was not proof against the allurements of pleasure, and the seductions and facile amours of a licentious Court, yet his better nature and

[1] Éléonore de Roye, eldest daughter and heiress of Charles, Sire de Roye and de Muret, Comte de Roucy, was born in 1535. Her mother, Madeleine de Mailly, Dame de Conty, was the daughter of Louise de Montmorency, sister of the Connétable Anne; and Louise de Montmorency by her second marriage with Gaspard de Coligny,

Maréchal de France, was the mother of the Admiral Coligny and of his two brothers, D'Andelot and Cardinal de Châtillon.

[2] For the origin of the title Prince de Condé, see Appendix of Documents, No. I.

[3] All his life long, 'le bon prince ayma autant la femme d'autrui que la sienne.' (Brantôme.)

the traditions of his family alike were calling him to a
military career. In that, more than at the Louvre, he
was to find still living the memory of the glories of his
House ; and the soldiery could not but accord a hearty
welcome to the brother of the victor of Cérisoles. In
the ranks the memory even of the Connétable was still
popular, and his crimes had been well-nigh forgotten in
his misfortunes. His exploits and his warlike qualities
were still the object of admiration. Of all the branches
of the Royal House, that of Bourbon had always been the
most military ; and it was an universally accepted tradition which Brantôme, notwithstanding his partiality to
another branch of the House, expressed in the following
memorable words :—' As for the Bourbons, they are all
gallant and brave, and have never been infected with
poltroon fever.'

France had just passed through a gigantic struggle, His first
marked by brilliant successes and by yet more startling campaign,
reverses. While the whole of Europe was bowing be- teer in the
neath the iron rule of Charles V., she had been able to Italy
retain her territorial as well as her political independence. (1551).
Despite blunders of every kind ; despite the wretched
state of her finances ; despite the inferiority of her armies
both as to numbers and organization, she had held in
check the colossal power of the House of Austria ; and,
ever on the verge of falling, she yet ever rose afresh
with incredible vitality. Her strange alternations of
weakness and heroism had extorted from the great Emperor those remarkable words :—' There is no nation in
the world which does more to ruin itself than the French,
and yet all turns out to its advantage ; God has both the
King and the kingdom under His special protection.'

The struggle had been suspended, not closed, when
Henri II. came to the throne. The Peace of Crespy had
been a mere truce, and in 1551 war broke out afresh in
Italy, as it were spontaneously, and without any preliminary declaration of hostilities. Condé, though but a
few days married, seized the opportunity; he had no
command; he could bring no men into the field; but he
asked and obtained leave to serve as a volunteer.

Armies were at this time in a state of transition. The
great advance already made in the use of fire-arms, the
new duties devolving upon the infantry, the encroach-
ments of the royal prerogative, and the influence of foreign
wars, had combined to break up the old feudal organization. But such regular troops as France maintained—
the cavalry, which was divided into 'compagnies d'ordonnance;' the infantry, consisting of French and Swiss
divisions,[1] scarcely numerous enough to keep the field
constantly in front of Imperial troops who were always
stronger in numbers and better equipped—these could not
by themselves either effect any decisive stroke or withstand any severe shock. When an attack was expected,
or, by the King's permission, was to be made, a crowd
of gentlemen-volunteers flocked in from every quarter,
to swell the ranks of the 'gendarmerie soldée,'[2] or of
the light cavalry. The less wealthy of these took their
place as 'anspessades'[3] in the ranks of the infantry.

---

[1] We omit mention of the légions
of François Ier, the institution of
which, however, marks an important advance in army organization.
His plan was imperfectly carried
out; and this force, composed of
very poor material (in a military
point of view), seldom appeared on

the field of battle, and when it did,
the result was unfortunate.

[2] Stipendiary cavalry. (See p. 10.)

[3] Anspessades, or lanspessades,
'lance spezzate,' broken lances. A
light-cavalry soldier, who having
lost horse and arms in some honourable engagement, had joined the

While such an accession of brave men who were trained
to the handling of weapons was an indispensable reinforcement to the commander, the absence of a system
of military rank, in which their position could be defined,
made their employment a matter of difficulty; and their
undisciplined condition, which was always troublesome,
frequently fatal, in an engagement, became, when for
any reason an expected battle did not take place, a
serious impediment. This was the case in Piedmont in
1551. The Maréchal de Brissac had already taken
Chieri and San Damiano, when the swarm of volunteers
arrived, among whom was Condé. It was known that
the Imperial troops were in good fighting order, and ably
commanded by Fernando de Gonzaga. An engagement seemed imminent. But time passed on without
swords crossing, and these fiery youths became impatient
of the delays which retarded the hoped-for action.
'If the generals hesitate,' said they, 'we will set them
fighting despite themselves.' Their foolish brains were
dreaming of all manner of wild enterprises, such as would
have compromised the safety of the whole army, when
Brissac, who had been informed of these projects, assembled the volunteers. He spoke like a father; he
appealed to their patriotism; he pointed out their duty.
His appeal was successful. Condé, who had already
distinguished himself by readiness as a speaker, replied
in the name of the whole body, although he was one
of the youngest of their number. He thanked the
Maréchal warmly, and declared their willingness to

ranks of the infantry, carrying the
pike till he could be better equipped,
was called an anspessade. This
name, which originally came from
the Piedmontese wars, extended to
all gentlemen who served in the infantry.

obey orders, so that they became eventually 'a very school of affection and kindly feeling.'[1] To encourage this disposition, Brissac authorised them to storm the Château de Saint-Baleing near Vulpiano. In this enterprise they acquitted themselves creditably; other surprises followed, which were almost always crowned with success. The army of Italy, although its theatre of war was of narrower dimensions and far less importance than it had been in former reigns, had never ceased to be an excellent military school. Brissac was a wise, active, and vigilant general; who was able to supplement, by the resources of his own skill, the insufficiency of the means at his disposal. His subordinates, almost all Gascons, Dauphinois, or Provençaux, were well broken-in to their work, bold, and gifted with that inventive genius common among the men of the southern provinces of France. Both officers and men excelled in the devices of petty warfare, so essential in an age when great strategic movements were almost unknown and almost always impracticable. It was here that were moulded the greater number of those well-skilled, indefatigable partisan soldiers who were to find a melancholy field for their experience in our civil conflicts. Among these old stagers Condé must have formed some useful connections and learned some valuable lessons. His ardour and perseverance became conspicuous. Montluc, in one of the most picturesque passages of his commentaries, represents him to us, in the middle of winter, working for two whole nights at the task of dragging the guns up the steep heights which commanded the Castle of Lantz.[2] But he was already showing himself less ac-

---

[1] 'Memoirs' of Boyvin Duvillars.   [2] On the Stura.

commodating in his temper than he was at the commencement of the operations; and he was beginning to prove 'not very easy to manage'[1] when the campaign came to a close.

It had lasted till late in the year, and the Prince, on his return to Court, made but a short stay. Henri II. was collecting an army on the frontiers of Champagne; and Condé, joining it, followed the King in that celebrated expedition which gave us, almost without striking a blow, possession of Les Trois Évêchés[2] (1552). This rapid conquest caused great commotion beyond the Rhine. Germany looked upon it as a revivification of the Gallic race. All German enthusiasm blazed up; the dissensions among the princes of the empire were for a time suspended. Charles V. took advantage of this unexpected unanimity. As early as the month of October in the same year, he appeared before Metz with a great army and formidable military train. But the intrepidity and genius of the great Duc de Guise saved the 'boulevard of France.' Condé and his brother Jean, Comte d'Enghien, surmounting all personal aversion and family antipathies, hastened to place themselves under his command. Entering the town among the first reinforcements, the two Bourbons were entrusted with the defence of the portion extending from the Porte Saint-Thibaut to the Seille, and acquitted themselves with equal courage and capacity.

Condé's conduct during these eighteen months of active service had drawn attention to him; and he returned to the army with a command.

France gained nothing by the defeat she had inflicted

He takes part in the conquest of Les Trois Évêchés and defence of Metz.

Campaign in Picardie (1553).

---

[1] 'Un peu malaysé à manier.'—Du Villars.   [2] Metz, Toul, an Verdun

CHAP.
L.

1553

Splendid
fight near
Doulens.
The King
confers
upon him
a 'compa-
gnie d'or-
donnance.'

upon the Imperialists under the walls of Metz. It had been one of the saddest characteristics of the reign of François Iᵉʳ that the inaction which followed upon every one of his great efforts had not only left his victories fruitless, but had given to the enemy an easy advantage over disbanded armies and unguarded frontiers. Henri II., who inherited his father's faults without his nobler qualities, displayed yet greater negligence. Whilst he was wasting in revelry and luxury the money which was needed to maintain troops and fortifications, Charles V., in his winter quarters in Belgium, was preparing to renew on the northern side of France the invasion which had failed on the eastern. Before we had taken one step in the defensive, he had already captured Thérouanne and Hesdin (1553). He had just laid siege to Doulens, when the Connétable arrived on the Somme with all the forces he could muster. The use of light cavalry was just then beginning to be understood, and this arm of the service was exactly suited to such gentlemen as did not belong to the ' compagnies soldées,' and were not accoutred like the line. These formed the staple of Montmorency's hastily collected army, and he lost no time in ordering them to the front : Condé and the Duc de Nemours divided the command of the force between them. They were supported by the Maréchal de Saint-André with five hundred gendarmes. At the head of eight squadrons, Nemours fell upon the enemy's advanced posts on the banks of the river Authie. He was soon engaged with the whole of the Imperial cavalry, which drove him back upon his reserves. Saint-André's gendarmes came up to his relief ; the enemy were checked, but not disordered, by this surprise, when Condé, debouching upon their flank with four squadrons, charged furiously and completely routed them. The Prince carried off the honours of the day, in which the Imperialists lost seven standards, thirteen hundred killed, and a few prisoners. The King, having joined the army shortly afterwards, rewarded this feat with a *compagnie d'ordonnance.*

This post was now of less importance than in the reign of Charles VII., when, on its institution, the *ordonnance* was commanded but by fifteen captains. Since that time the number had very greatly increased. At the date of our narrative each *compagnie* consisted of from five-and-twenty to an hundred *lances,* that is from seventy-five to three hundred men ; each *lance* comprehending one man-at-arms and two archers, besides pages, cutlers, valets, and other non-combatants. But the full strength was seldom attained, and the recruiting was much less select than formerly. The patronage too which the post of captain afforded, and the pecuniary profit which could be made out of it, caused it to be reserved for princes of the blood and persons of high degree. In general, birth was a surer recommendation to it than services, and the real command could be deputed to a lieutenant, who was always an experienced soldier. Condé, seeing many of the *noblesse* who were his inferiors both in age and rank promoted to this post at the very outset of their career, could not possibly think his appointment a very signal favour; but it secured him a definite position in the army, by which he was not slow to profit.

Shortly after the fight which we have just described, operations were suspended in consequence of the illness of the Connétable. The troops established themselves in winter quarters, and the execution of the scheme for

carrying the war into the enemy's territory was deferred
to the following year. At length, in the spring of
1554, Henri II. collected imposing forces for the invasion, in three columns, of the Imperial States. Condé's
company was ordered to Mézières, where the Duc de
Nevers was assembling the right wing of the army. It
was fortunate for the Prince that he now served under
his brother-in-law, who entrusted to him the command of
his light cavalry. But he does not appear to have found
any opportunity of distinguishing himself. The column
under Nevers, marching through the valley of the Meuse,
carried Givet, Marienbourg, and Dinant; while the left
wing ravaged Artois, and Montmorency led the centre
between the Sambre and the Meuse. The King concentrated his army before Namur, which he designed to
besiege. But the garrison of that city had been reinforced, and its investment was found to be an impos-
sibility in presence of the Imperialists, who had had
time to rally. The French fell back upon Cambrésis.
Condé, who was now under the command of Maréchal
de Saint-André, received orders to cover the retreat
with fifteen hundred horse. The post was a perilous
one, and near Le Quesnoy the rear-guard narrowly
escaped being captured. A thick fog concealed the
enemy's movements; the main body of the army had
just crossed the Escaillon and was in full retreat.
As Saint-André was upon the point of following, he
was surprised by the appearance of a body of five
thousand horse led by the Duke of Alva. Retaining his
self-possession, he immediately threw out skirmishers to
engage the head of the column, while with some of
his men he fell back upon an eminence which hid from

view the ford, and covered it with a screen of cavalry. The rest of the column, massed at the bottom of the narrow dell, and posted so as to be invisible to the enemy, crossed the river in haste, and deployed on a projecting bluff of the opposite bank. The Imperialists seeing this position occupied, believed that the French were preparing to resume the offensive, and engaged cautiously. When the last of our cavalry had abandoned at full speed the heights of the left bank, the enemy, unacquainted with the ground, found themselves arrested by the river and under the fire of ' arquebusiers '[1] concealed among the brushwood. The day was declining; and thus the rear-guard, thanks to the intrepidity of Saint-André and his comrades, joined the main body without any serious loss.

The King continued his westward march and laid siege to Renty, a place of some importance at that time from its position on the boundary of Boulonnais and Artois. Our troops encamped on both banks of the river Aa, and entrenched themselves. The Emperor also established himself between Merk and Fliembronne, less than a league to the north, in a strong position on a tributary of the Aa. Our left was covered by heights bordered with woods, which stretched behind it. Only through these woods was it possible for the enemy to approach to the relief of the town. On the twelfth of August, he detached a column to occupy them. But the

---

[1] These ' arquebusiers ' belonged to a mounted company, which had just been formed by the Duc de Guise. That great soldier, who perceived the important part which fire-arms must play in warfare, was applying himself diligently to the task of extending their use and perfecting their mechanism. We shall see how many of his victories were due to his judicious employment of them.

Duc de Guise, who commanded on that side, had posted there three hundred 'arquebusiers,' and their unexpected fire checked the advance of the Imperialists. Next day the attack was renewed by the whole army. The wood, after being held for some time, was abandoned by our infantry. But meanwhile the French cavalry had concentrated on the left bank; and when the enemy debouched upon the open heights, he was vigorously received, and in a second charge was utterly routed.[1] Unfortunately the Imperialists were not pursued as they ought to have been, and it was alleged that 'the retreat had been sounded by a blast of jealousy.'[2] Charles V. rallied his troops and fortified his camp. The King, having in vain offered battle afresh to the immovable Emperor, finding his supplies and munitions failing, raised the siege and disbanded his army in the month of September. The victory of Renty was therefore fruitless. But it was not the less a glorious one for the Duc de Guise. The sagacity with which he seized the right moment for withdrawing his infantry before it was overmatched, no less than the vigorous attack which arrested the deploy of the enemy on emerging from the wood, commands our admiration. This was the first battle at which Condé had been present; he and his gendarmes took part in the brilliant charges of the French cavalry.

His company remained during the following year on the northern frontier. The war, however, proceeded but

---

[1] Amongst other trophies four small cannon were taken, very light and easy to move, mounted upon four wheels, and drawn by horses. They were called 'the Emperor's pistols.' This was the first attempt at light artillery; but this excellent example does not appear to have been followed until the time of Gustavus Adolphus and his famous 'canons de cuir.'

[2] 'La conjonction des lettres et armes.' See also 'Histoire des ducs de Guise,' by M. de Bouillé.

languidly in that district, each side observing the other

without the wish to come to close quarters. In Italy, on the other hand, an engagement seemed imminent, and Condé returned thither as a volunteer. Since the time— four years back—that he had left Brissac's brave army, France had lost all her Transalpine allies. The Siennese, the last of the brave defenders of Italian independence, had been crushed after one of the most heroic struggles recorded in history. The whole energy of the war had been transplanted to Piedmont; and the Duke of Alva had boasted that he would expel the French thence within twenty days. Crossing the Ticino and the Sezia with thirty-five thousand men, he had relieved Vulpiano, and laid siege to Santhia, which covered the left of our line. Brissac, who was not in a condition to withstand such a storm, appealed for help, and a crowd of princes and noblemen flocked anew into his camp.

But the arrival of these reinforcements was seized by the Spanish general as a pretext for raising the siege of Santhia, where he had completely failed; and he was compelled to retreat with his army—now decimated by sickness and discouraged by this check—upon Vercelli. The Duke of Alva, a man of powerful intellect and indomitable courage, but slow, cold, and destitute of versatility, was unable to arrest the rapid movements of the French. While he was reorganizing his troops, we had already stormed Vulpiano, levelled its defences, crossed the Po, and taken possession of Moncalvo. The occupation of this place, following upon that of Casale, rendered us masters of Montferrat, and secured to us the whole line of the Upper Po. Brissac was unable to take part in the brilliant close of this campaign, the credit of

which, however, was solely due to him. Reasons of
health compelled him to resign his command, and, under
these circumstances, the presence of the volunteers had
once more, as in 1551, well-nigh compromised the safety
of the army. The King had fixed upon De Termes to
succeed Brissac. But this selection raised an actual
mutiny in the camp; everybody who had come from
Court refused to serve under a mere gentleman who was
not invested with the dignity of ' Maréchal de France.'
De Termes was obliged to yield, and the command was
bestowed upon the Duc d'Aumale, brother of the Duc de
Guise, and Colonel of the Transalpine light cavalry.
Condé had fruitlessly endeavoured to support De Termes,
and thus to defend the very first principles of military
discipline. At the same time we may be allowed to conjecture that the aversion of a Bourbon for a Lorrain
had some weight in determining his wise resolve.

Notwith-
standing
his ser-
vices, he
is refused
the Lieu-
tenant-
General-
ship of
Picardie,
which his
father and
his brother
had suc-
cessively
held.

But whatever motive actuated him, it seems natural to
expect that his conduct would have pleased the King.
But neither his respect for discipline, nor five years of
faithful and diligent services, could procure him the favour
of Henri II. Even those distinctions which appeared
most rightfully due to him were obstinately refused him.
The government of Picardie had been long entrusted to
Princes of the House of Bourbon, and his elder brother
had been appointed to it on his father's death. Now
Antoine de Bourbon had just inherited the throne of
Navarre, and the post of Lieutenant-Général of Guyenne
having been conferred upon him, he was obliged to resign that of Picardie. On placing his office in the hands
of the King, he begged him to bestow the appointment
upon Condé. A wise policy would doubtless have dis-

couraged the system of allowing provincial governments
to become hereditary in families, even, perhaps especially,
in families connected with the reigning House. But
maxims of this sort were as yet undreamed of; and the
petition of the Princes was at first received with favour.
The promise was even made, and the new King of Navarre was already preparing to cede to his younger
brother the title of Duc de Vendôme, together with a
portion of the estates which he possessed in the north of
France. But meanwhile a second negotiation had been
entered upon by the Court for the purchase of the
sovereignty of Béarn from Antoine. It was broken off;
and as a reprisal, the government of Picardie was suddenly refused to his brother, and given to Coligny;
Condé retained his name and his poverty.

He thus found himself, at the age of twenty-six, Gentleman of the Bedchamber and Captain of a company of
men-at-arms, without having obtained any of the lucra-
tive and honourable posts which he saw lavished around
him upon the relatives of Court favourites. This must
have been all the more galling to him because, in the
opinion of many, the war was at an end, or at all events
indefinitely suspended. Charles V. had retired from the
throne and the world; and the haste with which his
successors had just concluded the Truce of Vaucelles
(1556) seemed to augur a general peace. On the side of
France there seemed but little probability of its being
broken. Notwithstanding many blunders, the policy
which had been pursued since the accession of Henri II.
had been on the whole beneficial in its results. Our
successes had been more important than our reverses;
our gains had exceeded our losses. The truce, which to

a certain extent ratified our acquisitions, afforded us an excellent basis for a definitive settlement. But, contrary to all expectation, the actual course of events was the very reverse. The weak-minded Henri II., submitting in turn to the influence of each of the two factions which divided his Court, undid with one hand what he was doing with the other. At the very time that—acting on the advice of Montmorency—he was signing the truce, he was depriving himself of the power of abiding by its terms, in binding himself by a treaty with Pope Paul IV.,[1] and lending himself to be the tool of the joint ambition of the Guises and the Caraffas.

The Duc François was charged with the command of the disastrous enterprise to which his brother, Cardinal de Lorraine, had just committed France. The exchequer was emptied, and the other divisions of the army disorganised, for the formation of that which he was leading to Rome. But the Châtillons—not less ambitious—could not resign themselves to seeing their rivals in sole possession of the field. Coligny was anxious to inaugurate his government of Picardie by some brilliant achievement. Breaking the truce without a declaration of war, he attempted a *coup-de-main* on Douai, in which he failed, and only succeeded in carrying Lens, a fruitless and insignificant acquisition. Hostilities could not have been renewed more precipitately or less honourably.

The Duke
of Savoy
invades
Champagne and
Picardie
with
47,000
men
(1557).

This foolish conduct was not long in bearing fruit. In the first week of June (1557), the King of Spain assembled thirty-five thousand infantry, twelve thousand cavalry, and a large body of artillery at Givet. Philibert-Emmanuel, Duke of Savoy, was placed at the head of this

---

[1] G. Pietro Caraffa, elevated to the chair of St. Peter 1555.

army. The French Court hastened to throw supplies
into the towns nearest to the seat of war,—Marienbourg,
Rocroy, and Mézières; and all the troops which the
Italian expedition left at its disposal were concentrated
in Champagne under the command of the Duc de Nevers,
governor of the province. Condé had not taken part in
the Italian expedition, an enterprise which was designed
to redound solely to the glory of the House of Lorraine.
Forgetful of his just indignation, and glad to escape
from the idleness of the Court, he hastened to join his
brother-in-law, whose army, moreover, composed of but
indifferent material, scarcely amounted, in effective men,
to eighteen thousand foot and five thousand horse.

CHAP.
I.

1557

Condé repairs to the army. Commencement of operations.

The enemy, after a feigned assault on the newly-pro-
visioned towns, turned abruptly, carried La Capelle and
Vervins, and proceeded to menace Guise. Nevers,
moving parallel and to the south of the enemy's line of
march, succeeded in reaching Notre-Dame-de-Liesse,
where he was joined by the Connétable, who had come
to assume the command of the army. Here it was
discovered that the Duke of Savoy, passing Guise, had
continued his march towards Picardie. Coligny was
anxious to be first in the field in defence of his own
province; and, in compliance with his request, received
from Montmorency some light troops in order that, by
a rapid advance, he might occupy it without delay. On
the way he received intelligence that the Spaniards,
having just been reinforced by eight thousand English,
who had disembarked a few days before at Calais, were
investing Saint-Quentin. He repaired thither with all
speed, and had but just time to throw himself into the
town at night with a few of his cavalry. His infantry

lost their way, and were unable to follow him. The place was very scantily provisioned, and not even fully fortified; it became necessary to complete, under the enemy's fire, some works which were absolutely indispensable. The Admiral had not brought with him a single cannon, or even a musket. But his very presence was a powerful reinforcement.

Montmorency had closely followed Coligny; and on his arrival at La Fère, he learned at the same moment both the investment of Saint-Quentin and his nephew's entry into it. It was of the first importance that the town should be succoured at once, in order that it might detain the enemy till the French army could be effectively reinforced; and yet it was necessary to avoid a battle which, as things then stood, could only end in defeat. The nature of the ground and the positions occupied by the Spaniards admitted of both results.

Saint-Quentin lies on the right bank of the river Somme, which flows to the south of the town, through swamps and marshy bogs difficult to cross. On the south-west, a bridge, which had been broken down, joins the town to the suburb of L'Ile, which lies on the left bank. Half a league higher up, near the village of Rouvroy, the marshes are traversed by another causeway, —the only one in the neighbourhood at the time of which we write. The enemy had invested the place on the east, north, and west sides, leaving open the side next to the swamps, which were considered impassable. On the left bank he held only the suburb of L'Ile, and a mill, which commanded the end of the causeway to Rouvroy, and thus secured the communication between the Spanish camp and the suburb.

Montmorency was determined to reconnoitre the place
in person. On the eighth of August he arrived, with five
thousand men, at Issigny-le-Grand. Advancing by night
under the walls, he was enabled to communicate with
Coligny, to settle his plans in concert with him upon the
spot, and to explain them to a few trusted officers whom
he had brought with him, and for whom he was reserving
certain posts in the action which was impending. Among
these was Condé. The simplest and most reasonable
course would have been to attempt the relief of the town
by night, and to employ none but the troops intended to
enter it. But the Connétable preferred that his whole
army should take part in the operation. His plan was
to arrive at the Somme at daybreak, to drive back into
the suburb the Spanish corps stationed on the left bank,
to occupy the head of the causeway to Rouvroy, and
thus to cut off the communication between the two
banks, and by a feigned attack of artillery to draw off
the attention of the Duke of Savoy, who was encamped
at the west of the town, by the river side. At the same
time some boats, brought on carts from La Fère, were to
be launched at a point agreed upon with Coligny, so
as to introduce into the town supplies, together with a
reinforcement of two thousand men, commanded by
D'Andelot. It was hoped that all this might be effected,
and a retreat commenced, before the enemy had recovered from his surprise, and been able to force the
passage of the causeway.

Everything was in readiness for the tenth of August,—
St. Lawrence's Day. But unhappily a plan, fairly well devised, was not carried out with that vigour and precision
which were its only possible conditions of success. The

Somme was not reached till nine o'clock, instead of at daybreak. Instead of leaving at La Fère all the non-combatants, the army was accompanied by a crowd of camp-followers and sutlers, who were sure to increase greatly the difficulty of a retreat, and were already blocking up the roads with tumbrils. However, the Spaniards were taken completely by surprise, and were quickly mewed up in the suburb. Condé, with a few light troops, seized the mills on the right towards Rouvroy. Saint-André, to whom had been entrusted the feigned attack on the left, fell upon the tents of the Duke of Savoy, who had only just time to buckle on his cuirass and to make for the Comte d'Egmont's camp on the north of the town. But the boats which were intended to transport the reliefs, and which ought to have followed the vanguard, were lost in a crowd of baggage-waggons, and arrived too late.[1] When the attempt was made to launch them, they were swept by the fire of the garrison of the suburb and of the Duke of Savoy's retreating troops. Men and supplies were alike engulphed in the mud; and D'Andelot alone, with less than two hundred men, succeeded in reaching the town and in bringing to his brother the aid of his trusty sword.

Condé,
cut off on
the right,
is unable
to defend
the road to
Rouvroy.
Death of
the Comte
d'Enghien;
capture of
the Conné-
table and
flight of
the French
army.

The Spanish army, meanwhile, was rallying behind the causeway of Rouvroy. The fortune of the day depended on the way in which the French would defend this passage. But Montmorency imagined it to be much narrower than it really was, and instead of occupying in force this key of his position, he had merely stationed there a few 'reîtres.' Condé, posted at a little distance, perceived the approaching storm. Too weak and too

[1] 'Mémoires de Mergey.'

ill-supported to check the advance which was in prepa-
ration, he could only give notice of it, and ask for reinforcements.   The Connétable, very confident of success at
first, laughed at those who gave signs of some uneasiness
as to the issue, and jestingly replied that he ' would show
the enemy a trick of the old wars; ' until, his anxiety
increasing, and his hot temper getting the better of him,
he became absolutely savage in his bearing towards all
who brought him any intelligence or asked for orders.
At last he determined to send the Duc de Nevers with
three compagnies d'ordonnance to the support of Condé.
The enemy's columns were already debouching from the
causeway.   Condé, who held his position with the
greatest difficulty, besought Nevers to charge with him
at once, before the Spaniards had had time to complete
the passage of the river.   And perhaps this was the only
chance of saving the army.   But Nevers was bound by
the strict orders of the Connétable, who—not foreseeing
the consequences of this lamentable delay, and still
cherishing the hope of avoiding a general engagement—
had forbidden him, on pain of death, to charge.[1]   Condé
and Nevers were soon surrounded on all sides and cut off
from all possibility of joining the ' bataille.'[2]   Montmorency began to direct his course towards La Fère,
marching still in order of battle.   Seeing the enemy
beginning to occupy his line of retreat, he inclined to the
right, hoping to flank himself by the forest of Gibercourt.
But he was too late.   The pages and other attendants
who preceded and delayed the army in its retreat, attacked by the Spanish cavalry, fell back upon our troops

[1] ' Mémoires de Tavannes.'
[2] We have already stated that the centre or main body of the army was called the ' bataille.'

and threw them into the utmost confusion. The panic
soon became general. In vain did a few resolute men
try to stem the torrent. The first of these, Jean, Comte
d'Enghien, Condé's eldest brother, exclaiming that he
would never let himself be struck down from behind,
turned upon the enemy, and, throwing himself into the
thick of the victorious squadrons, 'answered those who
spoke of surrender with sword-thrusts, and died a true
Bourbon in heart and in blood.'[1] The Connétable too
fought, until wounded and overpowered by numbers,
he was compelled to yield his sword. The loss was
enormous. The French army was annihilated; the kingdom seemed to lie at the conqueror's mercy.[2] It is
said that the old Emperor, when in his retirement at
Yuste he heard of the event of St. Lawrence's Day,[3]
exclaimed immediately, 'My son must be in Paris.'[4]
But Philip II. was incapable of prompt and daring action.
He preferred capturing the places within his reach, and
forthwith pressed forward the siege of Saint-Quentin.
Coligny was ever great in adversity; his firmness, his
skill, and his bravery prolonged the defence beyond all

---

[1] Lestoile. This brave Prince
was thirty-one years of age. He
was an accomplished gentleman,
and his letters are those of a cultivated mind. His noble and melancholy face, of which Léonard de
Limoges has preserved for us a
striking likeness, in one of his magnificent enamels, was full of sweet-
ness and resolution. When he
was killed he had been scarcely two
months married to a young wife,
beautiful and wealthy, his cousin-
german, with whom he had been
in love for some years. He had
left her, almost on the morrow of
their wedding, that he might hasten
to the field.

[2] 'Paroissoit être en proye.'—
'Mémoires de Tavannes.'

[3] It is under this name that the
battle of Saint-Quentin is known in
Spain. And it was as a memorial
of this victory, and in honour of St.
Lawrence, that Philip II. gave the
form of a gridiron to that pile of stone,
as cold and gloomy as his own soul,
which is called the Escurial.

[4] 'Mon fils doit être à Paris.'

expectation.   And he was well supported by those who had rallied the remnants of the Connétable's army.

CHAP.
I.

1557

Condé and Nevers retreat. The former holds the field the whole autumn at the head of the light cavalry, and renders the greatest services.

Nevers and Condé, who had been obliged to manœuvre apart from the remainder of the army on the tenth, were enabled to reach La Fère the same evening.   It had required all their energy, and all the confidence with which they inspired their troops, to keep the men together and to force their way through the close ranks of the victors. Nevers, who had succeeded to the command, hastened to Laon, and supplied, as best he could, the neighbouring towns.   The gendarmerie was completely destroyed, but the light cavalry had not suffered so severely.   Condé rallied a few squadrons and immediately took the field again.   He kept it throughout the whole autumn, continually harassing the enemy, and attacking their foraging parties and escorts.   Almost all these raids were successful.   This is one of the finest passages in the Prince's military life.   So much activity and vigour on the morrow of so great a defeat astounded the Spanish generals. They gave up every important undertaking, and seemed so undecided in their counsels that Nevers thought he might venture on a fresh attempt to relieve Saint-Quentin. But he had relied too much on the supineness of his adversaries.   He was repulsed, and the town was at length captured; but the heroic Admiral surrendered to the Duke of Savoy a mere heap of ruins.   Le Catelet, Ham, Chauny, and Noyon met with the same fate.   But meanwhile the strength of Philip II.'s German troops was being daily diminished by desertions; and the English too had just withdrawn.   Added to which a really national movement was agitating France.   The conduct of the King, which from the first was admirable, had

sustained the spirits of all; and supplies both of men and
money were being raised in every quarter. As early as
the month of October, Philip II. left for Brussels, and
dispersed his army. At the same time the Duc de Guise
was returning across the Alps with the veteran bands
which he had so foolishly led into Italy. The nation
welcomed him as a deliverer, and the King conferred
upon him immense power and the title of his Lieutenant-
Général.[1]

Guise ap-
pointed the
King's
Lieu-
tenant-
General.
He takes
Calais and
Thionville
(1558).

It is well known by what brilliant achievements Guise
justified this high honour. Anxious to take advantage
of the universal enthusiasm, he put his troops in motion
in the depth of winter. Too weak to attack the towns
where the Spaniards were entrenched, he made a demonstration on the frontiers of Champagne and Picardie,
as if to prevent the revictualling of Ham and Saint-Quentin; and then, inclining to the left, he rapidly led his
army under the walls of Calais. In eight days (January
1558), he carried that town, which the intrepid Jean de
Vienne had held for a whole year against Edward III.
after the battle of Crécy, and which had been in the
possession of the English for more than two hundred
years. In the spring, he was before Thionville on the
Moselle, a place of great importance, and the occupation
of which would complete that of Les Trois Évêchés.[2]
The town surrendered on the twenty-second of June.

---

[1] The Prince de Condé asked for
orders from the new Lieutenant-
General of the kingdom in a letter
dated September 18, 1557. (Bibl.
imp., 'Mémoires du roi Henri II;'
orig. sign. autog.)

[2] This siege was difficult, bloody,
and very skilfully conducted. It
marks an epoch in the art of military engineering. It was there that
Montluc invented the *places d'armes*
in the trenches.

The *places d'armes*, in sieges, are
those wider spaces disposed here and
there in the trenches where bodies
of armed soldiers may be collected

In the history of these brilliant operations, Condé's name is scarcely mentioned. He had returned to the army in the King's suite: and no definite duty, no command was assigned to him. The rough winter campaign had been to him the occasion of a fresh mortification. The post of Colonel-Général of the light cavalry, which he had led with so much credit, had become vacant, and he thought he might solicit it. But the Duc de Guise wanted it for one of his friends, and to Guise nothing was refused. The Duc de Nemours was preferred to Condé, and the latter was thought to be compensated in being named Colonel-Général of the Transalpine infantry. This was no equivalent for the other appointment, in the opinion of the age, and it led to more than one repartee at the Prince's expense.[1] The infantry, however, was beginning to emerge from the undeserved contempt to which the old feudal world had consigned it. François Ier had understood the importance of the revolution which was taking place in military organization, and had spared no effort to assist and regulate its course. Among other measures he had determined that, in each army, the

---

under shelter, in order to repulse the sorties of the besieged, and to protect the men at work in the trenches. Otherwise the term *place d'armes* has various meanings in military phraseology. In a fortified town it signifies the principal open ground where the main guard is posted, and where the garrison may be mustered. It applies also to the fortress which supports the operations of an army, or portion of an army, in the field.

[1] 'Quand la Reine mère eut faict madame la Princesse de la Roche-sur-Yon sa damme d'honneur, le Prince de Condé luy voulut remonstrer [voyre s'en moquer, car il s'en aydoit] le tort qu'elle s'estoit faict .... à quoy elle respondit qu'elle ne pensoit pas plus se faire tort en cela, ny aux siens, que luy en la charge qu'il avoit autrefois prise de couronnel de sa belle infanterie et piedz puants de gens de pied, par la succession encor de deux gentilshommes qui estoient moindres que luy. .... Ce fut à M. le Prince à se taire. ...'—Brantôme, 'Grands Capitaines françois,' Disc. lxxx.

infantry should be united under the command of a colonel. And as there were two permanent armies, one Cisalpine, the other Transalpine,—that is in France and in Italy,—there were also two permanent offices of Colonel or Colonel-Général. These new posts had been accepted by illustrious soldiers. Bayard had not disdained to command infantry; and a Bourbon, the Comte de Saint-Pol, had been one of the first to follow his example. For indeed, at all times posts of danger have been posts of honour; and no command was more perilous than that of infantry. In action the colonel's place was in the front rank, where on foot, and pike in hand, he was more exposed than the bravest captain of the grenadiers would be in the present day. And indeed if the war in Italy had been still going on, Condé would have doubtless joyfully accepted this post. But, under the existing circumstances, the favour was an affront. Since the fatal issue of the Duc de Guise's expedition, France had scarcely been able to retain a few garrisons in Piedmont; she had no longer an army there, and very

1559. soon, by the Peace of Cateau-Cambrésis, she gave up to Germans and Spaniards that Italy which, for more than sixty years, had cost her so much blood and so many a glorious exploit.

The close of the campaign of 1558 had not corresponded to its brilliant opening. The Duc de Guise, occupied with the intrigues which were dividing the Court, had suddenly abandoned operations after the capture of Thionville. Diane de Poitiers, breaking her old alliances, had just joined herself to the party of Montmorency, and was endeavouring to ruin the House of Lorraine in the favour of the King, who was beginning to be alarmed at the popularity and influence of the conqueror of Calais. And while the latter was trying to baffle their intrigues, the Regency of the Low Countries, taking advantage of this respite, had again marched all their forces towards the west, and De Termes, surprised near Gravelines, had been completely beaten. Still there was no thought of recovering this serious check, and all that was done was to form a camp near Amiens. Everyone desired peace; the Montmorency party that the Connétable might be set free, the Guises that they might regain their influence at Court, watch over the internal affairs of the kingdom, and make themselves agreeable to the King of Spain. Some secret instinct, added to their own profound foresight, taught them that the support of this Sovereign would some day be necessary to them. After negotiations, which were too hastily conducted, the treaty was signed on the third of April, 1559. With the exception of Les Trois Évêchés, of Calais (and in reference even to this town there was a clause of restitution), of Turin, Pignerol, Chivasso, and one or two other small places in the States of the Duke of Savoy, which the King retained as a pledge for the submission to arbitration of his claims there, we lost all our recent conquests, as well as those of the preceding reign; all the rights claimed by our Kings were given up.

'A shameful Peace,' exclaims Tavannes, 'of which the illuminations were the funeral torches of King Henri II.!'

CHAPTER II.

1560.

Internal state of France on the accession of François II.; power of the
Guises.—The malcontents and the Protestants seek in vain to obtain as
their leader the King of Navarre.—Wrongs and position of the Prince
de Condé. He is intrusted with a mission; fresh injuries.—A conspiracy is revealed to the Duc de Guise.—'Conspiracy' of Amboise
(March 1560). — 'Le Capitaine muet' (the dumb captain). — Condé
repairs to the King.—Proceedings are taken against him; his indignant
reply; he quits the Court.—Nature of the conspiracy.—The Guises
have fresh cause of alarm; Condé goes to Nérac to his brother, the
King of Navarre.—The two Bourbons decline to attend the conferences
at Fontainebleau.—The King assumes a threatening attitude; disclosures of La Sague.—Notwithstanding the arrest of the Vidame de
Chartres and the insurrections of Maligny, Montbrun, and Mouvans, the
two Princes leave Nérac to attend the States at Orléans.—Measures taken
by the Guises.—Efforts on the part of Condé's friends to keep him
back. — Trusting to the King's word, he enters Orléans; his arrest
(October 30).—His trial; iniquitous mode of proceeding.—His haughty
bearing. The sentences of the 13th, 15th, 20th, and 26th November.—
Fruitless attempts to save him; firmness of the Guises; his execution
is fixed for the 10th December.—Illness and death of François II.
(December 5, 1560). Condé saved by the co-operation of Médicis and
of L'Hospital.

CHAP.
II.

1560
Internal
state of
France
on the ac-
cession of
François
II. Power
of the
Guises.

A VAGUE longing for change was now unsettling men's
minds. The principles of the Reformation were making
rapid progress; it was the aristocratic or the popular
cause alternately, varying with the traditions of each
province, and was covering France with a network of
churches, the power of whose organization was soon to
be manifested. The accession of a mere boy to the
throne, the humiliation of our country, the enormous

debts left by the late King, all combined to favour the propagation of the new thoughts; and while fierce persecutions were bringing to a climax the irritation of the sectaries, a revolution at Court was still further increasing the number of the malcontents. The Guises, who had been out of favour at the end of the last reign, were becoming all-powerful under their nephew François II.[1] The Queen-Mother, Catherine de Médicis, not so much from political forethought as from the vindictiveness of an injured woman, allied herself with them, that she might, in the person of the Connétable, strike at the friend of the Duchesse de Valentinois; and the Lorrains, who had now become the sole depositaries of the Royal authority, used their power with a haughtiness which it was hard for a nation, ever justly susceptible on the point of honour, to bear at the hands of a House of foreign extraction.

Antoine de Bourbon, who, like Montmorency, was in disgrace, who had almost openly renounced his former faith,[2] who more than anyone else had been fretted by the Peace of Cateau-Cambrésis—sacrificing, as it did, his claims on Lower Navarre—who was, in fine, first Prince of the blood, was looked up to as the natural leader and sure hope of the malcontents and the oppressed of every kind. Encouragements and offers of service were pressed

---

[1] He had married Marie Stuart (born December 7, 1542), who, by the death of her father, James V., became Queen of Scotland seven days after her birth (December 14, 1542). Marie de Lorraine, her mother, who was then Regent of her dominions, was the daughter of the Duc Claude de Guise, and sister to the Duc François.

[2] We learn from Beza ('Histoire ecclésiastique') that the King of Navarre was then much more 'affectionné à la religion' (attached to the Reformed faith) than his wife, Jeanne d'Albret. She 's'y portoit d'abord fort froidement' (was at first very coldly disposed towards it). Ere long the tables were turned.

upon him, and the bold counsels of his friends seemed
for a time to carry the day. He repaired to the Court,
surrounded by his relations, and followed by a numerous
retinue. It was hoped that he was about to assume the
attitude there of a man strong in his rights, and sure of
support. His well-nigh insulting reception at Saint-
Germain would have aroused in any other man the
keenest indignation. But though a brave man and ready
in speech, he was on this occasion utterly disconcerted.
After two days of humiliating delay, the Royal pleasure
was made known to him. Navarre complied without a
word. He accepted the mission of escorting into Spain
the Princesse Élisabeth—the betrothed of Philip II. On
his return from this embassy, during which fresh indignities had been heaped upon him, he retired to his
little Court of Nérac, and resumed anew his wonted life
of dissipation and frivolity.

'Disappointed of having for their leader the King of
Navarre, those who were urged onward by necessity
soon turned their eyes to Louis, Prince de Condé, a man
of high birth, prudent, brave, and poor.'[1] A near relative
of the Connétable, he was, next to the King of Navarre,
eldest of the Princes of the blood.[2] Too indifferent to
religion to have as yet taken either side in the contro-
versy, he yet was a favourite with the Reformers, of
whose views his wife, Éléonore de Roye, was a warm
adherent, and of whom his friends and allies, the Châtillons, were already the recognised leaders. In him
they would find no hesitation, no timidity ; but a keen
enthusiasm, a love of glory, and a turn for fighting ;

---

[1] D'Aubigné, 'Histoire universelle.'
[2] Another of his elder brothers
was still living, but he was, as we
mentioned above, in holy orders.

above all, a deep resentment for the neglect with which
his services in the field had been requited, and for the
insults which were daily rekindling bygone animosities.

Scarcely had Henri II. breathed his last, when, without
waiting for his brother's final desertion of the cause, he
protested loudly, in the name of the public welfare and
of the ancient laws of the realm, against the unjust
concentration of power in the hands of Catherine and the
Guises. The council, upon which, as a matter of form,
he had been nominated, listened, at first with astonishment, and afterwards with some degree of assent, to the
spirited and courageous words of a young man who was
supposed to care for nothing but love and war; and his
open and unexpected resistance to the measures proposed
was frequently successful. Thus it was owing to Condé's
opposition that François II. was not made to assume the
title of King of France, Scotland, England, and Ireland—
a step which the uncles of Marie Stuart were anxious
should be taken unexpectedly. They grew uneasy. Well
aware of the powerful influence which Condé might
exercise over the old servants of the Crown, they seized
the first opportunity that occurred to remove him from
Court.[1] Philip II. was still in the Low Countries, and
was about to embark on his return to Spain. Condé
was despatched in all haste to Ghent, to congratulate the
King of Spain, and to take, in the name of the new
King of France, the oath that he would observe the
recently concluded Treaty of Peace (August 1559). Just
as he was setting out, Cardinal de Lorraine handed to

---

[1] Despatch of Throckmorton, Ambassador, dated July 13, 1559. See
'A Full View of the Public Transactions in the Reign of Queen Elizabeth,' by D. Forbes. 2 vols. London, 1740–41.

him an order on the Royal exchequer for one thousand
écus. This was simply insulting to the Prince, whose
poverty was no secret; he was compelled to mortgage
his estates in order to keep up the dignity which his
embassy required.[1]　On the coronation of François II.
he had to submit to a fresh indignity.　If anything could
have consoled Condé for having been refused the government of Picardie by the late King, it must have been the
seeing it conferred upon Coligny, his kinsman and friend.
He had completely abandoned all thoughts of that dignity, when, during the coronation solemnities, Cardinal
de Lorraine informed the Admiral, with an air of mystery,
that the Prince had renewed his entreaties for it.　By
means of this false statement, the Cardinal hoped to induce
Coligny to resign his governorship, and to set him against
his cousin.　He was only partially successful.　After an
explanation, in which Condé had no great difficulty in
proving that he had been calumniated, the Admiral
tendered his resignation, and requested that he might be
replaced by him to whom he had formerly been preferred.
The King replied that he meant to confer Picardie upon
Maréchal de Brissac, and the two friends withdrew more
closely united and more deeply wounded than ever.

Meetings of the malcontents were increasing in number
in various parts of France.　Anxiety was becoming general; it extended to the Court, where there was no lack

---

[1] On August 5, 1559, Sébastien de
Laubespine, then Ambassador in attendance upon Philip II., wrote from
Ghent to the Duc de Guise to complain of the 'infinite inconvenience
occasioned by the retinue of Monseigneur le Prince de Condé, num-
bering not less than seven or eight
score.'　('Négociations sous François II,' published by M. Louis
Pâris; 'Collection of Unpublished
Documents.')　Had the Prince really
so numerous a retinue?　Or was
Laubespine desirous of amusing the
men in power by a jest at the poverty
of Condé?

of information, however vague and uncertain in its character. At length, when the King was at Blois, the Duc
de Guise received important and definite disclosures. A
formidable plot had been hatched. A Paris advocate,
named Des Avenelles, who had been solicited to take
part in it, had revealed it to the Duke's secretary. This
man must not be confounded with those low informers
whose perfidy and venality inspire us with aversion and
contempt. He was a sincere Protestant, and never
changed his religion. He was prompted neither by ambition nor by avarice; [1] but he was shocked at the nefarious character and the possible results of the scheme.
In the disinterested conduct of this advocate we see one
of the earliest signs of that stern and patriotic reverence
for law, hitherto unknown to the age, which was soon to
be so nobly exemplified in L'Hospital, and hereafter to
remain the tradition and the glory of the French law-
courts. Des Avenelles, however, mentioned but few
names, and gave but scanty details. Cardinal de Lorraine
proposed to assemble troops at once, and to take strong
measures. But his brother, who was cooler and less
easily alarmed, preferred waiting till the first blow should
be struck; and contented himself with removing the
King to the Castle of Amboise, where there was less
danger of surprise. He summoned thither the gentlemen
of whose fidelity he was sure; and soon had silently collected nearly three thousand horse. A fresh disclosure
enabled him to employ them to good account.

Simultaneously with the first measures of the Court,
the leaders of the conspiracy, though far from giving up
their designs, had begun to modify their plans, and to

---

[1] See De Thou, and even D'Aubigné.

expedite their proceedings. The day upon which they fixed was the seventeenth of March.. The dépôts of arms were prepared, and each of those engaged was already travelling to the rendezvous, when, as early as the fifteenth, small bodies of horsemen, sallying forth from Amboise, fell upon the earliest groups of the conspirators. The latter, arriving in small and scattered detachments from different quarters of France, were everywhere surprised by superior forces; the desperate but disunited efforts at resistance made by a few were easily put down, and by the eighteenth all was over. Most of the rank and file of men-at-arms who had taken part in the plot had been executed, drowned or hanged, without a trial. The massacre was terrible. The most prominent had been spared and conveyed to Amboise; it was necessary to put them to the question.

'The
dumb
captain.'
Condé
repairs to
the King.

It was already well known that everything had been organized under the command of a gentleman of Périgord, named La Renaudie, of equal courage and eloquence. He had just been killed in a skirmish near Château-Renaud. He was the acknowledged leader. But there was another mysterious leader, a great personage, who was never named, and was called 'the dumb captain.' At first the Guises had suspected the Prince de Condé. Great, therefore, was their astonishment when he arrived at Amboise shortly after the King. His bearing was so calm, and the suspicions that had been entertained against him were so slenderly supported by proof, that it was necessary to receive him in the customary manner. He was even intrusted with the defence of the Porte des Bons-Hommes, and François de Lorraine confined himself to stationing, as a security, at the same post, his brother the Grand

Prior and a few trusty friends. His enemies avowed that he took it very cheerfully.[1] Torture, however, compelled the prisoners to speak. La Bigue, secretary to La Renaudie, avowed that 'the dumb captain' was no other than the Prince de Condé. Others confirmed the statement. In the meantime, Maligny the younger,[2] a gentleman who was looked upon as one of La Renaudie's principal accomplices, and of whom it was intended to make a signal example, had succeeded in effecting his escape from Amboise. He was allied to Condé by the ties both of blood and friendship ; he had been cornet of his troop, and it was an equerry of the Prince's, named De Vaux, who had furnished him for his escape with one of his master's best horses.

Maligny's flight caused extreme vexation to the Court. Emissaries and instructions were despatched on all sides, in order to secure his arrest. Condé received orders not to absent himself; his papers were seized by the Grand Provost. His position was becoming day by day more critical. But his coolness and his high bearing did not desert him for an instant. At one time he thus answers some insinuation of Cardinal de Lorraine :—' My rank forbids me to conceal myself, as well as you to put interrogations prejudicial to me.' At another time, in presence of the irritated and threatening King himself, before his assembled council, the two Queens, the knights,

---

[1] 'Fit fort bonne mine.'
[2] Edme de Ferrières Maligny, called the Cadet Maligny, or Maligny the younger, born 1540, cornet in the Prince de Condé's troop in 1557, drowned himself in the Lake of Geneva in the autumn of 1560. His grandmother was an illegitimate issue of the House of Bourbon, and through his mother, Louise de Vendôme, he was connected with Condé, the Montmorencies, and the Châtillons. (See 'La Vie de Jean de Ferrières, par M. de Bastard.' Auxerre, 1858.)

the great officers of state, he appears, no longer as a
man under accusation, but as accusing others in turn :—
'Since I well know,' he exclaims, 'that I have enemies
about the person of the King, who are plotting the ruin
of myself and my friends, I have besought him to do me
the favour of listening to my answer in presence of this
assembly. And I hereby declare that saving the King's
person, that of MM. his brothers, that of the Queen his
mother, and that of the reigning Queen, those who have
reported that I was the chief and leader of certain
treasonable persons who are said to have conspired
against the King's person and estate, have falsely and
villanously lied. And waiving on this occasion my rank
as a Prince of the blood—a rank which I ever hold from
God only—I am prepared to compel them at the point
of the sword to confess that they are cowards and rogues,
who are themselves plotting the subversion of the Estate
and the Crown, to the protection of which I have a
better title than my accusers. If there is among the
present company any one who has promulgated this
report, and is willing to maintain it, let him do so on the
spot!'[1] The Duc de Guise rose and protested that he
could not endure to hear of so great a Prince being
calumniated longer, and offered to act as his second.
Condé, taking advantage of the impression made by his
spirited words, demanded and obtained permission to
quit the Court, which he immediately did.

Nature of
the con-
spiracy. Of his participation in the conspiracy there is little
doubt. And yet 'all did not come from him, nor yet
half of it.'[2]

---

[1] La Popelinière, 'Histoire de
France,' liv. vi.

[2] 'Tout ne venoit pas de luy, ny
la moitié.'—Montluc, liv. vii.

It was from the ranks of the Protestant party, now consolidated by its religious discipline, that an army arose, everywhere officered, and everywhere ready for action. Its soul and its head was Coligny. Prudent and self-restrained, he had not been implicated in the conspiracy. But he it was who, at a meeting at La Fertè-sous-Jouarre, after the King's coronation, had explained to Condé the organization of the Churches, the numbers of the Protestants, and their relations with the German Lutheran Princes;[1] and who at once enkindling his enthusiasm and restraining the impatience with which his many and fresh grievances filled him, had tempted him into a slower but surer course. It was then that relations were established between the Prince and the actual ringleaders of the only organized party which could furnish a solid basis of support in the impending conflict. The general dissatisfaction continued to swell the numbers of the sympathizers. Their object was to overthrow the power of the Guises, to obtain liberty of conscience, and, at the farthest, to place the King under guardianship; and not even torture could ever wring

---

[1] In the instructions addressed to the Bishop of Rennes, who had been sent as Ambassador to the Emperor (May 23, 1560), the King charges that prelate to seek interviews in his name with the Count Palatine, the Landgrave of Hesse, and the Duke of Wurtemberg, for the purpose of giving information to these Princes 'concerning a matter which seemed in some wise to concern them, which is, that in the troubles that have lately arisen in this kingdom, some of the rebels and seditious persons who, for colour and pretext of their conspiracy, put forward the question of religion, gave it commonly to be understood that they had communications with them; a thing which the King aforesaid would never believe.' . . . But the tone of the letter proves that since 1560 these relations actually subsisted, and gave much uneasiness to the French Court. The Bishop of Rennes was ordered to leave no means untried of abolishing them. (Imperial Library, Collection 'Colbert.')

from the conspirators an avowal of any other designs. It was asserted that the Protestant ministers wished to put Republican principles into practice, and to establish in France a government on the model of that of Geneva. It was said that the Prince de Condé was aiming at the Crown, and that already medals had been struck, bearing the inscription : 'Ludovicus XIII., Francorum rex.'[1] These statements seemed to have but little foundation in fact, and the Guises, despite all their exertions, could not succeed in gaining general credence for them. François II. alone remained in the belief that his life and that of his brothers was sought. It is true that the feeble and scrofulous young King was little known and little loved. It was vulgarly reported that in order to cure himself of a hereditary disease, he was in the habit of putting children to death that he might bathe in their blood. His brothers were still under age, and the prospect of a succession of regencies tended to increase the uneasiness of men's minds. Already at that time, in many a heart, disturbed by doubt, the political creed had been no less shaken than the religious, and it is far from impossible that vague aspirations may have mingled with the projects that were being settled. It is impossible to say what might have happened had the 'conspiracy' of Am-

---

[1] The medals were struck, according to some, at the time of the conspiracy of Amboise; according to others during the third civil war in 1568. Fontanieu (vol. cccxx. of his Collection) asserts that he had seen the silver coinage which the Prince de Condé caused to be struck with his name and effigy. Le Blanc, in his treatise on numismatics, described it as an *écu* of gold, with the head of the Prince on one side, and on the reverse the escutcheon of France with the legend *Ludovicus XIII. Dei grat. Francorum rex primus christianus.* But modern collections and numismatists assert that this coinage never existed, and reject the opinions of Fontanieu and Le Blanc, as founded on the misreading of a *douzain barbare* of the reign of Louis XIII.

boise resulted differently. For if the desired object had
been attained, it would soon have been left behind. But
whatever were its true aims, the attempt was culpable,
however susceptible of excuse. Had the repressive
measures which followed extended to none but the
leaders, it might be allowed us to pity the victims, without blaming the executioners. But it is impossible to
condemn too severely the atrocious cruelties for which
this affray afforded the opportunity, and the heart sickens
at the catalogue of sanguinary executions performed like
a pageant under the eyes of two Queens of France. The
only result of such proceedings was to embitter every
existing hatred, to bring to a climax the power of the
Guises, and to deepen the gulph which separated them
from the Bourbons.

On leaving the Court, Condé repaired to Ferté-sous-
Jouarre. Near Montlhéry, on his way thither, he met
Damville,[1] son of the Connétable, whom his father was
sending to attend upon the King. The two cousins,
without alighting from their horses, held a long conversation. The haughty bearing which Damville assumed after this conference excited the suspicion of the
Guises. Nor were other indications wanting to make
them uneasy. Montmorency had been charged with the
duty of announcing the result of the conspiracy at Amboise to the Parliament at Paris. The crafty old man,
while expressing himself in severe terms respecting the

[1] Henri de Montmorency, second son of the Connétable Anne, Duc de Damville, and subsequently Duc de Montmorency after the death of his father and of his eldest brother, became Connétable himself in 1595, in the reign of Henri IV., to whom he had rendered great services, and who used to call him his 'compère' (gossip). He was born in 1534, and died April 2, 1614. One of his daughters became the mother of the Great Condé.

rebels, had taken care to reduce the attempt in his de-
scription to the limits of a plot against the King's ministers and friends. This was not in accordance with his
instructions. At the same time the Spanish Ambassador,
Chantonnet, brother of Cardinal de Granvelle, earnestly
recommended the Queen-Mother to recall the Princes of
the blood to their share in the conduct of affairs, and this
advice was attributed to the influence which the Connétable still retained over Philip II. And lastly, Coligny,
D'Andelot, and the Vidame de Chartres,[1] all those, in
short, who were under suspicion, had, upon various
pretexts, withdrawn from Court. The Guises began to
fear that they had succeeded at Amboise in reaching
none but unimportant enemies, and to repent of having
allowed the more formidable to escape. They spared no
effort to secure once more the person at least of the
Prince de Condé. He, however, not feeling himself safe
on his own estates, had determined to join his brother.
Disregarding the invitations and fair words which he
continued to receive from the Court, he started for
Béarn, assuring the King of his devotion, but adroitly
keeping at a distance the messengers who were sent to
him. From that time forward 'the opinion arose that
he would cut out plenty of work for them, as indeed he
afterwards did.'[2] As soon as he reached Nérac the
malcontents flocked thither from all quarters. The

---

[1] François de Vendôme, Vidame
de Chartres, one of the most illustrious noblemen of the age, and the
last scion of his ancient House. The
elder branch had been extinct since
the close of the fourteenth century,
and the title of Comte de Vendôme
had been brought into the House of
Bourbon by Catherine, who in 1364
was married to Jean I., Comte de
la Marche. The Vidame François
was descended from a younger son,
who lived about 1310. His mother,
Hélène de Gouffier, was cousin to
the Montmorencies, to the Châtillons,
and to Éléonore de Roye, Princesse
de Condé.

[2] 'Mémoires de Castelnau.'

meeting of the Bourbons revived the hopes of all. The King's missives followed each other in rapid succession, pressing Navarre to bring his brother with him to Court, in order that he might clear himself of the accusations brought against him by 'those wretched heretics, who were charging him with strange things.' At the same time the tone of these despatches affected to be encouraging and almost friendly. They expressed the conviction that Condé would easily be able to prove the falsehood of the assertions made by these 'scoundrels.'[1]

There was a time at which the two Princes might have obeyed the orders of François II. without incurring much risk. The 'notables of the realm' were meeting at Fontainebleau. The Bourbons had more than one friend in this assembly. They might have presented themselves there with a considerable train, and there were not wanting about them gentlemen who were ready to follow them. Montmorency strongly advised them to profit by this opportunity; and he himself set them an example, by taking with him his nephews, the Châtillons; only he took care to bring with him an escort of eight hundred lances. Navarre and Condé made the excuse that they had not received notice in time; in short, they did not appear. The discussions at Fontainebleau were keen. Coligny spoke for the first time in the name of the Protestants. He presented and warmly supported a petition from the Reformers of Normandie. Then followed long harangues from the Bishops of Vienne and Valence against the irregularity and the immorality of the higher clergy and of the Court. To these petitions and orations Guise and his brother replied haughtily.

The two Bourbons refuse to attend the meeting at Fontainebleau.

---

[1] Various letters of Charles IX. See 'Mémoires de Condé.'

Still it was necessary to make some concession to popular feeling; and the King resolved that the States-
General should be called together, and named Meaux
as their place of session; promising that if the General
Council did not proceed to business, a national council
should take its place.

The King
assumes a
threaten-
ing tone.
Disclo-
sures of
La Sague.

The King, before leaving Fontainebleau, wrote again to
Navarre on the thirtieth of August, summoning him once
more to bring his brother. This time his letter was
couched in a less friendly tone:—'I should be very much
displeased,' concluded the King, 'if so unhappy a temper
should have made its way into the heart of a man of such
high birth, and so nearly related to myself; and I can
assure you that in the case of his refusing to obey my
orders, I shall know how to make him feel that I am
King.'[1] It was clear that they had obtained fresh proofs.
The arrest of the Vidame de Chartres, who was suddenly
thrown into the Bastille, explained everything. Condé
had despatched from Nérac one of his servants, named
La Sague, to carry letters to the Connétable, and to
Éléonore de Roye, who was then with her uncle. This
man, as he was passing through Fontainebleau, on his
return from Écouen, met in a tavern with a discharged
officer named Bonval, an old comrade of his in the
Transalpine infantry. As he thought that this Bonval
had some grievances against the Guises, and as he knew
him to be a man of determination, La Sague thought he
could win him over to his master's cause, and told him
all he knew, or thought he knew, of the schemes which
were being projected by the malcontents. Bonval pretended to be a convert, but went off and retailed every-

[1] 'Mémoires de Condé.'

thing to the Duc François, who immediately caused the Prince's messenger to be pursued; and he was arrested at Étampes. On his person were found letters from Montmorency and from the Vidame de Chartres. The Connétable's were unintelligible. But the Vidame's letters contained a promise to follow Condé in whatever he should undertake for the King's advantage. La Sague, under the threat of torture, confessed as follows: that the Princes were to set out with a large armed retinue, under pretext of appearing at Court in pursuance of the King's commands; that the Connétable was simultaneously to occupy Paris; and that other noblemen were to take possession of the principal towns of the kingdom. Lastly, he produced a letter which Fremyn d'Ardoys, the Connétable's secretary, was sending to Condé, which, although apparently of no consequence, revealed, when submitted to the action of water, words written in sympathetic ink. From this it appeared that Montmorency persisted in his resolutions; that he advised the Princes to come in great force to the States; that they must there obtain a sort of condemnation of the Lorrains, which must be at once ratified, willingly or unwillingly, by the King and the Queen-Mother. Fremyn added that many of their friends thought this plan impracticable; and preferred to the doubtful chance of the co-operation of the States-General, a direct and immediate attack upon the Guises by force of arms as soon as they arrived at Court. The affair once entered upon, the Montmorencies would pursue it. This is De Thou's account; and notwithstanding our confidence in the veracity of that great historian, we must confess that we are rather sceptical

as to the letter written with sympathetic ink. Perhaps
De Thou, in his anxiety to defend the course which his
father took in the subsequent trials, accepted on too
slight authority the version which was circulated by the
Court in order to justify its severities. There is no
doubt, however, that La Sague had made disclosures,
and that Condé's friends sought to penetrate the mystery of the revelations, true or false, of 'his Biscayan.'[1]
The Châtillons held a conference with the Queen-Mother
at Saint-Germain. The Dame De Roye had charged
them to implore Catherine to let them know the subject
of the charges brought against her son-in-law. Some
letters passed between them after this interview, and the
Dame De Roye ended by declaring that the Prince
should come, but with a powerful retinue. 'The King,'
they answered her, 'shall have one still more powerful.'

Notwith-
standing
the arrest
of the Vi-
lame de
Chartres,
and the
insur-
rections of
Maligny,
Montbrun,
and Mou-
rans, the
two
Princes
quit Nérac
for the
States-
General.

In fact, Antoine de Bourbon and his brother soon left
Nérac and journeyed leisurely to Orléans, the new place
of session appointed for the States-General. This resolution was surprising, for the aspect of affairs had
changed considerably since the time when the Connétable had advised the Princes to go to Fontainebleau.
Doubtless they did not know the full extent of the
revelations extorted from La Sague. But Montmorency
had written to Navarre, to justify himself for the part
he had taken in the arrest of that messenger, and for
having made any declaration which could implicate the
Bourbons in any charge; and the terms of his letter
were significant:—'You can well divine,' he added, 'to
what end all this tends.'[2] The Princes must have also
known that a counsellor of the Parliament, by name La

[1] 'Son Basque.'   [2] 'Négociations sous François II.'

Haye, who managed Condé's private business, had been arrested, conducted to Saint-Germain, and subjected to a minute examination on the twenty-second of September,[1] and that he was still in confinement. Lastly, they knew, above all, that the Vidame, a relative, a friend, and a great confidant of Condé's, had been in prison since the end of August, and that his trial was being urged forward with alarming precipitation. As it was impossible to refuse this nobleman the privilege of being tried by the knights of his order, a fresh creation was made on purpose to ensure his condemnation, and among that scandalous batch who completed the disgrace of 'a collar which fitted every beast,' the Court did not shrink from including the Italian Bentivoglio, to whom public opinion attributed the assassination of the Comte d'Enghien.[2] Other and more serious events followed in rapid succession. Maligny, the same gentleman whom Condé had assisted to escape from Amboise, had just, with a few men-at-arms, made an unsuccessful attack upon Lyon. At the same time, two brave captains, Mouvans and Montbrun, at the head of Huguenot bands, were stirring up Provence and Dauphiné. All these various risings, commenced without any combined plan, were easily crushed. Maligny and Montbrun escaped, but several of the associates of the former were arrested. As the Court was determined to establish, at all hazards, the complicity of Condé in this attempt, these wretches were not exempted from torture. One of them, a very young man, named La Borde, who

[1] 'Examination of an agent of the Prince de Condé.' Imperial Lib., Collection 'Béthune,' 8675. Printed among the 'Archives curieuses,' first series, vol. iv. The date found in the original is omitted in this edition.
[2] See chap. i. p. 21.

had been one of Condé's pages, was compelled to endure the most excruciating torments without uttering a word against his old master.[1] But others of them were not so silent, and the wretch[2] who had betrayed Montbrun was looked upon as an overwhelming witness against Condé.[3]

Precautions of the Guises.

The Duc de Guise, who had received timely notice, took measures of precaution with the promptitude and decision inherent in his character. The Cardinal, his brother, undertook the task of negotiating and cajoling when necessary. The King's body-guard, which had been doubled immediately after the conspiracy of Amboise, was reinforced by men chosen from the bands which had just returned from Scotland. The gendarmes were recalled to the interior, distributed over various points of the kingdom, and placed under the command of leaders whose decision, no less than their devotion to the Guises, could be relied upon. All who were suspected of indecision or of hostile predispositions were superseded, and D'Andelot encountered so many checks in the exercise of his authority as Colonel-Général of the infantry, that he was compelled to resign his post. He withdrew from Court. Maréchal de Saint-André was despatched to Lyon, and La Mothe-Gondrin to Dauphiné. De Termes was posted in the neighbourhood of Poitiers with two hundred chosen lancers to watch the movements of the two Princes.

---

[1] In the sentence subsequently pronounced by the Parliament, recognizing the innocence of the Prince de Condé, the Court reviews the official report of the 'questions et tortures baillées et répétées audit De la Borde.'

[2] D'Aubigné calls him D'Antoine; Allard ('Histoire de Montbrun') calls him D'Antriné (?). Most likely it was Antoine Bonym, whose evidence was reviewed by the same decree of the Parliament.

[3] The Anabaptists also tried to make a rising in Normandie in behalf of their barbarous doctrines; but Protestants and Catholics alike resisted them, and they were utterly defeated.

At last the King, passing through Paris on his way to the States-General, expressed his conviction, in an address to the Parliament, that the attempt at Amboise had been aimed against his person, and formally threw the responsibility of it upon the Bourbons. He immediately left for Orléans, whither he had been preceded by Cypierre, a man well known for his energy and harshness. The city was strongly garrisoned.[1] Cypierre[2] was the real commander of the town, but it was nominally under the Prince de la Roche-sur-Yon, who, being a Prince of the blood, was under suspicion, although his mild and submissive disposition rendered him an object of little dread.

All this, or at least the greater part of it, was known to the Princes, and all their true friends besought them to abandon their rash enterprise. As they drew near to their journey's end, Heaven sent them a final warning. Montpezat closed the gates of Poitiers against them as enemies of the State. But all the confidants of Antoine de Bourbon had been bribed by the Court, and kept urging him forward; they gave him to understand, as occasion arose, that he was not on his trial, that, in refusing to obey the summons of the King, he was commencing a civil war in which he would not have a chance

Efforts on the part of Condé's friends to induce him to remain.

---

[1] The infantry concentrated at Orléans amounted to four thousand, in twelve companies. On the day of his entry, the King was escorted by four hundred archers of his old guard, two hundred gentlemen, a strong body of Swiss, and the arquebusiers of his new guard.

[2] Philibert de Marcilly, Sieur de Cypierre, a gentleman of Mâcon, had served with much distinction in the wars of the last reign; and had been nominated by Henri II. governor to his second son, the Duc d'Orléans (afterwards Charles IX.). He died at the baths of Liége in 1565. He must not be confounded with René of Savoy, who was also Seigneur de Cypierre, and of whom we shall have to speak later on. The latter belonged to the Huguenot party.

of success, and that it would be madness on his part to sacrifice himself to his brother's interests. The latter, who was less accessible to these treacherous influences, was urgently importuned to decline accompanying Antoine should the latter persist in coming. He was repeatedly told, not without some truth, that the Guises would never attempt anything against the King of Navarre as long as Condé was alive to avenge him. But it was his nature to march straight forward into danger, and his loyalty could not tolerate the idea of perjury in his King. He trusted to his solemn promise, and that of his own brother, Cardinal de Bourbon. For no falsehood had been spared to diminish the mistrust excited in the minds of the Princes by the severe letter of the thirtieth of August, and the menacing language uttered to the Parliament. Further, what was to be done? They had exhausted every excuse for evading formal orders, and henceforth armed resistance was their only alternative. This, in face of the immense preparations made by the Guises, demanded means which they did not possess. So poor was the Prince that, in order to obtain a thousand *écus d'or*, his mother-in-law had been obliged to mortgage to the Connétable her château of Germiny. A few persons had indeed thought over the ways and means of maintaining a contest. Marillac, Archbishop of Vienne,[1] in a letter addressed to the Duchesse de Montpensier, who, like himself, was inclined to the new ideas, had pictured in eloquent terms the position of affairs, and traced a complete plan of operations for meeting the danger.

---

[1] Charles de Marillac was a great friend of L'Hospital. Like him, he was the son of an old servant of the House of Bourbon; he was an able negotiator and a man of eminent talents. Condé selected his brother, a few days afterwards, as his counsel.

He showed that the machinations of the Guises were directed against the whole House of Bourbon, all the members of which could easily be annihilated as soon as the two eldest had been struck down. He besought the Duchess to lay aside every secondary consideration, to make every possible effort to arrest the journey of Navarre and his brother, or at all events that of Condé, and at the same time to work upon Montmorency; to point out to him how greatly he was compromised by the confessions of La Sague; that if they were using him for the moment, it was that they might strike him down more surely hereafter; to arouse him, in short, from his inactivity, that he might call to arms the *noblesse* over whom he exercised great influence. He urged her at the same time to write to the Duc de Bouillon, her son-in-law, in order to win him to their side, to secure for Condé's wife and children an asylum on his estates, and to obtain, through his mediation, the assistance of the German Princes.[1] The Duchesse de Montpensier was deeply moved by this letter. She made some advances towards the Duc de Bouillon; but it was too late. The project was carried no farther; and it is said that Marillac, in consequence, died of grief.

The Court hastened to atone for the bungling insolence of Montpezat. In fact that officer had misunderstood his instructions. His orders were only to watch the Bourbons, without showing them any disrespect. If they declared themselves in revolt, or only prepared to turn back again, with a view to withdraw from Court, he was ordered not to shut the gates of a town against them, but to attack them, to treat them as enemies of the State,

---

[1] Thuanus (De Thou), lib. xxvi.

and give them no quarter. On this head the King's commands were precise. But as long as the two Princes pursued their journey peaceably, he was to bestow every possible attention upon them, and to omit nothing which might reassure them. And his instructions in this case were not less urgent.[1] Accordingly De Termes, who was Montpezat's superior officer, hastened to Poitiers in order to receive the Princes with all due honour. They continued their march. The same ill-timed caution which had kept them away from Fontainebleau when they ought to have been there, urged them on to Orléans when it was certain destruction for them to go thither.[2]

Condé,
trusting to
the King's
word,
enters Or-
léans.
His arrest
(October
30).

At Blois, Cardinal de Bourbon met his brothers, and guaranteed afresh their safety on the word of the King; next day, the thirtieth of October, they entered Orléans. From that moment the mask was thrown off. Not a single officer of State received the Princes. None of the usual honours were paid them. The streets were deserted, silent, and lined with troops. According to custom, Navarre presented himself before the principal gate of the Royal residence; but it remained closed. He had to submit to the indignity, and to make his entry on foot through the postern, between a double line of gentlemen looking insolently on. The King awaited the Princes in his chamber. Behind him stood the Guises and the

[1] This double part, which was assigned to all the officers who were stationed along the road that Navarre and his brother were to take, is distinctly laid down in the King's despatches to Burie, De Termes, and Montpezat; September and October, 1560 ('Negotiations under François II.').

[2] One of our best contemporary writers, to whom we owe so many true and spirited monographs of the sixteenth century, M. Vitet, believes that he has found the explanation of this inexplicable journey in a violent and reciprocated passion of Condé for Marie Stuart. The fact would not be incredible, but it remains up to the present time in the region of simple conjecture.

principal lords. Not a word, not a salutation did they vouchsafe. After a very distant reception, François II. led the Princes to his mother's apartments. There he questioned Condé sternly; but the latter, who was 'gifted with great courage, and who could speak as well as any prince or gentleman in the world, betrayed no astonishment, and pleaded his cause with many good and weighty arguments,'[1] protesting his own innocence, and accusing the Guises of falsehood. Upon his referring with dignity to the Royal word that had been passed for his security, the King interrupted him, and gave a signal. Brézé and Chavigny, the two captains of the guard, entered, and took the Prince's sword from him. He was conducted to a house in the town, near the Jacobin Convent, which was immediately barred up, crenellated, surrounded by soldiers, and transformed into a very bastille. He was kept in the most absolute solitude. His attendants were withdrawn. His wife, who had hastened to Orléans, could not obtain permission to see him. The King of Navarre had vainly endeavoured to obtain the custody of his brother. He was angrily refused his request. He himself, separated from his escort, was placed under surveillance in his own apartments. The same day, Grolot, 'bailli'[2] of Orléans, accused of favouring and professing the Reformed religion, was thrown into prison; and the Sieurs de Carouges and de Bailleul were despatched with a *lettre de cachet* to arrest the Dame de Roye, Condé's mother-in-law, and to conduct her to Saint-Germain.

The trial of the Prince commenced forthwith. A committee of magistrates, the same which had drawn up the

His trial.
Iniquitous proceedings.

---

[1] Castelnau.
[2] An office somewhat similar to that of mayor.

CHAP.
II.

1560

His in-
dignation.
Judgments
of the 13th,
15th, 20th,
and 26th
November.

indictment against the Vidame de Chartres, presided over
by Christophe de Thou (father of the historian), was
summoned from Paris, and charged with the examination.
The decisions were to be pronounced by the Privy
Council. All this was in direct violation of the pre-
cedents and ancient laws of the kingdom. As a Prince
of the blood, as a knight of his order, the accused could
only be tried by the Court of Parliament, with a due
proportion of peers and knights. The presence of the
King, who presided in person over the Court, gave to
these iniquitous proceedings an appearance doubly
odious. Accordingly Condé declined to answer the interrogatories ; he appealed from ' the King ill-advised to
the King better-advised.' Further than this, neither the
ominous procedure of his arrest, nor the rigour of his
captivity, nor yet the haste and illegality of the whole
conduct of his case, could subdue the intrepidity of the
Prince. His enemies failed to surprise him in one
moment of weakness ; and when officious proffers of
mediation were made to him, and it was hinted to him
that an interview with the Duc de Guise was not impossible, ' Interview ! ' he exclaimed. ' Between him and
me there can be none, except at the point of the lance ! '
At last, however, he consented to discuss the accusations
that were brought against him, in presence of Claude
Robert and François de Marillac, advocates in the Parliament of Paris, whom he had been allowed to retain as
his counsel. It was a great matter for them that he
should reply even so far, in order to keep up the appearance of a defended suit. This point once gained,
the affair might be allowed to go on without delay.
The panic was general. Everyone crouched before the

Guises; not a single voice in the council dared to speak
a word in defence of the life of Condé. His appeal, and his
successive protests, had been rejected by judgments of the
council, dated the thirteenth, fifteenth, and twentieth of
November. The answers of La Sague, of La Haye, and
of the Vidame de Chartres; the reports of the depositions
obtained under torture at Lyon; the evidence of two
wretches, a discharged tax-gatherer named Capolette, and
a certain Borianne, a priest who had been degraded, who
were both of them in prison for debt and crime, and had
offered themselves as witnesses in order to obtain their
discharge; these were summarily examined, and scarcely
sifted at all. On the twenty-sixth the Prince was sen-
tenced ' to lose his head on the scaffold.'

Still, when the time came for signing the sentence of
death, the old Comte de Sancerre, Louis de Bueil, flatly
refused to put his name to it, and the Chancellor de
l'Hospital, who could not openly break with the reigning powers, withheld his sanction under pretext of some
legal flaw. Duportail, a Councillor of State, followed
his example. These unexpected obstacles caused delay;
they irritated the Guises, but could not stop them; they
were determined to overbear all opposition.

Did François de Lorraine indeed cherish that supreme
ambition which his enemies attributed to him, and of
which his partisans made no mystery when they called
him the descendant of Charlemagne? Did he himself
look forward to that high eminence which his son was
to fail in attaining? A change of dynasty was no easy
work. The right of succession had been much more
firmly established in favour of the collateral branches in
the third race than it had been in the two former, and

CHAP.
II.

1560

Ineffectual
efforts to
save him.
Determi-
nation of
the Guises.
His exe-
cution
fixed for
Dec. 10.

the Royal House was very numerous.[1] But were the vigorous branches once broken off, it might be hoped that the old tree would fall without violent effort; had not the last scions of the first two Royal races been buried in the seclusion of the cloister?

Whatever may have been the projects, more or less fully formed, which were passing through the mind of the Duc de Guise,—whether he were urged on by his own passions or by the persuasion of Cardinal de Lorraine, 'who had a soul by no means pure, but very much defiled' (I quote the words of a Catholic writer),[2]—he had fully resolved to overthrow by force every obstacle which he might encounter, and to maintain, against all, the authority of which he and his brother, like the mayors of the palace of old, were the sole depositaries. Condé's execution was fixed for the tenth of December, the day on which the States-General were to open.

In vain did Éléonore de Roye devote herself to saving the life of her husband. Neither her efforts nor those of the Duchesse de Montpensier, who had not forgotten the advice of Marillac, nor the cutting reproaches cast by the old Duchess of Ferrara[3] upon her son-in-law, were

---

[1] It numbered at that time fourteen Princes still living, besides King François II.; viz.:—

The King's three brothers, Monsieur (Charles IX.); the Duc d'Anjou (Henri III.); and the Duc d'Alençon:

Antoine de Bourbon, King of Navarre; and his son the Prince de Béarn (Henri IV.):

Louis de Bourbon, Prince de Condé, and his three sons: Henri, who inherited his title; Charles, who died young; and François, the

Marquis de Conti:

Charles de Bourbon, the Cardinal, brother of the preceding:

Louis de Bourbon, Duc de Montpensier, cousin of the preceding, and his son, the Comte Dauphin (d'Auvergne):

Charles de Bourbon, Prince de la Roche-sur-Yon, brother of the Duc de Montpensier; and his son Henri, Marquis de Beaupréau, who died a few days after François II.

[2] Brantôme.

[3] Renée de France, daughter of

able to turn aside the fatal blow. The hopes which were
at first built upon the clemency of the King, and which
had even at Court been for a while encouraged,[1] had
utterly faded away. The Prince's death was certain, and
if his execution were postponed, if the life or liberty of
Navarre were still respected, it was doubtless only because it was hoped that the plan might be more safely
and completely carried out after the assembling of the
States-General. Besides which, was it not necessary to
give Montmorency time to arrive?

Condé, in perfect calmness, awaited death with patience. He was engaged in play with some of the officers
on guard about him, when one of his servants, who had
been allowed once more to attend him, pretending to
approach to pick up one of his cards, whispered in his
ear, ' Notre homme est croqué!' Restraining his emotion,
the Prince finished his game; and then finding an opportunity of speaking to his servant for a moment in private,
he learned from him that François II. was dead.

On the seventeenth of November the King was about
to mount his horse to go hunting, in order, it was said,
that he might avoid being present at the execution of
Grolot, when he suddenly felt ill. His illness at first
caused great alarm; but he soon so far recovered as to
be able to be present at the last judgments pronounced

CHAP.
II.
1560

Sickness
and death
of Fran-
çois II.
Dec. 5.
Condé
saved by
the co-
operation
of Médicis
and L'Hos-
pital.

Louis XII., and mother-in-law of
the Duc de Guise. She had embraced Protestantism.

[1] On the morrow of Condé's arrest,
Morvilliers, Bishop of Orléans, in
announcing the event to his nephew,
the Bishop of Rennes, who was
Ambassador at the Court of Vienna,
added:—' It is confidently asserted
that the King will not proceed
further in the matter, and that the
clemency of the King will be graciously extended to him in consideration of his youth.' (Bibl. imp.,
Collection ' Colbert,' printed in the
' Additions ' of Le Laboureur to the
' Mémoires de Castelnau.')

against Condé. But on the twenty-seventh a fresh attack came on. It was at first attempted to hide the serious nature of the malady; and the fainting fits were attributed to slight indisposition. But neither the uncles of François II. nor his mother were deceived as to his real condition. The King had but a few days to live. A legal minority was about to succeed the real minority. Catherine, who had long been neglected, found herself surrounded with obsequious courtiers; the pride of the Guises humbled itself before her; they hailed her as Regent, and promised her their support. Only it was necessary to strike down their common rivals. Before the King died, Condé's head must fall, and Navarre take his place in prison.

But L'Hospital was watchful. In that great soul and noble heart, the uprightness of the magistrate, the associations of family,[1] the honour of the statesman, reason, feeling, all alike had been outraged by this detestable trial. Already by judicious procrastination he had been able to delay the consummation of the crime. And now he was about to attain his object. He hastened to seek an audience of Catherine, and pointed out to her that in saving the Bourbons she would insure the independence of the Crown, of that Royal power of which she was about to hold the reins. A common policy united those two widely different natures; and this concord between subtlety and integrity saved the Prince de Condé.

The Queen, however, betrayed nothing of her intentions. She replied to the Guises in encouraging terms, and ordered the confinement of Condé to be made more strict.

---

[1] His father had been physician to the Connétable de Bourbon, and had accompanied him in his flight.

But she received Navarre secretly, and at the same time
wrote to the Connétable desiring him to hasten his
march. This 'cunctator,'[1] who had been long since
summoned to Orléans, but who well knew what designs
were being entertained against him, was travelling as
slowly as possible, and always, as was his wont, attended
by a large retinue. On receiving Catherine's letter he
made all haste. Finding on his arrival soldiers posted at
the gates of the city, he sent them away with threats of
the gibbet. All submitted to his orders; he entered, and
welcomed to his arms his niece the Princesse de Condé.
The King had just breathed his last.

[1] D'Aubigné's 'Histoire universelle.'

CHAPTER III.

1561—1563.

Condé repairs to La Fère after the death of François II.—He returns to
Court; he is reinstated by Royal declaration (March 15, 1561), and by
a decree of the Parliament (June 13); his formal reconciliation with the
Duc de Guise (August 24). Position of the Duc de Guise; Catherine
begins to favour him.—Montmorency, threatened by the States-General,
and disgusted with the party of innovation, allies himself to his
old enemies. Formation of the Triumvirate.—The members of the
Triumvirate secure the adhesion of the King of Navarre. The Queen-
Mother begins to favour the Protestants and the Prince de Condé.
—Decree of January (1562),—the first decree in favour of toleration.—
Irritation, and preparations for action on both sides.—Efforts on the
part of the Triumvirs to detach Condé from the Protestant side.—
Massacre of Vassy (March 1); Guise enters Paris (March 16); Condé
is compelled to quit Paris, making an appointment with Catherine
to meet him at Orléans (March 24).—He assembles his friends at
La Ferté-sous-Jouarre, wins over the Admiral to his side, and arrives
at Saint-Cloud with fifteen hundred horse (March 30).—The King
and his mother are carried off from Fontainebleau by the Triumvirs
and conducted to Paris.—Condé takes possession of Orléans.—The Protestant manifestoes, their risings in the provinces.—The Royal army,
seven thousand strong, advances as far as Châteaudun (June 1).—Condé
marches out of Orléans at the head of eight thousand men; his disappointment and indecision.—Negotiations set on foot by Catherine; the
Conference at Thoury, and the meeting at Talsy; Condé's rash promise
and speedy revocation of it.—Disloyal attempt to make a night-attack
('camisade') on the Royalists (June 3).—Capture and sack of Beaugency.
—Ravages committed by the Protestants; speedy decline of their
prospects. The Royal army, having received reinforcements, subjugates
La Touraine and Le Poitou.—Condé's unfortunate position in Orléans; he
divides his forces and urges forward negotiations with the foreign Princes.
—Siege and capture of Bourges by the Catholics (August).—Orléans is
placed in a state of defence.—The English at Havre; disastrous treaty
between them and the Protestants (September 20).—The Royal army
marches to the siege of Rouen.—D'Andelot succeeds in raising seven
thousand men in Germany; delays.—Capture of Rouen (October 25);
death of the King of Navarre.—Defeat of Duras at Ver, and other checks.

—Executions at Orléans.—Condé and Coligny alone resist the general
depression.—D'Andelot and La Rochefoucauld succeed in gaining Orléans.
—Condé marches forthwith upon Paris with fourteen thousand men (Nov.
11).—He lingers over unimportant operations; check before Corbeil.—He
arrives before Villejuif (Nov. 23); negotiations; 'Parliament' of Port-
à-l'Anglais.—Fight beneath the walls of Paris (Nov. 28); the Protestants
establish themselves from Vaugirard to Montrouge. Truce and fruitless
negotiations.—Unsuccessful attempts to surprise Paris (Dec. 5 and 7).—
The Royal army rallies and is reinforced; Condé retreats (Dec. 10).—
Various designs of Condé and his generals; they march towards Normandie to be near the English, by advice of the Admiral.—The army
marches very badly; it arrives at Dreux, where it had been anticipated
by the Catholics.—After a useless attempt at fighting on the 18th, the
Protestants on the 19th find themselves face to face with the Royal army.
The Admiral's mistakes. Battle of Dreux (Dec. 19); disposition of the
Royal army.—The Protestant army finds itself unable to refuse battle,
which is at once opened by the artillery without any previous skirmishing.
—Condé at once engaged with the cavalry of the main-body, forces the
Swiss batallion and breaks the squadrons of D'Aumale and Damville.—
The Admiral defeats the left wing of the Royal army with the cavalry
of the vanguard. The Connétable is wounded and taken prisoner.—
The Swiss, having rallied, rout the Protestant infantry ('lansquenets').
Second and unsuccessful charge of Mouy and the 'reitres' against the
Swiss.—Guise engages the Catholic vanguard; he throws Saint-André
upon the 'reitres,' and defeats the French batallion of the Protestants.
Condé and Coligny endeavour to support the 'reitres'; they are borne
down; Condé is taken prisoner.—Saint-André halts; Guise completes
the rout of the Protestant infantry.—Terrible rally on the part of the
Admiral; death of Saint-André; the Duc de Guise secures the victory
through the veteran French troops. Review of the battle of Dreux.—
The Duc de Guise treats Condé with courtesy.—Condé's conduct gives
some hope of peace; Catherine's unsuccessful efforts to conclude it.—Strict
confinement of Condé. The Admiral's movements.—Guise lays siege to
Orléans.—Attempts to obtain Condé's release; his resolute attitude.
Death of the Duc de Guise (Feb. 18, 1563).—Conferences at L'Ile-aux-
Bœufs (March 6 and 7). Notwithstanding the opposition of the ministers,
peace is concluded; Edict of Amboise (March 19).—Great dissatisfaction
of the Admiral and of the ministers; the Edict is confirmed.

WHEN the announcement was made to Condé that he
was free, he at first refused to leave his prison, intending,
as he said, to remain in it till his accusers had been in-
carcerated there. It was replied that all had been done
by express command of His Majesty; François II., on his
death-bed, had been pleased to make the declaration with

CHAP.
III.

1560
December

Condé re-
pairs to La
Fère after
the death
of François
II.

his own lips to Navarre. At length he resolved to set out for La Fère, a place which belonged to Antoine de Bourbon, and there to await the commands of the King. He was still surrounded by soldiers, but they were rather an escort than a guard. It was thought that the respect due to the memory of the late King called for his temporary absence from Court; and moreover Condé was determined not to make his appearance there otherwise than with all the pomp of a formal restoration to his honours.

e returns
Court.
e is re-
stated
r formal
:clara-
jn of the
ing
(arch 1),
id by a
cree of
e Parlia-
ent(June
, 1561).

At last he quitted La Fère at the beginning of February 1561, and proceeded towards Fontainebleau. He was accompanied by a large and brilliant cortége of friends who had hastened to congratulate him as he journeyed to Paris. At some distance from the Royal residence he left his suite, and advanced, accompanied only by La Rochefoucauld, his brother-in-law,[1] and the Sieur de Senarpont,[2] Lieutenant-Général of Picardie. On this occasion he was received with the accustomed honours. All the nobility of the Court, among them the Duc de Guise, came forward to meet him. On the morrow (March 15) he was admitted a Privy Councillor. The Chancellor de l'Hospital having, in answer to his appeal, pronounced that no proofs of the accusations brought against him had been adduced, the King acknowledged him innocent by a declaration, signed by all the members of the Council. An act of the Parliament of Paris, sitting as a Court of peers, confirmed this declaration. The sentence was pronounced on the thirteenth of June, in full session, on the report of four councillors, and on

---

[1] François, the third of that name, Comte de la Rochefoucauld and de Roucy, had married as his second wife (1557) Charlotte de Roye, Com-

tesse de Roucy, posthumous sister of Éléonore de Roye, Princesse de Condé.

[2] Jean de Mouchy.

the appeal of the Prince, who pleaded his own cause, the Procureur-Général being respondent. There were present in their places—on the right the King of Navarre, the Cardinal de Bourbon, the Duc de Montpensier, the Prince de la Roche-sur-Yon, the Connétable, the Duc de Guise, the Duc de Nevers, the Maréchal de Montmorency, the Maréchal de Saint-André; and on the left the Cardinals de Lorraine, de Châtillon, and de Guise.[1]

The tacit approval, however, which the Duc François had by his presence given to these formal proceedings, did not seem to Condé a sufficient reparation for his wrongs. He insisted on obtaining from him personally a public declaration, and an honourable reconciliation. It took place on the twenty-fourth of August at Saint-Germain, in presence of the King, the Queen-Mother, the Princes, and the Court. All had been arranged beforehand. The King was the first to speak. Guise next protested 'that he neither had nor would put forward any charge which was against the honour of the Prince ; nor had he been either the cause or the adviser of his imprisonment.' 'Monsieur,' replied Condé, 'I hold him or them to be scandalous and villanous who have been the cause of it.' 'I think likewise, Monsieur,' rejoined Guise, 'and the words concern me not at all.' Upon which they embraced each other, and the Secretaries of State drew up an official report of the ' appointement,' so

CHAP. III.

1561 June 13.

His formal reconciliation with the Duc de Guise (Aug. 24).

---

[1] The judgment applied also to the Dame de Roye (mother-in-law to the Prince, who had been arrested at the same time as himself) as well as to the memory of the Vidame de Chartres, who had died immediately on leaving prison, shortly after the death of François II. (Dec. 22, 1560). The extreme severity to which the Vidame had fallen a victim, was attributed to the resentment of Catherine de Médicis, whose love he was said to have rejected.

that nothing might be wanting to the cool, deliberate, and essentially official character of the ceremony. As it was being concluded, the Maréchal de Montmorency[1] appeared on the scene with a numerous body of friends and attendants, whom he had brought together to form an escort for Condé. This occasioned some sensation among the courtiers; but it subsided when the Connétable declared that since he had the honour of being so nearly related to the Princes de Bourbon, his son would have been much to blame had he acted otherwise. These words were a kind of courteous farewell which the old man was addressing to Condé; for their interests, which had long coincided, had now ceased so to do. It was indeed he who had brought about this reconciliation. It had seemed to him that the honour of his House necessitated its accomplishment. But after he had done what he considered was due to old relationships, he felt himself completely detached from all engagements with his nephew, and free to follow the fresh path which he had chosen. Guise, his ally for the time being, was well aware of this. He, too, felt that after this step his own position would be clearer and stronger. He was giving proof of moderation, was depriving his adversaries of the power of denouncing him as an enemy to the Royal House, and was diminishing the interest which attached to Condé. Thus the real advantage was on his side, and not on his rival's. Motives such as these were necessary to induce such a man to undergo whatever humiliation

---

[1] François de Montmorency, the Connétable's eldest son; a peer, Grand Master and Maréchal de France, Duc de Montmorency after his father's death; born 1530; married to Diane 'de France' (by an act of legitimation), a natural daughter of Henri II.; died without issue on May 6, 1579.

was implied in this proceeding; for there was no weakness in his nature.

The day after the death of François II. Guise had mixed with the crowd of courtiers with the calmness of Sylla descending into the Forum after his abdication of the Dictatorship. His enemies were triumphant. A fatal accident had dashed his power from his grasp at the very moment when he was about to exercise it with unprecedented boldness, to ensure the triumph of his policy and of his House. But he was too high-couraged to allow himself to be cast down, and too self-controlled not to adapt himself to altered circumstances. He waited; when once his supremacy had been overthrown, those who had been united against him by a common enmity, could no longer continue in agreement. Coalitions do not survive their own success. Catherine was the first to make advances towards him. She was becoming alarmed at the disposition of the States-General, which wished to confer the regency upon the King of Navarre. Notwithstanding his refusal to lay any claim to this post, notwithstanding the strictness with which he observed to the very letter the promises he had made to the Queen-Mother beside the death-bed of François II., a strong party was forcing him into power. The jealousy of Catherine awoke. The Duc de Guise had retained possession of the keys of the palace, and the command of the King's body-guard, in his capacity of Grand Master of the Household. Antoine de Bourbon maintained that this was an infringement of the prerogative of the Connétable. The Queen pronounced in favour of the Grand Master. Navarre threatened to quit the Court. The Duc de Montpensier, the whole of the Montmorencies and Châtillons

1561.
Position of
the Duc de
Guise.
Catherine
begins to
favour him

Montmc-
rency,
threatened
by the
States-
General,
and dis-
gusted
with the
party of
innova-
tion, allies
himself to
his old
enemies.
Formation
of the
Triumvi-
rate.

were to accompany him. He was already booted and spurred, and ready to mount, when he was informed that the Connétable had agreed to abide by the decision of the Regent and would remain with the King. This unexpected resolve changed everything; it was necessary to give way.

The Queen had appealed to the fidelity and devotion of Montmorency, and she found him all the more tract-able, inasmuch as his interests coincided with his duty. The provincial States had been convoked, and although the States-General had formally prohibited them from taking cognisance of the affairs of the kingdom, those of Paris, elected under the influence of the reaction which followed the death of François II., had taken into consi-deration the exhaustion of the exchequer. They had de-manded that account should be rendered of the presents made by Henri II. as well as by his son, and that the sums thus lavished should be refunded. And at the same time they encouraged the rest of the provincial States to make similar demands. These discussions in assemblies, themselves of small authority, yet deriving some importance from the existing state of public feeling, were sufficient to draw together those who before had been rivals; for all, with the exception of the Bourbons and Châtillons, having been loaded with tokens of their sovereigns' bounty, all were alike affected by these menaces. They agreed therefore to obtain a Royal declaration, which should include, in addition to other injunctions, a fresh prohibition to the States against in-terference in these matters. There were to be no more of those enquiries which from time immemorial had been the first business of our popular assemblies. But the warning was not without fruit. The Connétable was startled at the intentions which the Provincial States had disclosed during their brief sitting. Uneasy and alarmed, he withdrew definitively from those political and religious innovators whom he had at first appeared to patronize, and among whom were reckoned his nearest relations. And indeed he was not prompted merely by self-interest. The old man did not pretend to be a theologian, but he was a sincere Catholic, because Catholicism was the old religion and the religion of the King; those who wanted to change it became in his eyes enemies of the State. Such was the feeling of many at that time,[1] and if this attachment to a traditional faith was disfigured by violence and cruelty, it was because in that pitiless age it was given to few minds to understand, far less to practise, toleration. Alas! it is to be regretted that France, without breaking with her past, did not at that hour enter on the path of progress and reform! For a few steps taken with this view, at that critical era, would have perchance enabled our country to journey towards her future by a way where she might have experienced shocks less violent and ordeals less cruel. But if on the one hand liberty had to be achieved, on the other national unity had to be preserved, and we cannot unreservedly blame those whose resistance, often selfish, always narrow and bigoted, nevertheless arrested the dissolution of the French monarchy. Montmorency then renounced his former sympathies. His wife, Madeleine de Savoie, an ardent Catholic, and a secret enemy to the Châtillons, as well as his old friend the Duchesse de Valentinois, who had recently drawn closer to the Guises, through her son-

---

[1] See Montluc.

in-law the Duc d'Aumale, prompted him to take up this new position. In vain did his eldest son, a man of wise and moderate counsels, endeavour to keep him back; he concluded with the Duc de Guise and the Maréchal de Saint-André the compact which has become famous under the name of the Triumvirate. The successor of François II. had not yet been crowned; and already the great coalition which had been formed against the Guises, when they ruled under the name of that Prince, had been completely dissolved.

The Triumvirate secure the adhesion of Navarre.

The union of three men who seemed to represent the military nobility, the ardent Catholics, and the courtiers, was even more dangerous to the authority of the Queen-Mother than the phantom regency of Navarre. But political changes gave very little trouble to Catherine. Without affections, without principles, and without scruples, this Princess always held out the hand to the weaker party for the time being, as a means of escape from the dictation of the stronger. She turned once more to the Bourbons. The States had conferred upon Antoine the title of Lieutenant-Général of the King, and the command of the gendarmerie. He possessed the affections of the Protestants and was not disliked by the more moderate Catholics. But it was fated that this Prince should always bring his younger brother back to his former standing-point. Catherine found him committed to the Triumvirs, who had spared no pains to win him over to their side. They had had no difficulty in gaining the adhesion of his mistress, Louise de la Béraudière,[1] but they

---

[1] Louise de la Béraudière, Demoiselle du Rouet, daughter of Louis de la Béraudière, Seigneur de l'Isle Rouet in Poitou, and of Madeleine du Fou Vigean. She was maid of honour to Catherine de Médicis; she had a son by the King of Navarre, who was called Charles de Bourbon,

had experienced more trouble in securing efficient support from the King of Spain. Philip II. had never yet chosen to utter those encouraging words which they asked of him, nor allowed himself to show the faintest intention of reconstituting the Kingdom of Navarre in favour of the legitimate heir to that ancient crown. 'We will think of it,' he answered to all their insinuations, 'when he has exterminated all the heretics in France, and his own brother among them.' He ended, however, by giving them to understand that he might be induced, in the event of his performing signal services to the Catholic cause, to give up Sardinia to 'M. de Vendôme.' To this was added Tunis and other provinces of Barbary, of which it was easy to dispose, so long as there was no need to conquer them. All this formed a splendid imaginary kingdom, which was represented to Antoine as an earthly Paradise; and this dream of orange groves, of a lovely climate, of a soft and sensual life, allured him for the moment to forget his wild and mountainous Navarre, till he seemed to have sacrificed all nobler ambition to the pursuit of this chimerical vision.[1] Many other offers had been made to him, but this was, so to speak, the most substantial. Thus there had been talk of the crown of England, which, he was told, a Papal bull could easily transfer from the head of Elizabeth to his own. Finally he was offered the hand of Marie Stuart: Jeanne d'Albret being a heretic, there would be no difficulty in obtaining a divorce. But, let us say it to his honour, notwithstanding the passion which, it is affirmed, he entertained

and who became Archbishop of Rouen.

[1] 'On le badine ainsi, luy promettant encor

Des règnes, des chasteaux et des montagnes d'or.'—Contemporary Satire.

for the young and beautiful widow of François II., he
rejected this shameful bargain. At all events a few
vague hopes and treacherous counsels had sufficed to
determine his 'révolte.' [1] The Triumvirs had gained their
end, and had secured the support of the legal head of the
army.

The King of Navarre having become the tool of the
Catholic faction, it was necessary for Catherine to seek
the support of the Protestants. She would rather not
have gone so far; her character as well as her interests
kept her back from extreme parties; and moreover at
that time she was still under the salutary influence of
L'Hospital. But that great man was in advance of his
age. That moderate and truly national party, which he
was then vainly endeavouring to gather around the Queen,
had as yet no existence. It is not at the beginning of a
crisis that sound and just views succeed in coming to the
surface. Adopted by men who are enlightened but
timid and often a little selfish, scarcely avowed at first and
long ridiculed, they end by becoming the standard of the
majority. What taunts, what calumnies were the portion
of those who were called the politic party; those who
desired the welfare and the unity of the State, who opposed alike revolutionary changes and bigoted reactions!
But after more than thirty years of war and of miseries,
it was this party which triumphed, with the great Prince
who abjured Protestantism while he granted the Edict
of Nantes, that Henri IV., whose good sense and valiant
sword conquered France and saved it.

The
Queen-
Mother   Médicis had neither the strong arm, nor the noble
heart, nor the keen intellect of the great Béarnois. She

---

[1] D'Aubigné, 'Histoire universelle.'

was rather crafty than clever; and her tortuous policy had never an exalted aim. Behold her to-day an ardent Reformer. The Bishop of Valence preaches before her sermons of more than doubtful orthodoxy. Beza is received at Court,[1] and while the Catholic Office is sung in an almost empty chapel, a crowd of women and courtiers is pressing into the apartments of the Admiral or of M. le Prince to hear a Huguenot preacher. For, since his journey to Nérac, after the fray at Amboise, Condé had openly professed the new religion; during his confinement at Orléans he flatly refused to hear Mass, and he did not show himself at the coronation of Charles IX. that he might avoid attendance at the celebration of the Holy Sacrifice. He took, however, little part in the controversies of 1561, never withholding his protection from his co-religionists as far as he could legally extend it, but cautiously and without parade.[2] He seemed to be taken up chiefly with the cares and necessary steps which his reinstatement demanded. He was present at the sittings of the States which were transferred from Orléans to Pontoise; but he never spoke. The debates there had been animated, but, upon the whole, fruitless. There had been, as was then the fashion, long tirades against luxury, and lengthy criticisms of abuses without seriously reforming a single one. As regarded religion, the new views had found most favour; the Pope's delay in calling

[1] He had been presented at Court on the twenty-third of August, 1561, a fact which we learn from a letter written by him to Calvin. This curious document is preserved in the Library of Geneva, and will be found in the Appendix, No. II. In the passage concerning Condé we discover that mistrust with which the Prince was regarded by the Protestant ministers—a mistrust which we shall have occasion more than once to illustrate, and which greatly influenced Condé in many of his acts.

[2] See his letter to Lieutenant de Roye, dated Nov. 11, 1561 (Appendix, No. III.).

the General Council combined with many other causes to strengthen the party of movement. A national council, presided over by the King, was now demanded; it would have meant schism. As a compromise, it was proposed to hold a synod in which the ministers of the Reformed faith should be admitted to explain and discuss their doctrines.[1] This proposition, although it found no favour with many of the Catholics, was nevertheless advocated by the Cardinal de Lorraine, who had a great reputation for eloquence, and hoped for an opportunity of displaying his theological learning and oratorical powers. The Colloquy of Poissy therefore took place; each side left it more embittered against its adversaries, and more deeply compromised than before, by opinions which had been enunciated in the heat of debate. The law, however, was still very hard upon the Protestants. The Edict of Romorantin, enacted in 1560, which gave the Bishops power to take cognisance of the crime of heresy,[2] had just been succeeded by that of July, which visited with death those concerned in any meeting—armed or unarmed— held under pretence of religious purposes; forbad the administration of the Sacraments with any other than the Catholic ritual; and ordered heretics to be tried by the

---

[1] Touching the Council and the Colloquy of Poissy, the Bibliothèque impériale (Collect. Colbert, 390ᵉ) contains copies of a curious correspondence which passed between the Queen-Mother and the Bishop of Rennes, Ambassador of France at the Court of the Emperor of Germany. It appears from this how near the national council was to being called, even under François II. Some of these letters have been printed in the 'Additions' of Le Laboureur to the 'Mémoires' of Castelneau.

[2] L'Hospital has been warmly censured for lending his name to this edict. But this appeared to him the only means of averting from France the scourge of the Inquisition, and he endeavoured to modify its severity in practice by the instructions which he issued as to its application.

ecclesiastical courts; but those who were found guilty,
and were handed over to the civil power, were not to
receive a more severe punishment than banishment.

But early in January 1562, the deputies of the Parlia- Edict of
ments were summoned to Saint-Germain. After a few January (1562).
words from the King, and a long and splendid speech by First edict in favour
L'Hospital, it was resolved that the Edict of July should of tolera-tion.
be modified. The Protestants were still forbidden to
assemble in the towns, and to administer the Sacraments.
But, until it should be otherwise decreed by the Council,
they were permitted to assemble outside the towns under
the supervision of the civil power. Magistrates were forbidden to disturb them, as long as they observed the laws
and abstained from all demonstrations against the Catholic
worship.

Such were the chief provisions of the celebrated Edict Irritation and mutual
of January. For the first time the principle of toleration prepara-tions for
was laid down in an act proceeding from the Royal action on
authority. In the Privy Council the opposition had not both sides.
been very active. Catherine had skilfully made the most
of the provision for submitting all to the General Council
and of that which prohibited meetings in towns. What
was more, one of the agents of the Pontifical Government[1]
wrote that, ' in six months, or at most twelve, if the resolutions were carried out, there would not be a single
Huguenot remaining.' But outside the Court and away
from its influence, the impression produced was very different. The Sorbonne was in commotion. The Parliament of Paris refused to register the decree; and two

[1] Letter of Prosper Sainte-Croix, Cardinal Borromeo, dated Jan. 15.—
Bishop of Albe (afterwards Arch- ' Archives curieuses.'
bishop of Arles and Cardinal) to

Royal mandates were required to procure its passing.
The King of Navarre, who, as Lieutenant-Général had
signed the edict, at first supported it feebly, and afterwards, allowing himself to be led by his party, ended by
repudiating and condemning it. At the same time, in
order to punish his wife for her attachment to the Reformation, he endeavoured to deprive her of the guardianship
of her little son, and caused all the Protestant ministers
to be banished from Saint-Germain, where the Court then
was. At last he assumed so violent an attitude that
Jeanne d'Albret and the Châtillons prepared to quit the
Royal residence. Even Catherine took fright and sent for
Condé in all haste. He was just recovering from a very
severe illness in Paris, and was obliged to be carried in a
litter. When, upon his arrival at Saint-Germain, he became more fully aware of the proceedings of his brother
and the indignation of his own friends, he foresaw all the
consequences of such a state of affairs, and so strong at
first was his excitement, that it brought on a serious
relapse.[1] From this, however, he soon recovered, and
restraining the agitation of his heart, he boldly took the
part of opposition to Navarre. Every step that the latter
was taking in the path of reaction to which he had committed himself raised Condé higher in the favour of the
Regent. He became her most confidential adviser, and
was constantly at her side. If for a short time he was
absent from Court, it was to appear in the streets of
Paris at the head of five or six hundred horsemen, pistol
in hand, escorting in his own person a minister on his
way to preach; for this warlike demonstration was

[1] Sir Nicolas Throckmorton, English Ambassador, to Queen Elizabeth;
Feb. 16, 1562. (State Paper Office.)

needed to protect Protestant meetings. The irritation of
the populace of Paris, which was still Catholic, was
extreme, as appeared very plainly after the ' tumult' of
Saint-Médard,[1] which had just deluged with blood the
Faubourg Saint-Marceau—a sinister prelude of civil war.

Civil war! It was this of which all were thinking
and for which all were preparing: the Châtillons in
the retirement of their estates ; the Guises in Lorraine.
The latter, foreseeing that they might have to take up
arms against the depositaries of the Royal authority, were
seeking for support beyond the boundaries of France.
Their affinities with the Pope were but natural, and no
one for a moment doubted their friendship with the King
of Spain. But they were bent on making all foreign
alliances impossible to their opponents. They skilfully
cultivated a good understanding with the Protestant
Princes of Germany, making much of the dissensions
between the Lutherans and Calvinists, causing it to be
understood that it might be possible to come to an agreement on the basis of the Confession of Augsburg, and re-
presenting the sacramentarians as their common enemies.

[1] On the twenty-seventh of December, the Protestants who were
assembled at the Patriarche, in the
Faubourg Saint-Marceau, to the
number of three or four thousand, to
hear one of their ministers, named
Malo, sent to request the Catholics
who were assembled in the church
of Saint-Médard, that they would
silence the bells, which overpowered
the voice of their pastor. This request met with an angry reception,
and one of the Huguenots, it is
averred, was killed. Immediately his
comrades made an attack upon the
church, which they completely
wrecked, profaning the tabernacle
and the consecrated Host; several
persons were massacred ; and all
their lawless proceedings were carried on to a certain extent under the
protection of the watch and of the
civil officials, who sided openly with
the assailants. The excitement was
very great in Paris, when the facts of
the case became known; and in order
to satisfy the public, it was found
necessary to arrest the functionaries
who were accused of partiality for
the Reformers. Some of them were
afterwards executed.

Efforts on
the part of
the Trium-
virate to
draw
Condé
away from
the side of
the Re-
formers.

Cardinal de Lorraine and his brother made a journey into Alsace for the express purpose, and the King of Navarre was instructed to write a very pressing letter to the Duke of Wurtemberg.

The Triumvirate did not even despair of being able to detach Condé from the Reformers. How could it be believed that this brilliant nobleman, so devoted to pleasure and war, would give himself up to such low companionship? As for the Châtillons, it was only in keeping with their sombre and taciturn temperament. But Condé, so genial, such a good fellow, must he not be weary already of the formalities and preachments of the ministers? Ambition and temper had thrown him into union with the party; but the evil might yet be remedied; and no effort was spared to withdraw Condé from the fatal influence of his cousins. The aged Connétable reminded him of his almost paternal affection, which had so often been put to the test; the Maréchal de Saint-André called up reminiscences of past campaigns and of the dangers they had braved together—recollections always dear to a man of spirit; but all in vain. Recourse was then had to the means which had been so successful in the case of Navarre. The government of Comtat-Venaissin,[1] with which the Pope might invest him, was hinted at. But Condé was not so pliable as his brother, and was not to be bought over by such coarse baits as these. His old companions in the field and at Court little knew how haughty a spirit and how resolute a character was concealed under that brilliant and frivolous exterior. He remained immoveable.

Navarre, however, the only one of all the Catholic

---

[1] Avignon.

leaders who had remained with the Court, had some
difficulty in defending the ground. In vain did he ask
for modifications of the Edict of January; in vain did he
demand the summary punishment of an archer and of a
horse-patrol who had been arrested after the 'tumult' of
Saint-Médard, for having assisted and directed the Huguenots. His counsel was not listened to. His position was
no longer tenable. He appealed to his friends. Guise
left Joinville; and on his way occurred the skirmish
known as the 'Massacre of Vassy.'[1] This was the spark
which kindled all.

It was Beza who brought the sad news to Court.
Condé had entrusted him with his messages to the
Queen.[2] He demanded that the 'Massacreur' of Vassy
should not be allowed to enter Paris. Navarre took
the part of his friend, and lost his temper with Beza,
who quietly replied,—'Monseigneur, it is the habit
of the Church of God to endure blows; but, beware;
she is an anvil that has worn out many a hammer.'
Without declaring her intentions, the Queen wrote to
Guise her orders to join her 'peu accompagné' (with a
small retinue) at Monceaux in Brie, where she had taken

[1] On the first of March, as the
Duc de Guise was passing through
the little town of Vassy, the centre
of the Reformation in that district,
his men took offence at some Huguenots who were assembled in a
barn. The Duke proceeded thither
at once, either to put an end to the
service, or, as he pretended, to appease the tumult. But he was
struck by a stone which was thrown
at him, and his men, no longer able to
control themselves, attacked everybody and everything within their
reach. About sixty persons were
killed and two hundred wounded.
It is, however, very difficult to get
at the truth either as to the ground
or the commencement of this sanguinary collision, amidst the many and
conflicting narratives of which it has
been the subject.

[2] Condé had urged upon the Syndics and Council of Geneva that
Beza should be authorized to prolong his stay with him. See his
letter of Nov. 24, 1561 (Appendix,
No. IV.).

the young King. At the same time, with a view to disperse the Catholic leaders, she chose to send Saint-André
to his government at Lyon. She had been careful, a
few days before, in order to give a show of reason to
this order, to send Montluc to Guyenne and Crussol to
Languedoc. Saint-André insolently declared that he
thought his presence in Paris would be more for the
King's interest. Guise replied more respectfully, but to
the same effect. He made some excuse, saying something about a projected journey to Guyenne. In short,
he announced that he was not at leisure to perform the
Queen's commands. She did not mistake his meaning;
she tried to ward off the storm by concessions. The Connétable, who had lately arrived in Paris, expressed himself much displeased with his son the Maréchal, governor
of the city, who was accused of great partiality for the
Huguenots. After a vain attempt at influencing him, he
signified to the King of Navarre that he could not longer
place reliance upon his son. Catherine consented to
replace the Maréchal by the Cardinal de Bourbon. This
choice found favour with the Catholics, and yet Condé
might have apprehended a worse one.

The Cardinal was not in possession of his new government [1] before he who was to be the real master there had
made his entry into it. On the sixteenth of March, François de Lorraine had arrived in the city, with a retinue of
fifteen hundred gentlemen. The Connétable and Saint-
André had come to meet him with all their friends. The
people filled the streets and shouted enthusiastically, ' Vive
le duc de Guise!' It seemed as though they were wel-
coming a deliverer. In turning into the Rue Saint-
Honoré, this brilliant cavalcade found themselves face to

---

[1] He entered on it March 17.

face with a troop of five hundred horsemen. It was the
Prince de Condé returning from the Protestant Service
in the Rue Saint-Jacques. A thrill ran through both
companies. But, after the effect produced by the Massacre
of Vassy, the Lorrains wished to keep up an appearance
of moderation, and Condé was too weak in numbers to
think of attacking. The two rivals saluted each other
courteously, and passed on to their ' hôtels,' without any
hostile action.

The King of Navarre in his turn proceeded to lend to
the Triumvirate the support of his official character; and
in order that there might be no mistake as to his position,
he joined them in the procession of Palm Sunday, which
took place, with great splendour, on the twenty-second of
March. These shows and religious fêtes served only to
kindle the passions of the populace of Paris; their excitement was now at its height. Marles, Provost of the
Guild of Merchants, was despatched to the Queen to inform her of the public temper. He besought her to bring
the King back to Paris, and to allow the arms which were
in the Governor's custody to be distributed. Catherine,
persisting in her system of half-measures, refused his first
request, but granted the second: it is true indeed that
the thing would have been done without her permission.

Condé's position was becoming daily more critical. If
in some of the provinces the Protestants were gaining
recruits among the military *noblesse* and the active part
of the population, in Paris it was principally among the
most peaceful inhabitants that the Reformation found its
not very numerous disciples. So that it was a mere
handful of friends face to face with an armed and hostile
people. ' I believe,' says Lanoue, ' that if the novices from

Margin: CHAP. III.

1562
March 16.

Condé is compelled to leave Paris, after having appointed a rendez-vous with Catherine at Orléans (March 24).

the convents and the chambermaids of the priests alone
had presented themselves on a sudden, with sticks in
their hands, it would have made them (the Reformers)
draw rein.' Still the Prince had promised the Queen-
Mother efficient support, and he was bent on appearing
capable of so doing, on not beginning by an avowal of
weakness. At least he would not leave Paris without an
understanding with her. He therefore sent to her Hangest, Sieur d'Ivry, with a pressing letter proposing that
she should go to Orléans, where he would join her, and
whither therefore the legal seat of government would
then have been transferred. The Queen, terrified at the
designs which the Triumvirate were reported to entertain
against her, had already quitted Monceaux and was on
the way to Melun. Condé's proposal embarrassed her.
She was reluctant to give up the capital and to put
herself entirely into the hands of the Prince. Every day,
however, she wrote to him in the most pathetic strain,
beseeching him ' to save the children, the mother, and the
kingdom,'[1] but inwardly she hesitated to give him openly
her countenance; she thought she could once more gain
her end by a policy of intrigue and duplicity. She again
took a middle course, and conducted the King to Fontainebleau; thus she approached Orléans without going
far from Paris. But already Condé had been obliged to
leave that city. Left shamefully in the lurch by his
brothers, excluded in the most marked manner from the
councils where his rank entitled him to a seat, compelled
day by day to endure fresh insults, or to engage in a
struggle of which the issue could not be doubtful, he was

---

[1] Letter of the Queen-Mother to
the Prince de Condé (Bibl. imp.,
Saint-Germain, 171), printed with
several others in the 'Mémoires de
Condé.'

anxious at the least to save appearances and to quit Paris honourably. The Cardinal had long urged upon him to remove, in the interest of the public peace; and he offered to go provided M. de Guise went also. The offer was accepted; each kept his word. But while Condé hastened to Ferté-sous-Jouarre to assemble the chief of the Protestants, that he might hurry with them to join the Queen, Guise, who had already matured his plans, marched direct upon Fontainebleau, and was followed by his allies with four thousand horse. Both sides understood well how important it was to obtain possession of the King's person. To have him with them, was to brand the opposite party with the stigma of rebellion.[1] The Catholics were the first to be ready.

Condé had however made all possible speed. He had quitted Paris on the twenty-fourth of March; on the twenty-ninth he partook of the Lord's Supper at Meaux together with Coligny and some others. There had been some difficulty in gaining the Admiral; his old friends who were assembled with him at Châtillon had not found him very eager to comply with the Prince's summons. He had been for some time in retirement on his estates; he had not been, like Condé, excited by the events of the past few days; and being naturally phlegmatic and calculating, little given to rapid decisions, mistrustful both of the strength of the Protestants and of the word of the Queen-Mother, unwilling to take part against his uncle, tormented by honourable scruples which led him to view with regret the outbreak of a civil war, and perhaps too filled with a secret annoyance at finding

CHAP.
III.

1562
March.

Condé collects his friends at La Ferté-sous-Jouarre, urges on the Admiral, and arrives at Saint-Cloud with 1,500 horse (March 30).

---

[1] ' Quippe qui sic judicarent utri parti se rex et regina adjungerent, alteram quam deser*rent detestandæ re-   bellionis infamia notari.'—Thuanus, lib. xxix. 12.

himself reduced to being second in command on his own side, he would have preferred waiting and gaining time. But things had gone too far; his wife and friends were urging him on; he ended by 'mounting his charger' and joining Condé.

On the morrow, the thirtieth of March, the Prince and the Admiral were before the walls of Paris; a thousand gentlemen and three hundred 'argoulets' defiled in good order, three deep, along the ramparts from the Porte Saint-Martin to the Porte Saint-Honoré. The excitement was immense in the capital, where so speedy a return was not expected. The gates were hastily closed, and a pretence at defensive measures was made; further, the most serious step of all was taken in admitting immediately a garrison of fifteen hundred men, whom the magistrates had always refused to allow the Maréchal de Montmorency to place in the city for the mere purpose of maintaining order.

Condé had no intention of making an attack upon Paris. To respond to the appeal of the Queen-Mother, and to strengthen his cause by her authority and by the King's presence; this was the object he proposed, and which he was hasting to accomplish. He did not even halt before the great city, and he had already reached the bridge of Saint-Cloud, when he learned that he had been anticipated, and that the Triumvirs were at Fontainebleau. Nevertheless he pursued his journey towards Orléans, still hoping that Catherine would be true to her word and would find some means of joining him, or at least of communicating with him. And, moreover, his troop was augmenting beyond his hopes; on every side, as the news of the Massacre of Vassy and the excitement in Paris spread, the Protestant nobles had voluntarily put themselves in march with a few attendants. On reaching their friends, they were indeed a little disappointed to learn that the capital was lost and that the Guises were with the Queen. But when they saw that they were so large a body, and found at their head a Prince of the blood and all the Châtillons, as well as some of the De la Rochefoucaulds, De Rohans, and De Soubises, they recovered courage, and their confidence extended to their leaders.

Condé assembled two hundred horse on the bridge of Saint-Cloud and about five hundred on the Étampes side. He had thus altogether two thousand cavalry. These were not sufficient to attack the Triumvirate, although they already amounted to a considerable force. At any rate they thought themselves sure of Orléans, the geographical position of which rendered it, after Paris, the most important place in the kingdom. Tripier, Sieur de Monterud, was in command of it, in the name of the Prince de la Roche-sur-Yon. On learning the good understanding between the Protestants and the Queen-Mother, he had showed signs of favouring them. Condé therefore limited himself to detaching D'Andelot with two hundred horse to occupy the town, while he himself slowly pursued his march, waiting impatiently for the Queen's commands. He soon learned that the Queen had been obliged to yield. After three days spent in negotiations and entreaties, after having exhausted all the resources of her skill, in order to gain time, she had been compelled to bend before the iron will of the Duc de Guise. François de Lorraine, skilled in controlling himself, ready to concede to others the appearance of power, and caring himself

only for its reality, had interfered but little in the late
disputes. He preferred making a tool of the King of
Navarre, who simply followed the prompting of his ally,
but who, inflated by a show of importance, and covering
by the harshness of his language the weakness of his character, readily took upon himself the somewhat repulsive
part which he was required to play. The Queen-Mother
and her sons were first conducted to Melun, the château
of which being small and gloomy, but easy to defend, had
long been used as à prison. Subsequently, upon the news
of the approach of Condé and the increasing number of
his followers, they were hurried in a single day to Vincennes. The tears of the young King were a sufficient
proof of the violence which had been used towards him.
Next day he was taken to the Louvre. The Connétable,
who had preceded the Court to Paris, had caused the
meeting-houses which the Edict of January had allowed
to the Protestants to be sacked under his own eyes; a
proceeding which gained for him the nickname of 'Capitaine Brûle-Bancs.'

This news threw Condé into considerable perplexity;
the more so because the Queen's last letters had inculcated
peace and disarmament. The Triumvirs had manœuvred
well. The support of the Royal authority having been
taken from the Protestants, there was no longer any pretext for their remaining in arms. Other events put an
end to all uncertainty.

Tripier, the Governor of Orléans, on learning of the
King's return to Paris, had changed his tactics. He introduced into his citadel soldiers who had been sent by
Cypierre. D'Andelot, however, by means of a disguised
party, and of some secret understanding with the garrison,

was enabled to seize the Porte Saint-Jean, to establish himself there, and to repulse the first attempts of the Governor to recover it. But his position was a very critical one. The burgesses remained undecided; and he despatched a pressing message to the Prince. On the other hand, the latter was aware that D'Estrées, the ' Grand Maître ' of the artillery, was marching with all haste to the relief of Orléans. Condé was not long in deciding what to do. He dismissed Gonnor [1] and De Fresnes,[2] who had just arrived from Court with orders that he should present himself before the King immediately with his customary retinue. He protested to them that ' he was His Majesty's humble subject and servant, but that notwithstanding, having the honour to be of the blood royal, he could not believe it possible that the King could behave so unkindly towards him, as to command him to disband his forces when his enemy the Duc de Guise had been the first to take up arms and was still in arms at Court; in consideration of which he, the Prince, regarding what was being done in the light of a conspiracy of his enemies, did not intend to disband his forces until the Duc de Guise had laid down his arms.' [3] He then gave the signal to his followers to mount, and started at once. He was at Artenay. The six leagues which divided him from Orléans were passed at full gallop. Horsemen and baggage rolled over in the dust, without causing anyone to draw rein, amid the shouts of laughter of these foolish youths, and to the great amazement of peaceable travellers who were not expecting anything of the kind. ' It is,' cried the passersby, ' a meeting of all the madmen in France.' Tripier did

---

[1] Maréchal de Brissac's brother.
[2] One of the King's secretaries.
[3] Throckmorton to Elizabeth, April 10, 1562 (State Paper Office).

not defend himself, and evacuated the city. The burgesses welcomed Condé with cries of 'Vive l'Évangile!' The Protestants were masters of the 'nombril du royaume,'[1] and, as the worthy Lanoue, whose gravity deserts him on thinking of that happy souvenir of his youth, pleasantly adds, 'of the taps of the most delicious wines of France.'

It was a great thing to be in possession of so important a place, to hold the principal bridge over the Loire, and to be able to oppose to the Catholic capital a sort of Protestant capital situated almost equally near to those provinces from which any assistance was to be expected. The base of operations being now gained, both soldiers and money were needed for action. Condé had only from two to three thousand men, and sixteen hundred écus. He despatched a circular to the two thousand one hundred and fifty churches, claiming their assistance. He instructed the Admiral to apply to Cecil, that through the medium of the powerful Secretary of State, he might obtain the assistance which Queen Elizabeth had already led him to expect.[2] Another messenger was the bearer to Geneva of a letter from Condé addressed to 'his good friends, the syndics and council.'[3] The ministers assembled at Orléans wrote also; agents were despatched everywhere to enlist soldiers, levy subsidies, or, at any rate, to organise opposition to the payment of taxes. But it was not less important to allay the scruples that were agitating conscientious minds, to dispel the stigma of rebellion, to proclaim such views as could be avowed, and to assume the appearance of having a good cause. What party, in every

---

[1] 'In Orliens quasi nell' umbilico del reame di Francia.'—Davila.

[2] The Admiral to Cecil; Orléans,

April 11, 1562 (State Paper Office).

[3] 'Archives de Genève' (Appendix, No. V.).

civil conflict, does not claim for itself to be the sole defender of the rights and interests of the country?

It was with this view that a manifesto was immediately put forth. The Prince de Condé, the Admiral, the nobility and the knights of the order assembled at Orléans explained the object of their alliance. If, they said, they were ' compelled to take up arms, it was for the honour of God and the deliverance of their Majesties the King and Queen,' to insure the execution of the Edicts and of the measures resolved upon by the three orders of the kingdom; to prevent the money which was assigned by the States for the liquidation of the public debt from being put to any other use. They protested their respect for the King of Navarre, and declared themselves prepared to return to their homes if those who had taken up arms on their own authority were also disbanded. They further declared that they had chosen as their leader M. le Prince de Condé.

The mani-
festo of
the Pro-
testants.
Their
rising in
the pro-
vinces.

At the same time, in order to justify the appearance of being unprecedented and unwarrantable, which, despite its seeming moderation, this act displayed, they caused to be put in circulation the terms of an alleged compact between the Triumvirs, the Holy See, and the Catholic Kings and Princes, with the approbation of the Council of Trent, which had scarcely yet commenced its sittings. It was declared that the King of Spain was at the head of this league; that if the King of Navarre did not at once lend his support to the most decisive measures, his States would be handed over to the Duke of Savoy; that Guise and Philip II. had undertaken to see this carried out; that the Emperor and the Catholic Swiss Cantons were to exterminate their Protestant vassals or allies; that the

wealth of the Italian clergy and the produce of the confiscations made in France were to provide for the cost of
the whole enterprise. The destruction of all the sects,
and the extinction of the House of Bourbon; such was
the result aimed at by the league.

This document, however, was nothing but a stratagem
of war. There is no proof of its authenticity; but it is a
fair representation of the schemes which the Protestants
attributed to their adversaries. To these wild publica-
tions the Catholic leaders and the royal government,
which was in their hands, replied only by promulgating
afresh the Edict of January, to which was added a
single new clause, sufficiently justified by the state of
public opinion in the capital; to the effect that the
exercise of the pretended Reformed religion was inter-
dicted in Paris and its suburbs. It was the policy of the
Triumvirs, after having displayed so much decision in
their first proceedings, now to appear more moderate.
It was incumbent upon them to allay the apprehensions
both of the European Princes and of reasonable persons
in France, whom the abduction of the King had disgusted
and alarmed. The Protestants, however, were showing
themselves more powerful than had been expected, and
were reaping the fruits of the organization under which
they had been placed. Wherever they existed, however
few their numbers, they had risen. Before the end of
April, either by force or by the connivance of the authorities, they had occupied Dieppe, Havre, Rouen, Caen,
Le Mans, Blois, Tours, Poitiers, Bourges, and Lyon.
These places, all of them important, scattered throughout
the provinces where the Reformation had the greatest
number of adherents, were linked together so as to form

a chain of communication between Orléans and the
provinces in which they were situated. Throughout the
large extent of country which they embraced, especially
in the south, in Gascogne, in Languedoc, and in Dauphiné,
the struggle had commenced.

But it was in the heart of the kingdom that the question seemed about to come to an issue between the two
great armies which were gathering at Paris and at Orléans.
While these were making ready, the paper war continued.
The Protestants especially distinguished themselves by
the fertility and prolixity of their press; declarations,
confessions of faith, forms of prayer, protests addressed
to the Courts of Parliament, letters from Condé to the
Queen-Mother, to the King of Navarre, to the Duke of
Savoy, to the Lutheran Princes of Germany, to the Emperor; all these, with but few variations, harped upon
the same theme. Edited by Beza, or some of the other
pastors, rarely by Condé himself,[1] they were almost all
printed at Orléans, and copies of them disseminated in
great numbers. Never, since the invention of printing, had
that powerful engine been turned so largely to account.

The Triumvirs, on the other hand, changing their tone,
had presented a 'petition' to the Queen-Mother. This
was rather to be called a decree against the Protestants.
It was short, precise, harsh. They demanded in it the
extirpation of the sects and the revocation of the Edict
of January; and while pledging themselves, on their side,
to return to their homes as soon as the interests of religion
should have been secured, they demanded in turn that
'M. le Prince should be recalled from the position and the

---

[1] Some of them, we are told, even by the Bishop of Valence, a great con- fidant of the Queen-Mother. (See Appendix, No. VI.)

companionship in which he was at that time placed, and summoned to Court, since they were unwilling to believe of one of his rank anything unworthy of the blood of which he was the issue.'

They still temporized with Condé; and not only because they hoped to detach him from the Huguenots; it was, beside this, a device for making him an object of suspicion to his friends, and for sowing dissension among the leaders of the party.

The Royal army, 7,000 strong, advances to Châteaudun (June 1).

Words were soon followed by action. The Protestants were driven from Paris,[1] and on the first of June the Royal army advanced to Châteaudun. It numbered four thousand infantry, almost all belonging to the standing army, and three thousand lances, of whom eighteen hundred consisted of 'gendarmerie soldée;'[2] fifteen com-

---

[1] May 27. On the other hand, the practice of the Catholic ritual had been suspended in Orléans for more than a month previously.

[2] The 'gendarmerie,' as we have already had occasion to state, was the heavy cavalry, divided into 'compagnies d'ordonnance.' We have also explained (Chap. I.) what was meant by the term 'lance,' and given a few general hints as to the organization of armies in the sixteenth century. But in order to facilitate the comprehension of the detailed narratives which are about to follow, it may perhaps be convenient to explain here the different meanings which then attached to several expressions of military terminology. We regret that we cannot make these explanations as clear and precise as could be wished; for the absence of fixed rules, and of a systematic classification of the various degrees of military command, ren-

ders definitions of this kind very difficult. At the commencement of our religious wars, a captain (capitaine) of infantry and of cavalry was the real head of his company, and was almost independent, having over him none but merely temporary commanders, recruiting his own troop, and conducting its command according to his own pleasure. His 'compagnie' or 'bande' was in a certain sense his private property, and was the unit of military organization. The name 'bande' was generally applied to the infantry, and that of 'compagnie' to the cavalry. Each captain had his own banner or standard, which was called his 'enseigne' in the infantry, his 'cornette' in the light cavalry, and his 'guidon' in the 'gendarmerie' or heavy cavalry. The captain generally had under his orders a lieutenant, and another officer who carried his colours, and who thence

panies of Swiss, on the way to join it, were already in
Bourgogne, and Rockendorf was bringing twelve hundred
'reîtres' who had been enlisted in Germany; finally, it
was awaiting the arrival of some companies of Spaniards
which, by order of Philip II., the Regency of the Low
Countries was marching upon Paris. The title of Lieutenant-Général of the Kingdom gave the nominal command to the King of Navarre; but the real authority,
both political and military, was in the hands of the
Connétable and the Duc de Guise, more especially of the
latter.

Upon the receipt of the news of this movement, the
Protestant army quitted Orléans and encamped at the

CHAP.
III.

1562
June 1.

Condé
leaves
Orléans

derived his title ('enseigne' in the
infantry, 'cornette' in the light
cavalry, and 'guidon' in the 'gendarmerie' or heavy cavalry).[1] The
titles 'ensign' and 'cornet' are still
given to the sub-lieutenants of infantry and cavalry in the British army.

Next arose the custom of giving
to a troop the name of the banner
which headed it. A large body of
infantry was still called a 'bande;'
but a *company* of infantry, i.e. the
body commanded by a captain, was
usually called an 'enseigne,' and
a company of light cavalry a 'cornette.' The 'gendarmerie' alone
still retained the title of 'compagnie.'
Thus when, for example, an army
was said to be composed of forty
'enseignes,' thirty 'cornettes,' and
ten 'compagnies,' it meant that
there were forty companies of infantry, thirty of light cavalry, and ten
of heavy cavalry.

To sum up, the title of 'enseigne'
belonged alike to the standard of a

company of infantry, to the officer
who carried it, and to the company
itself, that of 'cornette' applied
equally to the standard of the light
cavalry, to the officer who carried
it, and to the company itself; that
of 'guidon' to the standard of a
company of 'gendarmerie' and to the
officer who carried it. The word
'compagnie,' when employed alone,
meant a company of 'gendarmerie.'
The words 'régiment,' 'bataillon,'
'escadron,' appear also in the military histories of that time, and are
used indiscriminately to denote a
temporary union of 'cornettes,' or of
'enseignes,' placed under the command of one common leader in a
campaign, or united for concerted
movements on the field of battle.

We shall see by and by when and
how regimental organization, in the
form familiar to us in the present
day, was applied to the French infantry.

---

[1] See *Othello*. Cassio was his 'lieutenant,' Iago his 'enseigne' or 'ancient' (ensign).

CHAP.
III.

1562
June.

rith 8,000
nen. His
;loom and
lesitation.

distance of two leagues from the city. It was composed of foot-soldiers from Gascony under Gramont, from Dauphiné and Languedoc, under the Vicomte de Rohan, and of French (i.e. men from the north and centre of France) under D'Andelot, in all about six thousand men, among whom were a considerable number of effective and veteran soldiers. Superior in infantry to the Royal army, its cavalry was neither so numerous, nor so well equipped and mounted, but it was for the most part composed of brave and well-trained gentlemen. The negotiations which had been set agoing to obtain the assistance of a body of foreign soldiers had hitherto proved unsuccessful, and there were no further reinforcements to be expected from the provinces. It was therefore on all accounts the interest of the leaders to come speedily to close quarters. It was advisable to profit by the astonishment caused by the first successes of their movement, by the ardour with which their troops were inspired, by the good discipline which prevailed among them, and by the equality in numbers and even almost superiority in efficiency of their forces to those of the enemy, rather than to wait till the latter had been reinforced, while the first blaze of enthusiasm should have burnt itself out, discipline have become relaxed, and money be exhausted. Condé was the man to see all this. Though he had not, like Guise, and even Montmorency, been accustomed to command large armies, he had nevertheless seen enough service in the field, and he had a sufficiently resolute character and sound judgment, to form and execute a vigorous resolve.

But in every age, even the most barbarous, whether men's minds are ruled by fanaticism or agitated by doubt, it is not without hesitation that a man of noble nature takes the final step in the disastrous path of civil war. He has weighed all, settled all, beforehand; he is convinced of the rectitude of his cause, or blinded by ambition and anger; still he cannot stifle the voice that speaks within his heart. He has ever before his eyes that vision of a weeping country which the poet calls up face to face with Cæsar on the banks of the Rubicon,[1] and his soul is filled with misgiving and with gloom. Such noble emotions were agitating the generous spirit of Condé. He too had had his visions and his ominous forebodings. Men told of weird apparitions which had crossed his path, of fearful dreams which had troubled his sleep; how ' as he was fording a stream, an aged woman, up to her waist in the water, out of which she seemed to arise, with hideous and wrinkled face, marched straight up to the Prince, seized his bridle, as though to gaze fixedly upon him, and then, letting it go, cried out, " Prince, thou shalt suffer, but God will be with thee and will deliver thee." He answered, " Pray to Him, my friend, for me," and remained awhile marvellously lost in thought. . . . . Afterwards he had a dream which he related to several persons, among others to Beza and to my father. It was to the effect that one day he fought three battles, and that after the fourth he found himself lying upon a heap of slain corpses.'[2] Once more his wife almost fell a victim to a frightful disaster. Having quitted Meaux at the same time as himself, to go to Moret, she had met on her way a procession.· Some of the young men of her retinue having insulted the sacred

---

[1] 'Ingens visa duci patriæ trepidantis imago.'—Lucani *Pharsalia*, lib. i. v. 186.

[2] D'Aubigné's 'Histoire universelle.'

ministers, the peasants rose in retaliation and pursued her little company with volleys of stones. The litter of the Princess was crushed to pieces, and she had barely time to reach Gandelu, when she was prematurely delivered of two sons. She arrived at Orléans almost in a dying state, with her eldest son.[1]

It was under the influence of these depressing feelings that Condé received fresh messages from the Queen. Catherine had gone with the King to the head-quarters of the Catholics; she was anxious to leave nothing untried which might avert the war, not from any horror of bloodshed, but because when once the struggle had begun, whichever side might be victorious, she must part with all hope of regaining power. She therefore offered Condé a conference with herself and the King of Navarre. The Prince, following the advice of all his friends, with the exception perhaps of the Admiral, accepted the offer. Apart from high quarters, and from local centres of irritation, there was in the mass of the troops so little enmity, that, notwithstanding the measures that had been taken to prevent a collision, and to keep the two escorts separate, they fraternized on amicable terms. It might have been taken for a halt of different troops in the same army. The interview took place at Thoury. It ended in nothing. Condé still demanded the dismissal of the Triumvirate; and Navarre, who had been duly schooled for the occasion, answered so harshly, that there was an end of the conference. The two armies now approached each other, and were scarcely more than two leagues

---

[1] Of these two children, born March 30, 1562, one died the next year, the other was afterwards brought up a Catholic, and became the third Cardinal de Bourbon.

apart. An engagement seemed inevitable, when negotiations were once more renewed. A somewhat better
understanding had been come to at last between the two
Bourbons; letters of a rather more cordial tone had passed
from the one to the other. Condé consented to hand
over to his brother the town of Beaugency, as a sort of
neutral ground, and offered to visit in person the Royal
camp. The King of Navarre promised that the Triumvirs
should retire to a distance, and that Beaugency should
be restored, if the negotiations proved abortive. Guise
entertained the proposal more readily than might have
been expected. He carried with him the Connétable and
Saint-André, both of whom, less far-sighted than himself, exhibited some degree of displeasure; and the three
quitted the camp. True, they did not go farther than
Châteaudun. The Duke saw clearly that, in the then
state of affairs, a friendly understanding was impossible;
still, he would not allow it to be said that he was an
obstacle in the way of peace.

Scarcely had the Triumvirate left, when Condé arrived
at Beaugency. He was conducted to Talsy, whither
Catherine, although suffering from a fall from her horse,
had come in fulfilment of her promise. After the preliminary compliments, the Bishop of Valence took him
aside. Everybody had thought, as did Condé himself,
that this prelate was devoted to the cause of the
Reformers. He was, however, only the creature of the
Queen, and like her he hoped to succeed in putting out
of the way all the leaders of public affairs, Catholic as
well as Protestant, in order to secure to Médicis undi-
vided power. His language was insinuating, but in-
definite; he counselled the Prince to bow to the evident

Interview
at Talsy.
Promise
impru-
dently
made, but
soon with-
drawn, by
Condé.

wishes of the Queen, whose interests were at one with his own. Next day Condé was joined by the principal officers of his army, Coligny, Prince Portien,[1] La Rochefoucauld, Genlis,[2] the Vicomte de Rohan,[3] Soubise,[4] Gramont,[5] and some others. Catherine received them very graciously, protesting her good-will towards them, but insisting upon the difficulty of arranging anything before the King attained his majority. She pointed out that the exasperation of the Catholics was great; it was necessary to make some sacrifices to the peace of the kingdom, and to give up for a time the exercise of the new religion. All this was said with a world of plausibility, and with such address, that Condé, losing his balance, declared at last that he and his friends would rather leave France than live without religion; that they begged his Majesty to allow them to do so, and to grant them leave of absence, if there was no other way of pacifying the kingdom. He was immediately taken at his word, and the King's majority was the term fixed upon for the expiry of their voluntary exile.

[1] Antoine de Croy, Prince de Portien. His father had quitted the Low Countries to settle in France. He had married a niece of Condé, Catherine de Clèves, daughter of François, Duc de Nevers, and of Marguerite de Bourbon. He died in 1564, and, despite his express recommendations, his widow married, six years afterwards, Henri, Duc de Guise.

[2] François d'Hangest, Sieur de Genlis, son of Adrien d'Hangest and of Françoise du Mas. This illustrious family of Picardie died out with that generation. The title passed on later to the family of Sillery.

[3] René, Vicomte de Rohan et de Léon, Comte de Porrhoet, cousin to Jeanne d'Albret.

[4] Jean Larchevesque, Seigneur de Soubise, last male scion of the House of Parthenay. His only daughter, Catherine, married, in 1575, the Vicomte de Rohan, whom we have just mentioned, and had by him the great Henri, Duc de Rohan.

[5] Antoine, Comte de Gramont, et de Guiche, ancestor of the Maréchal Duc de Gramont. He died in 1576. He was the brother-in-law of the Vidame de Chartres, François de Vendôme.

Their surprise was great; but they had no reply. The Protestant leaders returned to their camp sad and dejected. The intelligence of the issue of the conference was received there with amazement. Soon, however, the thoughtlessness of youth got the upper hand. They began to joke about the various occupations that each would have to adopt in order to live abroad. But wiser heads saw that the situation was no matter for laughter. When Condé officially communicated to the principal leaders assembled in council that of which most of them had been silent witnesses, a murmur of disapproval arose. ' He who deserts the game loses it,' said one. ' The land of France was our birth-place,' said another; 'it shall be our grave.' By unanimous agreement, they declared that the convention could not be carried out, and the Secretary of State, Robertet, who visited the camp in the evening, in behalf of the Queen, avowed ' that something more powerful than paper would be required to expel the Huguenots from France.' At heart, Condé was delighted at the compulsion thus put upon him. Emigration was ill adapted to the strongly marked characters of the sixteenth century. It was necessary to find some excuse for retracting the promise already made, and they were obliged to content themselves with rather feeble ones.

The next morning the Prince repaired to Catherine, told her what his friends had decided, and, to excuse his own submission to their wishes, spoke of the presence of the Duc de Guise at Châteaudun, and of certain letters which it was alleged had been intercepted; then, without further discussion, he abruptly broke off the interview.

It was the last stage of this absurd and make-believe attempt at an agreement. There were a few more

CHAP.
III.

1562
June.

messages interchanged. One of the gentlemen attached to Condé's suite, Bouchavannes,[1] came a few days afterwards to the Court at Vincennes with a passport from the Queen-Mother; but his mission, which was fruitless, seems to have had for its chief object the obtaining an interview with the English Ambassador, and the presenting, through his intervention, to Queen Elizabeth, an urgent entreaty for a subsidy.[2]

No one had been honest in the negotiation; but it is certain that the appearance of good faith was not on the side of the Protestants, and what followed was still more serious.

Somewhat treacherous attempt to make a night-attack upon the Royalists (July 3).

For more than a month 'Beauce had had two armies to assist her in gathering in the harvest.'[3] The country was getting exhausted, and the difficulty of finding provision had led the Catholic leaders to determine upon dividing their forces. There was a truce; and, what is more, the Triumvirate, with their numerous retinue, were absent from the camp. The Protestants, wishing to take advantage of these favourable circumstances, before the news of the final rupture should have brought about a change in them, resolved to make a 'camisade'[4] upon the Royalists as quickly as possible. During the day-time on the second of July, they marched to La Ferté-Alais; at sunset their soldiers, putting white shirts over their armour, that they might be able to recognise one another, moved off in two bodies. The first corps was under the command of the Admiral. He marched at the head of

---

[1] Antoine de Bayencourt, Sieur de Bouchavannes, a Picard, Lieutenant of the Prince de Condé's company.

[2] Throckmorton to Elizabeth.

Paris, July 23, 1562. (State Paper Office; French Papers; Appendix, No. VII.)

[3] Castelnau.

[4] Night-attack.

it with eight hundred 'lances,' who were to drive in the
advanced posts of the enemy's cavalry; twelve hundred
'arquebusiers' and two large battalions of 'piques' were
to capture the artillery. Condé commanded the 'bataille,' comprising one thousand cavalry in four squadrons,
and the remainder of the infantry. The country was
open and easy to cross. They hoped to fall upon the
enemy's camp about three o'clock in the morning, and to
surprise them before the reveil. But to prevent mis-
calculations in enterprises of this kind the troops ought to
be well trained and broken in for marching. A surprise
is seldom successful at the commencement of a campaign,
with soldiers freshly recruited or but recently brought
together. The Protestants found out this to their cost.
They moved slowly. There was some confusion; several
precautionary measures had been omitted. The guides,
who either became nervous or had been ill chosen, lost
the way. At daybreak they were still a league from the
rendezvous. D'Anville, who was in command of the
Catholic body-guard, was on horseback with his light
cavalry, and the sound of cannonading showed the Prince
that the enemy was beating to quarters. The surprise
had failed. Condé fell back upon Lorges, and the two
armies remained face to face without coming to close
quarters. At the end of two days heavy rains compelled
them to fall back upon former positions.

In order to give employment to his soldiery, whom he
was unable to pay, Condé resolved to attack Beaugency.
The Catholics had refused to restore this place, alleging,
not without good grounds, that as the truce had not been
declared at an end on the second of July, the attempted
'camisade' had been nothing but an act of treachery.

Capture
and sack of
Beaugency
by the Pro-
testants.

Beaugency was carried by assault; but this easy and somewhat feeble triumph did the Protestants more harm than good.

In the first outburst of religious enthusiasm they had subjected themselves to the severest discipline, and to habits of an austerity hitherto unknown in camps. Not an oath or profane expression was to be heard in the ranks. Nothing was taken without being paid for. In their camps neither gaming nor women were to be found. There were prayers morning and evening. The life was stricter than in a convent. But now that they had burst through the breach into Beaugency, the men from Provence began pillaging and sacking, the Gascons followed their example, and the French outstripped them both. No sort of excess was wanting; and those of the inhabitants who were of their own religion were no better treated than the rest.

They returned to Orléans in the utmost disorder. All the bonds of that splendid discipline of which they had been so proud were irretrievably broken. At the same time, bad news flowed in from the provinces. The Protestants had owed their success to their own boldness and to the panic of their adversaries. But when the first surprise had passed away, numbers began to be reckoned, and the majority was not found to be on their side. The reaction was speedy. They were unable to maintain the advantage they had gained, except in Dauphiné and Languedoc, where they were the stronger in numbers. They were unable, also, to gain possession of Toulouse; but they still had Lyon and Grenoble, and they had, above all, on their side, the Baron des Adrets,[1] a

---

[1] His campaign of 1562 is one of the most brilliant on record. But his career was like the flash of a meteor. Having quarrelled with the

man who was utterly devoid of principle, and who pushed his cruelties to the most odious refinements, but who was gifted with marvellous energy, and with some of the most striking qualifications of a soldier. Everywhere else they were rapidly losing ground. The ferocity of the Huguenots, in destroying everywhere, under the name of images, all objects of artistic and historical interest, 'the venerable securities of popular religion,'[1] excited the indignation of the multitudes who had been hitherto unconcerned. The leaders indeed felt how much this barbarous and childish fury was injuring their cause; but, in the lower ranks of the party, the tide of prejudice was too strong for them. Even at Orléans, at the very moment that their leaders and pastors had just disavowed and anathematized these new iconoclasts, and had accused the Triumvirs of stirring up these sacrilegious tumults, Condé was informed that his own soldiers were sacking the church of Sainte-Croix. He rushed to the spot, but his voice was not heeded. In a rage, he seized a musket and levelled it at a man who had mounted to the top of the porch to knock down one of the statues which adorned it. 'Monsieur,' exclaimed the soldier, 'have patience till I have overthrown this idol, and then, if you please, let me die!' The weapon fell from the Prince's hand. He thought he saw in this the finger of God.[2]

It was not only in the remoter provinces that matters fared ill with the Protestant cause. The Royal army, of The Royal army, having

---

Huguenots upon some point of amour-propre, or some pecuniary transaction, he subsided into a mediocre and obscure partisan.

[1] Lettres d'Est. Pasquier.

[2] H. Martin, whose splendid

'Histoire de France' we have constantly consulted. Although unable to share his opinions on all points, we cannot but bear testimony to the conscientiousness and lucidity of the work.

CHAP.
III.

1562
July.

received
reinforce-
ments,
subdues
Touraine
and Poitou.

which the nucleus was composed of regular and well-paid troops, had just received the expected reinforcement. Colonel Freulich had brought to it six thousand Swiss; the Rhingrave, twenty companies of infantry; Rockendorf, six troops of 'reîtres.' On the fourth of July, they stormed Blois. A detachment sent to the Duc de Montpensier, who maintained his position with great difficulty in Anjou, enabled him to recover Angers, and while the 'bataille,' under Guise and the Connétable, marched upon Tours, the rear-guard, under the orders of Saint-André, crossed the Loire to invest Poitiers.

This brilliant army had passed under the walls of Orléans, while Condé could do nothing to detain it. His troops were not in a state to take the field again. One common enthusiasm had rallied around him, from the most distant parts of France, the most zealous and the most ambitious among the Protestants. They had gathered in haste, with the cry, 'Dieu est bon capitaine!'[1] And they had reckoned on rapid successes, almost on miracles. The 'conferences' of Thoury and Talsy had somewhat cooled their ardour. The 'pilleries'[2] of Beaugency had given it the death-blow. Since that day, every fresh messenger from the provinces was a new source of anxiety. Each one trembled for his family, and longed to be at home to protect it. The southern infantry were the first to be attacked by a sort of home-sickness, and they began to desert in large bodies. More than once did Condé spring on his charger and gallop two leagues out of Orléans to overtake a band of these deserters. At his command they halted. As the Prince was 'in good sooth well-spoken and of a pleasant

---

[1] 'God is a good captain.'   [2] 'Plunderings.'

countenance,' they agreed to return. But the effect of this speech soon passed away; they were off again the next morning. The leaders soon became affected by the discouragement. There was a total lack of funds. They had coined money with the King's image, out of every metal they could lay hands on, either by robbing the churches or otherwise. This was, however, soon exhausted. They tried to sell the ecclesiastical property which they had procured, but could find no purchasers for it, even at the lowest price. The rivalries of the professions, the perpetual warfare between the gentlemen of the long and of the short robe, between the gown and the sword, complicated all these difficulties. The pastors were very numerous at Orléans. They claimed to direct everything in a war undertaken in the name of God, and endured but impatiently the supremacy of the Prince, without whose assistance they could not get on, but whom they wished to be a mere tool in their hands. Having no experience of practical difficulties, they laughed at or criticised the religious coldness of the gentlemen, their simpleness in the conduct of negotiations, and their weakness in action. To complete their disasters, the plague began to rage in Orléans. It became as impossible to maintain the army within the city, as it was to employ it without.

The leader of a party, compelled, as he is, to come to an understanding with all manner of private interests, and to satisfy all manner of persistently urged complaints, while yet he is deprived of all real authority over those who believe themselves or feel themselves to be absolutely necessary to him, is continually frustrated in the execution of his plans; and, in order to avoid the ruin or the desertion which threatens him, he must often either bow before wills which are very unreasonable, or else give up the prospect of obtaining services and sacrifices which he has no means of exacting. Condé had to face all the difficulties incidental to his position, even at a time when war was habitual, and when its consequences were generally understood and accepted. He gave way, and separated his troops. By so doing he at all events preserved an appearance of authority. Those whom he sent away, becoming his lieutenants in the provinces, could there maintain the cause, save some important places which they still held there, and organize resources for the reconstruction of the army. Soubise was sent to Lyon, Portien into Champagne, La Rochefoucauld to Angoulême, Duras[1] into Guyenne, Montgomery[2] into Normandie, whither already Morvilliers[3] had preceded him. In the meantime fresh energy was infused into the negotiations with foreign Princes. The new Vidame de Chartres, Jean de Ferrières,[4] had already been delegated to Elizabeth, and notwithstanding the opposition of the resident Ambassador, Paul de Foix, and of the Maréchal de Vieilleville, Ambassador Extraordinary, he had succeeded in obtaining encouraging assurances from that

[1] Symphorien de Durfort, Seigneur de Duras, Colonel of the legionaries of Guyenne, killed March 1563.

[2] The same who, in the tournament of the Porte Saint-Antoine, had mortally wounded King Henri II. He was taken in Domfront in 1574, and fell a victim to the unjust revenge of Catherine de Médicis.

[3] Louis de Launoy, Seigneur de Morvilliers, Governor of Boulognesur-Mer.

[4] Jean de Ferrières, elder brother of the younger Maligny whom we mentioned in the preceding chapter, cousin-german and heir of the Vidame François de Vendôme, one of the most indefatigable agents of the Protestant party. He was taken prisoner at sea while fighting against the Catholics, and was confined in the hold of a galley, and died there chained to the oar (1586). He was upwards of sixty-five years of age.

Sovereign. He was now joined by Robert de la Haye, the same magistrate who, in 1560, had shared the captivity of Condé. They were charged not to shrink from any sacrifice in order to secure to the party the active support of England. Finally, it was wisely judged that in order to ensure the despatch and direct the march of the 'lansquenets' and of the 'reîtres' which were expected from Germany, the presence of a man of the importance and resolution of D'Andelot was required. Condé remained in Orléans with the Admiral and a strong reserve, from which it soon became necessary to detach a considerable force in order to enable D'Ivoy[1] to defend Bourges.

For indeed that town was about to be besieged by the Catholics. All the cities of Touraine, of the lower Loire, and of Poitou had been captured, and the Government of Orléans, being thus cut off from Saintonge and Gascogne, could communicate with Lyonnais and Dauphiné only through Bourges. The whole of the Royal army was soon assembled before this city; but they were without ammunition, and Condé, who was not in a position to offer battle, tried to cut off their supplies. The cavalry which remained in Orléans took the field. One night the Admiral attacked, near Châteaudun, a great convoy, strongly escorted, which Cypierre was bringing to the besiegers. The escort was put to flight, and the powder and stores were destroyed. This was not the only success gained by this expedition. The Huguenot light cavalry brought back in triumph a personage whose arrival in the Protestant capital seemed to be the

---

[1] Jean de Hangest, fourth son of Adrien de Hangest, and brother of François, Seigneur de Genlis.

announcement of England's active co-operation, Sir Nicolas Throckmorton. Sir Nicolas no longer held the post of
ambassador, which he had filled for some years previously:[1]
in the month of July, he had requested and obtained from
Elizabeth his recall, having represented that he was no
longer safe in remaining in Paris. His farewell audience
had been granted him on the third of August.[2] Notwithstanding the uneasiness which he had at first expressed,
he did not quit Paris till the end of the month, and he
selected his route so cleverly that within a few hours he
fell into the hands of the Protestant cavalry. The latter
had not much difficulty in prevailing upon him to accompany them. No one believed his assertion of the force
put upon him; and as the fact that he was no longer the
representative of the Queen of England was either unknown or wilfully ignored, he was received at Orléans
with great ceremony. He was lodged with the Admiral,
and despite the strenuous remonstrances of the French
Government, notwithstanding the orders—at least the
formal orders—of his Sovereign,[3] he always found some
pretext for not leaving the Reformed army, which he
accompanied till the battle of Dreux.

[1] He had arrived in France as
Ambassador in May 1559, immediately after the Peace of Cateau-
Cambrésis. He was an active and
passionate man. In after years,
when in Scotland on sundry missions,
he was touched by the misfortunes
of Mary Stuart, and devoted himself
to her cause with an earnestness
which demands the more admiration
inasmuch as it was the effect neither
of love nor of religious sympathy.
Several of his relations perished
on the scaffold. He himself, says

Darcies, the chronicler of the reign
of Elizabeth, having quarrelled with
Cecil, 'was in great danger of losing
both his fortune and his life,' when
he died suddenly, immediately after
a supper at the house of Leicester; it
was commonly believed by poison.

[2] Throckmorton to Elizabeth,
July 23 and August 5, 1562. Eliza-
beth to Throckmorton, July 28.
State Paper Office. (Appendix, No.
VII.)

[3] French Papers. (State Paper
Office, *passim*.)

Coligny's happy *coup-de-main* was expected to lead to a decisive result for the safety of Bourges. The place was strong, tolerably well provisioned, and D'Ivoy had the reputation of being an energetic man. But he had had no news of late; and he was somewhat disheartened by the recent reverses of his party. The Triumvirs wished at all hazards to avoid a check. They offered him opportunely very favourable conditions—perhaps something more. D'Ivoy accepted them, and on the very day on which the Admiral defeated Cypierre, he capitulated.

The siege of Orléans seemed to follow naturally from the capture of Bourges. The city was enclosed only by a very bad wall, without outworks, without either a good ditch or a counterscarp. If they could press forward the siege before D'Andelot had had time to succeed in his negotiations, they might hope to crush, at one blow, the head of the party.

But those who were in possession of Orléans had not been idle. The wall had been furnished with many ravelins and other works. The islands in the Loire, too, had been carefully fortified. Nor was there any lack of men to occupy these hastily constructed works. Orléans contained twenty-two companies of infantry, amounting to three or four thousand picked men, who had remained behind as volunteers after their regiments had been disbanded; six hundred men of the garrison of Bourges, who had accepted the benefit of the capitulation; four or five hundred gentlemen, well mounted, brave, and accustomed to war; three thousand armed citizens, who were able to man the battlements; and this far from contemptible garrison was commanded by Condé and Coligny, who

CHAP.
III.

1562
eptember.

were not to be expected to yield so easily as D'Ivoy. The Admiral, more especially, had given proof at Saint-Quentin how well he could endure a siege, and was accustomed to say ' that there was no place in so bad a condition that it could not be defended, when three thousand men could be employed upon a sortie.'

he
nglish at
Lavre;
isastrous
eaty be-
ween
1em and
1e Pro-
estants
3ept. 20).

ept. 24.

Important news too had been received from Normandie. The English had taken possession of Havre and Dieppe, and were preparing to occupy Rouen. Queen Elizabeth had signed a treaty with the Huguenots, and had by Royal proclamation[1] made known her intentions with regard to all the ports of the province. This Princess, who was prudent, though ambitious, had long hesitated before taking any direct and active part in the affairs of France. From the very beginning of the disturbances, her Ambassador, Throckmorton, had openly, and not unnaturally, avowed his sympathy with the Reformers. He had announced to his Government, and greatly exaggerated, the assistance which the King of Spain was giving to the opposite party. He had urged that if England did not wish to see Philip II. in possession of Calais and all-powerful in France, immediate assistance must be rendered to the Huguenots; and Calais, Dieppe, and Havre[2] obtained as a guarantee. Elizabeth, however, distrusting the fancies of her Ambassador, threatened at home by conspiracies, not caring

---

[1] State Paper Office. Letter forwarding this proclamation to Sir Adrian Poynings in order to its publication at Portsmouth. In this Elizabeth further disclaims all intention of conquering Normandie for herself. There were afterwards keen discussions between the Protestant leaders and the Queen of England's ministers as to the meaning of the expressions in this proclamation. (Appendix, No. XIV.)

[2] Throckmorton to Cecil, March 14, April 10 and 17; to Queen Elizabeth, April 17. State Paper Office. (Appendix, No. VII.)

to increase, for the sake of doubtful results, the difficulties of her own position, and above all anxious not to compromise her rights over Calais,[1] received the overtures of Throckmorton at first with some coldness. Perhaps too she thought that by gaining time she could make a better bargain out of the claims of the Reformers. She confined herself therefore to addressing words of encouragement to Condé and the Admiral, accredited her Ambassadors to them,—a proceeding in itself of no small importance,—and gave a gracious reception to their letters and messengers.[2] But she took care to have Philip II. informed that she was lending them neither men nor money;[3] and flattering herself with the hope that she could, without risking anything, without opening her purse, without adventuring the life of a single soldier, become the arbiter of the destinies of France, she despatched to Paris two Ambassadors Extraordinary in succession, Sir Henry Sidney and Sir Peter Meautys. Their mission was to assure the Regent of their Sovereign's friendship, and to offer her the good offices of ' her sister' for the restoration of peace, but to the exclusion of ' any other prince or potentate.' Both these missions proved fruitless. Sidney and Meautys had great difficulty in travelling across France, were several times arrested, and did not reach the Court without considerable risk. Catherine

---

[1] By the Treaty of Cateau-Cambrésis, the restitution of Calais was guaranteed to her after a delay which was to expire in 1567, if during the interval she had not been guilty of any hostile act towards France. An article, rather ambiguously worded, left to the 'most Christian' King the power of compounding for this obligation by the payment of a heavy sum of money.

[2] Elizabeth to Throckmorton, March 31, May 10; to Condé and Coligny, May 10. State Paper Office. (Appendix, No. VII.)

[3] Cecil to Sir Thomas Challoner, Ambassador at Madrid, June 8. (State Paper Office; Spanish Papers.)

refused to allow that the Queen of England could step in between the King of France and his subjects. She declared that in case of need the King of Spain would render efficient assistance to her son, and would help him to restore order in his kingdom, if Condé and Coligny did not show themselves more reasonable.[1] Throckmorton, now left alone in Paris, which he was soon about to quit, and getting day by day more excited, renewed his solicitations with fresh ardour. Instead of exaggerating, as he had till now done, the strength of the Huguenots, he exaggerated their reverses. 'They want now,' said he, 'other things than words.' He represented that if the Queen did not determine upon giving them prompt assistance, they would lose the towns which they held in Normandie, and the gates of France would be closed to the English. If, on the other hand, Elizabeth were to adopt a prompt and energetic plan of action, the career of Edward III. was opening before the Queen of England.[2] This passionate appeal, in which some truth was mingled with many errors and misrepresentations, was not without effect in London. The Huguenot agents, the Vidame de Chartres with his indomitable perseverance, La Haye with his insinuating methods of proceeding, did not relax their pressure upon the Queen's ministers. Elizabeth took one more step, and recalled her Ambassador from Paris;[3] and then, as though alarmed at the effect which this measure produced in France, she

---

[1] Elizabeth to Throckmorton, April 28, July 16. Instructions to Sydney, April. Throckmorton to Elizabeth, May 8, August 5. Meautys to Cecil, July 27. (State Paper Office.)

[2] See the whole of Throckmorton's correspondence, preserved in the State Paper Office; French Papers, anno 1562. Several of them will be found in the Appendix (No. VII.).

[3] July 28, ibidem.

excused it upon grounds personal to Throckmorton,[1] and
announced the speedy despatch of a fresh envoy.[2] But
she had already made up her mind. At the beginning of
August the preliminary agreement[3] had been drawn up
between Cecil and the Vidame; English officers had gone
to inspect the fortifications of Dieppe and Havre;[4] and
La Haye had written to Condé to announce to him the
immediate arrival of six guns and a third of the sum he
had asked.[5] In short, as the position of the Protestants
was becoming day by day more critical, under the
pressure of circumstances, Cecil, having induced their
agents to yield to all his demands, concluded with them
the Treaty of Hampton Court. The Queen undertook to
place three thousand men in Havre, and, if required, to
furnish three thousand more for the defence of Rouen
and the castle of Dieppe. She also undertook to pay the
Protestants one hundred and forty thousand *écus d'or*.
But the fortress of Havre was completely handed over to
the Queen, and whoever should command it in her name
had the power of limiting the number of French, even
of Protestants, who should be allowed to reside in the
town. And she could be called upon to restore it only
after the restoration to her of Calais and the repayment of
the hundred and forty thousand crowns.[6]

---

[1] Throckmorton had been, as we mentioned before, for some time complaining of the insecurity of his life in Paris.

[2] August 17. The new Ambassador, Sir Thomas Smith, was despatched the following month. (State Paper Office.)

[3] An undated minute. (Appendix, No. VII.)

[4] Despatches of Sir H. Killigrew, from Havre, August 5 and 11; of Sir W. Woodhouse from Dieppe, August 11. Instructions to Horsey and Vaughan, August 30, &c. (State Paper Office.)

[5] August. No date as to day of the month. *Ibidem.* (See Forbes's Collection.)

[6] Dumont, 'Corps diplomatique du droit des gens,' vol. v. Part 1; Latin text. The minute is in English,

Condé accepted this shameful bargain. Men have not always the power of stopping short in the path into which their passions have drawn them. What had now become of the vehement accusations brought against the Triumvirs who were trusting to foreign aid? The Swiss and the Germans who were serving in the Royal army belonged to a class of mercenary troops that had for fifty years past formed part of every French army; the supplies furnished by the Pope had not been paid by cession of land, nor had the Spanish bands, who had recently entered Gascogne and Paris; and even if the fortresses in Piedmont had been evacuated, this was but the abandonment, unfortunate no doubt, but perhaps necessary, of claims which could no longer be maintained. But to throw open the ports of France to the English! To yield to these old enemies a single corner of that fatherland which for a hundred years they had devastated! To hand over to them the mouth of the Seine, when they had scarcely yet evacuated Calais! This was to recall the most sinister recollections of the wars of Bourgogne and Armagnac. Condé and Coligny endeavoured afterwards to wipe out the stain which this treaty left upon their memory. They pretended that they had not understood the nature of the engagements undertaken in their name with Elizabeth, and accused the Vidame de Chartres of having exceeded their instructions. But at the moment when the treaty was being signed they felt conscious of the unworthiness of their deed, and they were anxious to diminish its importance. 'They have expressly desired

corrected by the hand of Cecil, and preserved in the State Paper Office. Their despatch, signed by the Vi- dame de Chartres, is in the British Museum. (Cotton, Caligula, E. V., damaged by fire.)

me to say to your Majesty,' wrote Throckmorton to his Sovereign, 'that it would be a great reproach to themselves, and would be much resented in this realm, if your Majesty were, through them, to be put in possession of Havre, Dieppe, and Rouen, with six thousand men, solely for the purpose of retaining those places, and driving out from the flower of the Duchy of Normandie the King their Sovereign.' According to them, their only justification would be the conduct of the Queen of England. If the forces of Elizabeth were united to those which Briquemault and Montgomery had already assembled in Normandie to march immediately upon Paris, the occupation of Havre would no longer have that aspect of a mere selfish consideration of English interests which was so mortifying to the Huguenot leaders.[1] We may believe that the remedy would have been perhaps worse than the disease. In any case it never entered into the intentions of Elizabeth to follow this advice, and Condé was not mistaken as to the effect that the execution of the Treaty of Hampton Court would produce in France. The indignation was universal. Among the Protestants themselves, the ministers alone, who prided themselves upon a sort of Christian cosmopolitanism, had approved the treaty and insisted upon its ratification. But among the lay people the grief and humiliation were profound. Some, indeed,

---

[1] Throckmorton to Elizabeth, September 24. (State Paper Office.) Nevertheless, when the news that the treaty had been signed arrived at Orléans, Condé was desirous of testifying his gratitude to Elizabeth, and, notwithstanding his poverty, he ordered a beautifully mounted litter to be sent as a present to her, with two splendid mules. In order that the present might be in all respects welcome, he enquired of Cecil, through Throckmorton, 'what colours would be most acceptable to her Majesty.' Throckmorton to Cecil, October 15. *Ibidem.* (Appendix, No. VII.)

CHAP.
III.

1562
Sept.

gave up their adhesion to a cause so dishonoured. Morvilliers, to whom the Huguenots owed so much of their success in Normandie, and who had already thrown reinforcements into Rouen, when it was closely invested by the Duc d'Aumale, now retired to his estates, and became a simple spectator of a struggle in which his patriotism forbad him any longer to take part. His example was followed by Rouault de Gamaches and by others. The party writers tried to do away with this unfavourable impression, but their difficulty in doing so emerges from a cloud of verbose dissertations, in the innumerable pamphlets, letters, and manifestoes with which they continued to inundate France. At first they pretended that not the aid but only the mediation of foreign Princes had been sought; and then, when facts were too strong for such a misrepresentation, they explained, with naïve hypocrisy, that the English were not with M. le Prince, but at Havre, 'whither it has pleased her Majesty the Queen of England to send them, for the good zeal that she has for the glory of God, and the affection she bears to this sorely troubled kingdom !'

The Royal army marches to the siege of Rouen.

Thanks to the arrival of this reinforcement, so dearly bought, thanks to the delays of the Duc de Bouillon and to his own personal activity, Montgomery, who had succeeded Morvilliers, had bettered the circumstances of the Protestants in Normandie. This new position put an end to the hesitation of Navarre and the Triumvirs. Before entering upon the siege of Orléans, it was necessary to prevent the English from fully establishing themselves in France, and their Queen from becoming the sole and real head of the Huguenot party. This was a wise and patriotic resolution. It was deemed that a corps of

fifteen hundred horse and three thousand five hundred
foot would be sufficient to stop D'Andelot and to watch
the garrison of Orléans. This task was intrusted to the
Maréchal de Saint-André and the Duc de Nevers,[1] Governor of Champagne; and the Catholic army marched
towards Rouen.

D'Andelot had arrived in Frankfort at the very time *D'Andelot*
when Ferdinand was presiding there over the Diet which *succeeds in*
raising
had assembled for the coronation of his son, Maximilian, *7,000 men*
in Ger-
King of the Romans. Circumstances were unfavourable *many.*
to the Protestants of France, not only among the Catholic
Princes, but also among the Lutheran. No pains had
been spared to detach from the Huguenots the sympathies
which seemed to be naturally most drawn to them. On
the twenty-seventh of August, during the siege of Bourges,
the Sieur de Rambouillet had quitted the Royal camp in
all haste for Germany, in order that he might, at all
hazards, frustrate the negotiations that had been entered
into. His instructions, signed by the King of Navarre
and the other Princes, authorized him even to sacrifice
the Council, and offer to substitute for it a Colloquy which
should be presided over by one of the great Sovereigns of
Europe—the Emperor, the King of Spain, or the King of
France. There ' might be sought the means of coming
to a good understanding and sacred reformation . . ., and
instituting a public and Christian peace.'[2] The Cardinal

---

[1] François de Clèves, Duc de
Nevers, the son of him who acted
such a splendid part in the campaign
of 1557, and nephew of Condé
through his mother, Marguerite de
Bourbon. He had been very intimate with his uncle, and had at
first promised to join him at Orléans;
but, suddenly changing his mind, he
became one of the most ardent of
the Catholic party. He was killed,
accidentally, at the battle of Dreux.

[2] Instructions sent from the camp
at Bourges, August 27, 1562, to the
Sieur de Rambouillet, who had
been sent on a mission to Germany.
(Bibl. imp., Brienne, No. 88.)

de Lorraine had continued his intrigues, and indeed had gone so far in his advances to the supporters of the Confession of Augsburg, that he had become an object of suspicion to the Pope, and was very coldly received at Trent by the Roman prelates. The Calvinist envoys were to make a profession of faith before the Diet of Frankfort; it was recited by Jacques Spifame, the apostate Bishop of Nevers, a man utterly despicable, already in bad repute with his own party, whose mistrust was to cost him his life;[1] yet a clever, subtle, and eloquent man, who was particularly charged with the conduct of the negotiation, the success of which might possibly have been endangered by the roughness and violence of D'Andelot. After some days of waiting and discussion, the levy of men was authorized. But the execution of the measure was not easy. The agents of the Triumvirate multiplied obstacles; money and leaders were wanting; at last all was settled through the active co-operation of the Landgrave of Hesse, who supplied a hundred thousand *écus d'or*, and his own marshal, Rolthaufen, as commander of the little army. It was, however, only on the tenth of October, and not on the first, as had been stipulated, that D'Andelot was able to make his final muster at Bacharach. He brought with him nine troops of 'reîtres,' which made up three thousand three hundred horse, and four thousand 'lansquenets,' in twelve companies.

Capture of
Rouen
(October
25). Death
of the
King of
Navarre.

These delays were disastrous. Without reinforcements Condé could not stir from Orléans, and without prompt relief or a strong diversion, Rouen could not be saved. That place had been invested in September; the defence

---

[1] He was beheaded at Geneva, March 23, 1566, after a trial which lasted three days.

had been energetic and prolonged beyond all expectation; but at last, on the twenty-fifth of October, the town was carried by assault. Condé received, simultaneously with the tidings of its fall, that of the death of his brother the King of Navarre. Antoine de Bourbon died as he had lived, brave, undecided, and voluptuous. Struck down in the trenches, in a post of the utmost peril, he expired in the arms of Louise de la Béraudière, after having listened to the exhortations both of a priest and of a minister, without its being known by anyone whether he died a Catholic or a Protestant.

Such had been the relations between the two brothers that Condé must have been but slightly affected by this loss; that which concerned him most was doubtless the change it made in his own position. He found himself, owing to this event, the eldest of the Princes of the blood who was neither in infancy nor in holy orders, and he thus acquired the right of claiming a voice in the government of the kingdom. But, for the time, the King of Navarre's death served only to increase the power of the Triumvirs, since it deprived the Regent of the sole though feeble support that could enable her to restrain them, and gave them unlimited control over all the resources of the State. Condé remained the leader of a party, and of a party greatly dejected.

At the very time when Rouen fell, Burie and Montluc were beating and dispersing at Ver the levies that Duras had just made in the south, and which he intended to lead to Orléans. All resistance to the Catholic leaders ceased in Gascogne as well as in Guyenne, and the Protestants of those parts found their only refuge in the support of three energetic women, Jeanne d'Albret in Béarn, Jeanne de Genouillac, mother of Crussol, in Quercy, and Anne de Bonneval, mother of the celebrated Armand de Biron, in Agénois. The siege of Montauban had begun; that of Grenoble was being pushed forward with vigour. In Saintonge, La Rochefoucauld had been able, by means of the declaration of a synod, to calm the scruples of the Reformers, who were hesitating to take up arms against the King. He had made levies, and gained some advantages. He had already invested Saint-Jean-d'Angely, when the news of the battle of Ver forced him to raise the siege and proceed to rally the scattered remains of the bands of Duras. The Catholic ritual was re-established in La Rochelle, and all the country included between the Lower Loire and the Gironde was subjugated by the Duc de Montpensier.

Executions at Orléans.

These startling reverses, as they became known one after another at Orléans, excited there that feverish irritation which is sometimes taken for resolution and boldness, but which more frequently precedes despair. Some bloody executions had taken place at Rouen, and it was determined to make reprisals. The Master of Requests, De Selve, who was on his way, as Ambassador, to Spain, had just been carried off by a party, and taken to Orléans with the Abbé de Gastines, and Sapin, counsellor of the Parliament of Paris, who accompanied him. These, 'for lack of better,' were seized upon as victims. Selve, who had a brother in the Protestant army, was spared. The other two were hanged as 'accomplices in the conspiracy hatched against the King and the kingdom.'[1] Condé's

---

[1] Already in the month of August, the curé of Sainte-Croix at Orléans, an old man of seventy-five, who was found secreted in a garret, had been executed on the same charge.

signature was at the bottom of the sentence, and D'Aubigné, in relating the fact, repeats the following words of
his father: 'It is said that anger is half madness;[1] and
I say that in Princes it is complete madness!'

It was, however, not anger which had impelled Condé
to this useless and cold-blooded cruelty. The ministers
had demanded it, and he was compelled to disarm the
mistrust of that 'suspicious race.'[2] The Catholic leaders,
always skilled in fomenting the divisions which they
knew existed in the Protestant party, treated Condé with
an affectation of regard, and in a series of decrees pronounced against the Châtillons and their adherents (July),
the Parliament of Paris had formally excluded from its
sentence the person of the Prince, who was declared to
be a prisoner in the hands of the rebels. The handing
over to the executioner of a magistrate of that court was
the reply to these misstatements. Condé seemed more
deeply compromised than ever; it was a sad necessity
which thus compelled him to buy confidence at the price
of such culpable weaknesses!

A slight success had just at least lightened the de-
spondency, if it had not rekindled the courage, of the
garrison of Orléans. Dampierre, who had made a sortie
with fifty horse, had captured the baggage of the legate
on his way to the Council; the Cardinal, insisting upon his
diplomatic immunity, sent a trumpeter to demand it back.
Condé replied that an outfit so warlike and so magnificent
was ill suited to an ambassador of peace, accredited to the
successor of the lowly Peter, and that these riches would
be much better employed in defraying the expenses of

---

[1] 'Ira brevis furor.'

[2] 'Race soupçonneuse.'   'Genus   hominum   suspicax.'   (Thuanus, xxxiii.)

the war undertaken in behalf of religion; finally, that if the legate would cause the Triumvirs to refund the two hundred thousand *écus d'or* which the Pope had lent them, and would procure the recall of their Italian auxiliaries, he would restore the baggage intact.

This was but a scanty supply, and a very poor set-off against so many reverses. A fresh cause of uneasiness was agitating their spirits. They were without news of D'Andelot; they knew that Nevers was waiting for him with the army of Champagne, composed of fourteen companies of gendarmes, sixteen troops of 'argoulets,'[1] and twenty-five companies of foot-soldiers. Saint-André had just brought to Troyes nine companies of gendarmes, thirteen troops of light cavalry, and the legionaries of Picardie. What was to become of the little German army in presence of such forces? The news of its destruction was hourly expected. Condé and Coligny alone, whose resolution was unshaken, had calmly contemplated the probable issue. They had secretly agreed that if such a misfortune were to come to pass, the Prince, leaving the Admiral in command, should immediately set out in disguise, and, travelling by night, should go in person to implore the aid of the Lutherans. He was prepared to carry out this desperate resolve, when the news arrived that D'Andelot was only thirty leagues distant from them.[2]

Although suffering from fever and carried in a litter, this energetic man had himself directed the march of his soldiers. After traversing Lorraine, he betook himself to the mountains, and passing near the sources of the Seine, he came upon the Yonne through Bourgogne, leaving Nevers and Saint-André to continue their ar-

---

[1] A kind of light cavalry.   [2] La Noue.

rangements for stopping him in Champagne. He entered
Orléans on the sixth of November. Fortunate events
followed in quick succession; La Rochefoucauld arrived
at the same instant with three hundred gentlemen and
the relics of the bands of Duras. The Protestant army
was in a condition once more to take the field. 'Our
enemies,' exclaimed Condé, 'have taken our two rooks;
but I have good hope that this move we shall have their
knights.'[1]

He immediately marched out of Orléans with the
whole of his French troops, and joined the 'reîtres'
below Pithiviers, which was carried on the eleventh of
November. This prompt action was necessary, for there
was no possibility of finding sufficient supplies for the
Germans in Orléans, and there was no money to pay
them. They had, indeed, once hoped to procure some
from the Protestant zeal of the wealthy burgesses of
Geneva; but these good men feared to expose their city
to a risk greater than they durst undertake,[2] and limited
themselves to a 'civil reply.'[3] It was therefore necessary
to apply to the inhabitants of Orléans; a subscription was
opened, but with the usual fate of voluntary contributions
of this sort, it had produced but little, and the deduc-
tions from it had been excessive. All the sources of
supply which were still thought available had been laid
waste; it was necessary to live by plunder. This necessity was scarcely consistent with the injunctions of their
ministers as to the observance of discipline and strictness
of morals. Licence was now carried to excess; the

Condé
marches
upon Paris
with
14,000
men
(Nov. 11).

---

[1] Bourges and Rouen, an allusion
to the game of chess. The 'castles'
were then called 'rooks.'

[2] 'd'exposer leur ville outre leurs
facultez.'

[3] Appendix, No. VIII, 'une hon-
nête response.'

splendid regularity which had lasted but for a few days, in the first sortie, had vanished, never to reappear. It was resolved to march upon Paris, which was already— if I may use an expression borrowed from modern military phraseology—the 'point objectif' of the civil war. Condé had only six thousand cavalry, most of them French, good and tried, and eight thousand infantry, most of them German. No one as yet knew what the latter would prove themselves worth. They were in all fourteen thousand men. The artillery numbered eight pieces; five field-guns, and three siege-pieces. This was altogether but a slight equipment. But the Royal army, which at the commencement of the siege of Rouen numbered twenty-eight thousand men, was much reduced, both owing to the losses it had sustained and to the disorder which had ensued upon the capture of that city. It was still upon the spot, and only quitted it on the news of the Prince's movements. His plan therefore was to reach Paris before it; the capital, ill-provisioned, badly fortified, and occupied by a feeble garrison, was exposed to a coup-de-main. The success, however, of such a movement was very doubtful, and moreover, upon the approach of the Royal army, the Protestants were too few in number to hold so large a city, which was still ardently Catholic. They might, it is true, insult it and strike terror into it, ruin the suburbs, and, if necessary, give battle before the enemy could receive the reinforcements for which he was waiting. In any case they must march fast and straight upon their destination.

But in military affairs, how is it possible for a council of direction to adopt a simple, vigorous, practical scheme?

Every plan submitted to discussion is almost always
modified and fundamentally altered. The leader of the
Protestant army was, as we have said, far from being
free; he was bound constantly to consult the principal
men among his followers, and these gentlemen had no
notion of offering a modest suggestion, like that ventured
upon by a confidential officer in consultation with his
general; what they gave was a complete plan of the
campaign, set forth in almost dictatorial tones, and with
an imperative demand for its consideration. In order to
humour these obstinate and self-important men, a portion
of each scheme was selected, and the compromise which
resulted from this medley of projects was seldom successful. Thus, in consequence of a difference of opinion as to
the attack on Paris, it was agreed to march towards that
city, only taking the longest route, and stopping at every
hamlet on the way. By this means they combined all
the chances of failure, while they lost all the chances of
success. Étampes, La Ferté-Alais, Dourdan, Montlhéry,
were successively occupied and roughly treated. They
then turned to Corbeil, where Pavan was defending himself well behind good walls. Saint-André, who had
arrived from Champagne by forced marches when he had
learned that D'Andelot had passed him, but was too late
to save Étampes, threw himself into Corbeil. The siege
was not advancing, and time was passing, when Condé
received a friendly message from the Queen. The Princess, who had returned to Vincennes on the nineteenth,
requested him to make advances to her with a view to
negotiations for peace. This furnished a happy excuse
for withdrawing from an unpromising attempt. Firing,
therefore, ceased before Corbeil, much to the displeasure of

CHAP.
III.

1562
November.
operations;
check be-
fore Cor-
beil.

the English Ambassador;[1] and the Protestant army set out on the twenty-third of November, along the left bank of the Seine, while Saint-André's troops reached Paris by the right bank. A few shots were exchanged between the two banks, but without much harm to either side.

He arrives
before
Villejuif
(Nov. 25).
Negotia-
tions. Con-
ference of
Port-à-
l'Anglais.
On the twenty-fifth of November, Condé slept at the Abbey of La Saussaye, between Juvisy and Villejuif. Médicis had appointed him an interview on the following day at Port-à-l'Anglais.

The death of Antoine de Bourbon had served as a pretext for these fresh negotiations. The Queen had hastened to occupy the only ground on which she could resume the direction of affairs. Her first equerry, Saint-Mesmes, offered the Prince, on the part of the Queen, the post of Lieutenant-Général of the Kingdom for himself, and for his followers the re-establishment of the Edict of January, with certain modifications which were to be discussed at their interview.[2] Condé replied to the messenger that he should know how to take the authority of his brother, but ' without occupying his place or admiring his example,' alluding to the weakness with which Navarre had submitted to the direction of the enemies of his House. The interview he accepted, and kept his appointment; but, as the Queen was a little behind time, he returned to his quarters, alleging that he did not feel well, but letting it be seen that he was suspicious of some attempt against his person, while in reality he was apprehensive of being entrapped in some such snare as that into which he had fallen at Talsy.

[1] Throckmorton to Elizabeth, November 22. From Essone. (State Paper Office.)
[2] Throckmorton to Elizabeth, November 22. A first message, more vaguely worded, had been brought by Gonnor on the 11th. (The same to the same, November 20. *Ibidem.*)

The Admiral and the Connétable found themselves alone together at Port-à-l'Anglais, and on the following day, the twenty-seventh of November, Montgomery came with the Duc de Nevers to visit M. le Prince at La Saussaye. The conference was formal and without result, Condé pretending, in order to avoid discussion, that his indisposition prevented his talking; it did not, however, prevent him from bitterly reproaching Nevers, his nephew, for the breach of faith with which he charged him.

The Protestants began to feel that they must hasten. Guise had already arrived from Rouen. If he allowed the Queen to negotiate, it was only that he might gain time to rally the Royal army, of which a part had already joined; the remainder would follow. Montpensier and Lanzac were bringing, by forced marches, the Spanish bands and the cavalry which had been victorious at Ver. Condé resolved to 'try' the enemy at once. On the afternoon of the twenty-eighth, his advanced guard deployed before the Faubourg Saint-Victor, which had been hastily covered with some earthworks and trenches. About twelve hundred 'arquebusiers' and six hundred 'lances' were brought out of Paris. After a somewhat severe skirmish, M. le Prince ordered a general charge with perfect success. The Catholics gave way on every side; they behaved so badly that the Duc de Guise, who was in general very self-possessed, could not restrain his anger. He reproached his gendarmes, exclaiming that distaffs would become them better than lances. Strozzi, however, threw himself, with six hundred picked 'arquebusiers,'[1] into the enclosure of a mill, and stopped the

[1] These were the 'arquebusiers' (musketeers) belonging to the King's new body-guard, which were destined to become the nucleus of the French Guards. Filippo Strozzi was a member of the family of that name

advance of the victors. The day was declining, and the Huguenots were prepared rather for a reconnaissance in force than for a general assault. The retreat was sounded, and they contented themselves with taking up a position; the infantry with its left on Vaugirard and its right on Montrouge, which was occupied by Genlis. Portien held Gentilly with the advanced-guard. The Prince and the Admiral were at Arcueil with the cavalry of the 'bataille,' the 'reîtres' in their rear at Cachan and 'other convenient places.'

On the twenty-ninth and thirtieth, the Protestants placed themselves in line before their quarters, but without attempting an assault; and as the Catholics did not make a sortie, there was merely some firing, which was necessarily slight, on account of the weakness of both sides in artillery.

Had Condé caused the attack of the twenty-eighth to be supported more briskly, his troops would certainly have got possession of the Faubourg Saint-Victor; and there is no knowing what might have happened the next day. Several of his lieutenants were of opinion, not without some reason, that the success would have been a fatal one, and that the army, demoralized by pillage, would have been easily crushed. But then, why make the attempt if there were no hope of success? However, the chance, once lost, did not occur again. Reinforcements flocked into Paris; the terror, which had been so great the first day that it killed the President Lemaître, had rapidly subsided. The people of Paris

so celebrated for its devotion to Italian independence. His father, the heroic defender of Sienna, had been honourably rewarded with the bâton of a Maréchal de France. He himself was born in 1541, and fell in a naval engagement in 1582. He was a good soldier, and to him is due the definitive organization of the infantry into regiments.

had accommodated themselves to the situation with their traditional versatility. They laughed, they were merry at the expense of the Prince, who, having failed in taking Corbeil, thought he could take Paris; hence the proverb, 'He takes Paris for Corbeil.'[1] The shops were reopened; the academical classes of the 'Quartier Latin' had recommenced, and the noise of artillery which now and then reverberated in nowise interfered with the ordinary life of the great city.

This cannonading proceeded only from petty alarms given by the 'reîtres,' whose brains were somewhat disordered by the immoderate use of the wines of France; for an armistice had been concluded on the first of December, and on the second there had been an interview ('parlement') between the Queen and the Prince near a mill, at the end of the Faubourg Saint-Marceau. These negotiations were a source of considerable uneasiness to Throckmorton; he never left Condé, but watched him constantly, for he dreaded his bursts of patriotism. If he discovered in the conversation of the Prince some slight disposition to escape from the toils which held him in dependence on a foreign Power, he immediately reminded him of his engagements with England, and did his best to encourage him.[2] Elizabeth, informed of the hesitation of Condé, wrote to him on the occasion of the King of Navarre's death, and advised him to show himself more deferential towards the Admiral, who was always Throckmorton's main reliance.[3] Condé had to defend himself submissively, to send to the Queen a long apologetic

---

[1] Lettres d'Est. Pasquier. (State Paper Office.)
[2] Throckmorton to Elizabeth, November 20, 22; December 5, 13. [3] Elizabeth to Condé, December 4. *Ibidem.* (Appendix, No. IX.)

paper, and to protest 'that he would never finally decide on any step without informing her Majesty, that he might follow her counsel upon the matter.' [1]

There was, however, no foundation for the anxieties of the English Ambassador. On either side the sole object was to gain time. Médicis was undoubtedly as sincere in her desire for peace as it was in her nature to be. Undoubtedly also the gentlemen of lower degree were very anxious to be restored to their affairs and their families as soon as their sense of honour would allow them to return. They might be seen during the truces, meeting one another and conversing together, regardless of party, and with a freedom which the astonished Germans mistook for the commencement of desertion. But none of those whose opinion was of real weight were desirous of laying down their arms before they had more decisively measured their strength with their adversaries. The Catholics were negotiating in order that they might wait for their troops from Guyenne; the Protestants that they might reconnoitre the defences and prepare for a night attack.

Thus on the very evening—the fifth of December— when the truce was broken, all was ready for a coup-de-main on the Faubourg Saint-Germain, a quarter generally inhabited by the Protestants, and in which, notwithstanding their expulsion from it, their army had still some secret friends. The Duc de Guise, who suspected this design, had taken care to fortify the entrenchments, and to enjoin vigilance. But the weather was very cold, and the delay appeared long; the ranks by degrees grew thinner, and an hour or two after midnight there remained

---

[1] Condé to Elizabeth, Dec. 10. State Paper Office. (Appendix, No. IX.)

only the ordinary guard. Had the Huguenots then made the assault, their success for the moment would have been certain. Happily for their adversaries, or rather, perhaps, for themselves, they lost their way; and being overtaken in the country by the dawn, they hastened back to their quarters.

Negotiations were now renewed, with no better success or sincerity. Condé, not easily discouraged, wished once more to try a 'camisade' on the seventh of December. The word was given. His soldiers had already donned the white shirt, when a sinister rumour began to spread: —Genlis, who for some days past had inspired some distrust, and who had been unwillingly entrusted with the secret, had just passed over to the enemy.[1] It was therefore deemed prudent to abandon the scheme; but the excitement was great in the Huguenot camp. They believed that there was some conspiracy. All who were connected with the fugitive became the objects of ill-conceived suspicion. Even Gramont, who had given such noble proofs of his devotion to the cause, was compelled to clear himself, to declare his horror at the conduct of his late friend, and to offer to fight him in single combat.[2] To all the difficulties with which the chief of the Protestant army was already surrounded, there were now added distrust and bitter recriminations among his officers.

---

[1] Genlis always maintained that he had never revealed anything concerning the project with which he had become acquainted, and, in order to justify his defection, assigned all those excuses, longing for peace, and devotion to the country, which are never wanting to deserters. We must, however, bear in mind that he did not again take service, but retired to his estates. During the second civil war he appeared once more in the ranks of the Protestants.

[2] Throckmorton to Elizabeth, December 13. (State Paper Office.)

CHAP.
III.

1562
Dec. 10.

The Royal
army
rallies and
is rein-
forced.
Condé
retreats.

Their position was no longer tenable. Montpensier and Lanzac, after having passed through Vendômois and Perche, had crossed the Seine at Mantes. On the evening of the eighth, they entered Paris with seven thousand men. Guise now assumed the offensive. On the ninth he drove in the Protestant outposts, and intended to fall upon them with his entire force on the eleventh at daybreak. Condé anticipated him. On the morning of the tenth, he commenced his retreat in good order, marching upon Palaiseau, where he slept that night. He himself took the command of the rear-guard, which was not attacked. But even his presence and his efforts could not prevent his soldiers from firing their quarters and the villages along the road. It was the Germans who had set them this noble example. A foreign alliance always bears its fruits. They had set fire to Montrouge, under the strange pretext of being revenged upon Genlis, who had been quartered there.[1] All the rest imitated their example. It was necessary to execute some men that evening, and the irregularities were not entirely stopped till the day following.

Various
designs of
Condé and
his gene-
rals; on
the sug-
gestion of
the Ad-
miral, they
march
towards
Nor-
mandie, to
be near
the
English.

The Protestant army followed the road to Chartres, without any definite plan. On the fourteenth it halted at Saint-Arnoult,[2] and the chiefs consulted together as to their future movements. Some wished to besiege Chartres, but this suggestion was at once dismissed. Condé proposed a loftier and more daring resolution.

The Catholics, who had quitted Paris on the eleventh, had arrived before Étampes. The Prince was anxious to reinforce the garrison of that place, in the hope that

---

[1] See page 144.

[2] A village about eight leagues from Chartres and ten from Paris.

they would besiege it and that it would delay them for a
few days. During that interval, he would have marched
upon Paris, now clear of troops, with his whole force,
would have occupied the suburbs of the left bank, and
would have established himself there in a strong position.
The Triumvirs, in order to re-enter the capital, would
have been compelled to cross over to the right bank, and
he hoped that, before they were ready for him, he might
take advantage of the secret friends which he had within
the city, and of the terror which he had inspired, to treat
on advantageous terms. At all events, he hoped to be
able to retreat safely, after having caused his enemy much
material injury as well as a serious loss of prestige.

This scheme, which was not without some chance of
success, met with the inevitable opposition of the Admiral.
' Supposing,' said he, ' that we can seize the suburbs before
the return of the Triumvirs, they have strength enough
to place Paris in safety, and at the same time to hold the
country in our rear, to cut off our communication with
Orléans, and perhaps even all the means of retreat.
Rather than allow ourselves to be caught in such an en-
tanglement, why not make for Normandie ? We should
there find Queen Elizabeth's money, which we are so
much in need of to pay our " reîtres." Moreover, the
Earl of Warwick will be able to bring us from Havre
the artillery which we want for taking the towns, and,
above all, a large reinforcement of English infantry,
which will put us in a favourable position for giving
battle.'

The Admiral did not add that, in order to be successful,
it was necessary to occupy, in advance of the Royalists,
the Lower Seine, where they held no fortress, to establish

themselves there, and to wait for the English succours, without being compelled to fight. This opinion, however, prevailed, and Condé had to give way. He immediately despatched a letter to the Earl of Warwick, informing him of the decision, and urging him to cross the Seine at Honfleur and march to join him.[1] Throckmorton, who had strongly advised the march upon Normandie, and who took credit to himself for it with his Sovereign, also wrote to Warwick and to Elizabeth.[2] After having detailed to the Queen, and recommended to her, the demands of the Reformers, he added that they earnestly apologized for their conduct in the recent negotiations, and promised to be more circumspect in future, and more faithful to their engagements ; if they should capture any towns on the banks of the Seine, they would hand them over to the English as a pledge of their good faith, and as a security for the sums which should be advanced to them. It was, then, to open up a way to a foreign Power, and to establish it securely on our soil, that so much blood and courage were to be lavished !

The army marches very badly. It arrives at Dreux, where it had been anticipated by the Catholics.

They left the road to Chartres and took the direction of Dreux. The army marched very badly. For lack of money, they were compelled to give the Germans the advanced-guard and the best quarters, and the way in which these troops conducted themselves was not such as to conciliate a population already hostile. As they did not speak French, they sent out no scouts, and the army was without any tidings of the enemy. Further, they had an immense quantity of baggage-waggons, which nothing could induce them to leave behind, and which

[1] December 14. State Paper Office. (Appendix, No. IX.)
[2] December 13. *Ibidem.*

blocked up the roads and prevented their advance.
Finally, the small force of artillery was so badly horsed,
and so badly harnessed, that constant stoppages were
necessary for the purpose of repairing its furniture.

On the seventeenth they passed the Eure at Maintenon,
and the Prince slept at Ormoy, three leagues and a half
to the south of Dreux. The consequences of a bad organization were felt at every step ; for want of efficient
quarter-masters,[1] the advanced-guard and the light troops
under the command of the Admiral found themselves at
Néron, in rear of the quarters of the ' bataille' and a little
farther from the Eure.

On the other side of the river were the enemy. The
Catholics had followed the Protestant army, and, marching by the banks of the Voise and the Eure, were already as high up the river, notwithstanding the badness
of the roads. On the morning of the eighteenth they had
already passed their adversaries, had arrived at Mézières,[2]
and were occupying Dreux.

The Prince, on learning that the enemy's skirmishers had
been seen on the left bank of the Eure, gave orders for
all to be under arms. The advanced-guard once more
took up its proper position, and the army marched towards
Mézières, in the hope of crushing the enemy as they were
crossing the river. But they only came across a few
stragglers ; the Admiral maintained that there would be
no battle, and, as usual, gained his point. The army returned to its quarters at night without occupying the villages in front of it, without even reconnoitring. They

After a fruitless appearance under arms on the 18th, the Protestants, on the 19th, find themselves face to face with the Royal army. The Admiral's mistakes.

---

[1] 'Maréchaux des logis'—officers
who performed duties somewhat
analogous to those of the modern

staff.

[2] About a league east-south-east
of Dreux.

should at least have gained fresh ground, if they did not wish to come to close quarters.

On the nineteenth, two hours before daybreak, Condé was on horseback at the head of the 'bataille,' impatiently waiting for the advanced-guard to pass to the front, and sending to them message after message enjoining them to hasten. But the Admiral, persisting that there was no chance of an engagement, troubled himself very little about his orders, and did not appear for a long time with his troop, ' who had neither harness on their backs nor arms in hand.' The heavy baggage and the quarter-masters[1] were ordered to Tréon, where it was determined to halt for the night, and the march began. The strength of the army was within a few hundred men the same as it had been at the attack on Paris,—about thirteen thousand men, of whom eight thousand were infantry and five thousand cavalry.[2] An hour later the Admiral's scouts informed him that they could see a strong force on their own side of the Eure. Condé and Coligny gave the word to halt and 'lance in rest,'[3] and then ascended an eminence to reconnoitre the enemy. D'Andelot, although shivering from fever, and wrapped in a fur cloak, insisted on accompanying them. They discovered the whole of the Connétable's army posted in rear of the village of Nuisement, on the wooded slopes which at Dreux separate the Eure from the Blaise, and about a league to the right of the road on which they were. As this army seemed to the Protestant generals to be very advan-

---

[1] 'Maréchaux des logis.'

[2] Everyone knows how difficult it is for the most vigilant general, even now-a-days, with all the improved organization and means of control, to estimate at a given moment the precise strength of an army. What then must it have been in those days?

[3] 'Dresser les lances,' answering to the 'Draw swords!' or 'Fix bayonets!' of our day.

CHAP.
III.

1562
Dec. 19.

Battle of
Dreux.
Disposi-
tion of the
Royal
army.

tageously placed, they decided that it was better not to offer battle, and, on the advice of the Admiral, which, as usual, prevailed, they resumed their march for Tréon.

But Biron,[1] who was reconnoitring for the Catholic army, having perceived the Huguenots halt and put their lances into rest, warned the Connétable that if M. le Prince did not take up his position where he then was, of which he saw no signs, they would give battle within an hour. Upon this, Montmorency, quitting the confined position which he at first occupied, advanced across the open plain, which extends south of Dreux, and deployed his troops between the two villages of Épinay and Blainville, which are about two thousand 'mètres' apart. He had eighteen thousand men and twenty-two guns. As his cavalry was not numerous, he did not collect it together, but dis- tributed his two thousand horse between the battalions of infantry.

The right wing or advanced-guard, commanded by the Maréchal de Saint-André, rested on the village of Épinay, which was barricaded with carts, and outflanked its own left, the ground selected being still too narrow for the deploy of the whole army.[2] This wing was composed

---

[1] Armand de Gontaut, Baron de Biron, afterwards a Marshal of France, killed at the siege of Épernay in 1592. He was the senior 'maréchal de camp' present. His mother's views and his own tendencies made him an object of suspicion. His son it was, like himself a Marshal of France, who was beheaded in 1602.

[2] In order to understand how armies of considerable size could be disposed during the sixteenth cen- tury, in confined spaces, we must bear in mind how deep the ranks of the infantry then were. Generally one company, however numerous, formed only a single compact mass. The pikemen or 'corselets,' who formed the principal strength of it, were drawn up several ranks deep and fought in rectangles or squares, almost solid, the centre being re- served for the colours. If there were any 'arquebusiers' (sharp- shooters), they were divided into 'manches,' were drawn up in rear of the front ranks, and came forward to

of nineteen companies of gendarmes, fourteen ensigns of
Spaniards, twenty-two of veteran French bands, and
eleven of 'lansquenets.' Fourteen guns protected the
van. Damville, one of the Connétable's sons, and the
Duc d'Aumale, one of the Lorrain Princes, supported the
left of the advanced-guard with their two companies of
' ordonnance ' and with the light cavalry.

The dense mass of the six thousand Swiss, in twenty-
two companies, formed the centre, and outflanked slightly
the left of the advanced-guard. Eight guns were assigned
to them. The Connétable, with his gendarmes, placed himself between them and seventeen companies of soldiers from
Picardie and Bretagne (probably 'légionnaires'), which
were flanked by the cavalry of Sansac that formed the
extreme left.

The Duc de Guise had refused to take any command
in the army, in order that it might be made evident that the
war was not on his account, and also because he did not
choose to serve as Montmorency's second in command.
He posted himself with his escort in the centre of the
advanced-guard, between the Spaniards and the veteran
bands. The position was well selected.

While the Catholics were in this position, their ar-

fire, falling back immediately. Sometimes, too, the 'arquebusiers' formed
separate troops; their numbers as
well as their importance increased
considerably during the religious
wars, especially in the French corps,
and the need began to be felt of a
more complicated organization of
troops in the field, and often even of
an extension of line, although up to
the time of Gustavus Adolphus all
was still very confused. But the

Swiss, faithful to the traditions of
Granson and Morat, trusted principally to their 'piques' and their
'grosse phalange.' It appears that
at Dreux they only formed one
single battalion, and that not one of
them carried fire-arms. On the
mode of fighting at that time, see
Montluc, Tavannes, and others, passim, and especially the 'Discours
politiques et militaires' of La Noue.

tillery fired a few shots among the 'argoulets' who covered the Prince's right. The latter immediately faced about, and one company of 'reîtres,' which was within range, prudently inclined to the left to shelter themselves in a depression of ground. It was no longer possible to continue their flank march; despite the Admiral's predictions, an engagement was becoming inevitable, and neither he nor Condé were the men to refuse it. Besides, a battle in the open gave them a better chance than in woods and defiles, into which, had they advanced, they would towards evening have plunged, and where the superiority of the Connétable's infantry gave him an undoubted advantage.

The Protestant artillery therefore now advanced to answer the fire of the enemy's guns. The attempt, however, was but feeble, for it consisted only of four guns, the rest having been sent on, together with the baggage, to Tréon. The firing soon ceased, to allow the cavalry to pass. This was the only skirmish previous to the general engagement; there were none of those duels in which our ancestors delighted to display their valour and their skill in presence of two armies. 'Everyone was resolute,' says La Noue, ' reflecting within himself that the men whom he saw approaching him were not Spaniards, Englishmen, nor Italians, but Frenchmen, and even the bravest of Frenchmen, among whom were some who had been his own old companions, kinsfolk, and friends, and that in an hour they would all be killing one another; a thought which made each one shudder at the work, yet still without diminishing his courage.'

It had not been so easy as might be thought to the Protestant army to face to the right, although it was

CHAP.
III.

1562
Dec. 19.
army finds
itself un-
able to
refuse
battle,
which is at
once
opened by
the ar-
tillery
without
any pre-
vious skir-
mishing.

CHAP.
III.

1562
Dec. 19.

he cavalry
of the
bataille.'

drawn up in order of battle. In those days manœuvring was not much understood, and commanders seldom altered the position of their troops except to lead them to the charge. Some time was therefore necessarily spent in executing this movement and reforming the line. Moreover, as their line of march had not been exactly parallel with the line of the Royalists, it was found that, after the movement to the right, the Prince and the 'bataille' were nearer the enemy than were the Admiral and his advanced-guard.

It was after mid-day. Condé, impetuous and excited, would not wait for Coligny to get into line. He addressed a few words to his gendarmes: 'Comrades!' cried he, 'I mean to be the first in giving and taking blows ; and I pray God you may all charge as resolutely as my example shall show you how.' Then, leaving La Rochefoucauld with a hundred horse to support his infantry, he advanced at full trot with four hundred French 'lances,' and passing within the range of the enemy's advanced-guard, which did not move,[1] he fell upon the Swiss. Mouy[2] and D'Avaret attacked them in front, and he himself took them in

[1] Davila, 'Guerre civili di Francia,' says that Condé never saw the vanguard, whose right was hid by the village of Épinay, and their left by the Swiss phalanx ; that the Prince, in charging the Swiss, thought he was attacking the right of the Royal army. This assertion, which is of no great importance, has but little foundation, and does not appear in any of the contemporary accounts that we have seen. Davila is, however, an excellent authority on military operations, which he well understood, and which he had heard discussed and appreciated by good judges. In his narration of them, if he is not quite as exact, he is at all events more lucid than the Président de Thou.

[2] Louis de Vaudray, Seigneur de Mouy en Beauvoisis, a posthumous child of the House of the Seigneurs de Saint-Phale, and therefore generally called Mouy-Saint-Phale. He was one of the bravest men of his day. He was most treacherously assassinated in 1569 by the too famous Morvel, or Maurevert, 'the king's killer.' His son, Artus de Vaudray, was killed, in avenging his death, in the Rue Saint-Denis.

flank. The phalanx was divided. The Prince then hastened to his 'reîtres,' and divided them into two bodies. One of these he hurled at that living tower in which he had just made a great breach, and the long pistols of the Germans continued the work of destruction commenced by the 'furia francese.' The others he opposed to Damville and D'Aumale, who were coming up to support the Swiss. ·The heavy squadrons of 'reîtres' rode down the Catholic gendarmes, who were disposed 'en haies.'[1] D'Aumale fell, severely wounded ; Damville recovered himself by a junction with the vanguard, which had not yet stirred. One of his brothers, Montberon,[2] fell by his side.

[1] That is, formed in two or three very extended ranks, whereas the 'reîtres' were drawn up in several very close ranks. The 'reîtres,' recently levied in Germany, were the first cavalry that were armed with pistols, a weapon at that time quite new. They always charged at a trot, pistol in hand ; each rank discharged its pistols, and immediately wheeling round ('vire-voltait') and reforming in rear of the squadron, exposed the next rank. The sword was only used in single combats. Such was at least the proper use of the 'reîtres.' But as they were generally composed of but indifferent soldiers, they frequently fired all at once, and the greater part of their ammunition was fired into the air. At other times, under pretence of using their pistols more efficaciously, the whole squadron would change direction to the left before approaching the enemy, fire to the right, and then immediately wheel right about. They frequently met with reverses. But as they had experienced some success, and as this mode of warfare was highly convenient, the German gendarmerie or heavy cavalry had, while retaining their lances, borrowed from the 'reîtres' the fashion of charging at the trot and their deep formation. The French gendarmerie for some time resisted this innovation ; in the sixteenth century, and especially when they were few in number, as in the case of the Catholic cavalry at Dreux, they retained the old formation in two or three extended ranks. But the example of the 'reîtres' was gradually followed by the whole of the cavalry, and under the reign of Henri IV. the lance was completely abandoned in France. It was the immortal Sedlitz who gave to the cavalry all its power, by forming in two ranks and charging at full gallop, sword in hand.

[2] Gabriel de Montmorency, Baron de Montberon, fourth son of the Connétable. He was killed, it is

CHAP.
III.

1562
Dec. 19.

'he Admi-
il defeats
ie left
'ing of
ie Royal
rmy with
ie cavalry
f the
anguard;
ie Conné-
ible is
ounded
nd taken
risoner.

As soon as Coligny had seen that fighting had commenced, he had ordered his infantry to unite with that of
the Prince. He himself, wheeling to the right with four
hundred French 'lances' and six troops of 'reîtres,' charged
the Connétable's gendarmes. The latter were unable to
withstand the shock. The battalion of legionary troops
was broken, as also the contingent of Sansac. Montmorency endeavoured to resist the confusion, but his horse
was killed under him. Mounting another offered him by
D'Oraison,[1] a lieutenant of gendarmes, the gallant old man
was returning to the engagement, when he was again
struck down by a gunshot wound in the jaw. He was
surrounded and compelled to surrender. The fortune of
war threw him into the hands of Portien, who, although
a personal enemy, generously offered him his hand, and,
rescuing him from the ill-treatment of the 'reîtres,' conducted him safely out of the fray.

he Swiss
aving
illied,
out the
rotestant
nsque-
its.

The centre of the Catholics was now in complete rout,
and the Protestant cavalry was in hot pursuit of the fugitives. Some were making prisoners, others pushing on for
the baggage, the pillage of which attracted the 'reîtres'
and detained them a long while. But these victorious
troops had left behind them the great Swiss battalion,
which, though broken and decimated, still remained
firmly at its post.

Let us pause by the way to salute those heroic soldiers,
those models of honour and military fidelity, who, for
upwards of three hundred years, have mingled their
blood with ours on every field of battle.[2] Not a few

---

said, by one of the Prince de Condé's
equerries, with whom he had quarrelled at the attack on Paris.

[1] Antoine, Baron d'Oraison, Comte
de Cadenet.

[2] It is calculated that from 1480

of those who fought at Dreux, in the Catholic cause, were Protestants; yet not one of them deserted their colours or hesitated, just as, in after years, their children, born in a republic, were the last to die for the Royal government which they served. Their ranks had been devastated by the bullets, and broken by the tremendous shock; seventeen of their captains had been mortally wounded; all around them were flying; yet not one of them dreamed of flight. They rallied at the word from their surviving officers, picked up from the ground the gory shafts of their pikes, and advanced to recover their captured artillery.

The Protestant infantry which had remained behind had been posted according to nations, without regard to vanguard or 'bataille.' The German 'lansquenets,' four or five hundred strong, came forward to meet the Swiss; but the Lutheran Princes had not chosen to send the best of their soldiers. Their attitude already betrayed hesitation. La Rochefoucauld, left by Condé to support them with his company of 'ordonnance,' endeavoured to lead the way for them; but he was repulsed. 'It is an awkward thing,' remarks, somewhat humorously, in his memoirs, one who took part in this charge,[1] 'it is an awkward thing to attack such hedgehogs.' D'Andelot, who had been compelled by the violence of his fever to remain a simple spectator of the action, beheld those soldiers whom he had himself led through so many obstacles wavering and undecided. He sprang into the saddle, and, unarmed, rushed into the midst of them to urge them to close quarters. He too was unsuccessful. They lost heart before

to 1830, 750,000 Swiss served under   [1] Mergey.
the French flag.

striking a blow. Without waiting for the French battalion, three or four thousand strong, which was following them with the artillery, they took to flight and dispersed. About fifteen hundred of them reached the village of Blainville in a state of disorder. 'No such cowardly men,' cries Beza, 'had entered France for fifty years; and yet they were the finest looking troops in the world.'

Second and
unsuccess-
ful charge
of Mouy
and the
' reîtres '
against
the Swiss.

The Swiss had not yet seen the end of their trials. But their courage did not forsake them. Mouy, who had been the first of the Protestant army to join battle, was the first to rally his troop; he returned to the charge with his gendarmes. The Marshal of Hesse, Rolthaufen, who by himself worthily upheld the honour of Germany, supported Mouy with several troops of ' reîtres.' Once more they charged into the thick of the battalion. The great square was broken; but these noble fellows rallied into small and compact groups. When their halberds were broken they betook themselves to stones, which their powerful muscles made into terrible weapons, and retreating step by step they brought themselves into line on the left of the vanguard. Biron advanced to cover them with the light cavalry; Mouy and Rolthaufen were compelled to give up their attempt and to retreat to Blainville. This village, on which in the morning the left of the Royalist army had rested, now became the rallying-point of Condé's and the Admiral's cavalry. As the Admiral was being congratulated on their success, he pointed towards the right wing of the Catholics, and exclaimed, 'You do not then notice that black cloud which is about to burst upon us.'

Guise en-
gages the
Catholic
vanguard.

Beyond a few cannon-shots which at the commencement of the action had been aimed at the Prince's squad-

rons, it had seemed till now as though this right wing were
ignoring the fight that was going on under its eyes. Guise
was not its commander, but he was its soul. The Maréchal de Saint-André was wholly guided by his suggestions
and his orders. Guise, motionless and silent, was keenly
watching every movement in the action, making no reply
to the recommendations, taking no notice even of the
sarcastic remarks, of those around him. Men began to
murmur that he intended to allow the Connétable to be
crushed. Damville, whose brother had been killed by
his side, and who had under him now only a handful of
cavalry that had suffered severely, was compelled to be a
helpless spectator of his father's defeat. Damville kept
urging the Duke to charge, and as he persisted in his entreaties, Guise quietly replied, 'My son, it is not yet time.'
At last, when he saw the 'lansquenets' beaten, and the
'reîtres' and gendarmes of the enemy exhausted by the
resistance of the Swiss, a gleam of joy lit up his stern face;
'Now, friends,' he exclaimed, 'let us go into it; those
fellows are ours!'

At this signal, so impatiently waited for, Damville and He throws Saint-André
Saint-André set their cavalry in motion and marched to-
wards Blainville, driving before them Mouy and the 'reî- upon the 'reîtres'
tres.' Guise, ever prescient, sent the Royal 'lansquenets' and de-feats the
to their support; he posted the veteran bands as a reserve, French battalion
took with him the Spaniards and two hundred horse of the Protes-
which he had retained, and advanced to meet the French tants.
battalion of the Protestants. He was anxious, before following his ardent comrades, to cut off from Condé the support of his artillery and of his reserve of infantry. These
troops had not yet been in the action; but their isolated
position in the plain, and the defeat of the Germans, had

CHAP.
III.

1562
Dec. 19.

already shaken them. After a single discharge of their cannon and muskets, they abandoned their guns and took to flight. Guise left the Spaniards to complete this easy success, and hastened to join Saint-André.

Condé had received a wound in the hand, and could with difficulty manage his horse, which had also been struck by a bullet. Separated from his equerry by the fortune of the day, he had been unable to obtain a fresh mount. Notwithstanding this, upon the first movement of the Catholic right wing, he had hurried, with the Admiral, to the support of the 'reîtres,' without remarking the number of his followers. He had only been able to rally two hundred gendarmes, whose lances were broken and their horses tired out; still they were the steadiest of the men, those who had left off securing the prisoners and pillaging the baggage, and had returned to the field. But the Germans refused to stop their retreat; the 'ritmeisters'[1] declared that they could not wheel right about before they had reloaded their pistols, and continued their retreat at full trot. The French were driven back. The Prince and Coligny were unable to resist the rush; the pace quickened; it became a gallop, and they threw themselves, in disorder, into the woods to the south of Blainville. The Royal cavalry pressed them hard, killing or capturing all stragglers. Mouy was the first who was taken. Soon Condé rolled beneath his horse as it fell; he was immediately surrounded by Damville's gendarmes, who were burning for revenge, and compelled to surrender his sword.

Before continuing the pursuit through the woods, Saint-André allowed his troops to rest a little, and to

Condé and Coligny endeavour to support the 'reîtres;' they are driven back; Condé is taken prisoner.

Saint-André halts. Guise com-

---

[1] Captains of cavalry.

wait for the Duc de Guise. The latter had gone to take possession of Blainville, where some of the 'lansquenets' who had been defeated by the Swiss, had taken refuge. D'Andelot had rallied them in the farmyards of the village; but he could not prevail upon them to fight; they threw down their arms; he himself escaped with difficulty, and got to Tréon by a miracle. Guise returned to the Maréchal; the day's work seemed over: the enemy's general was captured; his artillery was in their power; his infantry were prisoners or defeated; his cavalry was broken. But just as the victors were preparing to despatch their light horse after the fugitives, a troop of 'écharpes blanches'[1] debouched suddenly upon their right flank.

After having passed through the wood at the entrance of which Condé had been taken, and also the dell on the other side, the Protestant cavalry, perceiving that it was no longer pressed by the Royalists, had halted on the eminence which commanded this dell. There they got into some sort of order; the 'reîtres' reloaded their pistols; the Admiral in a few words restored their courage; the energy which was once more apparent, both in his eye and voice, communicated itself to his soldiers. They returned to the charge, the French in the centre, the Germans at the two wings, and unexpectedly emerged from the other side of the wood. At first the Catholics thought that these troops had come to surrender themselves. But scarcely had they perceived them before they came to close quarters; and this was the most tremendous

pletes the rout of the Protestant infantry.

Terrible rally on the part of the Admiral; death of Saint-André; the Duc de Guise secures the victory through the veteran French troops.

---

[1] The Protestants had retained the white scarf which, before the civil war, was in general use in the French army. The Catholics, as a distinguishing mark, had conceived the unfortunate idea of adopting the red one of the Spaniards.

onslaught of the day. The leaders tried to encounter this unexpected storm. Saint-André was the first to rush forward. He was taken, and instantly fell, the victim of some private revenge. Guise himself was unable to restrain his cavalry; it gave way. But he reaped the fruit of his precaution. The veteran French bands, which he had left all day in reserve, came up at the double; their front was protected by numerous musketeers, whose well-sustained and well-directed fire decimated the Protestants and arrested their advance. Night had fallen; the white scarves could no longer be distinguished from the red. The Admiral retreated towards Neuville, still in good order, leaving to the rear-guard, at the post of honour, the remains of Condé's company and Bouchavannes, his lieutenant. Guise for some time followed him, less in order to attack him than to prove his own victory; but both men and horses were worn out with fatigue, and he returned to pass the night at Blainville.

The battle of Dreux lasted five hours. Of all those that were fought in our religious wars, this was the longest, the most bloody,[1] and the most hotly contested. It had three phases, or, in the language of our forefathers, three distinct charges.

[1] Several contemporary writers state that nine thousand men fell; others make the number five thousand. But even this second estimate is exaggerated. De Thou, who speaks of eight thousand killed in both armies, adds that the Protestants acknowledged only three thousand missing, without counting, however, fifteen hundred lansquenets whom the Duc de Guise had taken at Blainville, and whom he sent home again. The Admiral, on the other hand, writing to the Earl of Warwick and to Elizabeth almost immediately after the battle (December 21 and 22), avowed a loss of only eighty to a hundred horse (original letter, State Paper Office; Appendix, No. X.); but here the exaggeration in the opposite direction is so evident that the assertion carries no weight.

In the first, the Protestant cavalry, in very superior force, defeated the main body of the Royal army, and the Connétable was taken. But the Catholic right wing remained untouched; the Protestant infantry was cut off; the Swiss rallied, routed the German battalion, and, when charged for the second time by the cavalry, fell back upon the vanguard. The remainder of the Catholic army found that they had changed front, falling back upon their right which was at Épinay; the Protestant cavalry rallied at Blainville.

The right wing of the Royalists then moved forward, scattered the French battalion of the Reformers, captured their artillery, defeated their cavalry which was already fatigued, retook Blainville, and compelled the rest of the lansquenets to lay down their arms. The Prince de Condé was taken, and the engagement seemed at an end. This ended the second charge.

The third was the Admiral's splendid return to the attack. The Catholic cavalry had halted too soon, and the tremendous shock which they thus unexpectedly received well-nigh lost them the day. But the steadiness and the well-directed fire of the veteran French bands checked the Protestants, and forced them to retreat. The trophies of victory, the standards and guns, remained in the hands of the Catholics. The losses, however, were about equal on both sides; the two commanders-in-chief were taken prisoners, and the two armies quitted the field of battle.

The honours of the day belonged first to the Royal infantry, whose steadiness made up for the constant reverses of the cavalry. These honours were divided between the Swiss and the veteran French bands. The latter, a remnant of that infantry which for fifty years had been fighting in Italy and on our northern frontiers, were the especial favourites of the Duc de Guise, ' who understood infantry as well as any man living.' [1]   He had already much improved its organization, by subdividing the colonel's command, and grouping the bands under several ' mestres de camp.'   This was the rudimentary form of that regimental organization which was only completed in 1569 ; and this handful of brave soldiers were the nucleus of the ' vieux régiments,' those progenitors of the old French infantry, which, down to the close of their glorious career, continued to be the pride of our armies and the terror of our enemies. [2]

[1] Brantôme.

[2] In the spring of 1569, the death of Condé and of D'Andelot, as also that of the Comte de Brissac, having left Filippo Strozzi sole Colonel-Général, titular and effective, of the whole of the French Royal infantry, that able soldier profited by the opportunity to divide the ' vieilles bandes' permanently into four regiments.

Almost at the same instant the Huguenot leaders, in proclaiming as their general the young Prince of Béarn, appointed him a body-guard of two hundred picked men, chosen from among the Reformed infantry, giving preference to those of the veterans who, at the commencement of the civil war, had followed the fortunes of D'Andelot, their colonel.

One of Strozzi's four regiments became that of the French Guards. The other three were styled, in honour of the veteran bands, Picardie, Champagne, and Piémont. On the accession of Henri IV to the throne of France, his regiment of Protestant guards received the name of Navarre, and took rank after Picardie.

Such was the origin of the 'vieux régiments.' They retained their place on the right of the French infantry down to the republican organization into semi-brigades, and gloriously ended their long existence on the fields of Valmy and Jemappes, where they knew how to show our young battalions that path of honour which for upwards of two hundred years they themselves had trodden. They had preserved to the end of their career the traditions of their earliest days. It was only yesterday that I heard a veteran of 1792 detailing their last exploits; and, notwithstanding his many trials and his many great achievements, the eyes of the noble old man filled with tears as he recalled the following souvenir of his youth. It was an episode in the battle of Jemappes. The Duc de Chartres, who commanded the centre of the army, was leading the infantry to the attack of the forest of Flenu; this infantry was composed of old battalions of the line, and of battalions of volunteers who had not yet been 'amalgamated,' according to the expression then in

The Duc de Guise, who had made so judicious a use of these bands, was severely blamed by his contemporaries for having kept them in reserve till all the troops placed under the immediate command of the Connétable had been completely defeated. God alone knows what goes on in the heart of man; but such a base motive is very inconsistent with the great soul of François de Lorraine. To those critics, who doubtless were prompted by jealousy, he replied truly, that he was not commander-in-chief; that the right wing ought not to have gone into action before Montmorency gave the order; that he himself being left afterwards, by the fortune of the day, the sole judge of what ought to be done, had acted so as to insure the success of the Royal army; and that the issue of the battle completely justified his decision. The only reproach against him which had any foundation was that he showed himself too eager to destroy the remnant of the Protestant infantry, and thus that he allowed the Admiral to execute the movement which cost Saint-André his life and nearly lost the day.

The Protestant cavalry exhibited great courage; the 'reîtres' were never weary of expressing their admira-

---

use, and were distinguished by the colour of their uniforms, which were respectively white and blue. At the moment of the charge being sounded, the colonel of the fifth regiment of the line, an aged officer with white hair, looking back towards his troops and standing up in his saddle, exclaimed, waving his sword above his head, 'En avant, Navarre sans peur!' and the regiment repeated 'En avant, Navarre sans peur!' This was a souvenir of the Chevalier Bayard, 'sans peur et sans reproche,' who, in the wars in Italy, had commanded one of the first bands of French infantry, the nucleus of the 'vieux régiments.' The seventeenth regiment of the line, which was marching at a little distance, answered immediately by their war-cry, 'Toujours Auvergne sans tache!' The seventeenth of the line was that of D'Assas, the hero of Clostercamp.

tion of the series of conflicts in which it had been able to take part. 'We have a saying,' repeated Rolthaufen, 'that for pay one ought to go to the charge once, for one's fatherland twice, and for one's religion three times; but at Dreux I certainly charged four times for the Huguenots of France.' Condé had inspired his gendarmes with that fire which animated himself, and which in his great-grandson was destined to rise into genius. But the victor of Rocroy would have chosen his point of attack more discriminatingly, would have retained more control over himself and his men, and would not have allowed 'the black cloud' of the right wing to break upon a scattered army. Nevertheless the glowing courage of the Prince, and the boldness, as timely as it was dashing, with which he had made his attack and used to the best advantage a force, numerically the smaller, but superior in cavalry, were justly admired.

'he Duc
.e Guise
reats
'ondé
'ith
ourtesy.

The Duc de Guise was the first to recognise the merit of his rival with a well-timed courtesy which enhanced the splendour of his victory. He received the illustrious prisoner with a profusion of compliments when Damville on the night of the battle brought him to his quarters. He even professed towards this Prince of the blood, conquered and a prisoner, a respect which his pride would perhaps have refused to an adversary who was triumphant and successful. He placed at the disposal of Condé the humble cottage where he himself was quartered, apologizing for giving so poor a reception to so illustrious a visitor; but the loss of his baggage and the poverty of his lodging did not permit of his doing more. It was only after the repeated invitation of the Prince, that he consented to share with him the humble accommodations of the house. The two rivals sat down at the same table to a coarse supper; a single bundle of straw served as a couch for both; their animosity seemed not to have survived the combat; the one did not seem more inflated by victory than the other downcast by defeat; and men did not know whether to admire most the chivalrous generosity of the conqueror or the magnanimity of the conquered. They talked long together 'like intimate friends;' they discussed the various incidents of the day, and the condition of France. Either from a wish to repay by moderation the kindness of his adversary, or from dissatisfaction with his own party, Condé showed a conciliatory disposition that was not expected from him; and the next day, on despatching De Losse to the Queen-Mother to inform her of the battle, Guise sent word that the Prince seemed inclined towards peace. Two days afterwards, on the twenty-second of December, the Prince de Melphe, a Bishop of Troyes who had turned Protestant, arrived from Orléans and handed to Catherine a letter from the Connétable, who congratulated himself upon the reception given him by his niece the Princesse de Condé, and upon 'the good-will that there is in this company for having a good peace.'[1]

Médicis took good care not to neglect these hints. The issue of the battle of Dreux was a great blow to her authority. Left alone at the head of an army whose defeat he had changed to victory, delivered the same day by the fortune of war from his most dangerous enemy and from the most inconvenient of his friends, Guise was all-powerful. The opening of fresh negotiations permitted Catherine once more to take part in affairs, and if not to

---

[1] See Appendix, No. XI.

preserve a real influence, at least to contrive means for once more obtaining it. She therefore immediately set out with the young King. After stopping at Rambouillet, whither the Duc de Guise had led the army, and where he was officially declared Lieutenant-Général of the Kingdom, she went to Chartres, whither, by her orders, Condé had already been conducted from Dreux. The conferences commenced at once.

1563.

As early as the fifth of January, the Queen, writing to the Parliament of Paris, expressed her satisfaction at the amicable disposition in which she had found the Prince, and on the eleventh she sent word to Gonnor,[1] 'that she was arranging a meeting between the Prince de Condé, his brother the Cardinal, the Connétable, and the Duc de Guise to confer as to peace.' But these hopes, which had been built upon slight foundations, were not to be realised. The Duc de Guise refused to separate himself from the army; the people of Orléans demanded important hostages before they would allow the Connétable to leave; and above all it was found that Condé, while very conciliatory in manner, was in reality very firm. He persisted in his demand for the free exercise of the Reformed religion, and declared that, without that essential condition, peace was impossible. He further demanded that he should be allowed an interview with the Connétable, that he should be liberated on parole, &c. The Queen was compelled to answer that she would never tolerate the exercise of two religions, and that she would only give the Prince his liberty when all the places occu-

---

[1] Original letters preserved in the Bibliothèque impériale, and published in the 'Mémoires de Condé.'

pied by the rebels were given up.[1] She was, in fact, obliged to give some satisfaction to the strong Catholics, who were much displeased with her. It was no secret that she had received with an air of unconcern and almost of pleasure the first tidings of the battle of Dreux, when it was believed in Paris that the Royalists had lost the day ; that celebrated saying of hers which so well portrays both her own character and that of the age—'Well! we shall have to say our prayers in French '—had been heard and repeated. It was feared that 'she would pervert the Most Christian King ;' her regard for Condé, and her condescension towards him, were much criticised; 'she avoids the neighbourhood of Paris for fear she should have to place him in the Bastille, and yet she leaves him in an insecure and newly conquered district. . . . She does him the honour, obstinate though he be up to this day, of sending to him all the members of the council in a body to remonstrate with him in supplicatory terms, and beg him to have pity upon the affairs of this kingdom. . . . It seems,' adds the Spanish Ambassador, in the letter from which we have just quoted a few lines, ' that it is not M. le Prince who is the prisoner, but that he holds the rest in captivity.'[2]

Condé, however, was guarded, and that strictly. As early as the day after the battle he had been again entrusted to the care of Damville, who had given up his prisoner merely as an act of deference to the Duc de Guise, an act which the custom of the times did not render obligatory, and of which Guise had no wish to

CHAP. III.

1563 January.

Strict confinement of Condé.

---

[1] Interview of the twentieth of January between the Queen-Mother and the Deputies of the Parliament. ('Mémoires de Condé.')

[2] 'Correspondance Chantonnay.' ('Mémoires de Condé.')

take advantage. A special authority from the King had subsequently constituted Damville the legal custodian of the Prince. Who was more fit to guard that glorious captive than he to whom he was a kind of hostage for the life of his father? Three companies of men-at-arms and two of foot-soldiers were told off for this duty; there was constantly a sentry at the door of Condé's room and within it; but he was free to hold unrestricted communication with his valets de chambre; he was allowed pen and ink, and Perucel, the pastor, who had been captured along with him at Dreux, preached every day in his presence. It was thus that the Duke of Saxony and the Landgrave of Hesse had been treated by order of the Emperor Charles, when they were his prisoners after the battle of Mühlberg; and this precedent was closely followed in the case of the Prince de Condé.[1] The Queen Regent brought him in her train, thus guarded, from Chartres to Blois, and from Blois to Amboise, and ended by incarcerating him in the castle of Onzain, an old feudal fortress, situated about three leagues from the last-named city, and where the Comte de la Rochefoucauld had long held in close captivity an English nobleman, Lord Grey de Wilton, who had been made prisoner.[2]

[1] Smith to the English Consul, February 17, 1563. (State Paper Office.)

[2] *Ibidem.* William Grey, Baron de Wilton, had bravely but unsuccessfully defended Guines against the French in 1558. Made prisoner there, he was soon after liberated on parole, that he might bear to Elizabeth the first overtures of peace on the part of the Duc de Guise. Having loyally re-entered France on the completion of his mission, he remained in captivity after the Peace of Cateau-Cambrésis, being unable to pay the enormous ransom demanded by the Comte de la Rochefoucauld, whose prisoner he was, and who treated him most cruelly. He could only leave his prison by sacrificing the whole of his fortune. On his return to England he held a command on the borders of Scotland, and died Governor of Berwick-on-Tweed, in 1563. Darcies, 'Annals of Queen Elizabeth.' Forbes, 'Full View of the Public Transactions, &c.'

In this manner the month of January and the early days of February passed in fruitless negotiations, while there had not been for an instant any cessation of hostilities. Coligny had been declared head of the Protestant army, and he commanded it with as much vigour as prudence. He was not long in raising their fallen spirits, and as early as the twentieth of December, he drew up his astonished troops in line, as if to meet a fresh attack of the Royalists. As the latter, however, did not present themselves, he marched by short journeys towards the Loire, crossed it on the thirtieth, and encamped his army in Sologne and Berry, in order to recruit it. Guise, on the other hand, without heeding the operations of the Admiral, was preparing to lay siege to Orléans; and intending first to cut off all communications with the city, he proceeded to retake all the places of which the Huguenots had gained possession to the north of the Loire—Étampes, Pithiviers, &c. He then appeared before Beaugency, which he captured in like manner, and crossed the river with the intention of continuing his operations on the left bank. Coligny did not wait for him; he had not sufficient troops to give battle to the Royal army, and he had too many to shut himself up in Orléans. Leaving D'Andelot, with the infantry, to defend it, and entrusting to the Princesse de Condé the care of the Connétable, he reached Normandie with the French and German cavalry, that he might conquer that beautiful and rich province, where already he had secret friends, and thus secure for his party a solid base of operations, and put himself in a position to receive there the reinforcements of men and money which he expected from England. About the middle of February Guise commenced the attack on Orléans from the left bank of the Loire.

CHAP. III.

1563
February.
The Admiral's movements. Guise lays siege to Orléans.

CHAP.
III.

1563
February.

Attempts
to obtain
Condé's
release; his
resolute
attitude.

The Admiral, upon starting for Normandie, had despatched a party of men apparently with the object of
'rescuing' Condé; the only result of this was an increase
in the strictness of the Prince's confinement. The latter
managed, however, to win over two of his guard, and it
was arranged that, with their assistance, he should take
flight in the disguise of a peasant. But one of these men
divulged the plot to Damville, and Condé became aware
that all had been discovered, by seeing the unfortunate
soldier who was to have aided him in the enterprise
hanging from a gibbet beneath his windows. He was
deprived of his servants, and placed in solitary confinement: these rigorous measures raised the suspicion that
the Lorrains had not abandoned their plots against the
life of the Prince, and that the Orléans trial was about
to be repeated. Condé himself seemed at one time to
believe this, and as it was in his high-spirited nature to
grow more determined in the face of persecution, his language towards the Queen's agents became more haughty,
and his correspondence with his wife and with the pastors
and chiefs who had remained at Orléans was inspired
with the enthusiasm which was gaining influence over his
mind. 'I am quite prepared,' he wrote on the sixteenth
of February, to lose a life and to shed my blood for the
honour of God and the peace of His children. . . . If
my enemies cause my death, God will raise up another
leader, and will show favour, even to the end, to your
cause, which has become mine. . . . Continue to
labour that you may see peace secured to the kingdom of
God in this country, and our King honoured and obeyed.'[1]

But Catherine knew too well the Prince's character to

---

[1] La Popelinière.

hope to intimidate him, and she had too much need of his services to venture to drive him to extremities. On the other hand, the Montmorencies, who well knew that the safety of the Connétable depended on that of the Prince, would have made every effort to save the latter. And lastly, Guise did not view with displeasure the progress of negotiations which committed him to nothing, and which could only be a source of division in the Protestant party. The conferences were renewed. The Bishop of Limoges was despatched to Orléans, and two Huguenot officers, Boucart and D'Esternay, went to Condé. The question was to arrange for the interview between him and the Connétable. But fresh obstacles were every moment arising. 'My uncle,' said Éléonore de Roye to Montmorency, 'you do not understand our enemies ; they wish to do with you and with my husband that which the Parisians do with the reliquaries of Saint Marceau and Sainte Geneviève, which they never allow to come too near each other, lest their relationship should make them embrace so tightly that they can never be separated.'[1]

Nevertheless the siege of Orléans was pressed on vigorously.[2] The capture of the fort of the Tourelles had followed upon that of the Portereaux ; all the outworks had been taken, and the decisive assault was daily ex-

---

[1] La Popelinière.

[2] *A propos* of the siege of Orléans, here is a curious piece of information which I found in a despatch of the Ambassador Smith to the English council, and from which one might infer that some ingenious Huguenot had at that time invented a kind of bombshell : 'The garrison of Orléans, being short of lead, now loads its muskets with hollow projectiles of copper or bell-metal, which burst as they touch the ground, either upon alighting or at the first rebound ; this weapon causes terrible destruction, and strikes great terror among the Royal troops who have just occupied the Portereaux.' (February 17, 1563.)

pected, when, on the evening of the eighteenth of February, on his return from the direction of the day's operations, the Duc de Guise fell mortally wounded. An assassin, secreted behind a tuft of brushwood, had pierced his chest with three bullets. Six days afterwards this great man made a most Christian end, after having addressed to the King and to his children the most touching exhortations. For the second time, an accident, an unexpected death, checked the House of Guise in its ambitious career, just at the very moment when the goal seemed about to be attained; but this time fortune deprived it of the most illustrious and the bravest of its champions. From whatever point of view we judge the policy of François de Lorraine, we cannot but admire his noble qualities, and every Frenchman's heart will for ever honour the memory of him who saved Metz and won back Calais.

Médicis bestowed hypocritical regrets upon this glorious victim, and professed much horror at the crime which so well served her purpose; affecting great devotion to the Catholic cause, she gave orders to press forward the siege of Orléans, and even strengthened Condé's guard. In fact, a few violent Catholics had insinuated that the Prince had been privy to the crime of Poltrot; it was alleged that he had several times, within the last few days, asked whether M. de Guise was not killed or wounded;[1] but this calumny gained no credence. Poltrot formally accused the Admiral, Beza, and others of being the instigators of his crime; and, if their reply did not quite obliterate all the suspicion which rested on them; if it remained proved, according to the pithy and energetic language of D'Aubigné himself, that the reception given to the as-

---

[1] 'Correspondance Chantonnay.' ('Mémoires de Condé.')

sassin by them 'seemed like rejection and meant encouragement,'[1] yet no evidence could ever be found, no avowal extorted, which could implicate Condé; neither his contemporaries nor subsequent historians have ever classed him with the accomplices—active or passive—of the murderer.

Nobody was deceived by the Queen's orders as to the siege of Orléans and Condé's captivity; a speedy conclusion of peace was the inevitable consequence of the death of the Duc de Guise. The Catholic army remained without a leader. The aged Maréchal de Brissac, on whom it was wished to confer the command, was in a state of health which forbad his acceptance of it. For want of a head, all discipline became relaxed; everyone did just as he chose. The majority of the troops who occupied Les Portereaux, and the detachments which had been sent to the left bank, went in search of better and more comfortable quarters. There was soon nothing but the show of a siege. On the other hand, Condé, so haughty the night before, was on the morrow quite altered. He seemed as if he must give up the struggle, now that he had no foe worthy of him. 'I have just spoken to a little man,' wrote the Cardinal de Bourbon, on the fifteenth of March, 'who desires nothing so much as peace; it will not be his fault if we do not obtain a favourable one.' In fact, all were already agreed as to the interview so long talked of; the details had been settled in a conference between the Princess and the Queen, in which the latter had testified to Éléonore de Roye much kindness and affection.[2]

[1] 'sentoit le refus et donnoit le courage.'
[2] See (in Appendix, No. XII.) some unpublished letters relative to this negotiation.

CHAP.
III.

1563
Con-
ferences at
L'Ile-aux-
Bœufs
(March 6
and 7).

On the fourth of March Condé arrived at Blois, escorted
by ten companies of Swiss. He slept at a small tavern in
the suburbs, where he was treated and guarded as a prisoner. But those who saw him pass were struck by his
good looks, his gaiety, and even his stout appearance.[1]
On the sixth he was conducted to the camp at Saint-
Mesmin, and on the seventh Damville took him in a
carriage to the banks of the Loire, while the Connétable
was coming along the opposite side under the care of
D'Andelot. The 'parlement' was held in the middle of
the river, on the Ile-aux-Bœufs, a little below Orléans. A
room had been extemporized with tapestry, on board a
boat; but the uncle and nephew preferred conversing as
they walked up and down—everyone could see them and
no one could hear them. At the end of three hours
they separated, and were taken back, the Connétable to
Orléans, and Condé to the Catholic camp. On the eighth,
the conference was renewed, this time in presence of the
Queen. It was remarked by the attendants, on the arrival
of the Prince, that his sword had been returned to him.[2]
After a long conversation Montmorency remained there,
and the Prince set out for Orléans, each on parole. A
truce was concluded for a few days, and the preliminaries
of a peace agreed upon ; but Condé would settle nothing
definitely without the advice of his friends and political
supporters. On his arrival at Orléans, he assembled the
pastors and his chief officers.

Notwith-
standing
the oppo-
sition of
the
ministers,
peace is
concluded.

Was he to demand the unconditional restoration of the
edict of January? And if he could not obtain it without
modifications was he to give way? This was the only
important point which remained doubtful, — the only

---

[1] 'stowte and merrie.' Sir Thomas   Paper Office.)
Smith to Elizabeth, March 12. (State   [2] State Paper Office.

serious question on which he wished to have the opinion of the leaders of the Protestants. Seventy-two assembled ministers declared that it was impossible to accept anything that had been declined before the war; that any modification of the edict of January would be an irreparable wrong to the Churches; that it was not in the power of anyone to alter an edict which was the expression of the will of the States, and which had been carried in an assembly of all the Parliaments. They protested against every change which might be introduced into it. In vain did Condé plead the exhaustion of the kingdom; in vain did he insist that the essential principle, the free exercise of the new religion, would be maintained, and that it would be necessary to give to the peace the appearance at least of a compromise in order to secure its acceptance with the Catholics. The ministers were immoveable. But the gentlemen, who themselves were maintaining the whole weight of the war, thought otherwise, and the Prince, strengthened by their judgment, went on. He returned to the Queen. The agreement was concluded on the twelfth of March, and ratified by the Edict of Amboise on the nineteenth. The preamble expressed the hope that all would be settled by a 'sacred and free general or national council.' The King granted the free exercise of the new religion 'in the houses of all noblemen holding a "fief de haubert,"[1] and of all gentlemen holding a "fief,"' except those dependent on the 'seigneurs haut-justiciers,' who might exercise their right of forbidding it; in the cities where the liberty had existed before the seventh of March, 1562; and in the suburbs of one town in each bailiwick. An exception

[1] Tenure by service.

N 2

was made in the case of the City of Paris and the territory under the jurisdiction of its Provost and Vicomte.
All churches and ecclesiastical property were to be restored. Indemnity was granted for all moneys which had
been taken from the public funds. All pursuit was abolished. The law against armed assemblies was renewed.
On either side the foreign auxiliaries were to be discharged.

Great dis-
satisfac-
tion of the
Admiral
and of the
ministers.
The edict
is con-
firmed.

Condé and D'Andelot figured in the list of princes and
lords, ' by the advice ' of whom the King had passed the
edict. The name of the Admiral did not appear there.
Coligny had subdued almost the whole of Normandie, and
he was allowing his cavalry a few days' rest in the rich
plain of Caen, when he learned by a letter from Condé
that peace had been all but agreed upon; the Prince
begged him to return at once to Orléans to take part
in the negotiations. Setting out from Caen on the fourteenth of March, he took his journey, but without hurry-
ing himself, and not forgetting to capture the small towns
and Catholic châteaux along the road. When on the
twenty-third he arrived in Orléans, all was over. They
had not waited for his consent before signing the peace.
He found the whole city in a commotion and the ministers
in a state of exasperation. They, knowing well the weaknesses and the ' amorous complexion '[1] of Condé, accused
him of having yielded to the seductions of the Court of
Catherine, and of having listened to the whispers[2] of her
maids of honour. ' The treaty,' they persisted, ' is that
of a man with half his manhood in captivity.' Excited
by them, the populace had just destroyed all the sacred
buildings, which according to the treaty were to be

---

[1] ' amoureuse complexion.'
[2] ' d'avoir haléné ses filles d'honneur.'—D'Aubigné.

restored ; the church of Sainte-Croix alone was spared, ' because it contained the baggage of the reîtres,' naïvely enough remarks the Protestant narrator.[1] The Admiral joined in the clamour of the ministers, and did not attempt to restrain the violence of the populace.

There are few natures, even among the strongest, few minds, even among the most upright, who are not, during a lengthened course of opposition to an established government, involved, now and then, in some form or other of demagogic extravagance. Coligny did not always escape the fatal consequences of his position, and his language on this occasion contrasted strongly with his aristocratic habits and prepossessions. 'More harm has been done to the Churches by a stroke of the pen,' exclaimed he, 'than the enemy could have done by ten years of war ; the towns have been sacrificed to the nobility, and yet it is the poor who have led the way for the rich ; the latter have thought of nothing but pillaging and enriching themselves, and were always talking of desertion whenever things did not suit their fancy.'[2] This violent harangue was made in full assembly, in Condé's presence. Although the Admiral had made several allusions to that courtly temperament which could not resist a little flattery ; although he scoffed at ' those who allowed themselves to be cheated by the pretended conditions of the peace,' the Prince replied with moderation, repeated afresh the reasons which had decided him to accept the agreement, and reminded them that occupying, as he then did, the 'rank' of the late King of Navarre, he could do much more for the good of religion during peace. In fine, he offered to accom-

[1] La Popelinière.　　　　[2] La Popelinière. Beza.

pany Coligny to the presence of the Queen, and endeavour
to obtain some modifications of the edict. Fresh negotiations took place for this purpose ; Catherine consented
to tolerate preaching, not only in the suburbs but also
in the interior of the towns specified, as well as in the
private houses of the gentlemen of the territory of the
Viscomte and Provost of Paris.[1]   At the same time she
would not admit that these verbal concessions should
be inserted in the edict, of which the text must be retained.   Commissioners for its execution were appointed.
On the twenty-eighth of March, a public administration of
the Lord's Supper took place at Orléans.   Five or six
thousand persons, male and female, received the Sacrament.   The sermon was preached by Beza, who had taken
an active part both in the war and the negotiations.   He
reminded his hearers ' that exactly that day twelvemonth
they had received the Sacrament at Meaux ; that they
had then just united together for the defence of religion ;
that now they were receiving the same Sacrament on the
eve of their separation and of their return to their homes
to enjoy the freedom which God had graciously enabled
them to obtain for their consciences.   True, that liberty
was not so full as they could have wished ; but, such as
it was, they ought to thank God for it.'[2]   Next day Beza
set out for Geneva,[3] much less confident and much less
resigned in his private talk than he had expressed himself
in his sermons, and announcing that all was wrong, and

---

[1] Myddlemore (an English agent
in attendance upon the Prince and
the Admiral) to Cecil, March 30.
State Paper Office. (Appendix, No.
XIV.)

[3] Smith to Elizabeth, March 31.

Ibidem. (Appendix, No. XIV.)

[2] See (Appendix, No. XIII.) the
letter in which Condé announces
the return of Beza to the Council at
Geneva.

that he would not come back till matters were mended.[1]
The gentlemen and soldiery separated with much less
gloomy spirits. The joy of returning to their homes and
families surmounted every other feeling. At the beginning of April there was not a single Huguenot soldier
remaining in Orléans, and the King made his solemn
entry into it.

[1] Myddlemore to Cecil, March 30. State Paper Office. (Appendix, No.
XIV.)

CHAPTER IV.

1563—1568.

Condé announces to the Queen of England the conclusion of peace (March
8 and 17, 1563).   Elizabeth refuses to restore Havre.—Negotiations with
her; conduct of Condé, Coligny, and Catherine de Médicis.—Tardy concessions on the part of Elizabeth.—Siege of Havre (July 28, 1563); peace
with England (April 11, 1564).—Efforts and sacrifices of Condé to get
rid of the 'reitres' from the kingdom. — His fidelity to the Admiral,
who does not show, in the first instance, much appreciation of it.—He
continues to defend the interests of the Reformers.—In spite of L'Hospital,
the Queen-Mother gives herself up to the ardent Catholics; the King's
journey; Edict of Roussillon (July 1564); protest by Condé.—He wishes
to remain moderate, and blames the excesses even of the Protestants; both
sides are dissatisfied with him.—Condé's intrigues; his disorderly morals.
His relations with Calvin; warnings from Geneva.—His amours with
Isabelle de Limeuil and with the widow of the Maréchal de Saint-André.—
Sickness and death of Éléonore de Roye (July 1564).—Uneasiness of the
Protestants concerning Condé; rumours of an alliance between him and
the Guises.—Condé sides with the Cardinal de Lorraine in his quarrel
with the Maréchal de Montmorency (December 1564).—His arrival in
Paris (June 1565); his conduct increases the fears of the Protestants.—He
retains intimate relations with the Châtillons, and marries Mademoiselle
de Longueville (November 1565).—He is present as a friend to conciliation
at the small States of Moulins (Dec. 1565).—Fresh and extreme alarm of
the Protestants; movements of the Duke of Alva.—Condé, urged by the
Genevese and by his friends, demands and obtains an augmentation of the
army.—Ruses on the part of Catherine with a view to deceive and destroy the Protestants.—Favours shown to Condé : the King stands sponsor
to one of his sons (June 1567).—After the baptism, Condé is sent for to
Court.   Symptoms of an alliance.—Altercation between Condé and the
Duc d'Anjou; the Court throws off the mask.—Meeting of the Protestant
leaders; they resolve to take up arms.—Security of the Court.—The Protestants unexpectedly occupy Rozay and Lagny; the King quits Monceaux
and goes to Meaux (September 26).—He is there joined by the Swiss, and
quits it again during the night.—Attempted attack at Meaux (September
28).—The King arrives in Paris; Condé sleeps at Claye; his position and
plans.—His head-quarters are at Saint-Denis (October 2).—Fruitless negotiations —Condé summoned by a herald-at-arms.—Unsuccessful interview
with the Connétable.—Blockade of Paris.—The Protestant army, six thou-

sand strong, extends itself too widely.—The Catholic army, nineteen thousand in number, takes the offensive and clears the left bank of the Seine (November 4).—Skirmish in the plain of Saint-Denis (November 9). Consultation of the Protestant leaders. Condé resolves to accept battle.— Battle of Saint-Denis (November 10).—Position of the Protestant army before that city, between Aubervilliers and Saint-Ouen.—The Royal army marches out of Paris.—The Connétable's designs for surrounding the Protestant army.—Montmorency prematurely orders the simultaneous attack on the right and left; his attacks repulsed.—The centre of the Royalists is broken through by Condé; Montmorency mortally wounded. —The Catholics recover the advantage on all sides; but the confusion caused by the Connétable's fall permits the Protestants to retreat into Saint-Denis in good order.—The issue of the fight is honourable to Condé.—In the night the Reformers occupy afresh their quarters.— Condé marches off (November 13), places his wife in security at Orléans, and rallies the Poitevins at Montereau.—Reorganization of the Royal army commanded by the Duc d'Anjou.—It marches out of Paris.—The Protestants cross the Seine and the Marne and halt near Châlons. Truce.—Negotiations between the Court and Germany.—The Reformers march to meet their ' reitres,' pass the Meuse and the Moselle. Splendid order observed during the march. Great hardships. Condé's resolution.—Junction of Condé with Prince Casimir's troops (January 11, 1568); sacrifices in order to pay the ' reitres.'—Inaction of the Royal army ; they are unable to prevent Condé from bringing his troops back into Beauce. Remarkable order observed in the Reformed army.— Orléans relieved. Condé rallies the Gascons and Dauphinois, and finds himself at the head of thirty thousand men.—He invests Chartres (February 23). Siege of Chartres interrupted by peace (March 13).— Short Peace of Chartres, called the *paix fourrée.*—It is condemned by the Admiral, but supported by Condé.—Commencement of its execution.

WHILE Condé was negotiating for peace with Catherine and the Connétable, he might have expected that the opposition of the Admiral and of the Ministers would be less violent, and their reproaches less bitter, than he found to be the case. But he had other allies, and he could not conceal from himself that they would be even more difficult to satisfy. He was bound by a treaty to Queen Elizabeth ; and although he had never officially ratified the engagements that had been undertaken in his name, although he pretended not to be aware of their full import, he was obliged to take them into consideration. The complication was no slight one. How was it

CHAP. IV.

1563 March.

Condé announces to the Queen of England the conclusion of peace. Elizabeth refuses to restore Havre.

possible for him to remain faithful to all the engagements
with the Crown of England, now that he wished to conduct himself as a loyal subject of the King of France?

Immediately after the interview on the Ile-aux-Bœufs,
on the very day on which he had returned to Orléans
free, the eighth of March, Condé had written to Elizabeth
to inform her of what was occurring, and of his hope of
soon seeing peace re-established and liberty of conscience
secured. 'Now,' added he, 'you will let it be known
that no other reasons than simply your zeal for the protection of the faithful who desire the preaching of the
pure Gospel induced you to favour our cause.'[1] And on
the seventeenth of March, when the negotiation was
already almost completed, and its conclusion was only
delayed by the absence of the Admiral, he wrote once
more, 'We have suspended all negotiations until the
arrival of M. l'Amiral, till which time I have deferred
the discussion of that which concerns your private affairs,
not forgetting at the same time to broach the subject
and make some proposals to his Majesty. . . . We
shall all endeavour, as far as fidelity to our duty will
allow, to advise his Majesty to discharge all that can law-
fully be discharged.'[2] This appeared ominous language
to Elizabeth, and she resented strongly the moderate
counsels that were pressed upon her. She had, moreover,
other sources of information in addition to the correspondence of Condé and the Huguenot leaders. Besides her
own official Ambassador, Sir Thomas Smith,[3] who had

[1] Original. State Paper Office.
(Appendix, No. XIV.)

[2] *Ibidem.*

[3] Descended from a good family
in Essex, educated at Cambridge,
and subsequently sent to the Italian
universities at the King's cost,
Thomas Smith had become, through
the influence of the Duke of Somerset,
Secretary to King Edward VI., Dean

never left the Court in its wanderings, she had a specially accredited agent at the head-quarters of the Reformers, by name Henry Myddlemore.[1]   She knew, through them, that only very vague reservations in her favour had been made, and that the Prince de Condé displayed very little zeal in guarding her interests.[2]   She therefore charged her messengers to show Condé and Coligny how displeased she was with their breach of faith, and to caution them to keep their engagements; adding that, as for herself, she would consent to give up Havre only on the following conditions : the immediate restitution of Calais; the transmission of hostages who should remain for two years in London (the time considered necessary for repairing the fortifications of Calais); and the instant repayment of all the sums of money she had advanced to the Princes and confederated Lords.[3]

Immediately on the Admiral's arrival in Orléans, Smith and Myddlemore held several consultations with him and

Negotiations with England.

of Carlisle, and Provost of Eton. After having been deprived of all his emoluments by Queen Mary, he was once more employed by Elizabeth, and several times sent as Ambassador to France. He was appointed a Secretary of State in 1571, and died in 1577. Darcies calls him a 'wise and learned man.' He was the author of a treatise ' De republicâ Anglorum' and several other rather ponderous works.

[1] An old servant of Throckmorton accredited to the Huguenot leaders on February 2, 1563. He was frequently employed by Elizabeth on more or less confidential missions. Throckmorton himself, who was captured at Dreux, long held prisoner, and subsequently sent

to England, had left it again almost immediately on a mission to the Admiral. He had again joined the Protestant army on the first of March, but as soon as peace was talked of, he disappeared, and not daring to approach the Court, he left all his powers to Myddlemore, March 15. (Instructions to Myddlemore, February 2; to Throckmorton February 11; Throckmorton to Cecil February 21, March 1; Myddlemore to the Queen, March 30.   State Paper Office.)

[2] Smith to the Queen, March 12. *Ibidem.*

[3] Myddlemore to the Queen, March 30; the Queen to Smith, April 22, &c. *Ibidem.* (Appendix, No. XIV.)

CHAP.
IV.

1563
March.

Conduct of
Condé,
Coligny,
and Ca-
therine de
Médicis.

the Prince; and fulfilled their Sovereign's instructions.
Condé declared that he was the most unfortunate of men,
but that he had never known the clauses of the Treaty of
Hampton Court; that if La Haye and the Vidame de
Chartres had, in his name, made the enormous concessions
that were represented, he could not hold himself bound
by the acts of agents who had abused the carte blanche
which he had signed. He protested that next to his duty
to his King he had nothing so much at heart as the
interests of the Queen of England; he was ready to lose
his head in proof of this. But after having said again
and again that though the English troops had come to
Havre, it was solely to facilitate the King's deliverance
and the triumph of true religion, he could not possibly
lay before the Regent terms such as these, which would
not have any chance of being admitted or even discussed.
If Queen Elizabeth persisted, she would lose, not only
Havre, which she could never defend against the united
forces of the kingdom of France, but also all right to
claim either the restitution of Calais or a pecuniary
indemnification; and she would do an immense injury to
the cause of those whom she had addressed as her
'brothers' of France. If, on the other hand, she would
at once give up Havre, and would abide by the letter of
the Treaty of Cateau-Cambrésis, she would strengthen the
position of Condé and of the whole Huguenot party; it
should be arranged that the King and the Princes should
sign afresh the Peace of 1559; other hostages, much more
important, would be sent to London, and possibly even
Calais would be restored before the interval which did
not legally expire till 1567. What was at all hazards to
be avoided was a rupture between the two crowns; and

in order to avoid such a misfortune, Condé proposed a
mode which appeared singular enough: 'Why,' said he one
day to Smith, 'why should not your Sovereign marry the
Most Christian King?   He is more inclined to the Gospel
than is commonly supposed, and the union of the two
crowns would be a crushing blow to popery.'[1]   At every
meeting the Prince proposed some such fresh solution, or
rather reproduced the same suggestions under different
forms, with diverse developments, and always with a
warmth, a volubility, and even an eloquence, which did not
in all probability rest on very firm and sincere convictions,
but which his interlocutors could not help observing.[2]
These last indeed had never expected much active support
from him.   The temper of Coligny surprised them still
more.   The English had always counted much on him; he
had had more dealings with them than Condé; he had
often written and repeated that no peace was possible
without the consent of Queen Elizabeth,[3] and but lately,
when he so bitterly criticised the Treaty of Amboise, he
had appeared indignant at the neglect with which that
Sovereign's rights had been treated.   But he changed his
tone as soon as he had obtained some verbal modifications of the edict.[4]   He maintained, in opposition to

---

[1] M. Mignet is the first historian
who found in the State Paper Office
the despatches relative to this strange
proposal; he has referred to them
in his noble work on Marie Stuart.
Strange as the scheme may appear,
it was seriously put forward about
twenty months later, and this time
by Catherine de Médicis herself.
('Histoire de Marie Stuart,' vol. i.
p. 196; vol. ii., Appendices, p. 473.)

[2] Smith to the Queen, March 30,
31; April 1; to Cecil, May 19, 22.
Myddlemore to the Queen, March 30;
to Cecil, March 30, April 14, May 3,
1563. State Paper Office. (Appendix, No. XIV.)

[3] The Admiral to Elizabeth,
January 24; Smith to the English
council, February 17, March 21.
(Ibidem.)

[4] Myddlemore to the Queen and
to Cecil, March 30. Ibidem. (Appendix, No. XIV.)

the English envoys, the same opinion as Condé, in language less vivid and impassioned, but with just as much determination in his intentions and with even greater severity in his expressions. As he could not plead ignorance of the Treaty of Hampton Court, since he had subsequently signed another agreement in which that treaty was revised and confirmed,[1] he blamed the parsimony and delay of England. If, he said, he had received at a serviceable time, and at the dates agreed upon, the supplies of men and money which had been promised him, the Reformers of France would not have been reduced to this extremity of being compelled to accept the conditions of the peace just concluded.[2] And when he was threatened with the publication of the deeds which had been signed by him, and the consequent exposure of his disloyalty to the whole of Europe, he declared that he could not believe it possible that the counsellors of the Queen of England would persuade her to commit so great a blunder ; for the mere existence of these acts constituted on her part an aggression against the Crown of France (a case provided for by the treaty of 1559), and abolished *ipso facto* all her claims upon Calais.[3] It is in fact certain that Elizabeth, in taking possession of Havre and in limiting her intervention to the possession of that city, had done either too much or too little. She had committed a manifest breach of the peace, and she had not supported the Huguenots with sufficient energy to enable them to prolong the struggle, or even to evidence much

---

[1] The Queen to Smith, April 20. (State Paper Office.) This fresh agreement had been signed at Caen, after Throckmorton's last journey.

[2] Smith to the Queen, April 1. *Ibidem.* (Appendix, No. XIV.)

[3] Myddlemore to Cecil, May 17. *Ibidem.* (Appendix, No. XIV.)

religious enthusiasm in her countenance of them. It was in vain that all her agents, diplomatic or military, Warwick and Paulett as well as Smith, Throckmorton, and Myddlemore, all had deplored her indecision, and had pressed her to send more men and more money, if she wished 'to see the Reformers of France at her mercy.'[1] She had only, they said, doled out trifling sums of money, always tardily, and always less than she had promised; she had constantly ordered her officers to recall the detachments which had marched out of Havre, and to limit themselves to the occupation of that city;[2] she had so far pushed her economy, that when she had sent a thousand pioneers because they had not sufficient hands to carry out the fortifications, she had ordered an equal number of soldiers to be withdrawn.[3] The Admiral, unable to pay his 'reitres,' had been compelled to tolerate their depredations, which exasperated the country and disgusted the English who witnessed them;[4] he had been on several occasions obliged to suspend his operations that he might go to the mouth of the Seine to fetch the insignificant subsidies for which he had had to wait so long and which were granted to him with so bad a grace. And even the conduct of the commanding officers at Havre was a source of just indignation to the Protestants; all the

---

[1] Warwick and Paulett to Lords Dudley and Cecil, October 26, 1562; January 3 and 21; February 5, 8, 12, 15, 16, 26, 1563; Throckmorton to Cecil, October 30, December 14, 1562; February 21, 1563; Myddlemore to Cecil, January 24, 1563; Smith to Cecil, February 18, 1563, &c. (State Paper Office.)

[2] Instructions to Warwick, October 8, 1562; Warwick to the Queen and to Cecil, January 21, 23; February 4, 1563; Beauvoir la Nocle to Warwick, February 8, 10, 1563, &c. (*Ibidem.*)

[3] The Queen to Warwick, February 6, 1563. (*Ibidem.*)

[4] Myddlemore to Cecil, March 1, 1563. (*Ibidem.*)

French ships that happened to be in the harbour had been taken off to Portsmouth,[1] and the orders given to the garrison had been executed with so much rigour that the unfortunate Huguenots of Fécamp, Harfleur, &c., when pursued by the Duc d'Aumale, intreated in vain, on two different occasions, to be received into the city; a cruel refusal which delivered them defenceless into the hands of their persecutors.[2] Lastly, Condé had remained for three months in a harsh captivity which might have been violently and tragically ended at any moment by a criminal trial, and yet the prayers of his relations and friends, who besought Elizabeth to exert herself in his behalf, had only drawn forth from her the coldest and most barren expressions of sympathy.[3] The French Reformers had indeed some right to be surprised at a demand for the literal fulfilment of engagements which their allies had so imperfectly fulfilled.

As for Catherine, she seemed to amuse herself with these discussions, in which she had taken no part, confining herself to endeavours to increase the suspicions of the English Ambassador towards the Huguenots whenever she had an interview with him.[4] She had in the name of the King, her son, called upon Elizabeth to surrender Havre;[5] but she had no doubt that it could easily be

---

[1] Warwick to the Queen, November 4, 1562; Smith to Cecil, November 9. (State Paper Office.)

[2] Documents forwarded by Warwick, March 1563. (*Ibidem.*)

[3] Madeleine de Mailly to the Queen of England, January 4, 1563; the Princesse de Condé to the same, January 5, 14; Coligny to the same, January 24, 29; Condé to the same, February 17; the Vidame de Chartres and Briquemault to the English Council, January 22. The Queen of England to the Princesse de Condé and to Madeleine de Mailly, January 26, &c. *Ibidem.* (See Condé's letter, Appendix, No. XIV.)

[4] Smith to the Queen, March 31, 1563; to Cecil, May 12. *Ibidem.* (Appendix, No. XIV.)

[5] April 30, 1563. (*Ibidem.*)

retaken, and she preferred getting it back by conquest to seeing it amicably restored, since she would then feel herself perfectly at liberty to retain Calais. Briquemault having one day said to her that he would undertake that the English should evacuate Havre, if she would give one of her sons, the young Prince de Béarn, and the young Duc de Guise, as hostages for the restoration of Calais, 'I shall take good care not to do so,' she replied, laughing; and on Briquemault persisting, she requested him to go home to bed.[1] She consented, however, to send to London a Secretary of State, the Sieur d'Alluye,[2] with fresh propositions. De la Haye and Briquemault also made several journeys with letters from Condé and the Admiral.[3] All these envoys were received with much displeasure by Elizabeth, who requested that no more such ridiculous propositions should be made to her. She lost her temper with d'Alluye, and even told him that in occupying Havre, she had only intended to avenge the honour of England which had been compromised by the loss of Calais.[4] But when she learned through her ambassador that the Huguenot leaders had very little influence at Court,[5] and that they even talked of publicly disavowing the Vidame, in order to free themselves from all responsibility in connection with the

---

[1] Myddlemore to Cecil, May 17, 1563. (State Paper Office.) (Appendix, No. XIV.)

[2] A Robertet. Smith to Cecil, May 22; Myddlemore to Cecil, May 24, &c. *Ibidem.* (Appendix, No. XIV.) Cf. 'Correspondance Chantonnay,' in the 'Mémoires de Condé.'

[3] Myddlemore to Cecil, March 30. Condé to Elizabeth and to Cecil,

April 1; Smith to Cecil, May 28; Condé to Cecil, May 31. *Ibidem.* (Appendix, No. XIV.)

[4] The Queen of England to Warwick, June 4; to Smith, June 5; Myddlemore to Cecil, June 19. State Paper Office. (See for this last letter, Appendix XIV.)

[5] Myddlemore to Cecil, May 24; Smith to Cecil, May 26, &c. *Ibidem.*

unfortunate treaty of Hampton Court;[1] above all when Warwick had made known to her his uneasiness, informing her that Havre was surrounded by troops, that already several skirmishes had taken place, that the garrison was very short of victuals and decimated by the plague, and that, in short, he could not answer for holding out till supplies should reach him,[2] she immediately changed her tactics, and sent a new envoy to France, by name Dannett, with very ample powers. She consented to surrender Havre, and not to press the restitution of Calais any longer, provided she received good securities that that city should be restored within the interval fixed by the treaties. She demanded as hostages neither the King's brothers nor counsellors, but she asked for three sons of the German Protestant Princes, to whom France could give other hostages. She further would be contented with the repayment of half the sums she had advanced.[3] These conditions, had they been offered a few months sooner, would have greatly embarrassed the French Court, and the Huguenots could not but have warmly seconded their acceptance. But they had come too late. Dannett only brought back a vague answer from Condé,[4] and gave the most alarming accounts of the position in which matters stood.

Tardy concessions on the part of Elizabeth.

Elizabeth went a step farther. She pretended that she had never said she would keep Havre till Calais was

---

[1] Myddlemore to Cecil, May 3, &c. State Paper Office. (Appendix, No. XIV.)

[2] Despatches of Warwick dated May 18, 22, 27, 28; June 6, 7, &c. He however enjoined strict observance of days of fasting and abstinence, by the Queen's command, but their observance did not much augment the supplies of the place.

[3] Instructions to Th. Dannett, June 15, 1563. (State Paper Office.)

[4] Condé to Elizabeth, June 26. (*Ibidem.*)

restored, but only till Calais was accounted for to her.[1]
She no longer even particularised the guarantees which
she wished for its restitution, and no longer demanded the
immediate repayment of all or part of her advances ; she
only asked, both in case of the money lent and of Calais,
for good securities. Throckmorton was charged with
this new message. This was an unfortunate choice, for
he was very unpopular at Court, and suspected of having
been one of the greatest instigators of the recent troubles.
In any case, neither he nor Smith could be received by
the King, whom his mother had conducted to Fécamp, to
be nearer Havre.[2] The guns were already heard before
that city, which had been invested by the Maréchal de
Brissac. The soldiers of both religions pressed into the
besieging army. The Catholics and Reformers seemed at
that time to yield to a common impulse. 'From here to
Bayonne the universal cry is Vive France!' wrote Montmorency. The two 'enseignes colonelles' of D'Andelot
mounted guard side by side with the regiments of Charry,
Richelieu, and Sarlaboux, so devoted to the late Duc
de Guise, and when the veteran Connétable took the
command of the troops on the twentieth of July, the
Huguenot nobility crowded to range themselves under
his orders, rivalling in zeal and valour their late enemies.

Condé set them the example. He had hesitated long.
He had said that he would never draw his sword against
the Queen of England.[3] He had boasted to Smith of

1563
July.

Siege of
Havre.

Condé
takes part
in it.

---

[1] 'We never used such kind of
speche as we wold never deliver
Newhaven except we might have
Callice presently, but the phrase of
our speche hath been: except we
had reason rendered us for Callice.'—

The Queen of England to Smith,
July 6. (State Paper Office.)

[2] Smith to the Queen of England,
July 28. (*Ibidem.*)

[3] 'That his sword would never
cutt against the queen's ma^{tie}.'—

having refused the command of the army at the risk of losing the chance of being proclaimed Lieutenant-Général of the Kingdom, and of one day being promoted to the dignity of Connétable.[1] But when he heard of the avowal which, in an angry moment, Elizabeth had made to D'Alluye, he declared himself free as respected that Princess, and he no longer resisted the impulse of nationality by which all about him were being carried away.[2] While he protested his desire to contribute as far as he could to the restoration of peace between the two crowns, he shook off, not without some difficulty, Myddlemore, who had been ordered to attend him everywhere,[3] and joined the army. On his arrival in the camp he 'took up his post in the trenches,' and showed himself by the side of his cousin the Duc de Montpensier, a fiery Catholic. The English were not prepared for this sudden concord and this universal fervour. During a skirmish, Leighton, one of their captains, recognised a Protestant officer of the name of Monneins, with whom he had served in the defence of Rouen. 'What!' he exclaimed, 'when we are of the same religion, and a few months ago were fighting side by side, are we only to meet that we may cut each other's throats?' 'Monsieur,' replied Monneins, 'you are here by order of your Queen, and I of my King; the difference of religion is at an end, and every Frenchman of the one faith and of the other alike, is determined to spend his life and his power in winning back for the King all that was his own.' Alas! the brave

---

Myddlemore to Cecil, March 30. State Paper Office. (Appendix, No. XIV.)

[1] Smith to Cecil, May 12, 26. (*Ibidem.*)

[2] Myddlemore to Cecil, June 19. *Ibidem.* (Appendix, No. XIV.)

[3] The same to the same, June 29. *Ibidem.* (Appendix, No. XIV.)

Monneins was mistaken. The difference was not at an end, and the harmony was destined to fly away upon the wings of that wind which wafted the English ships from the coast of France, after the surrender of Havre.

The siege had been conducted with so much vigour that the garrison had been unable to hold out till the arrival of the fleet from Elizabeth with supplies. The capitulation was signed on the twenty-eighth of July, but without being followed by the restoration of peace. The state of war was maintained by a fresh royal proclamation,[1] and all the English agents and envoys, who had hitherto been free to travel all over France, were arrested.[2] Negotiations having soon after commenced, Smith and Myddlemore were speedily enough released.[3] But Throckmorton, against whom the French Government thought it had special grievances, was not liberated till the beginning of November.[4] And he was very soon afterwards again imprisoned at Saint-Germain, because the French hostages who, in execution of the treaty of Cateau-Cambrésis, had been sent to England, were still lying in the Tower.[5] But Throckmorton, though well guarded, obtained several secret interviews with the Queen-Mother, who was aware of his quarrel with Smith, and well knew how to turn to account misunderstandings between the two ambassadors.[6] Smith, on the other hand, tried to

Capitulation of
Havre
(July 28,
1563).
Peace with
England
(April 1,
1564).

[1] Smith to Cecil, August 16. War had been declared by a proclamation on July 6, but only with the object of regaining Havre.

[2] Despatches of Smith, Throckmorton, and Myddlemore, August 17, 18, 19, 24, &c. (State Paper Office.)

[3] Smith's despatches, September 14, 23. (*Ibidem.*)

[4] Throckmorton and Smith to the Queen, November 10. (*Ibidem.*)

[5] The same to the same, December 8, 1563; Elizabeth to Throckmorton, February 3, 1564. (*Ibidem.*)

[6] Throckmorton to the Queen of England, January 21, February 29, 1564, &c. (*Ibidem.*)

obtain the succour of the Admiral, who pleaded the difficulties of his position and would not interfere.[1] As for
Condé, he seems never to have taken any part in this
negotiation. Since the siege of Havre, he had broken off
all communication with the English agents, and Myddlemore himself, whom Stuart, a Scotchman attached to the
person of the Prince, had brought on one occasion to his
door, was unable to gain an interview.[2]

Peace was only concluded on the eleventh of April,
1564, at Troyes. The Queen of England lost all her
rights over Calais, and was obliged to content herself with
a hundred and twenty thousand crowns as the price of
the freedom of the French hostages.[3] Not considering
this sum as a payment made by the Huguenots, Elizabeth
reminded her ambassador by two subsequent despatches,[4]
to press the Prince and the Admiral on the subject of the
advances which she had made to them. But there is not
in the correspondence a trace of any answer or other
result of these demands, and the affair seemed to have
ended thus.

Efforts and
sacrifices
on the
part of
Condé, to
get rid of
the
'reîtres'
from the
kingdom.

The English, however, were not the only foreigners
whom, in their guilty recklessness, the Protestants had
introduced into the kingdom. There were still the
German reîtres to be got rid of, and they would not
leave France without their pay. And the King had less
money than soldiers. The edict of May (1563), which

---

[1] Smith to the Queen of England,
January 15, 1564. (State Paper
Office.)

[2] Myddlemore to Cecil, July 19,
1563. (*Ibidem.*)

[3] The peace concluded between
the two crowns was not re-established between the two ambassadors

of England. On the very day on
which the treaty of Troyes was
signed, Smith and Throckmorton
drew upon each other. They were
with difficulty separated. (Smith to
Cecil, April 13, 1564. *Ibidem.*)

[4] April 26 and May 2, 1564.
(*Ibidem.*)

enjoined the sale of all ecclesiastical property, till a sum yielding a revenue of a hundred thousand écus had been realised, was difficult to be carried out. The treasury was empty. Whilst waiting for their pay, the Germans ravaged our finest provinces. Condé showed himself sensible of the reproach which the conduct of his allies brought upon him, and left no effort untried to free his country from them. His pressing letters to the Prince Portien, who was in command of the reîtres, have been preserved to us.[1] But promises were not sufficient. He had to give security at Strasbourg and Frankfort for the pay. Nor did the Prince hesitate to make personal sacrifices for this end.[2] At last the Germans, tempted by an offer that had been made to them of employment in the Low Countries, quitted France.

In proportion as Condé displayed his honourable eagerness to fulfil the conditions of the peace, did he show himself faithful to those who had followed him through the war, devoted to the defence of their rights, and active in supporting their claims. Rigid and proud as he was in his relations with powerful antagonists, he knew how to forget the injuries of his friends ; and he only replied to the sarcasms and reproaches of Coligny by a fresh exhibition of courageous affection. On the fifteenth of May, 1563, finding that the Lorrains were about to appear at the Court to demand vengeance for the

Fidelity of Condé to the Admiral, who however does not at first exhibit much gratitude.

---

[1] Bibliothèque impériale, Collection Colbert. Most of them are printed in the 'Mémoires de Condé' (Lenglet-Dufresnoy's edition), and in Le Laboureur's additions to the 'Memoirs of Castelnau.'

[2] His own private fortune being insufficient, he had recourse to his relations. The Dame de Roye, his mother-in-law, was compelled to borrow at Strasbourg 6,600 florins (June 24, 1563). In 1622, the Prince de Condé, in order to release the heirs of the House of Roye, compounded for this debt, which, with interest, had accumulated to 81,264 livres.

death of the Duc de Guise, and to lay it to the charge of the Admiral in his absence, Condé made a speech in the council, and declared that he would regard as a personal insult any attack directed against his relative and friend. Seconded by François de Montmorency, he was so far successful that the matter was withdrawn from the jurisdiction of the Parliament of Paris, and referred, by appeal, to the Great Council. Hearing afterwards that Coligny, on an invitation of the Regent, had quitted his retreat at Châtillon and was on his way to Saint-Germain, he hastened to Essonne to meet him, and succeeded in stopping him. 'I have more care for his life than for my own,' he said to Myddlemore, 'and such is the state of matters here, that he is likely enough to have a pistol-bullet put into him in full Court.'[1] The Admiral showed but little gratitude for this kindness. He refused to see the Prince on the departure of the latter for the siege of Havre, and spoke bitterly of his 'weakness and pusillanimity,'[2] affecting in his talk, in the interests of Elizabeth, a revival of zeal which never indeed displayed itself in any serious actions, but which gained him the not very enviable flatteries of Throckmorton and Myddlemore.[3] But the magnanimity of Condé did not flag. The Guises, having obtained from the King a reply which to some extent favoured them, and which without condemning the Châtillons, left the sword hanging over their heads, the Prince proclaimed, in a solemn declaration on the thirtieth of August, that all which had been done by Coligny and

[1] Myddlemore to Cecil, May 17, 1563. State Paper Office. (Appendix, No. XIV.)

[2] Smith to Elizabeth, July 8, 1563. *Ibidem.* (Appendix, No. XIV.)

[3] Smith to Cecil, July 19, 1563, &c. (*Ibidem.*) See also the 'Correspondance Chantonnay,' in the 'Mémoires de Condé.'

D'Andelot had been done by his orders, and that he accepted the responsibility of it.   The bad temper of the Admiral subsided at last, and the intimacy between the two cousins was restored.

It was not merely to his friends of high rank that Condé gave his support.   The towns and individuals who appealed against the too frequent violations of the edict, always found in him a zealous defender.   There was no want of grounds for complaint.   Citadels were being erected at Lyon and Orléans.   In other cities belonging to their party the walls were being demolished.   Murders and crimes of every sort deluged the provinces with blood, and the Protestants seldom obtained justice for the outrages of which they were the victims.   Some of the governors had even taken into their pay irregular bands, sometimes even foreign soldiers, whose excesses were intolerable.   Languedoc long retained the memory of Damville's Albanians.   Condé, appealed to on all sides, addressed the Queen on the subject, himself presented deputations to her, and wrote letter after letter to the King's lieutenants.   Printed as well as manuscript collections still retain the memorials of his multifarious exertions, and contain a part of that voluminous correspondence which he carried on for the defence of his co-religionists.[1]

His efforts were frequently unsuccessful.   Médicis, without having as yet renounced her system of neutrality, was inclining more and more towards the extreme Catholics.   It was not from religious belief nor from exalted public spirit that she was attracted to this party,

[1] See (Appendix XV.) some of his letters, which have remained hitherto unpublished.

but merely from the narrow calculations of personal
ambition. Since the death of Guise, the Protestant
leaders, Condé and the Admiral, were the only men left of
whom she could be jealous. The official acts of the Royal
power betrayed her tendencies. One of the first edicts
forbad Huguenots preaching within five leagues of the
places where the King should halt during the progress
which he was then making through France. The change
was complete, and it seemed already long since the time,
still fresh in men's memories, when it was feared that ' the
Queen would convert the young King,' and the singing of
Marot's psalms was more frequently heard in the Royal
abode than that of the Catholic office. The most confidential agents of the Queen-Mother,[1] who had been despatched
at the commencement of the civil war with such very
different instructions, and now met the Court in the
provinces, could scarcely believe their eyes, and had
speedily to accommodate their acts and their language to
the altered state of affairs. L'Hospital alone remained
firm. But his star was waning. His influence, which had

as yet delayed the public promulgation of the Council of
Trent,[2] was powerless to prevent the issue of the Edict of
Roussillon (Aug. 1564), a decree which, under pretext of

---

[1] Among others, Crussol, the King's
lieutenant in a portion of Languedoc.
See (Appendix, No. XVI.) what he
wrote to M. de Gordes immediately
after he had paid his respects to the
Queen at Toulouse (March 10, 1565,
in an autograph postscript).

[2] See the letter in which the King,
who had been invited by the Catholic Princes to a meeting at Nancy,
that they might together take the
oath to observe the decrees of the
Council, refuses to obey a summons
of this kind, and justifies his conduct. Nothing has ever been written
more noble or patriotic. The pen of
L'Hospital is evident in every line.
We need not add that the supreme
decisions of the Council of Trent on
matters of dogma had nothing to do
with this question.

interpreting the Edict of Peace, modified it very considerably.

CHAP.
IV.

1564
Aug. 31.
Protest of
Condé.

Condé could not allow such an act to pass without addressing a protest to the Queen; in order that the character of it might be distinctly understood, he immediately caused it to be printed and circulated, accompanying it with a solemn declaration. He demanded that the Edict of Peace should be faithfully carried out, that there should be an end of all attempts to get rid of its letter and spirit by false and futile interpretations of it, and, finally, that the very grave crimes that were being committed shoul no longer go unpunished. And here he alluded to an occurrence which had justly shocked not only the Protestants, but every honest Frenchman. The Sieur de la Curée, a governor of a province, a Protestant gentleman, and lieutenant of the King in Vendomois, had just been assassinated by the Catholics of that country. The murderers were not prosecuted.

The tone of Condé's letter was firm and clear, but moderate. He always appealed to conciliatory measures, and made no secret of his strong desire and intention to maintain peace throughout the kingdom. He sincerely wished to show himself faithful to the engagements which he had undertaken previous to the Edict of Amboise. His acts were in keeping with his words. While he spoke out energetically against the murder of La Curée, against the violations of the edict, and against the outrages of the Catholics, he did not forget to reprobate the violence of his co-religionists, and when one of these, in a moment of fanatical excitement, snatched the consecrated host from the hands of a priest who was celebrating Mass in the church of Saint-Médard, the Prince expressed his approval

He wishes
to remain
moderate,
and blames
the excesses of
the Protestants.

of the wretched man's punishment. But it is not possible to be perfectly impartial with impunity; and, as is often the case with those who try to take a middle course in a time of unbridled passions, Condé found himself a mark for the reproaches of both sides.

The two
extreme
parties are
dissatis-
fied with
Condé.
On the one hand, his persistence in defending the rights guaranteed to the Reformers, in practising the new religion, in avoiding being present at the ceremonies of the old, drew upon him the anger of the extreme Catholics. The people of Paris, more especially, would not forgive him, and the municipal magistrates left no means untried to inflame the public excitement. The civil war became the subject of those military pantomimes which from time immemorial have been a leading feature in the popular pastimes of France, and these open-air performances used to be wound up amid universal applause by the execution of the Prince and the other Protestant leaders.[1] For several months Condé dared not appear in the capital, even in the suite of the King, and he was on more than one occasion compelled to remain almost alone at Vincennes and Saint-Germain in a ridiculous position, obliged to wait outside the barriers for the Regent, when he wished to confer with her.[2] Weary at last of such humiliations, he quitted Vincennes with the King on the occasion of a great Catholic holiday, and accompanied him to the doors of Notre-Dame. The crowd became excited when they saw the Prince bow to the King on his arrival at the door, and retire without entering the church. That evening a band of some hundreds of armed men

[1] Myddlemore to Cecil, May 24, 1563. (State Paper Office.)   1563.   *Ibidem.*   (Appendix, No. XIV.)
[2] Smith to Cecil, May 19, 22, 26,

assembled in the Faubourg Saint-Antoine with the most
sinister intentions. Happily Condé, on his return to
Vincennes, had joined the escort of Charles IX., and when
the assassins saw him on horseback by the side of the
King, they did not dare to attempt any outrage on his
person. They then made an attack upon the litter of the
Princess, which followed at a short distance. She was
saved by the presence of mind of her coachman. But one
of the Prince's gentlemen was killed at the carriage-door,
and several received injuries.[1] Every available means—
whether by intrigue or by violence—of opposing the
Huguenot Prince, was put into operation. Thus the
Pope had been asked to allow the Cardinal de Bourbon
to marry, in order, as it was said, 'tenir son frère en
bride' (to keep his brother in check), but really because
some astrologers had predicted that the children of the
Queen-Mother would not live, and there was a dread of
seeing Condé too near in succession to the throne.[2] This
strange negotiation fell through ; but it became known,
and revealed the feelings entertained towards the Prince.

On the other hand, the Protestant zealots could not
forgive his coldness. They accused him of a likeness in
all points to his brother the King of Navarre,[3] of 'sailing
between two currents and of playing the Machiavel.'[4] It
was not appeals to conciliation that they expected from
him, but inflamed language, perhaps incitements to revolt,

---

[1] Myddlemore to Cecil, June 17, 1563. (State Paper Office.) This incident is mentioned with less detail, and ascribed to another date, in Chantonnay's 'Correspondance,' and also in the 'Journal de Bruslart.' See 'Mémoires de Condé.'

[2] Letters of Prosper Sainte-Croix

to Cardinal Borromeo. ('Correspondance Chantonnay.')

[3] Myddlemore to Cecil, April 14, 1563. State Paper Office. (Appendix, No. XIV.)

[4] Smith to Cecil, May 19, 22, 1563. *Ibidem.* (Appendix, No. XIV.)

at all events an outspoken profession of his faith.[1] In their eyes, this great love of peace was nothing but the indifference of gratified ambition, or the forgetfulness of duty amidst the intoxications of pleasure. It must be conceded that if the public acts of Condé did not merit these reproaches, his private life justified the apprehensions of the Protestants.

He was still young, and had been for three years cut off from all amusement; he was exposed, after two separate seasons of captivity and many other trials, to all the seductions of the most corrupt court in the world; and he gave himself unreservedly to all the temptations of his ardent nature. How was it possible to believe that he could seriously occupy himself with the interests of religion, when he was continually hunting or tennis playing, and that with such eagerness that his health frequently suffered from it?[2] How could any reliance be placed upon the steadfastness of his faith, which had already, not quite groundlessly, been suspected of wavering? He was to be seen mingling with all these profane festivities, balls, tourneys, theatres, tilting-matches, distinguished among all his compeers by his skilful horsemanship,[3] his polite accomplishments, his noble bearing, and his 'bel gigneto;'[4]

---

[1] In a letter addressed to Condé, after the peace of Amboise, on the tenth of May, 1563, Calvin insisted on Condé's signing and making public in some way or other 'a short confession' which he had drawn up for D'Andelot to read at the Diet of Frankfort. Calvin, greatly excited by his conflict with the Lutherans, feared most of all that 'they would never cease setting snares to entrap Condé into that confession of Augs-burg which is neither flesh nor fish.' ('Calvin's Letters,' published by M. Jules Bonnet, ii. 507. Paris, 1854.)

[2] 'Correspondance Chantonnay.'

[3] See the 'Memoirs of Castelnau,' book v. ch. vi., for the account of the amusements at Fontainebleau.

[4] 'Dio mi guarda del bel gigneto del Principe di Condé!'—Contemporary Italian proverb.

surrounded by the treacherous ' squadron '[1] of the Queen-Mother's maids of honour, forgetting his own noble and faithful wife in the embraces of these frail beauties.

His amours were everywhere talked of ; Geneva was shocked at them.   Calvin had always continued on good terms with Condé.   After the Edict of Amboise, he had, adopting the point of view of the French pastors, strongly disapproved of the terms of the peace, and he had not concealed his feelings from the Dame de Roye.[2]   But he knew very well that Condé was necessary to his party. Fearing the effect which might be produced upon that hot temper by the revilings of his followers, he had begged him ' not to wonder that many others should wish to see a more favourable peace.'   And in a long and very remarkable letter,[3] he had used every endeavour to humour him, and keep up his courage.   He now wrote to him again, but in sad and stern terms.   Beza added his signature also to the letter, which thus addressed him, in the name of their afflicted church :—' In conclusion, Monseigneur, we cannot forbear to beseech you always, not only to use your endeavours in the cause of Our Lord Jesus Christ, for the advancement of the Gospel, and for the security and rest of the poor faithful, but also to show in your whole life that you have profited by the doctrine of salvation, and to let your example be such as to edify the good, and shut the mouths of all our gainsayers ; for in proportion as you are conspicuous from afar, in so exalted a position, ought you to be on your guard that there should be no cause in you for

CHAP.
IV.

1563–4

His rela-
tions with
Calvin.
Warnings
from
Geneva.

---

[1] Brantôme.

[2] 'Calvin's Letters,' ii. 497. In his fury, on his reading the conditions of the peace, Calvin, writing to Soubise, had called Condé a ' wretch ' (misé-rable). (*Ibidem*, ii. 495.)

[3] Of May 10, 1563 ; already quoted, p. 206.

them to retort upon us. You do not doubt, Monseigneur, that we love your honour as we desire your salvation; and we should be traitors if we concealed from you the rumours that are afloat concerning you. We do not think there is any harm in you whereby God has been directly offended; but when it is reported that you are intriguing with ladies, your authority and reputation are seriously injured. Good people will be scandalized; and the evil-disposed will make it a subject of mockery. That is a temptation which is entangling you and preventing you from attending to your duty; it cannot be but that it should lead you into worldly vanities; and it becomes you above all to be careful lest the light that God has given you be stifled and extinguished. We hope, Monseigneur, that this warning will be taken in good part, when you consider how much it is meant for your good. From Geneva, this thirteenth day of September, 1563. Your very humble brethren, Jean Calvin and Théodore de Besze.'[1]

Amours
of Condé
with
Isabelle
de Li-
meuil
and the
Maréchale
le Saint-
André.

This letter produced no effect. Condé seemed as it were carried away by a whirlwind of dissipation, and great was the scandal even for those days of licence and indifference, when at Dijon,[2] during the King's progress, in the Queen's own dressing-room, Isabelle de Limeuil, one of her maids of honour, gave birth to a son, the name of whose father she openly declared (May 1564). Catherine

---

[1] Bibliothèque impériale, Collection Dupuy, 102, copy.

[2] And not at Lyon, where all previous narrators lay the scene of this affair. The Court did not arrive at Lyon till the 9th of June, 1564. Now by the documents which we publish (see Appendix, No. XVII.) it is manifest that Isabelle de Limeuil was arrested at Dijon during the sojourn there of Charles IX. from the 22nd to the 29th of May that same year. The arrest could not have preceded the event which caused it.

de Médicis, 'who, however, was said to have ordered this girl to yield to the Prince's solicitations, for she was anxious to win him over,' was obliged to dismiss Mademoiselle de Limeuil 'from the troop,'[1] and even exhibited towards her an unusual degree of severity. Poor Isabelle was shut up under strict surveillance in a convent at Auxonne, and specially given in charge to the governor of that place. As she was of high birth, and even related to the Queen-Mother,[2] it was necessary to find some excuse for such rigorous and unwonted cruelty, and nothing less than a capital crime was alleged.

Isabelle was bold and outspoken. She was no less distinguished by her wit than by her beauty, and the vivacity of her repartees drew around her as many enemies as her personal charms attracted obsequious admirers. She indignantly resented the overtures of those who did not suit her fancy, and did not spare them her ridicule. Brantôme relates how she once rebuffed him who used to rebuff everybody else—Montmorency. For some time the butt of her attacks had been the Prince de la Roche-sur-Yon, who, despite his gout and his rather advanced years, may very likely have been a former and ill-used admirer, but against whom she had a special grudge.

This Prince was married to the lady-in-waiting to the

---

[1] Brantôme. See also De Thou, the 'Journal de Bruslart,' and the 'Additions aux Mémoires de Castelnau,' &c.

[2] She belonged to the House of La Tour d'Auvergne, to the branch of the Vicomtes de Turenne, Ducs de Bouillon, &c. Her grandfather, Antoine de la Tour, called Le Vieil, Vicomte de Turenne, Chamberlain to Charles VIII., had died February 14, 1527, leaving several children by Antoinette de Pons. From François, eldest son of the former, sprang, in the fifth generation, the great Maréchal de Turenne. From the second son, Gilles de la Tour, Seigneur de Limeuil, by Marguerite de la Cropte, Dame de Languais, descended:—three sons, who died without issue; Isabeau, or Isabelle, the subject of this note; and four other

Queen-Mother;[1] he thought, not unreasonably, that the Royal household was very ill-disciplined, and urged his wife to introduce into it some little ' reformation.' Limeuil reproached him with ' doing all the harm he could to the maids,' and with having caused her to be annoyed by questions and investigations as soon as he had suspected her pregnancy. She loudly expressed her hatred of him. One of the most assiduous amongst the gentlemen of the Court, Charles de la Marck, Comte de Maulevrier,[2] received, as did many others, the readily afforded confidences of Limeuil; but whether because he also had some secret grudge against her, or because of his habit of joking[3] about everything, he gave a strange interpretation to the expressions which the impetuous Isabelle allowed to escape her, and repeated them with abundant exaggerations. At first no heed was taken of the stories of Maulevrier, who was known to be a great bouncer, and utterly unworthy of credit; but suddenly these accounts seemed to excite attention, and the unfortunate girl found herself involved in a charge of having planned the poisoning of a Prince of the blood.

Two members of the council, two grave bishops, their Lordships of Orléans and Limoges, who were generally

daughters. The mother of Catherine de Médicis, Madeleine de la Tour, was of the same House, and married Lorenzo, Duke of Urbino.

[1] Philippa de Montespedon, widow of the Maréchal de Montejean, had married as her second husband Charles de Bourbon, Prince de la Roche-sur-Yon. The Princes of the blood were highly indignant that after this marriage she had accepted the position of a lady-in-waiting. She died in 1578.

[2] Born in 1538, he died in 1622. He was the second son of Robert de la Marck, Maréchal de France and Duc de Bouillon, called 'the young adventurer.' See what Brantôme says of him (vii. 387), and the account of one of his feats in the 'Additions aux Mémoires de Castelnau.' It is curious that he afterwards married as his second wife Antoinette de la Tour, younger sister of Isabeau.

[3] ' goguenarder.'

employed in the most important negotiations, received a
commission from the King to proceed to an examination of
the case. It was clear that there was a desire to go higher
than Limeuil, and implicate Condé in a villanous affair.
Catherine had gained nothing but a scandal in return
for her calculated laxity. She was determined to be revenged. It was already asserted that La Roche-sur-Yon
was not the only victim for whom poison was designed.
It was allowed to transpire that in the same nefarious
manner it was intended to despatch the aged Montmorency, to serve the ambition of Condé, who aspired to
the sword of the Connétable. But notwithstanding the
persistence of Maulevrier in his statements, it was found
impossible to elevate Limeuil's fault to the height of a
state crime. All that could be done was to drag her
about for several months, from Auxonne to Mâcon, from
Mâcon to Lyon, and from Lyon to Vienne, with great
precautions, lest she should be rescued, for her persecutors
believed, or affected to believe, that her intrepid para-
mour would spare no pains to carry her off. But the
Prince contented himself with writing very affectionate
letters to her: he had already obtained possession of the
child,[1] and promised to acknowledge it; but it appears
that he had some doubts on this point, and some jealousy
of a Sieur du Fresne, Secretary to the King.[2] Besides,

[1] This child died shortly afterwards.

[2] Florimond, one of the Robertets,
Sieur du Fresne, Secretary of State,
died in 1567. Another Robertet,
Florimond, Sieur d'Alluye, his cousin,
was Secretary of State at the same
time as himself, and died in 1569.
The public shared Condé's doubts :—

‘ At multi dicunt quod pater
Non est princeps, sed est alter
Qui Regi est a secretis ;
Omnibus est notus satis.’
Satire quoted in the ‘ Additions
aux Mémoires de Castelnau.’ On
the whole matter see Appendix, No.
XVII.

he was already at that very time engaged in another intrigue with Marguerite de Lustrac, widow of the Maréchal de Saint-André, who had conceived for him a violent passion. Such was at that time the licence which existed alike in opinions and morals, that a man of the rank of Condé, a prince who was justly considered a man of high honour, could, without exciting the surprise, and almost without eliciting the disapproval of anyone, accept an almost regal present from one of his avowed mistresses. The Maréchale de Saint-André gave him the estate and magnificent château of Valery,[1] which her luxurious husband had rebuilt and decorated with that richness and elegance which characterize almost all the precious remains of our sixteenth century architecture. It must be added, that the Maréchale's daughter was betrothed to Condé's son[2]—a fact which somewhat modifies the singularity of the gift, but which also shows how utterly deficient it was possible for even the noble natures of that time to be in some of the finer shades of delicacy.

Sickness
and
death of
Éléonore
de Roye
(July 23,
1564).

In thus publicly exposing the licentiousness of his morals, Condé not only violated those eternal laws which no man is entitled to transgress, and which even the immorality of the times was no excuse for his forgetting, but he showed himself ungrateful. He owed at least respect and consideration to the wife whose devotion to

---

[1] Valery is situated in the department of the Yonne. This château continued to be one of the favourite residences of the Princes de Condé, and was the last resting-place of all the most illustrious of them in after years. During the middle of the last century, however, it lapsed, as her portion, to Mademoiselle de Sens,

a princess, by whom it was sold.
[2] The deed of gift was not confirmed till after the death of Mademoiselle de Saint-André. It comprehended not only Valery, but all the property of that young lady. See, on this subject (Appendix, No. XVIII.), a letter from Cardinal de Châtillon, dated July 4, 1564.

him had never wavered in hours of the utmost peril. Éléonore de Roye had quitted Orléans in a state of utter prostration; her health, which had been till then sustained by her courage, but was yet undermined by so many anxieties and fatigues, could no longer bear up against the grief which the conduct of her husband caused her. While in retirement on her estates, still suffering from the effects of the accident which she had met with at the commencement of the civil war, she was, in addition to all this, attacked by small-pox, which could not be completely cured. After a few months her case became hopeless. Condé, informed of her dangerous state, at last hastened to her side. His heart was not quite corrupted; and by that bed of sickness he saw and repented of his faults. And although he could not undo the ill that he had done, at least the genuine sorrow which he evinced, and the assiduous and affectionate attentions which he lavished upon the dying sufferer, must have sweetened her last moments.[1]

Éléonore de Roye was deeply regretted by the Protestants. Her private virtues and her heroic qualities had been the admiration of all. But the Reformers chiefly loved to see in her a zealous convert, who had done not a little to win over her husband to their cause, and keep him steadfast in his attachment to it. Her death severed one of the links that bound them to Condé. What would become of the Prince when the first burst of his grief had subsided? His impressions, it was well known, were more violent than lasting, and his friends feared lest his

---

[1] She died July 23, 1564. ('Épistre d'une demoiselle françoise à une sienne amie, dame estrangère, sur la mort d'excellente et vertueuse dame Léonor de Roye, princesse de Condé. 1564.' Small 8vo.

voluptuous habits should soon once more gain the mastery
over him, and the growing licentiousness of his morals
should extinguish in his heart every vestige of religious
zeal. In fact, it soon became known that Isabelle de
Limeuil had been set at liberty,[1] and that Condé had renewed his connection with her, that he had received with
a very bad grace the advice that Coligny had given him
upon the subject, and had laughed at the ministers who had
talked of excommunicating him.[2] But what the Reformers
most dreaded was a new family alliance which might
change the position of their former leader, and draw him
off in another direction. Their alarms on this head soon
became serious.

Hardly had the grave closed upon the late Princess,
when a thousand reports were afloat concerning the intentions of her husband and the solicitations by which he was
beset. To begin with, public rumour betrothed his eldest
son, the Marquis de Conti, and his sister,[3] respectively to the
daughter and son of the late Duc de Guise.[4] The Marquis
de Conti had, it is true, as we have already stated, been promised to Catherine d'Albon, daughter of the Maréchal de
Saint-André; but she had just died suddenly, and her unexpected end was ascribed to a diabolical crime on the part of
her mother. She had broken, it was alleged, by poison, the
projected union between the two children, with a view to
facilitate the success of her own aspirations to the hand of

---

[1] Or carried off by some friend
of the Prince de Condé, if the English Ambassador is to be believed.
(Smith to Cecil, April 10, 1565.
State Paper Office.)

[2] See (Appendix, No. XIX.) an
Italian letter drawn from the stores
of Simancas. ('Archives de France.')

[3] Marguerite de Bourbon, born in
1556, died young.

[4] Catherine de Lorraine, born in
1552, afterwards Duchesse de Montpensier; Henri de Lorraine, Duc de
Guise, born in 1550. (See 'Correspondance Chantonnay.' Letter of
June 16, 1564.)

Condé. Nothing, therefore, stood in the way of the double
connection which the newsmongers had invented or propa-
gated, except the extreme youth of the parties, the elder
of whom was only fourteen. These rumours, however,
gained but little credit, and when it was found that
offers were being made from a different quarter to the
young Henri de Lorraine, they completely fell to the
ground. But other rumours, more important, and perhaps
with more foundation, were already in circulation. These
had reference to Condé himself, whom they espoused at
one time to the daughter of the late Duc de Guise,[1] at another, to his widow, Anne d'Este, still very beautiful;[2]
others again united him to the young and captivating
Queen of Scots, who had left so many souvenirs at the
Court of France.[3]

It was now no secret that the Guises, deprived of
their influence through the death of the illustrious head
of their House, were anxious for union with Condé;
and he himself, who was never rancorous against a fallen
enemy, seemed not indisposed to an alliance. The
Cardinal de Lorraine, on his return from the Council

Condé
sides
with the
Cardinal
de Lor-
raine
in his
dispute
with the
Maréchal

---

[1] Letter of M. de Losse, Governor
of Lyon, to M. de Gordes, Lieutenant
of the King in Dauphiné, May 12,
1565. ('Archives de Condé.') See
Appendix, No. XVI.

[2] De Thou, D'Aubigné, &c.

[3] 'She (Marie Stuart) informed me
of the offers made to her by several
Princes . . . .; and some of her
subjects wished to put before her the
Prince de Condé, who was then a
widower, in order to unite the
House of Bourbon with that of Lorraine in closer friendship. . .' ('Mémoires de Castelnau,' book v. ch. xi.)

'. . . . le cardinal brigue
Trafiquer une fausse ligue
Avec le prince de Condé.

Il fait au prince avoir envie
D'épouser la reine d'Escosse,
Et toujours de promesse fausse,
Il paist ce prince débonnaire.

Il faisoit mener cette affaire
Par deux moinesses sœurs du prince.'

('Épistre du coq à l'âne' ('Letter
from the cock to the ass') in the
'Additions' of Le Laboureur to the
'Mémoires de Castelnau.'

CHAP.
IV.

1564
December.

le Mont-
norency
Dec.
564).
of Trent, had passed through Soissons, where the Prince had been living in retirement since his wife's death in company with his sister Catherine, the Abbess of Notre-Dame. Their meeting, it was affirmed, had been very cordial. On leaving Soissons, the Cardinal went to Paris. He had scarcely arrived when the Maréchal de Montmorency, Governor of the Ile-de-France and his personal enemy, expelled him by force from the city, under pretext that the prelate had violated the edicts in being accompanied by a body of armed retainers. This raised a great commotion; the Maréchal's soldiers had grossly illtreated the escort of the Lorrain; one of his servants had been killed. D'Aumale joined his brother at Meudon; Montmorency, on the other hand, summoned his friends, and Coligny was among the first to obey the summons. But Condé took the Cardinal's part, and openly blamed Montmorency. He spoke out at once, 'This is too much if it is intended for a jest; too little if it is in earnest.'

Condé
arrives at
Paris
June
565).
His
attitude
ncreases
he fears
of the
Protest-
ants.
This unexpected language set people thinking. It seemed the foreboding of a new policy, the confirmation of rumours already widely circulated, and the first result of the mysterious interview at Soissons. It was soon bruited in Paris that Condé was arriving with a large following, to bring back by force the Cardinal de Lorraine and the Duc d'Aumale—'his cousins,' as it was carefully added. The Maréchal de Montmorency thought it right to march out of Paris, with all his troops, as if to give battle; but he met no one except the Prince, attended by a small escort, and having no intention but that of passing through Paris to join the King at Bayonne, and there pay his respects to the Queen of Spain. Condé expressed himself much hurt by this display of force, and

the Maréchal, not a little embarrassed, pretended that
he had only wished to do him honour, and hastened to
disperse his imposing cortége. During his stay in the
capital, which lasted seven or eight days, the Prince
was visited by the principal authorities, and the tone of
his conversation was carefully noticed. The Bishop of
Paris received from him the assurance that he would
protect the ecclesiastical hierarchy, and that he regretted
that which had taken place on the entry of the Cardinal
de Lorraine. To the Parliament, which complained that,
in contravention of the edict, there had been preaching in his house, he declared that these sermons had not
been authorized by him, and that he had not been present
at them.

The Reformers ' exhibited great jealousy' at this state
of affairs; 'many were alienated thereby, or at least
abated somewhat of the desire that they had to do him
service,'[1] and they vented their annoyance in a series of
stinging lampoons.[2] They were, as we have already
stated, unjust and ungrateful. There is nothing to prove
that Condé ever seriously contemplated a union by marriage with the House of Lorraine. But in any case, if he
did 'bind himself afresh' to his former rivals; if he

---

[1] M. de Cadenet à M. de Gordes,
June 14, 1565. ('Archives de Condé.')
This letter contains most of the
details which we have given. We
also give, farther on, some more
quotations from it. M. de Cadenet's
point of view was just, and his intimacy with the House of Montmorency gave him good opportunity
of reliable information. (See Appendix, No. XVI. Also the 'Journal
de Bruslart.')

[2] 'Who has not seen the sonnets
which they put forth against the late
Prince de Condé? Was he not accused of being a Sardanapalus, in a
word, a man who, being given up to
all kinds of dissipation, was betraying their cause?' ('Warning of the
English Catholics to the French
Catholics,' 1586, a very violent but
a very remarkable pamphlet by the
leaguer advocate Louis Dorléans.)

refused to take part in all the quarrels and to share all the passions which were raging around him, it was because he was sincerely desirous of endeavouring to obliterate the traces, and prevent the renewal of the civil war, ' being so amiable a prince, that he will never support anything but that which is reasonable and for the peace of the King's subjects.'

Condé
continues
on inti-
mate
terms
with the
Châtillons.
He marries
Made-
moiselle de
Longue-
ville
(Nov. 8,
1565).

He showed himself just and kind to all ; he sought to protect all the oppressed, and although justly wounded by the suspicions of which he was the object,[1] he remained true to his convictions. Thus, at the very moment when the Protestants were crying out most vehemently against his speeches, and against his interviews with the Cardinal de Lorraine, he appeared in close consultation with D'Andelot, and ' making it openly manifest that he wished to keep inviolate the friendship between himself and Messieurs de Châtillon.' The maintenance of these relations ought to have reassured the Protestants, or at all events diminished their bitterness. But soon a fresh incident happened which put an end to all conjectures. Condé, yielding to the strong representations of his friends and the advice of Jeanne d'Albret, broke with Isabelle de Limeuil and with the Maréchale de Saint-André, who both soon found consolation,[2] and made

---

[1] This appears from a letter addressed by him to the Vidame de Chartres on November 6, 1565, at the time of his second marriage. He complained bitterly of the Vidame's mistrust of him, of ' the charity of the talkers.' (Bibl. imp., Collection Dupuy ; printed in the ' Vie de Jean de Ferrières,' by M. de Bastard. Auxerre, 1858.)

[2] Isabelle de Limeuil married Scipion Sardini, Baron de Chaumont-

sur-Loire. He was a Lucchese, one of the Italian adventurers who, by the favour of Catherine de Médicis, made their fortune in France.

The Maréchale de Saint-André was married again to Geoffroy de Caumont. Still Condé in 1568 took upon himself to recommend her interests to the judges. (See his letter to M. de Morvilliers of May 17, 1568, Appendix, No. XX.)

choice of a new wife, Françoise-Marie d'Orléans-Longue-ville.[1] It was then seen how disinterested had been the acts which had been the subject of such harsh reproaches; for after he had resolved on this course, he still persevered in the same impartial and conciliatory course of action.

We have stated that Condé was repairing to the King when he passed through Paris in May 1565. But a fresh order countermanded his journey; either because he was really too late, as was said, to see the Queen of Spain, or rather because it was wished to prevent the presence of an inconvenient witness at the interview at Bayonne. The Prince did not join the Court again till the twenty-first of September, 1565, at Niort. He went thither to inform the King of his approaching marriage, and to ask for His Majesty's sanction. He was very cordially received, and as he was on the point of leaving with his betrothed, that their marriage might be performed according to the rites of their common religion, in a house of Jeanne d'Albret's, the Queen-Mother detained him,[2] and insisted on the ceremony taking place at Court on the eighth of November. There was nothing very remarkable in this. But Catherine went still farther. Jeanne d'Albret, the Duchess of Ferrara, the Prince and the new Princesse de Condé, having caused a sermon to be preached by one of their ministers within the walls of the Royal residence, the Cardinal de Bourbon remonstrated indignantly, and high words arose between him and his brother. The Queen-

---

[1] Posthumous daughter of Fran-çois d'Orléans, Marquis de Rothelin, a cadet of the House of Longueville, and of Jacqueline de Rohan. Her brother, Léonor d'Orléans, had been the heir of the Dukedom of Longue-ville since 1551. She survived her husband many years, and died in 1601.

[2] Journal of Smith the Ambassa-dor, September 19 to October 15, 1565. (State Paper Office.)

Mother took Condé's part, and the Protestant service was authorized at Court, on condition that it should be performed with closed doors, and that the Protestant Princes should bring none but the ladies and gentlemen of their own suites.[1] Thus did Médicis commence that course of duplicity which was to dissipate the fears and lull to rest the vigilance of the Reformers. They were becoming anxious as to the projects which might be entertained in conjunction with the ministers of Philip II., and as to the measures which, one after another, were to be taken for the disorganizing and restraining of the Huguenots. It was therefore necessary that public attention should be distracted. For nearly two years had the King been travelling here and there throughout France, and everywhere his presence had merely sown the seed of fresh mistrust. Catherine was anxious to conceal the actual results of these progresses, to bring them to an end with a conciliatory ceremonial, and to make it appear that they had resulted in the union of parties and reform of abuses. Such was the end aimed at by the assembling of the ' small States' of Moulins in December 1565. All the members of the Royal family, the Guises, the Montmorencies, the Châtillons, the ambassadors from sovereign Courts, the trésoriers-généraux and the principal officers of finance, as well as many other important personages, were summoned to that town. A few companies were disbanded and a few pensions suppressed. L'Hospital delivered a magnificent speech and made courageous efforts for ' the better ordering of public justice;'[2] Co-

---

[1] Smith to Cecil, December 11, 1565. (State Paper Office.)

[2] This speech was one of the greatest oratorical triumphs of L'Hos-pital, and the celebrated ' ordonnance de Moulins,' one of the foundations of our system of jurisprudence, was sufficient to render his name illus-

ligny exchanged the kiss of peace with Anne d'Este,[1] and
Cardinal de Lorraine 'came to terms' with the Maréchal
de Montmorency. Condé had been one of the most active
in bringing about this reconciliation, from which many,
more sanguine than prescient, anticipated great good 'to
the peace and concord of the realm.'

'Provided there be no padding about it!' wrote one of
the witnesses of that scene.[2] In fact, men had already
noticed the silence and the expression of countenance of
the young Duc de Guise during the interview of his
mother with the Admiral. His 'oncles d'épée' had
taken care not to be present at it. It was soon seen that
the interview had not produced those results which it
had been hoped. The excitement which had been spread
throughout Christendom by the incursions of the Turks and
the siege of Malta had contributed more to the momentary maintenance of domestic peace than that theatrical
and insincere reconciliation. The fire was smouldering
beneath the embers, and was now and then showing itself.
Violence and feuds had broken out afresh in the Comté
de Foix and elsewhere, giving occasion, as is always
the case, to mutual and passionate recrimination. The
Huguenots believed, or affected to believe, that a vast plot
was being hatched against their leaders, and appearances

---

trious. But his political influence
was already almost null, and he was
deprived of the seals of office after
the second civil war. Even at
Moulins indignities had been heaped
upon him, and he remarked sorrow-
fully to a magistrate who was complaining of some misrepresentation,
'I have found by experience that in
this reign it is the honest men who
are calumniated.' (Letter from the
Sieur de Brianson to M. de Gordes,
January 21, 1566. ('Archives de
Condé.' See Appendix, No. XVI.)

[1] Widow of the Duc François de
Guise.

[2] Montjay, a gentleman attached
to the suite of the Cardinal de Châtillon. (Letter of January 17, 1566,
to M. de Gordes. 'Archives de
Condé.' See Appendix, No. XVI.)

CHAP.
IV.

1566–7
seemed to favour their suspicions. Jeanne d'Albret and D'Andelot had been successively threatened, and a highwayman of the name of Simon de May had just been arrested, who, it was said, had been hired to assassinate Coligny. This wretch was executed; but the mistrust of the Protestants had been aroused. They watched with uneasiness the proceedings of the Catholic Powers. The Pope, having abandoned his intention of taking measures imitated from the twelfth century, against Jeanne d'Albret, tried to strike her down by other means, by dividing into two the bishopric of Bayonne and thus sanctioning the separation of the two Navarres. At last, in the beginning of the year 1567, it became known that a large army was assembling in Italy and was marching across Savoy, under the command of the Duke of Alva.

Condé,
pressed
by the
Genevese
and his
friends,
asks and
obtains
from
Médicis
the reinforcement of
the army.
Condé had gone to pass a few days with D'Andelot at Tanlay in Bourgogne, when he received a pressing message from Geneva. The stronghold of Calvinism was menaced, it was alleged, by the Duke of Alva, and application was made to him for prompt succour.[1] The fears of the Genevese passed away, for the Spanish army continued its march upon Flanders across Franche-Comté; but its movements were still an object of anxiety to the French Protestants.

It was known that the rising of the 'gueux'[2] had been put down. It could not therefore any longer be the affairs of Flanders which rendered this imposing demonstration necessary, but rather some secret design against France, or, at all events, against the Reformers. Had not these movements been preconcerted with Médicis, and

---

[1] Thuanus, book xli.
[2] The name assumed by the National party in Flanders.

were not men now about to witness the first steps towards carrying out the plans decided upon at Bayonne?

Urged forward by the pressing entreaties of his friends, Condé went to the Queen in the hope of clearing up the misgivings which, despite his confident tone, were now filling his mind. He demanded that the kingdom should be placed in a state of defence, that the army should be reorganized, that a new treaty should be concluded with the Swiss,[1] and that the country should hold itself in readiness to support, or even to enter upon, a war with Spain. Catherine's replies were perfectly reassuring. She consented to everything. Brissac's bands, already directed against the Marquisate of Saluces, were stopped in Lyonnais and Dauphiné. Orders were given for an immediate levy of six thousand Swiss, and a corps d'armée was formed on the frontiers of Champagne. 'To take away all suspicion,' D'Andelot received the command of this; and he 'beat his drums in Paris to fill up his complement of men. There was no talk but of war.'[2]

Davila has detailed, with a mixture of satisfaction and admiration, all the devices which Médicis invented in order to mislead and reassure the Reformers, during the time she was plotting their overthrow. At the very moment that she was conspiring at Bayonne for their destruction, she was receiving very graciously a deputation from the Protestants of Bordeaux, was allowing L'Hospital to speak the language of toleration and dignity, and

Devices of Catherine in order to ensnare and destroy the Protestants.

[1] Calvin had always supported an alliance with the Swiss. In his letter of May 10, 1564, he said: 'And since, Monseigneur, I have heard that an alliance with the Swiss is talked off, I beseech you, for the King's good, see that it be speedily effected. . . . .' He was very anxious that Geneva should be included in it.

[2] Various letters addressed to M. de Gordes. (See Appendix, No. XVI.)

was making a display of the protection she extended to
Jeanne d'Albret. She ostentatiously refused to open the
passes of Dauphiné to the 'tercios' of the Duke of Alva;
but she took good care that this general should find depôts
of provisions ranged all along the frontier. D'Andelot
received from her a command on paper; but he was
perpetually being trammelled in the exercise of his office
as Colonel-Général of infantry, and the bâton of Maréchal
was given to another person. And finally, the Queen
succeeded in contriving that the Huguenots themselves
should ask for the assembling of the very troops who
were intended to crush them. The violent temper of her
son, however, had nearly betrayed her. When the
Admiral and the envoys of the Lutheran Princes of
Germany came to ask Charles IX. to make a definite
concession of liberty of conscience to his subjects, the
young King had replied with a haughtiness and an anger
which boded much; but Catherine managed to atone for
this thoughtless outburst with such consummate skill, that
the eyes of even the most sagacious were blinded, and
Condé, 'di natura assai pronta a ricevere la varietà del-
l'impressioni,'[1] was more completely ensnared than anyone
else.

Favours
granted to
Condé.
The King
stands
godfather
to one of
his sons.

Personally, too, the Prince was now the object of a
constant system of artful schemes and flattering attentions.
The government of Picardie, the refusal of which he had
felt so deeply on a former occasion, had been conferred
upon him immediately after the Peace of Amboise. Other
favours, of slight importance, but bestowed in such a
manner as to make their value felt, had rendered it easier
to put him off in case he should proffer more important

[1] Davila.

requests. The Comté de Rotrou was erected, in his

favour, into a ' duché-pairie,' under the title of Enghien-le-Français, in order to preserve in his family a name already rendered illustrious by his two brothers.[1] At last, his second wife having given birth to a son, the King consented to become godfather to the child, and allowed the Admiral, in consideration of the difference of their religion, to represent him at the font.

The baptism was celebrated in June 1567, at Valery, where the Prince had assembled all the principal nobility and gentry among the Reformers, 'so that it was a most distinguished assemblage, and was well entertained by the said Prince, and amused by various innocent pastimes.' In the interval of hunting and other pleasure-parties there was much said concerning the 'agitations in Flanders,' and the measures prescribed by the King's injunctions. Everyone was preparing for war; but it was for a foreign war, 'which may well bring about a better union among us,' and if some of the company could not conceal their suspicions and their apprehensions as to the cause which ' all these projects would take,' yet still no concerted plan of action was resolved upon.[2]

The fêtes were still proceeding, when Condé was sent for afresh to Court. The Montmorencies, the Guises, the Châtillons were all there. The King had summoned them all, it was reported, to consult with them as to the

---

[1] The Comté d'Enghien, situated in the Low Countries, then belonged to his nephew, the Prince of Béarn (Henri IV.), by whom it was shortly afterwards sold.

[2] These details as well as the passages quoted are taken from a letter addressed to M. de Gordes by the Comte de Sault on his return from the baptism, June 30, 1567 ('Archives de Condé'). He was a Protestant nobleman who was one of the first to take up arms two months afterwards. He was killed at Saint-Denis. (See Appendix, No. XVI. Cf. Castelnau, La Popelinière.)

means of opposing the incursions of Spain. Never had the Prince been more cordially welcomed; never had the union between all the great men of the nation seemed more complete. 'I have this day seen the King,' wrote a magistrate who had just arrived at Saint-Germain,[1] 'holding the head of Monseigneur the Prince in his left hand, and that of Monseigneur the Cardinal de Bourbon in his right, and trying, as a jest, to force them to knock their foreheads together. Monseigneur d'Aumale was caressing Madame la Connétable, and Madame la Maréchale de Montmorency was present; Monseigneur le Maréchal himself exchanging amiable attentions with Monseigneur d'Aumale. Monseigneur le Cardinal de Châtillon was not far off. In short, all, without distinction, seemed on such good terms that I hope never again to see any great discord in France.' Four days after, the good president might have been present at a very different kind of scene, and have brought away from it, it is to be feared, rather less satisfaction and enthusiasm.

Altercation
between
Condé and
the Duc
d'Anjou.
The Court
casts off
the
mask.

At the time of the Orléans negotiations, Catherine had promised Condé the 'degree' of the late King of Navarre, that is, the rank and authority of Lieutenant-Général of the Kingdom; and this promise was one of the principal arguments which the Prince had used to urge upon his co-religionists the acceptance of the conditions of the peace. When the Edict of Amboise had been executed, Condé claimed the fulfilment of the promise. The Queen replied that nothing could be attended to till the English

---

[1] Truchon, first president of the Parliament of Grenoble. Letter to M. de Gordes of July 4, 1567. 'Archives de Condé.' (See Appendix, No. XVI.)

had been expelled; and when Havre had been re-
captured, she pressed forward the declaration of the
King's majority. There was no excuse for opposing such
a resolution. Condé was obliged to submit, and took the
oath of allegiance together with the other Princes. Since
then France had doubtless been in an unsettled state, but
no breach of the peace had occurred; there was no force
in the field, and as the King governed, or was reputed to
govern, in his own person, the state of the kingdom did
not call for the nomination of a Lieutenant-Général. But
now that a foreign war was imminent, Condé renewed
his claims. He demanded the Connétable's sword, which
Montmorency, owing to his advanced age, seemed disposed
to resign into the hands of the King; or at all events the
command of an army, a post to which his office, as
Governor of one of the most exposed provinces, namely
Picardie, seemed especially to call him. The Queen only
gave an evasive reply; but that very evening her second
son took the Prince aside, and demanded of him in loud
tones by what right he desired to usurp a dignity that
should belong only to himself; then, after some words
uttered in a menacing tone, retired without waiting for a
reply. The Duc d'Anjou was scarcely more than a boy;
and although he was already the object of his mother's disastrous favouritism, he had as yet exhibited no symptoms
of such unwonted and precocious ambition. Evidently
he had been schooled how to conduct himself. Condé,
surprised and irritated at this unexpected outburst, demanded some explanation of it. But the mask had been
already thrown off; there was no more talk of war with
Spain or of the formation of an army. ' What will you do,

CHAP.
IV.

1567
July 10.

Meeting
of the
Protestant
leaders.
They
resolve
to take
up arms.

then, with the Swiss?' asked he. 'We shall find abundant employment for them,' was the reply.

The Prince immediately, on the tenth of July, quitted the Court, making no secret of his deep displeasure; [1] the bandage had fallen from his eyes. He was followed by the Châtillons; a few leading Protestants were called together. They met twice, at Valery and at Châtillon. Their opinions were at first unfavourable to an armed resistance; notwithstanding all their grievances, they were willing still to wait. Condé had received from the Queen-Mother a reassuring and almost cordial letter. She assured him, ' on the faith of a Princess and of a woman of honour, that neither he nor his friends had anything to fear as long as her son would listen to her advice.' [2] Moreover, they were conscious that they were ill-prepared. Little was known of the intentions of the German Lutheran Princes; and if the English Ambassador, as was his wont, fanned the flame, if he still urged on the Huguenots to open resistance, [3] he had given them no hope of succour from his Sovereign. It might well be believed that Queen Elizabeth had not forgotten the results of her first intervention,—fruitless expenses, a fresh

---

[1] 'Monsieur le Prince has left this morning on his way home. It is whispered by several that he has sustained some great disappointment, which I leave to those who know more about it than I do. At all events, I don't think I am doing wrong in repeating what a thousand people have said—that he went away very gloomy and dissatisfied. (Guyon to M. de Gordes, Saint-Germain-en-Laye, July 11, 1567. 'Archives de Condé.' See Appendix, No. XVI.) ' The Prince of Condé went this ix of

July miscontentyd from the courte.' (Norreys to Cecil, Paris, July 10. State Paper Office.) This Norreys had replaced Smith, and had been received as English Ambassador by the King of France in the month of February 1567. See the note relative to this person, p. 262.

[2] Norreys to Cecil, August 23, 1567. State Paper Office. (Appendix, No. XXI.)

[3] The same to Queen Elizabeth, August 29. Ibidem. (Appendix, No. XXI.)

check of her armies, the final surrender of her claim upon Calais, a fearful plague which the garrison of Havre had brought back, and which had overspread England.[1] These, it must be allowed, were not encouraging recollections to her. The leaders of the Protestants of France could not therefore count upon active support from that quarter. But later tidings received from Court changed their first resolves. The Swiss were still advancing; two thousand of them were to be marched upon Paris, two thousand upon Orléans, and two thousand upon Poitiers. As soon as these cities had been garrisoned, the Edict of January was to be recalled and replaced by one of Draconian severity; the Protestants must be prepared to expect the most violent measures. The excitement was intense in the little assembly; but they still hesitated, and Condé exhibited great reluctance to be the first to break the peace. It was proposed by some that the Protestants should take possession peaceably of Orléans, and from thence should address respectful remonstrances to the King, making public at the same time, by means of a manifesto, the state of affairs; they would then be out of all immediate danger, and yet would avoid the appearance of rebellion. But Coligny reminded them that the peaceable occupation of Orléans was no longer possible, for the city was commanded by a citadel built since the last troubles, which must be taken by sheer force, under penalty of not being able to enter the city, or of being immediately dislodged from it. In his opinion there was only one way open to them—to attack the Swiss, to defeat them, and then to expel from France the Cardinal de Lorraine. And when it was objected that that prelate

[1] Darcies, ' Annals of Queen Elizabeth.'

never left the King, and that very soon His Majesty would be surrounded by the Swiss—'What does that matter?' exclaimed the fiery D'Andelot; 'who can possibly suspect us of aiming at the King's sacred person? At all events we should thus be nearer to him, and should be better able to enlighten him on all points, and to obtain reliable terms of peace.' This advice was approved, and a rendezvous was arranged for Michaelmas Day, the twenty-ninth of September, at Rosay in Brie.

The time and the place were selected in consequence of information gathered concerning the movements of the Court and the progress of the Swiss. It was hoped that the time and place would enable the Protestants to put a stop to the advance of the Swiss by a battle, and thus to be the first to surround the person of Charles IX., who was to pass the autumn with his mother at Monceaux, not far from Rosay. To seize the person of the King was always the first object in a party-struggle; for to succeed in this attempt was, in some sense, to give to the rebellion a show of legitimacy. The Protestants remembered what advantage their adversaries had gained by a coup-de-main of this sort at the beginning of the first civil war; and, notwithstanding the difference of circumstances, they hoped to be equally clever and equally fortunate.

Security of
the Court.

Complete secrecy was the one indispensable condition of success. The precautions necessary to ensure it were not unwisely taken. The leaders in the plot separated. No appeals were made except to perfectly trustworthy men, and all was managed surreptitiously. But it is impossible absolutely to prevent all disclosures in an enterprise of this kind, prepared nearly two months beforehand

and necessarily known to so many. Warnings reached the Court from all sides. At first they were treated with contempt. The Huguenots seemed so depressed, and the Court so strong in the force collected, that it seemed as though there were nothing to fear from them. Yet still the warnings multiplied. There was an unwonted degree of activity on the high roads. Several members of the Royal household had met on the way Protestant gentlemen, who tried, with some confusion, to conceal their cuirasses and arms beneath their travelling-cloaks. This information occasioned some uneasiness. Spies were sent to find out what was going on at Valery. Condé was alone, entirely taken up with his greyhounds and his hunting. At Châtillon, the Admiral was thinking only of his vintage, and D'Andelot was peaceably employed in planning new walks in his park at Tanlay. The Court grew tranquil again. Those who had sounded the alarm were treated as turbulent spirits,[1] and on the twenty-third of September the King wrote thus to the governor of a province:[2] 'It is impossible to live more peaceably than we do; there is not even a rumour of agitation.'

Three days afterwards, this security was succeeded by the keenest anxiety. Four hundred Protestant noblemen had arrived at Rosay. Condé and the Admiral, with a large force, had taken possession of Lagny on the twenty-

---

[1] ' .... I have no doubt that where you are you have not escaped your share of the alarms which during these last days have been given us, and that you have recovered from them with the same determination as we, namely, that we have clearly satisfied ourselves that they were only the lies and inventions of a few turbulent spirits who were only too anxious to see us once more surrounded by the troubles from which we have escaped....' (Robertet, Secretary of State, to M. de Gordes, Lieutenant of the King in Dauphiné. Monceaux, September 21, 1567. 'Archives de Condé.')

[2] M. de Gordes ('Archives de Condé.')

CHAP.
IV.
———
1567
'he King
uits Mon-
eaux for
Meaux
Sept. 26).

sixth of September. The King at once quitted Monceaux, a solitary country-house lying in the midst of an open plain, to throw himself into Meaux. All the Swiss who were to have been quartered for the night at Château-Thierry were hastily summoned thither, and the Maréchal de Montmorency was despatched in the direction of the Protestants to learn their designs and to try and arrest their progress. He found them all assembled at Torcy on the twenty-seventh of September, and was amicably received by them; but he was unable to induce them to abandon their projects. This conference, however, had delayed the confederates sufficiently; and when, towards evening, Condé proposed starting in order to get before the Swiss, he was too late; they were just entering Meaux.

At Court the whole day had been spent in discussions and in council. The Connétable urged strongly that the King should remain at Meaux; he had nothing to fear there, having with him the Swiss, and having other troops within speedy call; a retreat would be undignified, and would probably bring on an action, the issue of which no one could calculate; for the confederates, having once crossed swords with His Majesty's escort, could never hope to be forgiven such a crime. The Queen seemed at first to approve of this advice, but, either through weakness or deeply calculated craft, she yielded to the entreaties of the Cardinal de Lorraine, and in the evening again assembled a fresh council at the house of the Duc de Nemours. It was pretended that news had arrived of the reinforcement of Condé's troop, and of an impending attack. It was therefore resolved to leave Meaux. In vain did the courageous Chancellor exclaim that this was risking the life of the King, betraying the country's cause, and shutting out all hope of peace. The Court took its own way, and L'Hospital was never forgiven that speech.

The Swiss had arrived during the night. After three hours' rest they were ordered to arms, and they were told that the King relied on their fidelity and courage to open to him the road to Paris. These brave men answered by shouts of joy. Although they had marched twelve leagues the day before, they started off singing, and at such a pace that by daybreak they were already four leagues from Meaux.[1] They marched by the side of the high road, in order that they might not form into file, but retain their order of battle; the King was in the centre with an escort of his gentlemen; others on horseback rode as vedettes in advance and on either flank. All these noblemen were not fully armed, but wore only their steel caps and swords. About sunrise two hundred horsemen appeared to the left; the Prince de Condé rode forward from their ranks, and approaching bare-headed, begged leave to speak to the King. He received no answer, but a movement was perceptible in the column. The Connétable had caused Charles to pass over to the right flank, and in a few seconds the Prince found himself only confronted by a line bristling with pikes—the Swiss.

D'Andelot soon after joined Condé. Between them they had no more than five or six hundred horse. What could they do, with so small a troop, against six thousand of the best infantry in the world, supported by nearly

CHAP. IV.

1567 Sept. 28.

He is joined by the Swiss and departs during the night (Sept. 28). Attempt at Meaux. The King reaches Paris. Condé sleeps the night at Claye.

[1] According to Castelnau and the Duc de Bouillon, the King did not quit Meaux before the 29th; De Thou says the 28th. But I find among the correspondence of M. de Gordes, already quoted, a letter from the King announcing to him 'the wretched conspiracy and enterprise of his subjects.' This letter, commenced at Meaux on September 28, closes with a postscript dated from Paris the same day and written with different ink. The same letter was sent in duplicate on the 29th. (See Appendix, No. XXII.)

eight hundred cavalry? The King's departure from Meaux, and especially the arrival of the Swiss, had disturbed all the arrangements of the conspirators; they had not assembled half their followers. Nevertheless, either through enthusiasm, or through vexation, they divided into four troops, and appeared as though preparing to charge the strong battalion. On each side some of the gentlemen began skirmishing, 'but more with words than blows.' And now they were becoming excited; the Swiss began to kiss the earth and to perform their usual ceremonies indicative of their readiness for a general engagement. At last the young King, full of ardour and fury, drew his sword and prepared to charge with his gentlemen. Montmorency stopped him, and while he 'stood his ground'[1] with the Swiss, Charles IX. and his suite moved forward by a cross-road which led to Paris. The King soon met D'Aumale, Vieilleville, and some others, who had hastened to his help with all the men they could muster, and being by this reinforcement of his escort placed out of all danger, he reached the capital in a few hours.

The Swiss resumed their march, harassed rather than attacked by the Protestant cavalry. In the evening they arrived at Le Bourget, having only left behind them, since quitting Château-Thierry, about thirty men. Condé returned to sleep at Claye without having obtained any actual result, but not without having endangered his cause by a serious insult to Royalty. Charles IX. never forgot that the Protestants 'had made him journey from Meaux to Paris at a pace faster than a walk.'[2]

---

[1] 'faisait ferme.'

[2] Montluc. From this time for-   ward the hatred of Charles IX. to the Huguenots is discernible in his let-

The confederates remained three days at Claye, waiting, as they said, an answer to the petition that they had handed to the Maréchal de Montmorency, but really for the purpose of assembling their forces, and organizing them for action. Condé's plans had been promptly formed. He intended to hold the open country as near to Paris as possible, to stop the provisioning of the towns and the detachments which were joining the Royal army, —in a word to blockade the capital and the Court. He hoped that hunger would change the mind of the Parisians, and that thus the King, under pressure of a revulsion in popular opinion, would be compelled to grant him a favourable peace. If not, he would try to force a battle which might prove successful, before the whole of the Catholic troops should have time to unite. With the small army under his command, this was a course full of danger for himself and for such of his party as were in the field; but it was the best, perhaps the only one which he could take. While he was thus drawing the attention of his enemies upon himself and compelling the Royalists to draw all their forces towards Paris, the roads were open for the passage of the reinforcements which he had asked from Germany, or expected from the south of France; and lastly, the Huguenots could take possession of some important fortresses which would prove most useful to them should his army encounter a defeat.

As the Prince recollected that in the first troubles, out of so many places which had been held at first, his friends had not retained a dozen by the end of two months, he had recommended them not to think of occupying more

CHAP.
IV.

1567
Position
and plan
of Condé.
His head-
quarters
at Saint-
Denis
(Oct. 2).

ters as well as his acts and speeches. (See Appendix, No. XXII., his let-ter of October 8, 1567, to M. de Gordes.)

than the principal ones. Their success was complete at Orléans and at La Rochelle. The last war had demonstrated the importance of the former of the two cities; as for the latter, it presented an excellent base of operations in the west, and very valuable maritime resources. The capture of Montereau stopped the arrivals from the Yonne and the Upper Seine; Lagny closed the route from Brie; a small army which Montgomery and the Vidame de Chartres were bringing from Poitou occupied Étampes and Dourdan, and was on its way towards the bridge of Saint-Cloud, intercepting Beauce. Finally, Condé took up his head-quarters at Saint-Denis on the second of October. All the mills on the north side of Paris were burnt.

Fruitless
negotia-
tions.
Condé
summoned
by a
herald-at-
arms. Un-
successful
interview
with the
Conné-
table.

The Connétable had summoned to Paris the bands of Strozzi, who was in Picardie, as well as those of Brissac, who had already left Lyon. He had also called for the succour of the Duke of Alva; a regiment of volunteers was being recruited in Paris. Being cautious by nature as well as on principle, he was determined that every chance should be on his side; his forces were already superior to those of the enemy; but he did not think fit to make use of them before the arrival of the reinforcements which had been promised him, 'holding it manifestly imprudent to imperil the whole body politic by risking a doubtful engagement with madmen, whose only counsel now is their desperation, and their only wealth their arms and horses.'[1] Moreover, he continued to negotiate. He had discountenanced the retreat from Meaux, and regretted its consequences. He now wished to repair

[1] La Noue.

them, and to prevent the King 'from becoming alto-gether a puppet of the Guises.'[1]

Through his influence, Vieilleville and Morvilliers were commissioned to carry to the confederates overtures of peace ; but the only result of two interviews was a lengthy and vaguely worded petition, in which the rights of the aristocracy and questions of political reform took up as much space as the most justly founded complaints ; in which the privileges of the nobles were claimed side by side with liberty of conscience and the assembling of the States-General, the whole mingled with violent diatribes against the Guises, and against 'those Italians who, like vultures, were sucking the blood of France.' The allusion to the Queen was not to be mistaken. She understood it and never forgot it. The most zealous advocates of peace were compelled to be silent ; the petition could not even be discussed. But a herald-at-arms with the fleur-de-lis on his coat was sent to Saint-Denis, and presented himself there with a pomp long disused. There, in a loud voice, in the midst of the general surprise, he summoned, in the King's name, the Prince and ' other principal leaders and officers of a certain armed assemblage to present them-selves forthwith before the King, to render to him that obedience commanded and ordained of God, or to declare and avow promptly their sinister and iniquitous design, in order that upon their making the aforesaid declaration, the King might provide for it.'

The confederates were affected by the solemnity of this summons. They had had no misgivings in attacking the very escort of the King, but they hesitated to declare themselves enemies of his crown ; they had not shrunk

---

[1] 'Guisard.'—D'Aubigné (with a play upon the word 'Guise').

from an outrage upon majesty itself; and now a mere formality made them hesitate. They were afraid of the effect which this step might produce both in France and abroad; it might even stop the ' reîtres ' from coming to their assistance. So the next day a letter was sent to the King, of a very different character from those which had preceded it. This time there were no more pompous demands for a radical reform of the government. The Protestants confined themselves to a respectfully worded statement of grievances and a petition for their redress. The advocates of peace began to hope once more. The Connétable offered his nephews an interview, which took place at La Chapelle. But although Montmorency was far from wishing to push matters to an extremity, his excitable temperament rendered him very unfit for a work of conciliation. To the first words uttered by Condé, he replied loudly that the King would never tolerate two religions. The party instantly broke up. The Protestants had gained once more the right to say they were fighting for liberty of conscience.

Blockade of Paris. The Protestant army, 6,000 strong, extends its line too far.

Meanwhile the operations of the blockade proceeded, and the effects of it began to be felt in Paris. The Reformers had received reinforcements. Whatever obstacles D'Andelot had encountered during peace, in the exercise of his functions as Colonel-Général of the infantry, he had nevertheless regained some considerable influence over the veteran bands. In answer to his appeal, a good number of arquebusiers quitted Paris, Metz, and other garrisons to join him. A few levies made in Normandie also arrived very opportunely. Above all, Montgomery and the Vidame, after a feigned attack on the bridge of Saint-Cloud, had seized all the boats on the Seine, and had been enabled to cross at Saint-Ouen on the twenty-fourth of October.

The little army thus attained an effective force of four thousand infantry and two thousand cavalry. Condé was at Saint-Denis, covered on his front by Genlis, who occupied Aubervilliers. Clermont,[1] after having captured Charenton, had filled the river with piles and other obstacles, and had fallen back upon Le Bourget, where the extreme left was posted. The Admiral with the right wing held Saint-Ouen, and communicated by means of a bridge of boats with the detachments sent along the left bank as far as Argenteuil, and even Dampierre. All was succeeding so well with the Protestants, and the execution of their plans had met with so few obstacles, that they thought they might extend themselves farther. D'Andelot was despatched with five hundred horse and a good body of arquebusiers to occupy Pontoise. It was hoped thus to make the blockade still closer, to stop the advance of Strozzi, who was on his way from Picardie, and above all to protect the army against an imaginary incursion of the Spaniards. But the Duke of Alva never made his appearance; Strozzi had already passed; the surprise at Pontoise failed, and the absence of so large a detachment was destined to cost the Reformers dear.

Provisions could no longer be brought into Paris; and loud murmurs arose there, not unreasonably, against the inactivity of the Connétable, who with a tenfold superiority in numbers was allowing himself to be blockaded

The Catholic army, 19,000 strong, takes the offensive

---

[1] Antoine de Clermont, Marquis de Resnel, added to his own his mother's name of Amboise. He was half-brother of Prince Portien, and was killed in the St. Bartholomew massacre by his cousin the famous Bussy.

CHAP.
IV.

1567
and clears
the left
bank of
the Seine
(Nov. 4).

with impunity. Besides, there was a favourable opportunity for action ; Strozzi and Brissac had just brought up
their forces ; the Parisian regiment was under arms, and
the Royal army was now raised to a strength of sixteen
thousand infantry under eighty-four ensigns, supported
by three thousand cavalry. Above all, they were aware
of the serious mistake the enemy had made ; Montmorency
determined to profit by it.

On the fourth of November, a column which had made
a sortie from Saint-Cloud captured the corps-de-garde
which protected the bridge of boats at Saint-Ouen, burnt
the bridge, took Argenteuil, and swept the whole of the
left bank of the Seine below Paris. The victualling of the
capital was secured.

On the ninth, the advanced-guard of the Catholics
occupied La Chapelle. A reconnaissance was made in the
plain, which attacked and completely routed the main
guard of the Protestants. Dampierre, lieutenant of the
Admiral's gendarmes, was killed in the skirmish. All
night long bodies of light cavalry kept alarming the
Reformers in their quarters, in order to keep them from
reposing and to harass them. The Connétable was
anxious to give them battle next day, the tenth of November, the vigil of the Feast of St. Martin, one of the
patron saints of the French Crown.

Consulta-
tions of
the Pro-
testant
leaders.
Condé
decides to
accept
battle.

Condé had decided to accept battle. The question had
been warmly discussed by the leaders of his army.
Some wished to evacuate all the advanced posts, to fall
back upon Saint-Denis, and there to maintain themselves
by skirmishing till the arrival of D'Andelot. Others were
urgent for an immediate retreat. They called to mind
that they had not a single cannon ; that their infantry
numbered three thousand men, almost all arquebusiers,

without a single corps of pikemen which could hold the
field ; that the separation of D'Andelot had reduced their
cavalry to eighteen troops, amounting only to fifteen
hundred fighting men ; that they were moreover mounted
on ' courtauds,' or horses of small size, and very badly
equipped ; for, if the plan had not been devised of pulling
off hinges and gratings in order to enable the farriers
to make with the iron thus obtained heads for the poles
that had been intended for the tents at the fair of Landit,[1]
they would have had great difficulty in bringing any
lances into the field. Was it with such equipments as
these that they could hope to hold the ground against
the twenty thousand men and the splendid artillery of the
Royal army ?

But the Prince had replied that almost before they had
fallen back upon Saint-Denis they would be hemmed in
and surrounded by the enemy, separated from D'Andelot
and inevitably captured. As for an immediate retreat, it
would be impossible for them to march northwards,
having no fortress in that quarter. They must either
draw to the south towards Orléans, or once more ascend
by the valley of the Marne to meet the Germans ; but in
either of these movements they must of necessity expose
their flank to the Royalist army, which would then be
certain to attack them, and that in the open plain, under
circumstances most unfavourable to them ; so that their
defeat would be certain. On the other hand, while they
remained under the walls of the capital, they were profiting
by all the advantages of their position ; an army so numerous and composed of such heterogeneous elements as

---

[1] An old and celebrated fair which used to be held at Saint-Denis.

that of the Connétable could not possibly march out of a large city like Paris in an orderly and compact manner; the several corps would fall into line slowly and not simultaneously, and might thus, by means of a few well-timed and well-managed charges, be defeated in detail; the days, too, were short, and the sun would have set before the enemy could effectively bring to bear the whole advantage of his great numerical superiority. Their success might, it was true, be only momentary; but it would give them great prestige, and would at least diminish the inconveniences and dangers of a retreat. This counsel, which was adopted by the Admiral, prevailed.

Battle of
Saint-
Denis
(Nov. 10).
Position of
the Pro-
testant
army in
front of
that town,
between
Auber-
villiers
and Saint-
Ouen.

This decision had been arrived at during the night between the ninth and tenth, and they were still deliberating on the subject 'in the saddle,'[1] when, shortly after daybreak, their scouts arrived with the information that the Royal army was debouching from the Faubourg Saint-Denis. The Protestant generals had only just time to get to their posts in all haste. Leaving in Saint-Denis his small troop of pikemen, Condé drew up the 'bataille' in front of that town, between Aubervilliers and Saint-Ouen, forming thus a kind of living curtain between two bastions. As he had so few men, and had to fill up a very extended line—about three thousand five hundred 'mètres'—he had formed his cavalry 'en haye,'[2] in single line. Some companies of arquebusiers covered the flanks and joined those who were holding the two villages. The Admiral, supported in rear by Saint-Ouen, with the cavalry of the advanced-guard, was protected on the right by small

---

[1] 'Le cul sur la selle.'—D'Aubigné.   [2] See note, p. 157.

woods and gardens filled with infantry. The cavalry of
the rear-guard, under Vardes and Genlis, was before
Aubervilliers; the ground not offering them on this side
any point d'appui, they had occupied a mill a little in
advance of their left; a ditch with an épaulement, dug
between this mill and the village, concealed a line of
arquebusiers.

This very simple order of battle was so well suited to
the positions they occupied, that the little army was
drawn up long before the Royal troops, who were
marching out of Paris in a single column, had deployed
into line.

The Connétable had not expected that the Protestants
would accept battle in the open plain, broken only by a
single paved road, without any ditch on either side. He
supposed that, alarmed by the reconnaissance of the previous day, they would have entrenched themselves in
their quarters, and at most have there tried to maintain
their position. His plan was to capture simultaneously
the two villages which protected the right and left of the
Reformers, and then to attack Saint-Denis with his whole
force. A few companies of ordonnance and a few of the
arquebusiers, supported by the Parisian regiment, he
thought would be sufficient to dislodge the Admiral from
Saint-Ouen; this left wing was commanded by the Duc
de Nemours and the Duc de Longueville, by Thoré, and
several others. Aubervilliers, which was thought to be
better defended, was to be bombarded by the artillery,
which was to be supported on the left by the Swiss, and
on the right by the French bands, as well as by the
gendarmes of Cossé and Biron. Still farther to the right,
Damville and D'Aumale, with their companies of ordon-

CHAP.
IV.

1567
Nov. 10.

The Royal
army
marches
out of
Paris.
Tactics of
the Ad-
miral to
surround
the Pro-
testant
army.

nance, were to turn the flank at Aubervilliers and to march straight upon Saint-Denis. Upon Saint-Denis was also to be directed a powerful squadron which the Connétable, accompanied by his eldest son, commanded in person. He intended to advance between the two attacks, and there subsequently to effect a junction with the victorious troops of the two wings.

Mont-
morency
prema-
turely gives
the order
to com-
mence the
attack on
the right
and left.
These
attacks
repulsed.

The Catholic cavalry was already taking up its position in front of La Chapelle and of La Villette. The fine tall horses of the gendarmes, their splendid armour, their uniforms and standards emblazoned with crosses, contrasted singularly with the modest equipment of the Reformers, with their plain white surcoats and their mean-looking animals. A battery of fourteen guns, placed on the heights of La Villette, had just opened fire upon Aubervilliers, when Montmorency, surprised and seemingly vexed at the position the enemy had taken up, without waiting for the effect that this cannonade must have produced, without even waiting for his infantry or the whole of his cavalry, gave the order for an immediate attack.

Cossé and Biron were the first to advance towards Aubervilliers, but they were stopped by the ditch which had been dug in front of the village. Genlis chose this moment to charge, and drove them back in disorder, without the possibility of their artillery, which had been covered by this movement, being of any use to them. Damville and D'Aumale, who took the place of the first squadrons, were equally unfortunate.

On the side of Saint-Ouen, the Admiral's troops had resisted, with like success, the attack of the Catholics. Coligny, in pursuing the retreating gendarmes, met the regiment of Parisians, who, 'gilded like chalices,'[1] were trying to form line with the inexperience of amateur soldiers who had left home that morning. The affair was over in a moment. The volunteers, who were unprepared for such a reception, could not resist the charge of the veteran Protestant soldiers, and fled in disorder. 'They long remembered it.'[2]

At the centre the Connétable had drawn up his cavalry in two lines. The first was led by his eldest son; he himself commanded the second, and was advancing in that order against the Prince de Condé, when the latter, leaving a third of his force to oppose the front line of the Catholics, wheeled past him with the pick of his men, and bursting suddenly upon the left flank of the second line, charged it with such fury that in an instant the great squadron was broken. The Connétable's horse rolled over; Stuart, the Scotchman, summoned him to surrender; but all the answer he got from Montmorency—'whose men deserted him, but not his valour'[3]—was a blow from the hilt of his broken sword, which fractured his jaw. At the same moment the old man fell, mortally wounded by a bullet which passed through his body. Condé's anticipations were coming true. Success was crowning the valour of the Protestants. 'If my master,' exclaimed the Turkish Ambassador, who from the top of Montmartre witnessed this terrible conflict, 'if my master had only a thousand of those white surcoats to place at the head of each of his armies, the universe would not hold out against him two years.'

But a complete victory would have been a miracle;

---

[1] 'Bien dorez comme calices.'—D'Aubigné. [2] La Popelinière.
[3] D'Aubigné.

CHAP.
IV.

1567
Nov. 10.

day on all
sides; but
the con-
fusion
caused by
the loss of
the Conné-
table
allows the
Protest-
ants to re-
enter
Saint-
Denis in
order.

and already the fortunes of the day were changing.
Genlis and Vardes, exhausted by three engagements, were
no longer able to move before Aubervilliers, and were
receiving, without reply, the fire which the artillery had
reopened.　The Catholic gendarmes were rallying around
the Swiss and the veteran bands who had just taken up
line, and were preparing for a fresh and decisive assault on
the village.　On the other hand, the Admiral had pursued
the Parisians too far, and taken in flank by Chavigny with
a fresh body of horse, he had just been completely routed.
He himself had been run away with by a hard-mouthed
horse, and thus had been lost sight of by his own men,
who fancied that he had either been taken prisoner, or
was being concealed by some friend; for three days
search was made for him in Paris.　Finally, the Maréchal
de Montmorency, having routed the Protestant companies
who were opposed to him, was offering battle to the victorious squadron of the Prince.

Condé was just about to be utterly defeated, when
along the whole line of the Royal army a rumour spread
that the Connétable had been wounded and captured.
On this news his sons, Damville and Thoré, hastened to
his assistance, taking with them all the gendarmes who
were fighting with them on the two wings.　No order
was given, no one before the action having been appointed
as lieutenant to the jealous Connétable; and no Duc de
Guise was there to fill his place and repair his omissions.
The relics of the Protestant advanced-guard were no
longer pursued, and were enabled once more to join the
'bataille;' the Catholic infantry, having been left unsup-
ported to the attack of Aubervilliers, could not prevent
Genlis from retreating almost unmolested from the village.

Thus all the cavalry of the Reformers met at the centre, and while the enemy was hastening to the relief of Montmorency, Condé was extricated, at the very moment when his horse fell dead under him from the stroke of a lance. Nightfall overtook the Royal army in the midst of unutterable confusion. Favoured thus by darkness and by the disorder, the Protestants slowly retreated upon Saint-Denis.

The Catholics remained masters of the field. The Protestants could not claim a victory; but, considering the unequal forces, the mere fact of not having declined battle was honourable to their valour, and it was a glorious achievement to have accomplished an orderly retreat after having given to the enemy a series of temporary checks. They had, no doubt, been aided by the mistakes of their adversaries no less than by the good fortune which had deprived the enemy, at the most critical moment, of the Connétable. But they had shown that they knew how to profit by the favours of Providence,—and in this consists often the secret of success. Condé could claim the chief share in the honours of the day, and could repeat with pride the old Latin proverb, 'Audentes fortuna juvat.'

Shortly after midnight, the silence which reigned in the plain apprised the Reformers that the enemy had reentered Paris. They immediately mounted their horses, and before daybreak they were in their old quarters of the day before. On the morning of the eleventh, D'Andelot, who had returned, on the evening of the battle, from his expedition, dashed across the plain with five hundred horse, made a demonstration against the Catholic corps-de-garde at La Chapelle, and carried fire up to the very walls of Paris, without any sortie having

Marginal notes:

CHAP. IV.

1567 Nov. 10.

The result of the battle is glorious for Condé.

The Reformers retire to their quarters during the night.

been made to repulse him. The Connétable had not
survived his wounds. His death, by leaving the command
vacant, and the field open to every intrigue, paralysed the
Royal army.

On the other hand, the Prince, having made this first
display of his force, and having succeeded in discouraging
the enemy, did not choose to maintain any longer a position so uselessly perilous. Profiting by the forced inaction of the Catholics, he withdrew from before Paris,
and hastened to meet the reinforcements which were
being sent to him from Germany.

Condé
strikes
tents on
the 13th,
places his
wife in
security at
Orléans,
and rallies
the Poite-
vins at
Montereau.

He set out on the thirteenth of November,[1] directing
his course first towards Montereau, where he had appointed a rendezvous for a contingent of eighteen troops
of cavalry and twenty-seven of infantry which Poitou
and Guyenne had just furnished to him. He had also
another reason for this march. Before advancing far into
the east, the Protestant leaders, wishing to place in safety
those whom they held most dear, without uselessly sepa-
rating their forces, had resolved to assemble their families
in Orléans, and to fortify that city only, where also the
troops from Provence, from Dauphiné, and from Gascogne
were to meet. But they had first to gain Orléans. The
Princess, the Admiral's wife, and the wives of the gentlemen from the north or east of France, could not reach
Orléans without passing near Paris and exposing themselves to the risk of being captured by some Catholic

[1] According to some historians, on
the fifteenth of November. But in a
letter of the fourteenth, the King
announced that the Prince de Condé
had commenced his retreat on the
thirteenth, at seven o'clock in the
evening. ('Archives de Condé.' See
Appendix, No. XXII.) It is most
likely that the Protestants did not
uselessly prolong their sojourn under
Paris.

corps. All these ladies therefore joined together to form a sort of convoy, the passage of which was facilitated by the movement on Montereau. They were met by the Protestant army on the second day of their journey. On meeting his wife, Condé received sad tidings. His mother-in-law, the Marquise de Rothelin, disregarding all warnings, and trusting to the substantial walls of her château at Blandy, had refused to quit that place, and had retained with her three of the Prince's children, as well as several of his friends. She had just been treacherously surprised by her nephew D'Entragues.[1] Her house had been sacked. She herself, her grandchildren, and the inmates of the château had been carried off prisoners to the Louvre.

La Rochefoucauld joined the confederates. He brought with him four guns[2] and nearly ten thousand men recruited in Poitou and Guyenne. Pont-sur-Yonne was captured, and the army marched back towards the Seine, leaving in Montereau a rear-guard of seven companies, under the command of Renti, to dispute for a time with the Catholics that important post, and draw them off from the siege of Orléans, which was not yet in a position to hold out.

For now the Royal troops had marched out of Paris. The Court had speedily recovered from the shock of the

Reorganization of the Royal

---

[1] François de Balzac, married to Jacqueline de Rohan, Dame de Gyé, niece to the Marquise de Rothelin. He married as his second wife Marie Touchet, and became the father of the Marquise de Verneuil.

[2] The Protestant artillery was thus composed of six pieces; 'two large double cannon, a large culverin, which went by the name of the Queen-Mother, and three field-pieces, which they named the Queen's maids, or pets.' ('Journal of the Movements of the Army of the Prince de Condé, &c.' State Paper Office.) We have made several quotations from this curious document, the great length of which has prevented our inserting it in full in the Appendix.

CHAP.
IV.

1567
Nov.

army, com-
manded by
the Duc
d'Anjou.
It quits
Paris.

Connétable's death.   That event in securing to the ardent
Catholics an undoubted preponderance, at the same time
favoured the designs of Catherine relative to her beloved
son.   The disappointment, too, at the fruitless issue of
the battle of Saint-Denis was forgotten ; success, it was
thought, would be none the less sure and complete by
being retarded ; for this time it was in no danger of being
compromised by a spirit of conciliation.   The glory of ex-
terminating the heretics was reserved for Monsieur, and
on the seventeenth he was appointed Lieutenant-Général
of the King.   Médicis had skilfully demonstrated the necessity of cutting short all the rivalries which divided the
leading generals of the army, by placing at its head a ' son
of France,' and it was hoped that wise counsels might
make up for the utter inexperience of the young general.
Moreover, he gave promise of serviceable and even of
brilliant qualities.   Although he had within him even then
the germ of that deep depravity which was destined so
shamefully to sully the throne of France, it would be un-
fair to confound the attractive person of the Duc d'Anjou
with the gloomy portrait of Henri III.   Above all, he had
no lack of soldiers.   The Margrave of Baden sent him
' reîtres ' from Germany, and D'Aumale had just started
for Lorraine, in order to open up the road for them by
arresting the progress of those troops which the enemy
was expecting.   Nevers was bringing the veteran bands
of Piedmont and some Italian troops ; D'Aremberg was
only a few miles from Paris with a contingent furnished
by the Duke of Alva.   But Monsieur could have dispensed
even with these reinforcements ; and, without waiting for
them, he put his army in march on the track of the Protestants.

Followed, although at some little distance, by the Royal troops, Condé perceived that he was in danger of meeting fresh obstacles on his line of retreat, and of finding the passages across the river strongly guarded. The Duc de Guise had collected a small army in Troyes, and was preparing to defend the Seine. The confederates therefore made a feigned attack on Sens, and, while Guise was advancing to the succour of that town, they rapidly pushed on to the banks of the Seine, captured Bray and Nogent with great audacity and success, crossed the river, drew back upon Bray the detachment which held Montereau, broke the bridges, and advanced towards the Marne. As soon as they had reached the right bank, they drew in the rear-guard, rallied their whole force at Épernay, and then, without going far from the river, advanced slowly into the plain to the east of that town, that they might avoid Châlons.[1] Meanwhile overtures of peace had been made, and for several days some communications had been exchanged through a certain captain named Combault, who had been captured at Bray, where he was in command for the Duc de Nemours. At last propositions of a more serious nature came from the Court through the Marquise de Rothelin. The Queen, in order to win over Condé, had

CHAP.
IV.
1567
Dec.

The Protestants cross the Seine near Châlons. Truce.

---

[1] There are in the Bibliothèque impériale several letters from Condé to the King, to the Queen, and to the Duc d'Anjou, relative to these negotiations; among others one dated from Bray, December 7, one from the neighbourhood of Épernay, dated December 16, and two from Saint-Martin, dated December 17. (See Appendix, No. XXIII.) Saint-Martin is on the Marne, about twenty-two kilomètres from Épernay and eleven below Châlons. Sarry, where the extreme left of the Reformers was surprised some days afterwards, is also on the Marne, about six kilomètres above the last-named town. It is therefore probable that, while negotiating, and before they had decided upon any plan of operations, the Protestants had marched slowly towards the east, in order to get beyond Châlons, which had been all along occupied by a Royal garrison.

CHAP.
IV.

1567
Dec.

Negotia-
tion with
the Court
and with
the Ger-
mans.

set his mother-in-law and children at liberty. A truce was concluded, and the leaders of the Reformers began to deliberate.

Should they wait there for the issue of the conferences, and run the chance of having to give battle in the plains of Châlons with the forces then available? Should the infantry remain shut up in the towns which bordered on the Seine and Marne, while the whole of the cavalry went quickly to fetch the Germans? Should they march with the whole army to meet the latter? Such were the three plans, on one of which they must decide. But in order to appreciate their decision, it must be understood on what terms the negotiations were conducted with the German Lutheran Princes.

It was to the Elector Palatine, their old ally, that the confederates had appealed. He had hesitated considerably as to sending them reinforcements. The King's deputies had produced letters written by several Reformers, expressing their satisfaction with the way in which the conditions of the peace had been observed, blaming the ambition of Condé and the Admiral, and averring that religion had nothing whatever to do with their having taken up arms, but that it was a mere rebellion. The Elector, in great perplexity, sent to Paris to learn the real state of matters, and on the return of his ambassador, convinced that the question of religion was not so foreign to the dispute as had been represented, he despatched his soldiers towards Lorraine, under the command of his second son, Casimir. He was a very young general, being only twenty-six years old; but he was full of ability and fire, and spoke French as well as he did German.[1] When

[1] 'Industrius et acer, gallicæ linguæ et maternæ ex æquo peritus.'

the Bishop of Rennes was about to make a fresh remonstrance, the Elector Palatine had replied that his son was
of age, and he would not prevent him from going ; that
Condé and his associates had taken up arms in defence of
the King's most Christian Majesty and to secure the good of
his subjects ; and that in going to his assistance, his son remained faithful to the traditions of his family, which had
always been well disposed towards the Crown of France.[1]

These details were known to the confederates. They had
just arrested the younger Lanssac, who had accompanied
the envoy of the Elector on his journey to France, and
who was on his way back to Court with the despatches
containing the information just detailed. Such being the
case, was it possible to hesitate any longer ? If Condé did
not at once go to meet the Germans, their enthusiasm
would be very likely to cool down, and the Protestants
would lose the help they so ardently desired. Were they
to give battle ? That was not to be thought of till they
had received the reinforcements. Were they to wait for
the issue of the conferences ? That would be to display
great simplicity ; for the Court was only negotiating in
order to delay the Protestants from action, and thus gain
time for Monsieur to come up to them and surround them.
Whilst they were parading the Cardinal de Châtillon from
town to town, without giving him any answer, without
making any definite overture, Nevers was bringing up
nearly ten thousand men to the Duc d'Anjou, and already
portions of the Royal army, debouching from Châlons,
were appearing on the right bank of the Marne. At
length, on the last day of the armistice, and before its

N . . . . to Cecil, Strasbourg . . . .   Hatfield,' London, 1740, fo.
1567. 'A Collection of State Papers   [1] 'Hatfield Papers.'
. . . . left by W. Cecil . . . . from

CHAP.
IV.

1567
Dec.

The Re-
formers
march to
meet their
'reîtres,'
and cross
the Meuse
and the
Moselle.
They
march
in splendid
order.
Their great
hardships.
Condé's
firmness.

conclusion had been proclaimed, Brissac suddenly seized the château of Sarry, which covered the left of the confederates; and the next day the latter began their march.

They had abandoned the disastrous project of leaving their infantry on the Marne, which would have been to hand it over to certain and unnecessary destruction. The Admiral, who had suggested this course, had yielded to the powerful reasons by which Condé had opposed it. But, in order to ensure rapidity of movement, the Prince had taken care to assemble, for several days past, all the horses which could be brought together, and had caused them to be distributed among the companies of infantry. The best animals had been reserved for a troop of picked arquebusiers, which D'Andelot had raised, and which he commanded in person. It was thus possible to reach the Meuse by forced marches and in good order. Condé led the way with the 'bataille;' the Admiral, with his corps, followed; the light cavalry, under Mouy, brought up the rear, and was supported by D'Andelot's mounted arquebusiers.

The army crossed the Meuse at Saint-Mihiel and continued its route towards the Moselle. The cold was intense, provisions scarce, the hardships great. Their courage had been buoyed up by the hope of meeting the 'reîtres;' but now they had arrived in Lorraine, they could find no tidings of the Germans. Even the most stout-hearted gave way to gloom and anxiety. Desertions seemed impending. Already Clermont d'Amboise and Genlis had disappeared, the former 'without even bidding them farewell, and with little colour of excuse;' the latter 'requesting leave of absence to go to Picardie, where he could be of great service,' but in a tone which admitted of but one

reply. These were grievous examples. Condé and Coligny alone contended against the general discouragement,
the latter always serious, and sternly rebuking the least
murmur; the former always amiable, stimulating afresh
their drooping cheerfulness by his merry suggestions and
ever-ready repartees.[1] Thus one day, when a grumbling
officer asked him whither he was leading them after this
fashion, he replied, 'We are going to join our allies.'
'And what if we do not find them?' 'Well then, we
shall have to blow upon our fingers, for it is very cold.'
A hearty laugh arose from all the bystanders, at the expense of the indiscreet questioner.

They had just crossed the Moselle at Pont-à-Mousson,
when the vedettes announced to Condé that they had
sighted an immense body of men on the march. The
Prince at once sent out to reconnoitre. Might it not possibly be the Royal army, of which he had not for several
days had any tidings? He was making arrangements for
fighting, at all risks, when he perceived approaching towards him the young Count Palatine and his staff. The
two armies had, without knowing it, been for some hours
marching parallel to each other. Casimir had brought
to the aid of Condé six thousand five hundred horse, three
thousand foot, and four field-pieces.

The Protestants of the two nations welcomed each other
joyfully. But, after the first embraces and the first excitement of delight, an anxious thought cast a fresh cloud
upon the countenances of the French. Their prudent
brothers of Germany declared that they would not stir till

Meeting
between
Condé and
Prince
Casimir
(Jan. 11,
1568).
Sacrifices
in order to
pay the
'reitres.'

---

[1] '. . . Quæ tamen Condæi, ut
erat natura læta, humanis ac festivis
sermonibus, inde gravibus Colinei
increpationibus repressa sunt.'—
Thuanus, book xlii.

they had received an instalment of the sum that had been promised them. The exchequer of the army was empty, and the purses of its leaders not much better furnished. Such, however, was their spirit, and so urgent their need, that no one kept back a single trinket or a single crown-piece. From the Prince, who was the first to sacrifice his gold chains and his plate, to the very poorest groom who gave up his last mite, they all, to a man, joined in the general sacrifice, and ' that brave band of beggars '[1] produced among them upwards of a hundred thousand livres. The Germans then consented to go forward.

The Royal army had not taken any steps to prevent this junction of forces. When the Reformers had begun their retreat from Épernay, there were not wanting flat-terers who represented to Monsieur that he had driven the Huguenots from France,[2] and he, who was already inclined to an indolence very inconsistent with the hard-ships of a soldier's life, had stopped at Châlons to cele-brate his easy victory. When it became known at Court that the little army of the Reformers had effected its re-treat unmolested, and that Condé was on his way back, reinforced by nearly ten thousand men, the inactivity of the Royal army became the theme of general indignation. The blame was cast upon the advisers of the Duc d'Anjou, and their place was supplied by others, who were deemed more capable of enforcing discipline and of giving a wise direction to operations. The new Catholic generals thought that the Protestants would make for Bourgogne, in order to avoid the districts which they had already exhausted. Monsieur therefore threw supplies into the towns on the Marne and the Seine, and prepared to march,

[1] D'Aubigné.   La Noue.

with his remaining troops, parallel to the Reformers, intending to wait till their lack of money and provisions
should have disorganized their army before giving them
battle. But the Protestants, that they might not be reduced to want, had taken such precautions as were almost
unprecedented in those times, and are always difficult to
carry out. The credit of these is due to Coligny. Possessed of a logical intellect and a capacity for organization, he was accustomed to say in discussions about
bringing an army into the field, 'We must begin the
creation of this monster at his belly.'[1] He had collected
a considerable number of pack-horses, had distributed
some of them among the several companies for the transport of the baggage, and told off others for the commis-
sariat service. It was strictly forbidden to exceed a
certain number of beasts of burden; regular distributions
of provisions took place on certain days and in fixed
quantities, and foraging was effected wherever it was
possible. A regular system had also been carried out
respecting quarters; the infantry was always to take the
centre, massed in heavy columns; the cavalry was to be
cantoned in the surrounding villages; every night these
cantonments were to be barricaded and entrenched; detachments of arquebusiers were to be mixed with the
cavalry; and, finally, a rendezvous was appointed in case
of an alarm. On the march the army was always to be
preceded at some distance by an advanced-guard of
twelve hundred cavalry, the half of whom were to be
armed with the arquebuse.

Owing to this combination of arrangements, admirably

[1] La Noue.

conceived, and very remarkable for that age; owing, moreover, to the firmness and foresight which were brought to bear upon its execution, the Protestants were able to pass without much inconvenience through districts which were entirely hostile to them, to march always compactly, almost in sight of the enemy, in good order and in excellent discipline, and without being exposed to surprises from dispersion when in quarters. They thus arrived unmolested in Beauce, after having passed the Marne near its source and the Seine above Châtillon, and then reached Orléans by Auxerre, Bléneau, and Montargis. They had not been stopped by the enemy's towns. They had been careful to avoid useless expeditions, and the only one that they did risk had resulted in their repulse at Crevant. It is melancholy to have to add that they avenged this check by the massacre of the inoffensive inhabitants of Irancy. The Royal army, on the other hand, notwithstanding its numerical superiority, had not been able, or did not dare, to offer them battle, and that long and splendid march had been marked by only one single engagement. The Italian garrison of Châtillon-sur-Seine had expected great results from a few foot-traps which they had dispersed about the fords; but the snare was soon discovered, and did not cause much loss. Still it made some little delay, of which the Italians took advantage to make a brisk attack upon the rear-guard. Condé was already in quarters at Ancy-le-Franc; but upon hearing the firing, he immediately despatched to the scene of action a few troops of ' reîtres;' and Schomberg, the German, soon returned with two ensigns which he had captured. To reward him, and to encourage his fellow-countrymen, the Prince placed around his neck the only gold chain which he had retained, and which, as a badge of his rank, he was accustomed to wear.

Orléans had been seriously menaced during the expedition into Lorraine. But, as had been ordered and foreseen by Condé, the Gascons and Dauphinois, under the command of Mouvans and 'the seven viscounts,'[1] had arrived in time to relieve the city; and, not satisfied with their success, had proceeded to invade Touraine. They had already captured Blois and Beaugency, and were besieging Montrichard, when they received the order to join the army, which had just gone into cantonment in Beauce, and of which the full strength thus amounted to upwards of thirty thousand men.

Orléans
relieved.
Condé
rallies the
Gascons
and the
Dauphi-
nois, and
finds him-
self at the
head of
30,000
men.

It was not five months since Condé had commenced the campaign with only eighteen hundred horse. At the head of a party which was poor and feeble in numbers, threatened by a formidable coalition of the French and Spanish Courts, he had opened the campaign by a bold and as it were desperate stroke. He failed, yet without losing his courage; for a whole month he kept at bay, with a handful of men, a large and disciplined army, fought a heroic battle which covered him with glory, and finally seized upon the opportunity which fortune gave

[1] The Vicomtes de Bourniquet, Montclar, Paulin, Caumont, Serignan, Rapin and Montagut, commonly called 'the seven viscounts,' because they were united by a cordial agreement, were the principal leaders of the Protestant party in Rouergue, Quercy, and Albigeois, as Mouvans was in Provence, Montbrun in Dauphiné, and D'Acier, younger brother of Crussol, in Languedoc. All these partisans had taken up arms at the opening of the second civil war, and, notwithstanding the efforts of the governors of the provinces, they had succeeded in effecting their junction. After several operations, conducted with remarkable intelligence, and after one or two reverses, they had divided their forces on the urgent representations of the Princesse de Condé. Montbrun and D'Acier remained to sustain the cause of their party in the south; Mouvans and the seven viscounts marched towards Orléans.

CHAP.
IV.

1568
Feb.

him to escape from a critical position, and fell back upon the Moselle, without allowing himself to be attacked. This long and trying retreat, and the well-planned and well-conducted march by which he subsequently returned into the very heart of France, would have been remarkable in any age. In short, the rising of the provinces was directed to a clearly defined issue. Instead of allowing the insurrection to exhaust itself in isolated efforts, the leaders of the cause received orders to aim, above all, at uniting their forces and concentrating them towards a single point. Thus it came to pass, that in the month of February 1568, Condé found himself at the head of a large and splendid army.

Condé invests Chartres (Feb. 23). Siege of that city interrupted by the peace.

It was now his turn to desire a battle. It was the object of Monsieur to avoid it. The latter, moreover, had not crossed the Seine, and by the time the Protestants were at Orléans, he had re-entered Paris, continuing to wait for the time when the Protestant army should break up for want of money and supplies. Had Condé consulted only his enthusiasm, he would at once have gone in pursuit of him. The capture of that great Babylon had always been the dream of the Protestants, and at this time, as we have said, its capture seemed to them to be the legitimate consummation of their success, the close of the whole civil war. Moreover, it had been the intention of the Prince to march straight upon Paris after his junction with the Germans. The difficulty of the return through Champagne, and the necessity of rallying the Gascons, had induced him to abandon this plan; and now again he felt compelled to postpone it. He preferred to adopt a course which permitted him to give the Parisians and the Court a severe shock, or to force Monsieur to

take the field again and accept battle. Having accomplished twenty leagues[1] in two days, he arrived under the
walls of Chartres with three thousand horse, and invested
the town on the twenty-third of February. But he had
not been able to prevent D'Ardelay from introducing a
detachment which raised the garrison to the number of
four thousand men. Operations commenced at once.
Condé wished to hasten the siege, and, notwithstanding
the inferiority of his artillery (he had only nine guns), the
breach appeared practicable at the end of six days.

The assault was about to begin, when it was perceived
that a solid intrenchment had been thrown up behind the
breach and mounted with cannon. The besiegers then
set to work to divert the course of the Eure, which
worked the water-mills in the town, and although
Linières, who carried on the defence with much vigour
and intelligence, had erected some windmills, he soon
found himself short of supplies. Pressed more closely
than ever by solicitations and reproaches, Monsieur could
not allow the key of the granary of Paris to be captured without striking a blow. Nevertheless, he judged it
sufficient to send La Valette there with eight hundred
horse and a few companies of Italian infantry. Condé,
informed of this step, sent the Admiral, with the whole
of the cavalry, to meet him, and the reinforcement was
surprised at Houdan and cut to pieces. It seemed that
there was nothing for Chartres but to capitulate, when
the news arrived that a peace had been signed on the
thirteenth of March.

The King put into force once more the Edict of
Amboise, and suppressed the restrictions which had

---

[1] About fifty miles.

been introduced in the interval between the two civil
wars. The Prince and his adherents were re-established
in all their property, emoluments, and dignities. Condé
was 'designated and reputed a loyal kinsman, and a
faithful subject and servant of the King.' The Reformers
were to disperse, to restore the towns which they held,
and to discharge the Germans immediately. The King
advanced the hundred thousand *écus d'or* due to these
latter. He bound himself, by a secret article in the
treaty, to disband *at some future time* his foreign troops
and a part of the French troops.

The peace
is con-
lemned by
he Ad-
niral.
Such were the principal terms agreed upon at Lonju-
meau between the negotiators on either side, through the
mediation of Norreys, the English Ambassador.[1] When
this treaty was submitted to the chiefs of the Protestant
army, the Admiral attacked it violently, and this time
most reasonably. It would be madness, he said, on their
part to lay down their arms and give up their towns
without any security, or any guarantee beyond an empty
promise. The attack at Meaux and their successes, could
only have envenomed the hatred which had been long

---

[1] Sir Harry Norreys, created Lord
Norreys in 1589. His father, who
was suspected of being in the good
graces of Anne Boleyn, had been
executed in the reign of Henry VIII.
His grandson, created Earl of Berk-
shire, died without male issue. The
barony of Norreys passed into the
Bertie family, and is now the
courtesy title of the eldest son of the
Earl of Abingdon. De Thou states
that the mediators of the Peace of
Chartres were Sackville, Lord Buck-
hurst, and Guido Cavalcanti the
Florentine. But these two persons
were not sent to France till 1571,
to present the congratulations of
Elizabeth to Charles IX., on the
occasion of his marriage. It was
then that they began to negotiate
for the marriage of the Duc d'Anjou
(Henri III.) with their sovereign, a
negotiation which was speedily interrupted by the massacre of St.
Bartholomew. Darcies ('Annals of
Queen Elizabeth') and other English
historians state positively that Norreys was the mediator; and this
assertion is confirmed by the correspondence preserved in the State
Paper Office. This mediation was,
however, of little importance.

cherished against them, confirmed the determination of
the Court, and tightened the shackles which they had gone
to war to break. This peace was only an instrument for
crushing them more efficiently. Was it then so absolutely
necessary for them to accept it? No doubt the ranks of
the Gascons were being diminished by desertion, the
Germans were not paid, and were, by their marauding
propensities, which it was impossible to check, exaspera-
ting the population. But they were certain of capturing
Chartres, and its capture would restore their spirits, furnish them with abundant resources, and perhaps enable
them to undertake the siege of Paris. It was not for
them, he urged, at the moment when they were gaining
so many advantages, to accept such a treaty.

Condé nevertheless ratified it. Despite Coligny and
the evidence he adduced, public opinion in his camp was
far from being opposed to peace, and it seemed difficult
to him to maintain his army any longer. In the first
place, the King having put the Edict of Amboise into
force, there was no pretext for continuing the war; and it
was repugnant to the feelings of the Prince thus to prolong it without apparent reason. For 'he loved his
country and had pity on the people,'[1] says a contemporary
writer, who assuredly was not given to considerations of
'pity,' and was not favourable to the Huguenots.[2] He
sacrificed, therefore, the results which he might have derived from his splendid campaign to a kind of generous
impulse and a wish to alleviate the sufferings of his
country. Assuredly it is not for us to blame his noble
resolution. But it is before entering upon war that the

Condé ratifies it, and its first conditions are put into execution.

---

[1] 'Il aymoit sa patrie, et avoit pytié du peuple.'
[2] Montluc.

sufferings which it entails should be thought of. To stop short at the point which the Protestants and their army had now reached, and in face of the influences which then ruled the Court, was not the way to secure a lasting peace, but only to ensure a fresh conflict longer and fiercer than before. It must therefore be conceded that Condé then 'made a false step.'[1] There seemed to be something wanting in his nature, as well as in his fortune. He never allowed himself to be beaten, but he never had the power or the skill to be really a victor. In adverse or in critical circumstances he was firm, full of resources, and truly great; but he failed in decision and prescience in ordinary times or when fortune smiled upon him, and, nobly gifted as he was, it must be allowed that his heart was larger than his intellect.

The ministers of his religion had therefore good reason to complain of the levity and incapacity which at this juncture he displayed as a party leader. But they did him an injustice in again accusing him of sacrificing the interests of their cause to his personal love of pleasure. And this time they had no excuse for such calumnious charges; for there were no fêtes, no rejoicings of any kind. When the treaty had been signed, the negotiators silently withdrew, and ' the short peace of Chartres,' the ' patched-up peace,'[2] as it was called, was ratified without éclat by an edict of the twenty-third of March. The maids of honour could have had nothing to do with it; Condé did not even appear at Court, and contented himself with thanking the King for the peace, by a letter,

---

[1] 'fit un pas de clerc.'—Montluc.

[2] It has been sometimes called the ' lame and unsteady' (boiteuse et malassise) peace. But this is a mistake. The latter designation was applied to the peace of 1570, negotiated by the Sire de *Malassise* and Biron the *Lame* (le Boiteux).

respectful indeed, but short, cold, and almost ironical in its final paragraph. 'Hoping,' he added, 'that your Majesty will show yourself careful to see it carried out.'[1]

After having disbanded his French troops, he went to Orléans to arrange for the departure of the Germans, the restitution of the cities, and the despatch of the Protestant commissioners, who, in conjunction with the Royal commissioners, were to be present at the registration of the edict in the provinces. A few days later the ' reîtres,' who had been paid off, and hired by the Prince of Orange, were on their way to the frontier. All the cities on the Loire and in Auxerrois in the occupation of the Huguenots were handed over to the lieutenants of the King, and Condé withdrew to his estates.

[1] Letter dated March 30. (Appendix, No. XXIV.)

APPENDICES.

APPENDICES.

———◦◦◦———

UNPUBLISHED DOCUMENTS.

I.

Origin of the Title Prince de Condé.

IN the archives of the House of Condé there is a copy of the marriage contract of Louis I., Prince de Condé, and Éléonore de Roye. The Prince is there styled Louis de Bourbon, and there is nothing to show precisely either whence he derived, or at what time he assumed, the title which he left to his descendants. The earliest official document with which we are acquainted in which this title is given to him, is the Procès-verbal of the Bed of Justice which was held January 15, 1557.[1] The name of Condé itself is frequently met with both on the map of France and in the pages of Père Anselme: Condé-sur-l'Escaut, Condé-en-Brie, Condé-sur-Noireau, Condé-en-Barrois, &c.; it has been the title or the patronymic of more than one family, unaccompanied, for the most part, by any very clearly distinctive addition. Of all these seigneuries of Condé, two certainly lapsed to the race of Bourbon-Vendôme; the one derived from the ancient House of Châtillon-sur-Marne, the other from the family of Luxembourg.

Marie d'Avesnes, only daughter and heiress of Guy d'Avesnes, seigneur de Condé, &c., was married about the year 1225 to Hugues de Châtillon, Comte de Saint-Paul. Their heirs were Guy, Jacques, Hugues, and Jeanne de Châtillon; the last-named was married to Jacques de Bourbon, first Comte de la Marche. Jean de Bourbon, the issue of this marriage, received as his share of the inheritance the seigneurie of Condé, and becoming by marriage Comte de Vendôme, left the title of Condé to his second son, Louis, paternal grandfather of the subject of these pages.

---

[1] Du Tillet, *Recueil des Roys de France.*

It is nowhere stated explicitly that the seigneurie just spoken of was that of Condé-sur-l'Escaut, but all the possessions of Marie d'Avesnes were in that district.   Finally, Père Anselme mentions a deed of the date 1326, executed at Condé-sur-l'Escaut by Jeanne d'Argies, wife of Hugues de Châtillon, seigneur de Condé.

On the other hand, the seigneurie of Condé-en-Brie, after having belonged to the House of Coucy, then to the House of Châtillon, descended to Pierre de Luxembourg, Comte de Saint-Paul, whose daughter and heiress, Marie, married as her second husband François de Bourbon, and became the mother of Charles, Duc de Vendôme.

The last-named Prince would seem, then, to have possessed the two seigneuries of Condé-sur-l'Escaut and Condé-en-Brie.   Which of the two was the origin of the title borne by his fifth son ?   On this point the chroniclers of the family are not agreed.   The best known among them, Desormeaux, in some MS. notes which are now before me, declares it to be 'beyond all doubt that the first Prince derived his name from Condé-en-Brie.'   Indeed, in the marriage contract of Louis I., mentioned at the beginning of this note, the seigneurie of Condé-en-Brie appears in the list of the possessions of the Prince. He owned a château there, where he often resided, and executed various deeds, whereas there is no official document relating to him known to exist, in which any mention is made of Condé-sur-l'Escaut.

But another librarian of the family, L'Huillier, who, though a tedious and very dull writer, has left in MS. many historical and genealogical memoirs, of which Desormeaux has often made use, declares himself in favour of Condé-sur-l'Escaut; and the Convention seemed to be of the same opinion, by its naming that place ' Nord-libre.'

We shall leave to more learned genealogists the task of solving this question, which though doubtless of little importance, our love of historical accuracy would not suffer us entirely to pass over.[1] We will confine ourselves to placing on record here :—

(1.) An analysis of the marriage contract between the first Prince de Condé and Éléonore de Roye.   He is here styled, as has been stated, ' *haut et puissant prince, Louis de Bourbon, fils de feu bonne mémoire Charles, en son vivant duc de Vendôme, et de dame Françoise d'Alençon, son épouse.*'   His friends present were :—

His brothers, ' *Anthoine, duc de Vendôme, avec Jeanne, princesse de Navarre, son épouse ; Jean de Bourbon ;* '

---

[1] See the *Histoire généalogique de France* and the *Histoire de la Maison de Châtillon-sur-Marne,* by Duchesne, *passim.*

His uncle and guardian '*Louis, cardinal de Bourbon, primat de France, archevesque de Sens, évesque duc de Laon.*'

The Seigneur and Dame de Roye assigned to '*leur fille aînée, Léonor, douze mille livres de rente, pour en jouir par le dit futur époux de six mille livres pour le jour des espousailles, et des autres six mille livres après le décès desdits seigneur et dame. . . . Et où il ne surviendra aucuns enfants mâles desdits seigneur et dame, en ce cas, ladite demoiselle Léonor de Roye et ses enfants viendront à leur succession comme aînés et principaux héritiers. . . . Et en ce cas, le second enfant masle issu de ce mariage, et après son décès le tiers, et consécutivement tant qu'il y aura aucun enfant mâle après ce premier sera tenu de porter le nom et tiltre de Roye, et ses armes écartelées avec celles de Bourbon. . . . Et sur ce, a ledit seigneur duc de Vandosme dit et déclaré que, par le partage puis naguères accordé entre luy et lesdits seigneurs, Jean et Louis, ses frères, audit Louis sont écheues les terres et seigneuries qui s'ensuivent. C'est à sçavoir : la Ferté-au-Coul et vicomté de Meaulx, Condé-en-Brye, Ailly-sur-Noye, Sourdon et Braye, la Basecque, les transports de Flandres, trois cens trois livres huit sols deux deniers tournois, qu'il est tenu par ledit partage assigner en fonds de terres.*' A dowry of four hundred livres was guaranteed to the bride, and charged upon the aforesaid lands, '*et spéciallement sur lesdites terres et seigneuries de Condé et la Ferté-au-Coul. . . . Fait et passé à Nisy-le-Chastel, par-devant nous, etc. . . .*' (n.d.) [Copy from an abstract on paper, signed by the notaries who received it, July 1, 1664.]

(2.) The titles of the same Prince as they appear in a lease granted by him 'au chastel de Condé-en-Brye,' November 1, 1558 : '*Loys de Bourbon, prince de Condé, comte de Roucy, vicomte de Meaulx et seigneur de la Ferté-au-Coul, chevallier de l'ordre du Roy Monseigneur, capitaine de cinquante lances de ses ordonnances, capitaine et colonnel général des bandes françoises estant pour le service de Sa Majesté delà les monts.*' [Archives du département de la Marne.]

II.

Théodore de Bèze to Calvin.

Saint-Germain, 25 août 1561.

Monsieur et père, j'arrivay en ceste cour il y a deux jours, où je vous puis asseurer que j'ay esté receu avec un fort grand accueil de tous les plus grands, qui ne me baillèrent loisir de souper pour les aller trouver. A l'entrée, je trouvai le chancelier que sçavez,[1] qui vouloit avoir l'honneur de m'avoir introduict. Force me fut de le suyvre, mais ce fut avec un tel visage qu'il congnut assez que je le congnoissois. Cela ne dura guères, car il n'y avoit que trois pas d'un cabinet à l'entrée duquel je trouve Monsieur, que je n'eus pas le loisir de saluer, que voicy le roi de Navarre et Monseigneur le prince de Condé, qui se jettent sur moy avec une fort grande affection, ce me sembla ; de là, je voy auprès de moy le cardinal de Bourbon et puis le cardinal de Chastillon qui me tendoient les mains.

Quant au roy de Navarre, la somme du propos fut que j'avois grand'peur que bientost il ne fust pas si joyeux de ma venue, s'il ne se délibéroit à faire aultrement. Il se print à rire, et je luy respondy que c'estoit à bon escient qu'il y falloit penser. Ce propos fut environ de demye heure, qu'il fut nuyct, et s'en allèrent chez la Royne, et moy avec ma troupe, cent fois plus grande que je n'eusse desiré, fut conduict chez madame la princesse et madame l'admirale, que je trouvay merveilleusement bien disposées. Le lendemain, qui fut hier au matin, je fis une exhortation au logis de Monsieur le Prince, en laquelle grande et honorable compagnie se trouva, mais non pas le prince, car il estoit empesché après son apoinctement avec celuy que sçavez,[2] par le moyen de celle que pouvez penser.[3] Je ne sçavoys rien de tout cela, et ne le sceuz qu'il ne fust faict. Après dîner, estant mandé par luy en son cabinet, il m'en faict tout le discours et m'en monstre l'acte par escrit, portant en somme que sa partie luy a desclairé en présence de la Royne et du conseil qu'il n'estoit aulcunement cause ny motif de la détention d'iceluy. Sur quoy, le prince a dict qu'il tenoit pour meschants tous ceulx qui en auroient esté cause. 'Je le croy ainsy, a respondu l'aultre, et cela ne me tousche en rien.'—Voylà tout. Estant enquis qu'il m'en sembloit, je respondis que les responses me sembloient ambigues, mais qu'en telles affaires je me rapportoys à ceulx qui entendoient mieux ce qui concernoit l'honneur de son rang ; quant à sa querelle particulière, qu'il sçavoit assez à qui il en falloit remestre la vengeance, mais que nul ne pouvoit estre tenu pour amy de Dieu, s'il ne se desclairoit ennemy des ennemys jurés d'iceluy et de son Église en ceste qualité. Sa response fut telle que nous aurions occasion de louer Dieu de tout ! Mais que cela soit ferme ! Au faict, il fust sorti de grands maulx de ces privées affections, et pourveu que ce ne soit occasion de passer plus oultre, je ne suis

---

[1] L'Hospital. That good man was treated with equal injustice by both the extreme factions.

[2] The Duc de Guise.

[3] The Queen-Regent.

point marry que tels mystères ne soyent meslés parmy ce que nous pourchassons. Voylà donc l'issue de toute ceste esmeute que nous craignions, sinon qu'elle tire après soy quelque queue.

Vostre entier et humble serviteur en Nostre-Seigneur,

TH. DE CHALONNAY.

(*Bibliothèque de Genève.* Ms. 117. Original.)

I am indebted for this document, as well as for several others, to my learned friend M. Jules Bonnet.

III.

The Prince de Condé to Lieutenant de Roye.

Saint-Germain-en-Laye, 11 novembre 1561.

Monsieur le lieutenant, je croy que n'ignorez poinct combien de peines et de temps le Roy et son conseil ont emploié pour remédier et pourvoir aux séditions qui pourroient advenir touchant le faict de la Religion, ne les édictz passez sur ce faictz, prohibitifz à tous, d'une part et d'aultre, de se mesfaire ou mesdire, mais vivre en union et paix; toutesfois, à ce que j'entens, ces édictz ont eu bien peu de lieu en la ville de Roye, par la négligence ou affection d'aulcuns des principaulx ministres de la justice, qu'il n'est à craindre qu'il ne sorte beaucoup d'inconvéniens, si de bonne heure n'y est pourveu, pour la mauvaise volunté d'aulcuns tendans à sédition, qui font plusieurs injurieuses menaces à ceulx qu'ilz pensent estre de la Religion, ce qui ne se feroit (comme il est aisé à croire) s'ilz n'estoient portez ou favorisez de ceulx qui ont la principalle authorité en la ville; et d'aultant que cela est plus à craindre, aussi est-il besoing y obvier promptement, et partant veulx-je bien vous faire, sur ce, entendre l'intention et volunté du Roy, suivant ses édictz et ordonnances, qui est que s'il se trouvoit qu'il y eust aulcuns si téméraires ou adventageux de faire prescher ou assembler ès rues ou lieux publicz, ou qui prennent temples ou abbatent images, que incontinant et sans vous enquérir de quelle religion ilz sont, ne avoir esgard à personnes quelz qu'ilz soient, ayez à user contre eulx de toutes les voies de rigueur qu'on pourra; si toutesfois ilz sont ou estoient en leurs maisons, n'aiez à vous en enquérir d'aventaige, maiz cloyez l'œil, gardant, au surplus, les édictz et ordonnances faictes sur la correction des séditieux. Et afin que les aultres officiers du Roy, gouverneurs et eschevins de la ville y puissent de leur part faire leur debvoir, leur communiquerez la présente, pour fin de laquelle, etc.[1]

IV.

(Le Prince de Condé) à *messieurs et bons amys messieurs les Syndiques et Conseil de Genève.*

Saint-Germain-en-Laye, 24 novembre 1561.

Messieurs et bons amys, congnoissant le sain et vertueux zèle que vous portez à l'avancement de la gloire de Dieu et le desir que vous avez que sa pure doctrine puisse prendre pied et racine en ce royaume, ainsi que desjà nous commençons à en voir les apparences claires et grandes, j'ay pensé, puisque Nostre-Seigneur a faict si heureusement prospérer le voiage que y a faict Monsieur de Beaze, duquel il s'est servy comme de son instrument à l'édification de son Église, que pour la conservation d'un tel et si savoureux fruict, vous ne trouverés mauvais que nous l'ayons retenu encore pour environ quatre mois auprès de la Royne ma seur;[2] et pour ce qu'en luy proposant ce retardement, il a faict vertance grande sur l'obéissance qu'il vous doibt et veult rendre, affin de luy lever de ma part toutes les difficultés et excuses qu'il pourroit sur ce alléguer et prendre. Je vous en ay bien voulu escrire ceste lettre pour vous prier très-affectueusement au nom de Dieu, Messieurs et bons amys, non-seulement luy permettre tel séjour par deçà, mais expressément le luy ordonner et enjoindre. Ce faisant, oultre le bien et profict commun que vous moiennerez à la France, laquelle s'en sentira infiniment gratiffiée de vous, je le tiendrai si estroittement et particulier en moy que jamais je n'en oublieray le plaisir et l'obligation, pour le recognoistre généralement envers le corps de vostre république, ou en privé envers les membres d'icelle, par tous les bons et dignes offices dont vous me vouldrez requérir et emploier, ce que je feray tousjours d'aussy bon cueur que je supplie le Créateur, etc.

(Archives de Genève. Original.)

---

[1] (Bibliothèque impériale. Mss. 8696, fol. 3. Original.) *du règne du roy Charles IX.*   [2] Jeanne d'Albret.

V.

(Le Prince de Condé) à messieurs et bons amys messieurs les Syndiques et Conseil de Genève.

Orléans, 11 avril 1562.

Messieurs mes bons amys, vous ne trouverés estrange s'il vous plaist si non-seulement les bruicts des choses advenues en ce roiaume depuis trois sepmaines en ça, mais aussi quelques lettres sous le nom des Majestés du Roy et de la Royne ou d'autres, ont prévenu les présentes. Car ce qui nous a retardé n'a esté par faulte d'asseurance que nous avons de vostre desir et affection d'entendre tels affaires et de nous y ayder aussi, mais nous avons mieulx aymé estre tardifs en actendant que Dieu apaisast ces troubles par quelque moyen plus aisé, que d'estre trop légers à espandre les estincelles d'un feu si dangereux. Or, Messieurs, quant au discours de toute la matière, nous vous prions la vouloir entendre par la déclaration que nous en avons faicte à la vérité, et laquelle nous vous envoions pour estre bien pesée et considérée, comme nous desirons que toute la crestienté en ayt la congnoissance, en quoy faysant nous espérons que vous trouverez notre cause si juste, estant conjoincte avec la religion que nous avons commune avec vous, et touchant de si près la conversation de la couronne et maison de France, de laquelle vous estes anciens amys et alliez, que au lieu d'adjouster foy aux bruicts qui courent au contrayre, mesme aux lettres que nos ennemys font expédier à toutes heures selon leur apétit, d'autant qu'ils tiennent le Roy et la Royne en captivité, vous ne ferez difficulté de favoriser à ceux qui sont tout injustement oultragez, pour vouloir maintenir l'honneur de Dieu et les édicts du Roy, vostre ancien amy et allié. Voyla pourquoy nous vous avons envoyé expressément ce gentilhomme présent porteur, et de vostre nation, pour vous prier autant qu'il vous est possible de l'ouyr et bien entendre, et sur ce nous octroyer ce que nous vous demandons, et que nous espérons obtenir de vous comme juste et raisonnable, et comme concernant mesme vostre estat, pource que l'ambition de nos ennemys connue nous asseure que ce n'est pas à nous seuls qu'ils en veulent, mais que plus tost ils ont embrassé tout le monde par leur insatiable cupidité. Messieurs nos bons amys, nous nous recommandons à vos bonnes prières et de toutes vos Églises, après avoir prié, etc.

(Archives de Genève. Original.)

VI.

Both in Père Lelong (*Bibliothèque historique de France*), and in the *Catalogue de l'Histoire de France*, recently published by the Trustees of the *Bibliothèque impériale*, will be found a very imperfect list of pieces printed by the Reformers in the course of this year, 1562. These little pamphlets are scarce; but the most important of them have been reprinted in the *Mémoires de Condé*, or in other collections. In this place we will merely insert two unpublished autograph letters of the Prince de Condé, written during the earlier months of his occupation of Orleans. They are characteristic of the turn of his mind, and the peculiarity of his style of composition.

The Prince de Condé to the Queen.

Orléans, April 19, 1562.

[Early in this month the populace at Sens had risen at the instigation, it was said, of Cardinal de Lorraine, archbishop of that diocese; a hundred of the Protestant inhabitants had been massacred, their houses pillaged, and their church pulled down. The Prince de Condé wrote to the Regent to demand justice upon the murderers. His letter is printed in the *Mémoires de Condé* (iii. 300) with some variations. The original concludes with the following postscript, which has not been published.]

Madame, la connesance que jé de vostre bon naturel me donne asurrance que si estes an lyberté, comme il plait à Vostre Magesté nous faire antandre, que ne léserés ynpuny le fait sy ynhumain quy sait esséquté à Sans; vous asurrant quy let besoin dan faire une bonne jeustysse pour faire conestre à tous vos seuges que senet pas vostre vouslonté, mas campt nestes tres fachée, et pour sela que leur faires connestre la fauste quyl lon fait de si cruelemant tué vos seuges et ronpre vos esdis pour satifaire à leur pasion trop donmagable pour ce reosme, au regar de l'inportance caporte après soy telle essemple.

Vostre très-humble et très-obéyssant seuget et servyteur,

LOYS DE BOURBON.

(*Archives de Condé.* Original autogr.)

The Prince de Condé to the King of Navarre.

[Undated, but evidently written before the commencement of hostilities, or immediately upon their breaking out.]

Monsieur, campt je nores jamays eu connessance de lonneur et bien quy vous plait me porter, la lestre quy vous a pleu m'escryre par Monsr de Losse[1] man rande ases bon témonnyage, puys que je vois la pene que portes de celle cator jendure. Sy par le passé jé resu tant de faveur de vous davoyr fait connestre mon ynnosance, à plus forte résont jespère que médres à faire parrestre que ne pance faire chose quy fut contre mon onneur, lequel jespère conserver plus cher que ma vie propre. Campt à lanvye caves de me voyr, je vous an remersie très-humblement; car je vous prommes domme de bien que ne seres a mon esse fin à tant que me trouve auprès dé vous, jouyssant de vostre bonne grace. Je vous suplie de crere que la boue, où pances que suys tonbé, ne m'a soullié la réputasion quy deut vous donner quelque mecontanteman; car an pancée ny anne-fait, je ne commys chose qui fust constre le Roy et la Rène et vous; quy me fait tenyr pour asurrer que me trouveres net et desireus de vous faire servyce aussy fidel que serviteur que ores jamays. Dieu veuille, Monsieur, que bientot nous puyssions voyr Monsr lamyral et moy auprès de vous ou bien cheu nous, sy set lieu quy vous soit plus agréable; car vous connestres que préferres vos commandemans à mes vouslontés, et pour gage sy vous plaist me faire tant donneur de prandre de mes anfans pour mestre an sacryfice, pour vous faire conestre que vous veus randre parfaite obéyssance et contanter. Sy vous crères se que vous dira Monsr de Losse, auquel je dit des moiens bons pour vous mestre an repos.

Vostre tres-humble et très-obéyssant frère et serviteur,

LOYS DE BOURBON.

(*Archives de Condé.* Original autogr.)

VII.

In the following Appendix will be found a collection of despatches and other documents extracted from the State Paper Office in

[1] Jean de Beaulieu, Seigneur de Losse, captain of the guard to the King of Navarre, was present during his last moments. He remained with the army after the death of that prince in the capacity of *Maréchal de camp*, was entrusted by the Duc de Guise with the mission of carrying to Paris the news of the victory of Dreux, and received on that occasion the command of a *Compagnie d'ordonnance*. He took part in the Conference at l'Ile-aux-Bœufs, where the preliminaries of peace were agreed upon, in March 1563. After the siege of Havre, he obtained the command of the Scottish company of the Royal body-guards, and served at Lyon in 1565, and elsewhere. He died in January 1576.

London (French Papers), relating to the period between March 1 and November 1, 1562. They are printed in chronological order, without reference to the order in which they are noticed in the body of this work.

It may be mentioned here that under the title of 'A Full View of the Public Transactions in the Reign of Queen Elizabeth,' Dr. Forbes published in 1740 a large portion of the documents relative to our subject, contained in that rich store. All that is here subjoined is a selection of such of the unpublished documents as appeared most interesting.

Throckmorton to Cecil.

(EXTRACT.) March 14, 1562.

Heere be strange discourses and great expectations what shall become of the world heere. The king of Navarre, the duke of Guyse, the constable, the cardinall Ferrare, the three marshalles of Fraunce, St-André, Brysac and the Thermes, the cardinall of Tournon, and all their favereurs and followers be conjoynid fermelie together to overthrowe the protestant religion, and to exterminate the favereurs thereof, whiche enterprise and desirid pourpose is pousshyd forwardes by th'ambassadeur of Spayne heere, and Spanishe treateninge and countenances. The Quene mother, assistid with the quene of Navarre, the chauncelor, the prince of Condé, the cardinall Chastillon, the admirall, Monsieur d'Andelot and their followers and favereurs, do yet countenance the matter on our syde. I praye God the Quene mother do not stripp her coller: she will the better persiste in her good devotion if Mons. de Foix there may understand nowe and then at the Quenes majesties handes, that Her Majestie dothe allowe and lyke this godlie inclination in the Quene mother. . . .

Sir, I do assure youe it is high tyme that the protestantes be countenancyd and sustaynid, lest all quayle, and of this be youe assuerid, that the favereurs of the protestant religion do make as greate accompte of the Quene my mistresse favour and supporte as the papistes in this realme do as moche feare the Quenes Majestie and her force, as they do presume upon the king of Spaynes ayde. The kinge of Spayne makith this accompte for his proffitte to norishe and countenance the papistes heere as his faction, and therefore it importeth the Quenes Majestie, to do the lyke to the protestantes heere and so to make them her faction.

Queen Elizabeth to Throckmorton.

(COPY OF MINUTE.)   March 31, 1562.

Right trustee and well beloved, we grete you well.

We have of late had some consideracion of the proceedings in that state, and havinge founde by your advertisements the same to tende to such a perilloose change, we could not but have good regard therto in tyme, and therfor have we delated the matter with the french ambassador here, who could not tell us certenly of any such particularities as you have advertised, but saied that he had cause to feare the change of some persons there. We required him to advertise the Quene mother and the prince de Condé how well we allowe of there constancy, and how dangeroose we think it to be to the kinge of Navarre to separate himself from them, and to wyne which those that have sought his ruyne, and can take no proffitt but by his decaye. We have touched to him a late example in this realme of the overthrowe of the last duke of Somersett by dissention with his brother; we have also required him in our name to comefort and encourage the Quene mother, the quene of Navarre and the prince of Condé to shew their wisdome and constancyes, and not to gyve the adversaries power or comeforte by their declyning. And for that we meane to assure them and the admirall of our intent to stand constantly, and therby to comefort them in their good intents, we have thereon mete that you shuld sete occasion to speke with the Quene mother, the prince de Condé, and the admirall apart, acertening them that we have also imparted our mynd to the embassador here resident, and to the Quene mother you shall saye that . . . as longe as she shall not meane any other partialitie, but the weale of hir sonne, and quyetnesse of the realme, it is not to be feared, but she shall avoyde all the practises and devises of such as shall seke but their owne glorye and wealth, with ambytion. Finally, as you shall fynde it mete, ye shall make hir assured of our amytie and asistance by all good meanes possyble. You shall do the like to the prince of Condé, and advise him from us that he in no wyse yelde in so good a cause as he hath, to adjoygne himself to such as he knoweth shall take benefytt by his decaye, and lett him remember that in all affaires, second attempts be ever more dangeroose than the first; how he hath escaped once he knoweth therein Goddes goodnesse, and now the same God shall assyste him, if he yelde not to practises, wherewith we thinke suerly he shall be plentifully assalted, as well with flatery and vayne promyses, as with threatenings.

Lykewyse you shall in our name, affectuously salute the admirall, and assure him that his wisdome and constancy hetherto in all his manners and actions hath desserved and hat great commendacion in the world, and therefore he may not now in Goddes cause (wherof his conscience beareth him so good wytnesse) forynte, but use his wisdome towards the furtherance therof, and to lett him understand that one of the causes, why we did not presently follow the advice of the Quene mother opened by him to you for sending to Trydent, was for that untyll we might understand the meaning of the princes of Almayne, we wold do nothing to discorrage them or to comeforte the adverse parte, but after we shall heare from them, we will omytt nothing that may furder the common tranquillitie of christendom. We wold you should make him as assured of our good will towards him as though he were our owne naturall kinsman, and because the courte is not neare Parys, so as ye must of purpose make a journey thither, you shall take occasion of your going to the courte upon this occasion as followeth, etc.

Throckmorton to Cecil.[1]

April 17, 1562.

Sir, by that tyme you have redde and well perused this my dispatche to Hir Majestie, I thinke you will be of mynde not to thinke meete that Hir Majestie make any *long progresse from London*, but rather you will thinke convenient to intende and give order *for warly preparacion in tyme*, then to apply pleasures and hunting matters, wherunto I knowe for your parte you are not greatly dedicate. You muste bothe *besturre you* at home, but specially *abrode*, and so worke which all your frendes which speede, and in tyme, that *the king of Spaine* againe may be well occupied, and have *his hand full* in cace *he will ayde the papist of this country*, for there liethe our daunger. It may so chance as the Quenes Majestie may make *her profit of these troubles, as the king of Spaine dothe* and intendeth to do, for if they fall *to catching on his side and the duke of Savoye* on his side, the Quenes Majestie may not be *idle*, nor be laste ready. I know assuredly *the king of Spaine doth* greathly eye and practise *to put his foote in Calais; our frends the protestants in this countrey* must be so handeled and dandeled as in case *the duke of Guise, the conestable, the marshall Saint-André, and that secte* do minde, as I feare they do, *to bring in the king of Spaine into this countrey, and to give him possession of some port* and forts, that then the protestants,

---

[1] The words in italics are in cypher in the original.

eyther for their owne surety and defence, either for despite and desire of revenge, or for good will and affection *to the Quenes Majestie and hir religion, may be moved and induced to give the Quenes Majestie either* possession of Calais, Dieppe or Newhaven, all whiche these, or any of the whiche I care not thoughe we had. But this mater must in no wise *be moved either directly or indirectly* to any of them or their ministers, as yet *whosoever* shall come and treate which youe, for the matter will fall out more aptly and conveniently of itself *upon their demands of aide, such purse and contenance, and the more metely when the prince of Condé and the protestants* shall perceive that the *papists do mynde to bring in strangers into this realme, and to gyve the king of Spaine interest in all things.* I wold rather it shulde so come to passe *that the prince or the protestants shuld offer the Q. Ma*ᵗᵉ *entrey or possession of any of their places, then that it shuld be by us desyred.* Remember, I pray you, what good Her Maᵗᵉ discret and sincere proceedings did worke *in Scotland,* and this we have for avantage that we shall deale which true and faithfull men, I meane *the protestants; and they* which double and crafty men, *I meane the papists.* I think, er it be long, a *gentleman of good credit, very honest, and one that doth know you well, shall be sent thither to the Queenes Maj*ᵗᵉ *shortly, from the prince of Condé, th' admirall and Mons*ʳ *d'Andelot,* and shall have *commission and instructions to treate which the Quenes Maj*ᵗᵉ *further* in these *maters.* You must bethink you where to bestow *him secretly when he comith thither that he may so do his businesse,* as it may *be kept secrett.* Harry Middelmore shall, upon *his arrywall,* gyve you knowledge of yt; *he is a gentleman of the King's privy chamber, and the same that the bisshop of Orléans and Mons*ʳ *de Oy did demannd of Q. Mary to be rendrid to the Fr. king,* who was then *fled into England for religion.* Sʳ Peter Meautes *was his harbinger and his host when London was searchid for him.* He can tell you his name, but he saith he hath good cause to know yours.

Sir, I have written a few words to the Q. Maᵗᵉ to be pleasd for her owne service to send *me credict either by M*ʳ *Gressams meanes, or by M*ʳ *Guido Calvacanti, for the some of fyve or six thousand crownes, of the somme of wish money I will take employ, and bestow so much from tyme to tyme,* and no more then shal be necessary and convenient for Her Majᵗᵉ service. It were verie necessary that the Q. Majᵗᵉ shuld sent unto me which speede *her letters, addressed to the Q. mother, to the king of Navarre and the prince of Condé,* and the subject of therin so conceyvid in general termes as may serve for this tyme, and for Her Majᵗᵉ purpose, *referring the credence and*

furder declaracion of her mynde to be by me unto them, and to every
of them, *and the delivery of the same letters,* and declaracion of the
same credict *to be referred to my discretion,* declared in Her Maj^te
letter unto me, *to be delyvered or not delyvered, and to be spoken and
not spoken* as I shall see occasion heere offred.   I have appointed my
cosin Middelmore to attend upon you for the dispatch of the said
billes of credict.

Throckmorton and Sydney to Queen Elizabeth.

May 8, 1562.

It may please your Maj^te, by my letters of the seconde of maye
youe might perceive that the bushopp of Orleans and Monsr de
l'Aubespine were not retourned from the prince of Condé hither,
sence whiche tyme, the IIIIth of this present, the sayd busshopp
and secretarie l'Aubespine retournid to the courte, who brought
which theim for answer that the prince wold neither disarme nor
dispose his forces, but uppon suche condicions as Your Majeste, by
my former advertisements dothe understande, and hereuppon betwixt these parties more rigoreus actes be shewid in sondrie
partes of this realme to the faverours of either syde. . . .

And having written this farre, minding to dispatche the same
to Your Maj^te, I was advertisyd the said III^de daye of this monethe
that sir Harrys Sydney was arryvid in this towne, and come
as farre onwardes on his waye towards my lodging as Saint-
Marceaux gate (not farre distant from my sayd lodging), wher by
the garde of the sayd porte (being towns men) he was detaynid and
not sufferid to passe anie further, but was there the space of two
longe howers, kept in suche sorte as neither he might come to me
nor send to me.   Hereby Your Majeste may perceyve the furious
and malicious insolencie of this people, the small consideracion they
have of the honnour, privilege and libertie due to ambassadeurs.
Immediatlie, as sone as I knewe of his arryvall at the sayd gate, I
sente one of my servants to the courte, to declare to the Quene
mother and the kinge of Navarre that Your Maj^te ambassadeur,
being arryvid in this towne, was otherwise usid and entreatid then
was agreable to the good amytie betwixt Your Maj^te and the Kinge,
or agreable to the King honnour to treate one ambassadeur, otherwise then the conte of Russy and their ministers were usid in
Englande.   Further and without delaye, as sone as my servant
could speake which the kinge of Navarre, and that the sayd kinge
had signified the matter to the Quene mother (who were together

in councell), the sayd kinge and Quene mother sent the mareschall Momorencie, gouverneur of this towne, to take ordre in this matter, and to punishe suche as were cheifs of Mr Sydneys empeachements. In the meane tyme, the ambassadeur of Portugall, coming to take his leave of me (passing by the sayd gate), founde sir Harrys Sydney there, and so handled the matter that sir Harrie Sydney and he, the sayd ambassador together came to my lodging from the sayd gate a horseback, not being sufferid to bringe his carriage nor any of his staff with him, untell the sayd mareschal Momorencie arryvid there, who toke ordre that his trayne and carriage was immediatlie sufferid to passe, and also toke two of the principalls with him, and commyttid theim to prison.

. . . .

Mr Sydney and I accompaynid with Mr de Carres and these gentlemen, went to the courte (beinge at the Louvre) the Vth daye in the after none. And being brought unto the King presence (who was accompaynid with the Quene his mother, the duke of Orleans, the king of Navarre, the prince of Roche-sur-Yon, the duke of Guyse, the constable and manie other greate personnages as well women as men), I, Your Maj^te ambassador resident, declarid to the Kinge and the Quene his mother together that Your Maj^te, his good suster, being desyrous to let him, your good brother, and the Quene his mother, your good suster, understande, in this tyme when his realme was troublid with garboyles, your good affection and sincere amytie howe to reduce the same to repose and tranquillitie, and therefore had sent this gentleman s^r Harrie Sidney, in greate diligence, to testifie the same Your Maj^te good will unto them bothe, as it shuld appeare more at large by his lettres and creance. Then I, s^r Harrie Sidney, presentid Your Maj^te lettres to the Kinge and the Quene his mother, and declarid so farre furthe unto theim according to my instructions, as tendid to the declaration of Your Maj^te good will and affection to appease these troubles, divisions and tumultes in his realme, and for as moche as I, and sir Nicholas Throkmorton, Your Maj^te ambassadeur resident, consulting together uppon our instructions, haiving regarde to the present tyme and state of things heere, thought good for the better advancement of your service, that it shuld be better to differe the opening of the points of your advise for an amiable composition of the great difference bewixt these parties, and for reducing this realme to repose and quyetnes, untill we might perceyve howe the generall declaracion of your good minde in these matters were accepted at the Quene mothers hande, and wether there wold appeare in her anye desyre to understande the particularities of Your Maj^{te} opinion in that behalfe. Uppon whiche respects I procedid no further then is before sayd, saving that Your Maj^{te} had given me and my collegue in charge to employe ourselves in this affayre, as faythfullye and diligentlie as if it were Your Maj^{te} owne cace.

The Quene mother answerid 'I thanke the Quene my good suster, for the shwres of her good will and assueryd amytie to the Kinge my sonne, and to me in this tyme now, when his realme is vexid with troubles, and a frendshipp nowe shewid is more wortie a great deale good acceptation, then when things be calme, and when there is not so great neede thereof: whiche kindnesse, I truste, neither my sonne nor I for my parte will ever forgett. I have, sayd the Quene mother, understande by the Quene your mistress ambassador resident heere, sence the beginning of these troubles, the Quene my good suster's affection and sincere amytie to the Kinge my sonne and me, and nowe do by your legation finde the same bothe well confirmid and well augmentid; therefore the Quene my good suster may be well assuerid she shall finde, at the Kinge my sonne's handes and myne good correspondencie of this good will, and albeit we have good cause to take verie thankfullie the Quene your mistress procedings, and friendlie offers towards us in this tyme for the appeasing of these inconveniences, yet we truste (sayd she) that we shall not have neede to employe my good suster's healpe and her ministers in this matter, for the prince of Condé beinge the King's neere kinsman and the admirall being the King's councelor and good servant, will, I truste, be so well advised that they will condiscende to reason, when it is offerid, and not obstinatlie persiste in suche opinions and procedings as may occasion the troble of the Kinge my sonne's realme, their own ruyne and dishonnour. The King hathe sent thither latelie unto theim suche condicions as they can not but accepte, if they be well advised, and therefore I do not doubte but all shall be well and amyablie endid, but for as moche as the kinge of Spayne (having married my sonne's suster and my daughter and therefore my sonne's good brother and allie) hathe offerid, to represse these desordres and troubles, to ayde the Kinge my sonne, and to recouvre again due obedience unto him, XXX thousands foetman and VI thousande horse payd of his owne charge, and lykewise the duke of Savoye and other our allies, hathe offerid greate ayde and succour in this cace, all which their offres and kindnesses we have good cause to take in good parte, though we shall have, I truste, no neede to use theim, nor employe theim, so in like manner for the good opinion we do conceyve of the Quene, your

mistress' good devotion towards us, the King my sonne and I wold APP.
be glad to hear her advise and offre in this matter howe to stande VII.
us insteade upon all eventes, and therefore I pray you, said the
Quene mother, Messieurs les ambassadeurs, open the same unto us.'

Then I, Your Ma^te ambassadour resident, sayd unto the Quene
mother:

'Madame, albeit some other princes, frendes and allies to the
kinge your sonne and youe, have offerid nowe when your realme is
vexid with troubles and partialities, risen as well for matters of
religion as for particular causes, ayde and succours of men of
warre in greate nombres with advice to proceede by force of armes
in these matters, the Quene our mistress, your good suster geving
place to none in good affection and sincere amytie to the Kinge her
good brother and youe, dothe not thinke good to followe these other
princes your frends steppes in this matter, nor to make offre to youe
at this tyme of anye ayde and succours of men of warre to ende
these trobles; but Her Ma^te thinketh rather the beste waye is, and
moste profytable for the Kinge her good brother, for youe and for
his realme, to seeke the waye of composicion amyablie, and not to
proceede against your subjects, as youe wold do against your
enemies, and howe so ever other princes do grounde their judge-
ments and opinions to advise the Kinge and youe to use rigour in
this cace, the Quene our mistress dothe thinke that the better and
more sounde councell is neither to employ strangers against your
own subjects, nor your subjects against themselves, if the matter
may be any other wise compromidid. . . .'

The Quene mother answerid:

'I can not but allowe verie well of these, my good suster's advises,
and to be playne with youe, her councill in this matter is agreeable
to the articles and condicions whiche we have sent latelie to the
prince of Condé and th'admirall, trusting they will be so well advisid
as to accepte theim, for hitherto I have taken theim for good servants to the Kinge; but if they refuse these reasonables condicions,
I must be inforcid to think otherwise of theim, and the Kinge, my
sonne, muste be compellid to proceede by waye of force to have
obedience of his subjects, for it is not to be lykid, nor to be sufferid
that these outrages and insolence whiche be daylye commyttid,
shuld have anie longer continewance, as the killing of one of the
king's gouvernours of his provinces, being a knight of th'ordre, the
taking of his towne and keping therein as they do daylie in all
partes of this realme; the spoiling of churches and breaking of
images, contrarie to their own promesse. It shall therefore be meete

that all these insolences be laid down, and the force out of all mens handes but the Kings my sonnes, that he may have th'autoretie and obedience which is due unto him. Some of these greate personnages which the prince of Condé dothe desyre shulde retyre from this courte, have bene counsailours to the Kinge my father, to the Kinge my late sonne and be counsailours to my sonne the King that is nowe. All which and everie of theim hathe done great service to this realme, and have great estates in the same as they are well worthie, and therefore not meete to be commandid to retire theimselves from the courte. Neverthelesse they be so wise, so honnorable and so well affected to the quyet of this realme, that of theimselves they have offerid and have desyrid me that they may retyre theimselves to their own houses. Now on th'other side, if the prince of Condé will not accepte reason when it is offerid, and content him with enough, the Kinge must be dryven to employe all his frendes,.as well strangers as others, to compell these men to reason and to their dutie.'

. . . .

Then I, Sir Harrie Sydney, did Your Ma^{te} commendacions to the duke of Orleans, who askid me hartelie howe Your Ma^{te} did, in whom there did appere to me verie greate towardness for his age.

This done we toke our leave of the Kinge, the Quene mother and the duke of Orleans. Then we repayrid to the kinge of Navarre, who was not farre from the Kinge, unto whom I, sir Harrie Sydney, presented Your Ma^{te} letters and hartie commendacions, and declairid unto the sayd kinge in effecte the same matter, which I had before declairid to the Kinge and the Quene his mother, having respecte to the sayd king of Navarre person as the King's principall counsailor.

The sayd king of Navarre thankid Your Ma^{te} for your gentle visitacion and acknowledgid that he was readie and willing. to do Your Ma^{te} service, bounde thereunto, as he sayd, for the good amytie and susterlie love it pleased you nowe to shewe to the King his souverayne in this tyme of trobles, and also for the honnour and favour youe had manie wayes and manie tymes, and nowe lastlie of all shewed unto him for his particuler, and in th' ende of this talke, the sayd kinge seemid to taxe more bytterlie (though not by name) the prince of Condé, and his doings, saying that the Kinge his souverayn shuld be dryven to use his force against suche insolent doings as wold no otherwise be reformid.

Then I, Your Ma^{te} ambassadeur resident, declarid unto the said kinge that in as moche as we had declarid at good lengte Your Ma^{te} opinion and advise for the best quyeting and ending these troubles, to the Quene mother, who we are sure wold declare it unto him, we wold put it unto his choice whether we shuld reitterate the same unto him agayne, for Your Ma^te had geven us in charge to communicate the matter onlie unto the Quene mother and to him, onles by their ordre we shuld declare it unto others.

The Kinge of Navarre answerid: 'In as moche as you have declarid it unto the Quene mother, it shall suffice and I shall take an other tyme to talke further with youe at more commoditie.'

Then I, sir Harrie Sydney, saluted on Your Ma^te behalf the prince of Roche-sur-Yon, principall gouvernour to the Kinge, who gave Your Ma^te his most thankes with offre of his services.

The like, I, sir Harrie Sydney, did to the constable. . . .

Then I, adressid myselfe unto the duke of Guise, unto whom I did Your Ma^te hartie commendacions, and told him that I had from the same in charge to saye unto him, that as well in respecte he was the quene of Scotland, your good suster and cousin's uncle, unto whom Your Ma^te professid assuerid amytie and frendshipp, as also for that he was a nobleman and of Your Ma^te good brothers pryvey councell, with whom you had professed also lyke amytie and mutuall intelligence, youe were desyrous to let him knowe that Your Ma^te did repute him in the nombre of your good frendes, and in like manner was desyrous that he and his shuld make accompte of youe and your friendshipp, as of one that he and they did repute well affected unto theim.

The duke of Guyse humbly thankid Your Ma^te, and sayd that your favour and good affection unto him and his was rather of your grace then of their deserving, but there was nothing to him more acceptable then that he did perceave your susterlie love and amytie to the Quene his niece, unto whom he had the honnour to be uncle, and so requyrid me, sir Harrie Sidney, that I wolde assertayn Your Ma^te that he was readie and willing to do youe service and pleasure.

.   .   .   .

Throckmorton to Cecil.

May 8, 1562.

Sir, you may perceave by thys dyspatche the state of thyngs here, and how perhapps Mr Sydney and I may be employed yn the matter of the composicion of these trebles; therfore I pray you, uppon all events, lett us have sent hyther, with some dilygence, Hyr Ma^tes commyssion or instruction, to auctorise us, and to instructe us of owr dutie and procedyngs, together with Hyr Ma^tes letters of creance to the prynce of Condé and the admirall of Fraunce, in case

the Kyng and the Quene hys mother so employ us in thys affaire :
uppon whatt grownd we be lett to imagyne any suche matter you
may perceave by owr letter to Hyr Ma^{te}. . . .

Whatt somever the conte of Roussy hathe their reaportyd of all
the prince of Condé weaknes, and of the likelyhode of his defeat, I
can assur you att thys dyspatche he ys the strongest partie, and in
suche state his matter stadeth, that these men wold fayne have a
reasonable end, thoughe yt were with some dishonnour. Sir, I pray
you, hold to your hand to kepe Hir Ma^{te} in good opinion with the
prynce of Condé, and th' admyrall, for, when all hys don, theyr
might be her welfare. . . . Thys I am suer of, that all other prynces,
mynysters, wyll empeache what they can to lett that nether the
Quens Ma^{te}, nor none for hyr shuld deale any thyng in the accord
and composicion of thyse dyfferents. By our nexte you shall perceave more.

Queen Elizabeth to Throckmorton and Sydney.

May 10, 1562.

(MINUTE IN CECIL'S HAND.)

Right trusty and wel beloved, we grete you well. We have
receaved II pacquetts of lettres, the one dated the second of this
month from you, our ambassador resident, the other the VIIIth of
the same from you both. By the latter we perceave how discretly
you have discharged your dowties in communicatyng of our mynd
to the Quene mother and how wisely you have proceded to procure
to yourselves, as our ministers, the creditt of entermeddlyng in this
matter, if otherwise it shall not be compounded by there owne mes-
sengars, and if it shall to come to pass that you shall be used herin,
than we wold ye shuld circonspectly behave yourselve, to kepe our
creditt and your owne on both partes, and to prescribe you any
particular negociation with the one parte or the other we can not
directly from hence, because the particulareties ar not knowen to
us, and though they wer at this instant wryting, yet the same ar
subject to such variation from howre to howre, that we can not express any direct and particular waye for you to procede, but generally
we referr you to use your discretion to bend all your actions to bryng
the matter to an end rather by your mediation, than to permitt any
stratagem, prince or potentat, to intermeddle in it, and as you fynd
the cause so to furder that which is most agreable for our weale and
service, whereof we know there needeth not any large declaration.
We have herewith sent you lettres of creditt for you and the prince
of Condé, and another to the admirall, and if you shall by order of

the Quene repayre to them, you may delyver with our harty commendacions, and assure them both that we are desyroose to have
such an end as might tend best to the tranquillitie of christendom,
and the restitution of Christ church. Of your doings and pro-
cedyng, and of occurrances there we require you to give us frequent
advertisement by one meanes or other. . . .

*   *   *   *   *   *   *   *

Queen Elizabeth to the Prince de Condé.

(MINUTE.)   10 mai 1562.

Très-cher et très-amé cousin. Au commencement de ces troubles-
là advenuz entre vous et autres grans personnages du royaume, nous
estions bien marrye; mais, voyant que tant de sages gens se trou-
voient en chascune partye, il nous donna bonne espérance de ne
pouvoir longuement durer. Toutteffois, trouvant maintenant le vent
de ce tout contraire (qui nous a donné cause de plus grant regret),
avons envoyé expressément M. Henry Sydney, chlr, un de noz féaux
serviteurs et conseillers, président de nostre conseil au pays de Galles,
devers nostre bon frère le Roy vostre souverain et la Royne sa mère
pour leur faire entendre nostre advis en quelle manière ces querelles
et controversies d'entre vous se pourroient composer sans effusion de
sang. Nous avons donné mandement exprès audict sr de Sydney et
à nostre ambassadeur là résident, de y employer en nostre nom le
travail et sens selon ce que nous y avons advisé, par quoy eux, ou
l'un d'eulx, auront occasion de traicter avecques vous en cest endroict. Vous requerons les vouloir croire et d'interpréter et prendre
les choses qu'ilz, en nostre endroict, vous mectront en avant, en telle
part que nostre principalle intention en est, assavoir à l'honneur de
Dieu très-puissant, secondement au repos et tranquillité du royaume
de nostre dict bon frère en ce son jeune aage, et outre ce, au bien de
vous et de vostre maison, estant si proche en sang à nostre bon frère
le Roy très-chrestien. Quoy faisant, nous espérons que grand bien
s'en suivra à toutes parties qui sont bien disposées.

Queen Elizabeth to Throckmorton.

(MINUTE.)   July 16 1562.

Right trusty and wel beloved, we grete you well. Uppon the
alteration of the matters there in France, whereof both you by your
letters of the XIIth of this month hath advertised us, and by the
french ambassador yesterdaye we understande we have, by advise of

our counsell entred into such consideration therof, as we have differed our jornaye northward, and have for satisfaction of the Quene of Scotts, our sistar, sent sir Herry Sydney, knight, in post with a sufficient assurance graunt und (*sic*) our hand and great seale, that we will, by God's leave, mete with hir the next yere at Yorck or there about, at any tyme that she shall appoynt betwixt the XXXth of maye, and . the last of august then following. We have also, partly uppon our owne consideration, partly uppon some indirect speche of the french embassador, thought mete presently, to send an ambassador of II of our privee counsell of good authorite to the kyng there, to motion that theis troubles in France might rather take some end by treaty and colloquy than by sword and bloode, and yet before we will send the said embassade on there waye, we wold that you shuld fele the Quene mother's disposition therin, ether indirectly as a thyng wherof you ar advertised by your frends of creditt here, or if ye see nede, for more certenty of hir mynd, ye maye deale directly with her from us, to fele hir mynd, and if she shall not utterly mislyke it, you maye saye we will not forbeare to send thither such persons as shall have creditt for there authorite and indifferency with other part, onely to move a reiteration of treaty and colloquye.

Our meaning is that herin all hast possible be used to have knowledge, and therfore in any wise ritorn to us answer without any delaye of tyme. The french embaxador here hath informid us that the breach of the accord now at Bogancye shuld arrise of the prince of Condee's part in this sorte, that the admyrall and his brother, Monsieur d'Andelott, with sondre others coming to (of that part) speak at the Quene mother, wer content to yeld for quietyng of the realme to depart out of the same, and so to remayn, untill the King shuld come to age, having licence to receive the prouffyts of their lands for ther sustentacion ; and so returning to their camp, they founde the multitude so moche offended herewith, that the prince send her worde they could not performe that which had been yelded unto, whereuppon the Quene mother advertised the duke of Guyse and his parte ; and so they proceded with the armie towards Bleise. He sayth also that the Quene mother offered to the prince that it shuld be permitted to hym and his partie to use their religion in their private houses, so as no preaching, nor other their actions in their religion wer used in any open assemblies or congregacions, either in churches or otherwere, wheruppon the prince wold not assente, so as by theis tales it shuld appere that the breache grewe on the parte of the admyrall, and therfor the Quene mother willed the embassadors to informe us that, uppon these occasions, she was compelled to bryng in force of strangers, as Switzers and others. Now how the truth of this matter is, indede we wold gladly have you to enquire and to advertise us as soone as you maye.

Throckmorton to Queen Elizabeth.

July 23, 1562.

. . . The daly despyghts, injuries and threatenyngs put towards me and myne by the insolent ragyng people of thys towne dothe so assuer me of myn owne dystrucion as I am not ashamyd to declare unto your Ma^te that I am afferd and amasyd, and by so moche the more as I do see that, nether auctoritie of the Kyng, Quene hys mother, nor other person can be saynctuary, ether for me or suche as these furyos people do malyce. I can not justly ley any laste to the Kyng, to the Quene hys mother, nether to all hys councelors, as thoughe they were careless of my saffety, havyng sene, by them, sondry expresse commandements, govyne as well to the Marishall Brysacke (and by hym to others) for my suerty and good usage, as also to others havyng auctoryte yn thys towne, but all to no purpose, for, not only in my case, but in all others, the prynce's commandment ys daily despituously contemnyd and broken, not forbearyng to kill daly, yet almost howerly, bothe men, women and children, notwithstandyng any edict or defence to the contrary, under payne of deathe. I do therfore most humbly beseche Your Ma^te, lett yt not offend you, that I do declare my feare and trewly the grownd thereof. Par avanture yf some wer ponysshyd for these murters and insolences (as theyr ys non) yt wold be a terror to others, not to commytte the lyke. But the King and the Quene hys mother, ar so farr from ponyshyng these ragyng people, as they are glad so to be gardyd at boy de Vyncennes for theyr owne suerty and advoyd the danger and bloddy hands of these Parysyens. The pryncipall offycer of thys realme, and yn my judgement the beste councelor (I meyne the cheanseler), ys as moche threatenyd and yn as grett danger of hys lyffe as I am, and yett he ys lodgyd at a village hard by the courte, wheare he ys forcyd to have the Kyng's gard of Swysses to gard him, whom the Parysyens have threatenyd to spoyle and kill in his lodgyng. The force in armes ys yn the people's hands, not only here, but yn all vylagis in other placis. The Kyng, nor the Quene hys mother, nether dare nor have meanes to rule them. The force of men of armes, souldyers and strangers, ys at the kyng of Navarr, the duke of Guise and constable's devotion, wyche be at Bloys to vanquyshe the prynce of

Condé, and some do not lett to say that, with the provocation of the cardynal in courte of parlyament, these grett personagis before namyd do anymate this madd people to do these excesses and worse. Verely I do thynke they do use to grett connivance. . . .

. . . .

Sir Peter Meautys to Cecil.

July 27, 1562.

. . . I arrived at Parys the XXVI of this present at night, and being theare strictlie examynid at myn entring, and also at my outgoing (as in tymes past hath not bene used), and so being accompaned with dyvers harquebusiers of the guarde unto the Quene's Matie ambassador's house, as it sholde then seme of courtesye. With whome having communycated my hole dispatche and negociation, he for many respects thought not good, being utterlie ignorant before of my commyssion, that I sholde go to the courte with my letters of creance directed to the King and his mother, and the rather because that Monsr de Vieleville is present-lie dispatched from hence into England in so amyable sorte as he is, nether dothe the said ambassador think good, both for the daungier of the weys and for the great suspition that may arryve if I wer intercepted, that I sholde goo to Orleans, and speciallie because that I have no letters of creance to the prince nor admyrall, wether because my leguation shall, as the case standeth, be nothing accept-able unto the prince of Condee, so as this my doings might be an occasion t'altre the prince's good devotion from the Quene's Matie, wherfor th'ambassador doth think good that I have sum letters of creance to the prince and admyrall, and also for all events, to serve an other tone, that I sholde also have Her Ma^tes^ letter to the duke of Guise, the king of Navar, and the conestable, that Her Majestie most earnestlie desireth them to take sum reasonable ordre with the prince of Condee, and also with th'admirall, as well for the cace of religion as for the amyable composition of all quarrels and differences amongst them, and I to use the lyke language on Her Ma^tes^ behalf to the duke of Guise that Her Matie desired he sholde not entre into jalosye and suspition of her amytie to the quene of Scotland his nieace, albeit the entrevue agread upon to have taken place this summer was deferred to the next yeare, at what tyme the matter was fully accorded to taike place without any faile.

Articles presented to the Queen of England by the Prince de Condé.

Août 1562.

Qu'il plaira à S. M. la Royne accorder à Mgr le Prince :
Premièrement, une déclaration en bonne forme :

Que pour la préservation des villes de Normandie S. M. mectra six mil hommes en terre ;

Que S. M. prendra les villes du Havre et de Dieppe en sa protection et garde ;

Que, s'il est possible, sa dicte Majesté mectra des hommes en la ville de Rouen, en remectant cela au jugement de son lieutenant, et au cas qu'elle n'y puisse mectre des hommes, fournira vingt mille escuz, oultre les cent quarante mil ;

Qu'elle recevra aux villes du Havre et Dieppe et aux environs en sa protection les gentilshommes et autres fugitifs des églises réformées ;

Qu'elle tiendra les subjects du Roy, tant des dictes villes que des environs, en leurs biens et libertez.

Qu'il plaise à S. M. pourveoir d'entretenement convenable aux gentilzhommes qui sont dedans le Havre selon leurs qualitez.

S. M. promect de ne se désemparer poinct de la ville du Havre sans le consentement exprès de Monseigneur le Prince, et sans que les gentilzhommes soient remiz en leurs biens.

On supplie très-humblement S. M. qu'entre les seuretez soit exprimé le cas que mondict S^r le Prince, ou Monsr l'admirall, vinssent entre les mains de leurs ennemys ;

Que sa dicte Majesté ne fera accord sans le consentement de Monseigneur le Prince, et sans icelluy ne prendra Calais de la main de ses ennemys ;

Qu'il sera loysible de tirer les marchandises qui sont au Havre et les vendre.

Articles entre la Majesté de la Royne et Monsr le vidame de Chartres, touchant la manière de délivrer la ville du Havre au sieur Adrian Poinings, cappitaine de Portsmeu.

Août 1562.

Monsieur le visdame s'en yra à Portsmeu, et de là s'en reviendra icy ou ira à quelque maison de quelque seigneur ou gentilhomme là voisin, pour n'en bouger jusques à ce que tous les articles qui s'ensuivent ne soyent accompliz.

Premièrement, ledit sieur visdame donnera ordre que sitost que ledit Sr Adrian Poinings arrivera devant ladite ville du Havre, que la principalle tour, qui est assise devant ladicte ville, à l'entrée du Havre, avecques toute l'artillerie et munitions à icelle appartenant, sera délivrée entre les mains et possession de telz capitaines et souldatz que ledict sieur Adrian Poinings assignera, que se fera en telle sorte que lesdicts capitaines et souldatz en auront paisible possession et en seront maistres. Item que le jour que ledict sieur Adrian et les souldatz anglois seront descendus en terre, ilz auront baillé entre leurs mains autant de boulevers et fortz de ladicte ville que le temps avant mitt le souffrira.

Item que le jour suivant que les gens de S. M. seront entrez en ladicte ville, les soldatz françoys ne se mesleront aucunement de la garde d'aucun boullevert, muraille, platte forme, fortresse, artillerie, ou d'aucune autre chose appertenante à la défense de ladicte ville, ains permectront les Anglois d'en avoir entièrement la possession et en user à leur volunté.

Item que toute l'artillerie et munition appertenant au Roy, estantz là pour la défence de ladicte ville, sera délivrées par inventaire audict Sr Adrian, ou à celuy lequel il assignera, et ce d'estre faict dans XXIIII heures après l'arrivée là dudict sieur Adrian.

Item que tous les souldatz françoyz, qui sont dedans ladicte ville, partiront d'icelle dedans deux jours après l'entrée des souldatz anglois (si elle ne soit assiégée), pour aller secourir Rouan, ou faire quelque autre entreprinse, ou en cas qu'ilz ne pourront partir à cause de telle siége, de le faire aussitost qu'ilz le pourront.

S'en ira aussi avecques eulx quelque nombre des Anglois, si ainsi sera jugé nécessaire du lieutenant de S. M. ou dudict Sr Adrian Poinings, à la voulenté desquelz le tout sera remis. Et quant aux habitans de ladicte ville, S. M. permectra leur faire le mesme bon traictement qu'elle faict ordinairement à ses propres subgectz, et eulx, si elle vouldra, y feront serment de y rester fidelz.

Throckmorton to Cecil.[1]

Orléans, October 15, 1562.

Sir, you maye perceave by my letters to Hir Majestie, uppon what respects *I have made somme difficulte at this time to accompanye sir Thomas Smithe to the corte* and to present him. You maye also understande in what tearmes things be here, and *how longe it will be before the prince of Conde can departe this towne to go to the fieldes,* therby you maye perceave *howe I am to seake what I shall do;* therfore yt maye lyke youe to move Hir Ma^{te} that I maye knowe hir

---

[1] The passages in italics are in cypher in the original.

order and pleasure for my further proceadings, and weather *I shall remayne for some tyme in this towne* untyl you maye see *somme further progresse in these matters, or weather I shall accompanye the prynce of Conde to the fyelde when he shall departe hence, which will be a matter for me very dangerose if this case* spede not well, and so suche as be alreadye here en well affectyd unto me wolde my distruction (as there be inoughe) *may be these my doings have some coulor to execute their malice* upon me, or weather Hir Magestie pleasure shal be *that by hoke and by croke, and by as good meanes as* I can, I shall adventere to convey myselfe fourthe of this contrey secretly and by sleyght. . . .

And nowes, Sir, you see that the *protection, garde and defence of Diepe, Newhaven and Roan (if there be any hope left of Roan or that the same be gardable)* restithe only *in Hyr Majestie's hands.*

I trust there will be so good order gaven there redelye and in season *as the holde of the honor, suretye, profite and reputation, which is taken already and wonne by the possession of those peces,* shall not be lost for lacke of good conduct, wyllyngnes *and succoured in tyme.* I coulde wysh that everye noble manne, gentilmanne and *good Englishman were as redy and willing to employ their lifes, helpes and goods to prosecute this good enterprise* spedely, as many be amongst them to *enjoye the pleasures and ease of their contrey,* which be not accompanyed with so much honor, suertye and profett as the *achiving of this enterprise is, and then I myght trust that* forthe, without delaye, XII or XV thousands of our nation *should be* quickly on this syde, a horseback and on foote in good order, which power, by the grace of God, shulde, I ame suer, make a honorable ende of these matters. Sir, watsomever any man saye, Hir Majestie nowe must in no wise *waxe colde, spare nor recule,* for therby dependethe bothe great honor and great perill. Suffer not *your papistes at home* to hoorde up rytches of what qualitye or estats somever they be, but lett them spende and *the protestants* have charge and serve. *Putt your shippes to the sea, command the navigation, lett the french men bothe upon the coast and at the sea smarte in any wise.* . . . Looke about you for to advoyde *papisticall sedytion, accord practises at home, suffer no lyttle sparke thereof to enflambe; take hede of the Scottishe movings and practyses, admonishe th'erle of Mar and the lorde of Ledington to loke to themselves,* and well to beware of treason. *Th'erle of Sussex muste be provydend also, for the house of Guise, with the good advice of the cardinal Ferrare, have layed their baytes in England, Scotland and Ireland to move trouble* and sedytion, in which practises the cardinall Granvel, his brother the resident ambassador here, and the bushope of Aquila be conjoyned and associate. Sir, *the prince of Conde and the admirall hathe,* at this *dispatche,* sent a *cipphre to serve* betwixt *the Quene's Majesie and them,* upon all events, *which they do desier* maye eyther remayne in Hir Majestie coustodie or yours. *The sayd prynce and admirall* hathe desyerid me to make *their affectuouse comendacions* to you *and to my lorde Robert,* and to tell as the Q. Maj^{te} shall durynge *their lives* have of them two willing servants, so you and my sayd lorde Robert shall have *two assueryd frends of them why lest they lyve.* I do perceave the prince dothe mynde to provyde Hir Maj^{te} a fayer litter, with two beautifull moylettz, and a coche shall be sumptuouslye coveryd, and therfor *the sayd prince* dothe desier my lord Robert and you to advertise *him,* by me, what coullors in your opinions shall be moste agreable to Hir Maj^{te}. I do perceave *by him and by the admirall, they do mynde to present you* with some thinge from hence, which they think you want there, and may be agreable to youe, and to conclude I will saye unto you both, and by you unto Hir Maj^{te}, not knowinge what *may become of me* in this casuall state and tyme wherin I am, that the amytie *of the sayd prince, admirall,* of the house of *Chatillon,* ys as worthye to be by Hir Majestie valuyd, embracyde and entertaynyd as *any frendsship in Fraunce of all the house of Bourbon.* I do *think him the wysest and the most sincere prince,* and amongest the noblemen I doo esteame the *admirall* and his *brotherne* the wysest, the most vertuous and most sincere men that be of any apparence in this realme. *The prince* and the noblemen before spoken of be also *most hatefull and most fearyd to the Spanyard and the papists.* .   .   .

VIII.

Minute of Deliberation of Council of Geneva.

4 août 1562.

Ont esté receues lettres du prince de Condé dattées à Orléans du 23 de julliet, par lesquelles après s'estre asseuré de la bonne affection que Messieurs ont à soustenir la querelle de la religion, il les suplie de se déclarer à présent et vouloir adjouster foy à ce qui de sa part leur sera proposé par Monsr Calvin. Surquoy Messegneurs les syndiques ont raporté en avoir parlé avec Monsr Calvin, qui leur a remonstré que la volonté du prince est qu'on responde pour eux la paye de deux mille pistoliers pour troys moys ou qu'on presse l'argent.

Aussi a communiqué les lettres que luy a escriptes ledict S^r prince, par lesquelles il le prie de requérir Messieurs à la levée de gens qu'il fait en Allemagne, ou à tout le moings respondre la somme qui sera requise.   Aussi a monstré autres lettres que luy en a escriptes Monsr l'admiral tendant à mesme fin.   Et leur déclara que la somme pourroyt estre de plus de soixante mille escuz.   Et luy en estant par eux demandé son advis, il se trouva fort perplexe, parce qu'il ne voudroyt pas qu'on le fist pour la grandeur de la somme, et aussi ne sçait comme on le pourroyt refuser.   Toutesfois qu'il seroit d'advis qu'on fasse responce que si ceux de Basle veulent fiancer, Messieurs se constitueront rèrefiances, s'asseurant que ceux de Basle ne le voudront pas faire, et que par ce moyen on les pourra renvoyer honestement.   Ce qu'estant entendu de tous, a causé grande facherie, tant pource qu'il est impossible de fournir à telle somme, en cas qu'il la fallust amender, et que ce seroyt cause de la ruine de la ville, que aussi pource qu'on desire de leur pouvoir assister en tout ou partie. Par quoy a esté résolu qu'on ne se mettra point en telle peine et qu'on n'exposera point la ville en dangier outre noz facultés, et partant qu'on aye bon advis pour leur faire quelque honneste response.

(*Registres du conseil de Genève.*   Volume de 1562, fol. 94, v°.)

IX.

Despatches and documents extracted from the State Paper Office, London (French Papers) between November 20 and December 16, 1562.

The Prince de Condé to the Earl of Warwick.

Du Plessis, 21 novembre 1562.

Monsieur le conte, ce m'a esté ung très-grand plaisir d'avoir entendu de voz nouvelles par la lettre que m'avez escripte du VIe de ce mois, et plus encore de la bonne affection en laquelle je vous retrouve disposé à vous employer en la querelle que maintenant je soustiens à l'encontre des ennemys de l'Evangille, usurpateurs de l'auctorité du Roy, mon seigneur, et perturbateurs du repoz publicq, de quoy je ne veulx oublier à vous en randre le condigne remerciement que vous méritez.   Je puis vous dire que si l'incommodité des passaiges nous ont jusques icy empesché de recevoir lettres l'un de l'autre, j'espère maintenant que Dieu me faict la grâce d'estre en la campaigne et à huict ou neuf lieus de Paris, si bien pourveoir à rendre les chemyns faciles que les moiens nous seront aysez, non-seullement de nous visiter par lettres, mais aussi, s'il plaist à Dieu, de bientost nous entreveoir. Cependant, d'aultant que c'est à ce coup qu'il nous fault à bon escient évertuer de rompre les desseings et entreprinses de noz dicts ennemys, où je m'attends de recevoir du costé de la Royne, vostre royalle maistresse, l'un des meilleurs se-cours, ainsi que desia elle a fort bien démonstré au très-bon com-mencement ; je vous prieray de vostre part, Monsieur le conte, tenir la main envers Sa Majesté qu'elle continue en ung tel et si sainct vouloir, si que de brief et les hommes et l'argent que nous en at-tendons puissent bien arriver, luy faisant particulièrement entendre le besoing que nous en avons et l'utillité qui en proviendra, ainsi que je m'asseure vous vouldriez voluntiers faire, qui me gardera vous en faire plus longue persuasion.

Queen Elizabeth to the Prince de Condé.

4 décembre 1562.

Puisqu'il a pleu à Dieu tout-puissant de rappeller de ceste vie nostre bon frère, le feu roy de Navarre, de l'âme duquel Dieu vueille avoir mercy, nous sommes ejouye que la place que ledict feu roy tenoit pour le Roy très-chrestien, nostre bon frère, en ce son jeune âge, soit (comme il semble) par la providence divine, venue par nature et ordre à vous, ne doubtant rien que comme dès le com-mencement de ces troubles avez cherché d'avoir la personne dudict Roy très-chrestien et de la Royne sa mère mise en pleine liberté, et avec ce le royaume gouverné selon les loix et ordonnances d'icelluy, ainsy vueilliez maintenant, sur ceste présente augmentation d'autho-rité à vous dévolue, persister, continuer en ce mesme pourpos, et dresser tous voz actions à l'honneur de Dieu tout-puissant et au bien du Roy et de son royaume, en quoy nostre assistance ne vous fauldra point. Et nous vous advisons, en bon escient, d'avoir bon esgard de n'escouter à ceulx qui vous tiendront aucunes raisons ou persuasions de décliner de l'asseurer de stable conjunction de voz *fidelz et ap-prouvez amis* et bons serviteurs dudit royaume, comme nous jugeons que M^r *l'admiral* et *ceulx de sa maison* sont ; car nous pensons as-seurément que quelconques qu'ilz soient qui vouldroient ce faire ne veulent user leurs raisons à autre fin que à vostre ruyne et destruction, et ce vous escrivons icy, non sans quelque raison ; pour le reste nous vous prions donner crédit à nostre féal serviteur, messire Nicholas Throckmorton, qui sçait tout nostre intention en toutz noz affaires avecques vous.

Queen Elizabeth to Throckmorton.

(MINUTE.)   December 14, 1562.

. . . For your further information, we *send to you the copye*
of the articles concerning our possession of Newhaven, as we have
them *signed* and *sealed by the prynce of Conde.* Whereuppon ye
maye, as you see can, use the matter towards the prynce, allegyng
that we meane not to utter the same to any person *to doo*
hym or his any dammage, but because he *sameth to take hold of the*
words of our protestation which be generall, and doo conteyne sufficient
matter *for us to demand Callais.* Ye may, as ye see meete, as of
yourself, privatelye deale with hym and the admyrall that they doo
so use us, having for there sake adventured the breakyng of the
treaty and entred into unkyndness both with the king of Spayne
and the french kyng, as the world doo not condene them of ungrate-
fulness, and hereafter occasion us to forbeare intermedlyng with
any of there consels, in what nede so ever they shall be. If they
shall thynck that there shall be any *blott in them, that by there meanes*
we shall recover Callais, they may so use the matter as it may be
delyvered to us by order of justice, because the treaty was broken
in kyng Francis tyme, *and so lett the world to understand that the*
enterprises of the house of Guise wer the cause therof.
On the other part, those men *shall* not conclude with there adversaryes, than we wold that ye shuld therein comefort them to persist, and uppon intelligence had from them, we will lett them
playnely know in what sorte we may ayde them to bryng there
adversaryes to some better reason. . . . . We have gyven sufficient
order to Newhaven to have it garded ageynst all events. Wherin
the most perill is, the contynuance of so *grete* a number of Frenchmen
in that towne, whom we *heare whithall though dangerously,* because
we wold *not offend the prynce* nor his frends, and therin we pray
you have some conference *with the prynce, informing* hym of our
gratuite towards his frends, who shuld utterly perish, *if by our*
meanes they *wer not both preserved from the ennemy,* and ayde with
victualles out of England.

M. de la Haye to the Prince de Condé.

14 décembre 1562.

Monseigneur, la peine où nous sommes est indicible pour n'avoir
de voz nouvelles, veu le mescontentement qu'a Sa Majesté de n'avoir
communication de voz affaires, ny par delà par la voie de son

ambassadeur, ny par deçà par la vostre, comme il est raisonnable qu'il se fasse suivant les accordz qu'elle asseure garder de sa part, continuant à la démonstration de la bonne volunté qu'elle porte à la deffence de vostre cause, de laquelle on ne l'a peu demouvoir par quelques offres et conditions advantageuses qu'on luy ait sceu présenter d'ailleurs ; s'asseurant aussi sa dicte Majesté que vous ferez le semblable en son endroict, et que vous ne conclurez rien en ceste cause qui luy est commune avecques vous sans l'en advertir. Parquoy, Monseigneur, nous vous supplions très-humblement de bien poiser la faveur de telz amys pour les inconvénients que doibt prévoir tout homme qui considère combien les choses qu'on pense le plus souvent bien asseurées sont subjectes à mutation. Nous vous en avons par plusieurs foys escript, et bien au long, et mesmement par une dernière depesche envoyée par Caen.

Monseigneur, nous vous supplions très-humblement penser en quel ennuy peuvent estre ceulx qui sont icy de vostre part.

The Prince de Condé to the Earl of Warwick.

Saint-Arnoul, 14 décembre 1562.

Monsieur le conte, attendant que la commodité se présente plus propre de vous pouvoir voir et deviser privément avecques vous, envoiant maintenant ceste depesche en Angleterre, je n'ay voulu oublier à vous ramentevoir le besoing que nous avons de joir de vostre secours, auquel j'espère, moïennant la grâce de Dieu, me joindre de brief, pour par après mectre quelque fin à tant de calamités. Si Monsieur le conte de Montgommry est de retour avecques quelques forces, je serois bien d'advis que, pour vous devancer, vous vous acheminissiez droit à Honnefleur pour plus faciliter le chemin et à l'une et à l'autre armée.

The Prince de Condé to Queen Elizabeth.

Saint-Arnoul, 16 décembre 1562.

Madame, j'ai receu avec très-grand contentement les deux lettres qu'il a pleu à Vostre Majesté escrire, l'une du seziesme du passé, et l'autre du présent, ainsy que j'estois prest de vous depescher ce porteur pour vous faire incontinent et bien au long entendre ce qui s'est négotié en l'abouchement qui est ces jours passez intervenu prez Paris entre la Royne mère et moy, bien que noz adversaires, desquelz ne procède que déguisement de vérité, ayans en main toutes commoditez et ministres propres pour exécuter toutes leurs volontez, n'auront pas failly, usans de leurs artifices accoustumez, de peindre ce faict de faulses couleurs et faire servir à leurs passions et advantage ; négotiation de paix laquelle vous pourrez, Madame, entendre au vray simplement comme elle s'est passée, *par le discours que je envoye présentement, lequel vous démonstrera au doigt et à l'œil en quel devoir je me suis mis et me suis condescendu à toutes les plus douces et raisonnables conditions,* dont je me suis peu adviser pour essayer *mettre une bonne, ferme et seure paix en ce royaume et l'exempter des calamitez dont il est affligé, n'ayant demandé autre chose que la liberté des consciences avec la conservation de l'honneur et la seureté des biens et personnes de ceux qui se sont employez en ceste cause, sans avoir regardé du tout des advantages que je pouvois lors avoir sur mes ennemys pour* le desir que j'avois de parvenir à ceste effect, sans aussy avoir voulu faire *instance du lieu qui de droict me apartient en ce royaume, et qu'on ne me peut tollir, ce qui servira pour le moins à justifier davantage mes actions, à découvrir la malice de noz ennemyz et le but de leurs mauvaises intentions, et à nous esmouvoir de poursuivre ceux qui n'ont autre fin proposée que la ruyne de l'Église de Dieu et de la relligion de tous ceux qui en font profession,* et généralement de touts les subgectz du Roy ; en quoy j'espère, avec l'ayde de la Majesté divine, *et de la vostre, m'employer tellement, sans m'arrester désormais à parlement et négotiation, que malgré eux Dieu sera servy par tout ce royaume et ses serviteurs exemptz de leur violence et cruautez ; vous suppliant au reste très-humblement,* Madame, vouloir rejecter *la faulte de ce que vous n'avez plus souvent de mes nouvelles sur l'incommodité et difficulté des chemins et passages,* ensemble vouloir croire que je n'eusse jamais entièrement conclue aucune chose *en ce faict sans première n'avoir adverty Vostre Majesté, pour sur ce suivre vostre conseill. Et où cy aprèz telle négotiation interviendroit,* à quoy toutes fois je me suis résolu de n'entendre *aucunement si autre chose ilz ne vouloient mectre en avant, ceste lettre vous servira,* Madame, *de gaige et asseurance que je ne conclurai jamais rien sans en avoyr vostre advis, ny accorderay chose quelconque qui vous touche sans vostre consentement, estant en oultre bien* délibéré de me conduire tousiours *par le conseil de Mons' l'admirall et ceux de sa maison pour les cognoistre des plus gens de bien et plus affectionnez qui soyent de ce royaume,* aussy d'ajouster foy à tout ce que me fera entendre *maistre Nicolas Throgmorton de vostre part, duquel j'ai desia entendu ce que vous luy aviez donné charge de me dire, qui vous fera entendre ma response.*

X.

The Admiral of France to Queen Elizabeth.

Auneau, 22 décembre 1562.

Madame, sinon qu'il nous fault recevoir patiemment tout ce qu'il plaist à Dieu nous envoyer et nous conformer en toutes choses à sa saincte volunté, je desirerois bien d'avoir ung meilleur subgect pour escrire à V. M. que celuy qui se présente, qui est que le XIXᵉ de ce moys, Monsieur le prince de Condé, desirant mectre une fin aux troubles et désolations qui sont en ce royaume, aprocha de si prez noz ennemys, que sans regarder à l'advantage du lieu et au nombre des gens de pied et d'artillerie qu'ilz avoient, il leur donna la bataille, en laquelle Dieu a permis qu'il ayt esté pris, mais ce a esté avec si grande perte et ruyne de leur cavallerie que la plus grant part de leurs chefs et principaux capitaines ont esté pris, tuez et blessez, et la nostre, qui est demeurée entière et qui a faict l'exécution sans avoir perdu plus de quatre-vingts ou cent chevaulx, est en ceste résolution de poursuivre l'entreprinse présente de tout son pouvoir et de toutes ses forces. Et parce, Madame, que Monsieur le Prince vous a faict cy-devant entendre son intencion, et que nous vous avons tous telle asseurance en la vertu et bonté de V. M., au zèle que vous avez tousiours démonstré avoir à l'advancement de la gloire de Dieu, et aux grâces que Dieu a mis en vous, dont nous avons assez de cognoissance et expérience, je n'ay voullu faillir de vous suplier très-humblement, Madame, de vouloir, maintenant que la nécessite et l'occasion s'y présentent, nous donner le secours qui nous est nécessaire, selon que vous entendrez de Mʳ de Briquemault, lequel il playra à Vostre Majesté ouyr, et le croire de ce qu'il vous dira, tant de ma part que de toute ceste compaignie, qui espérons que, par vostre bon moyen et avec l'ayde de Dieu, qui marchera devant nous pour combatre pour sa querelle, l'yssue en sera si heureuse que il sera servy par tout ce royaume, et le Roy obéy de tous ses subgectz avec ung repos et tranquillité publique.

(*State Paper Office.* French Papers.)

XI.

The Connétable de Montmorency ' a la Royne, ma souveraine Dame.'

Orléans, 22 décembre 1563.

Madame, Madame la Princesse, aiant esté advertie de la prinse de Monsieur le Prince son mary, m'a prié vous escripre et supplier très-humblement estre contente que Monsieur le prince de Melphe [1] voyse vers vous et que je luy bailasse une lettre à ce qu'il vous plaise estre contente de le veoir et l'ouyr, vous asseurant qu'elle est si travaillée et affligée qu'il est impossible de l'estre davantage. Et je suis prisonnier en sa maison, là où elle me faict si bon traictement que je tien ma vie du soing qu'il luy a pleu me faire. Par quoy je vous supplie très-humblement de vostre bonté accoustumée avoir extrêmement recommandé mondit seigneur le Prince, comme je sçay qu'il vous a pleu luy porter tousiours fort bonne et grande affection ; et . . . que Nostre Seigneur a voulu que les charges de ceste bataille soient passées, en sorte que, j'espère, il en réussira une bonne paix, qui est ce que plus vous desirez en ce monde. Madame, je suis blessé d'une harquebuze en la machouere et d'un coup de pistollet. J'espère en Nostre Seigneur estre bientost guery et en estat de vous pouvoir faire service là où je n'espargneray ma vie, vous suppliant, Madame, avoir la connestable extrêmement recommandée. . . .

(*Autogr.*) Madame, Monsieur le prynce de Melfe vous fera antendre la bonne voullenté quy a an ceste compagnye d'avoyr ugne bonne pes. Je vous suplye, Madame, d'avoyr pour byen recommandé Monsyeur le Prince.—Vostre tres-humble et très-obéyssant subgect et servyteur,

MONTMORENCY.

Madame, je vous suplye que ce jantyllomme voye Monsyeur le Prince, vous aceurant que je suys sy byen trété que je vous suplye d'avoyr celles de Monsyeur le Prince pour recommandé.

· (*Archives de Condé.* Original ; signature and ten lines autograph.)

---

[1] Antoine Caraccioli, Prince de Melphe, was descended from an illustrious and well-known family, which still exists in the kingdom of Naples. His father, Jean Caraccioli, having espoused the French cause, quitted Naples along with our army, and received the Maréchal's bâton in the year 1544. He subsequently became Governor of Piedmont, and died at Susa in 1550. Antoine, at first a Dominican friar, afterwards a Carthusian monk, and in 1538 Canon of Saint-Victor of Paris, in 1543 Abbot of the same, became in 1551 Bishop of Troyes. He early gave signs of an inclination to the Reformed faith, but he did not abjure till after the Colloquy of Poissy. Of dissolute morals, of a vacillating and uncertain temper, he was always suspected of insincerity, and in particular of disloyalty in the negotiations with which he was entrusted after the battle of Dreux and during the siege of Orléans. He afterwards confessed as much in an apology which he addressed to the Protestant ministers (*Mémoires de Condé*, v. 47). Beza, in his history, passes a severe censure upon him. He died, in 1569, at Châteauneuf-sur-Loire.

XII.

The *Mémoires de Condé* contain a great number of documents relating to the negotiations which preceded the Peace of 1563. The four following letters have never been published.

The Princess de Condé ' a la Rayne.'

Sans date.

Madame, n'ayant peu congnoistre mon oncle Dendelot et ceste compagnie avec moy, l'intansion et voulonté de Monsieur mon mary par la lectre quy la escrite à Vostre Magesté touchant Monsieur le prince de Guynvylle, c'est se quy nous faict suplyer très-humblemant Vostre Magesté ne trouver mauvelx que ne fasions nulle réponse que premyèremant ne ayons envoyé vers ledict seigneur sur se entendre résolumant son avys ; et pour cest effect vous suplions très-humblemant, Madame, quy voùs playse donner congé à se porteur, quy est à luy, que pryvémant et en partycullier il en puysse resevoyr sa voulonté. Car c'est une chose de sy grand importanse que ne povons passer plus avant à répondre iusque à se qu'ayons sa résollusion, et n'est pour prolonger le moyen d'avoyr une pays, mays seullemant pour randre les choses plus clères et asùurée ; car c'est se qu'en se monde desyrons plus que de la veoyr bien faicte, et par se moyan avoyr la liberté de Monsieur mon mary, pour luy et moy plus que jamays nous amployer à vous fayre très-humble servyse, supliant Dieu, Madame, que bien tost se bien tant desyré, soit donné à Vos Magestés et à tous vos subgects avec très-heureuse et longue vye.

Vostre très-humble et très-obéissante subjecte et servante,

LÉONOR DE ROYE.

(*Archives de Condé.* Original autograph.)

The Prince de Condé ' a la Rene.'

Amboise, 28 février 1563.

Madame, vous avés peu voyr et connestre derremant mon yntansiont pour le partemant de Monsr le conétable par la dernyerre lettre que jé escryte à Vostre Magesté et ausy à ma femme, quy me gardera, aient surssela toujours ungne opinyont, an fère long discours de ma vouslonté, vous supliant très-humblemant de crère comme je voys que lavès cru que je necrys deun et fais antandre daustre, et cossy peu voudres-je antretenyr Vostre Magesté à négosiasiont disversse, et quy plus ma fait pancer quy ne vousdre à se que leur ó mandé, et pourres par saiste foys fère antandre sy condescendre: sait que disse quyl le veullie tous y consantyr; quy me fait fort peu esperrer quyl le veullie permetre; vous supliant très-humblemant, Madame, crère de moy que ne desire rien tant au monde que davoyr de Vos Magestés les moiens pour vous fère connestre que ne soryes anploier homme en vostre reosme quy plus desire voir une bonne pais que je fais, et quy plus desire vous fere ung bon servyce que moy, suplient Dieu, Madame, quy me fasse la grâce que le puyssyez bien crère, et vous donne autant de con-tantemant que vous an desiré. Danboysse, se dernier jour de feuvryer.

Vostre très-humble et très-obéyssant suget et servyteur,

LOYS DE BOURBON.

(*Archives de Condé.* Original autograph.)

The Prince de Condé to the Princess.

Amboise, 28 février 1563.

Veu les lettres cavés de moy resue, vous avés peu connestre mes yntantiont; par coy sait à moy follie vous an fère antandre davan-tage; car pour la mort de Monsr de Guysse quy a été tué sy myssérablemant, l'opynyon ne met nullement changée, et de vous an escryrre davantage se seret abus, veu la ressolution que seus d'Orléans on tous prysse de ne léser partyr Monsr le connetable; vous prient tous de bien considérer les meschanssetés que saiste guerre tire après elle, quy et bien ung suget pour tous desirer la pais: suplien seluy quy tyen les cuers des roys et des hommes quy les disposse an resevoyr les moyens et reculler seus quy vousdront aler au contrayrre et chatié seus quy n'y vousdront antandre. Car anvers Dieu et leur roy méryte grande punysiont. Je masurre que vous amployrés an tous se que pourrés, se que vous prye fère de toutte votre puysance; car sait une requête que vous an fais de tout mon cuer; car je ne desire ryen tant comme une bonne pays quyl ne soit point fainte et quy soit à loneur de Dieu et servyce du Roy proufitable; quy sera la fin de saiste lestre, après avoyr à tante et oncle pressenté mes bien afecsionnée recommandasion à leur bonne grace et quy vous doint à tous autant de contantemant que vous an desiré.

Danboyse, se dernyer jour de fevryer.

Votre bien afecsionné et bon mary,

LOYS DE BOURBON.

(*Archives de Condé.* Original autograph.)

The Prince de la Roche sur Yon to the Queen Regent.

Amboise, 3 mars 1563.

APP.
XII.

Madame, si je me trouvay en peyne, recevant votre commande-
mant, venir en ce lieu, encores plus quant je my suis veu, estant si
peu instruit comme toutes choses estoit passées entre vous et mondit
Sᴿ le Prince qu'il a fallu je l'aye apris de luy mesme. Car vostre
lettre ne tandoit principalemant que pour la déclaracion de la sienne
ambigue qui m'a montrée et a assuré n'a ryen mandé que de
mesmes ce qu'il a escript à vous, Madame, et à Madame sa fame, et
que la mort de Monsieur de Guise, qu'il a autant pris à cueur que
de son propre frère, estant mort son amy, et qu'à son fils il ne le
pardonneroit, desirant sa punition où ny espargnera sa propre vye
au chastiment de sy meschant acte, m'assurant ladite mort ne l'a
faict changer d'opinion, ne moins l'affection qu'il a à vous obéir en
tout ce qui vous playra, soit pour l'aboucher avecques Monsieur le
connestable ou aultrement, pour s'acheminer à la paix; mais il
crint, come il avoit dit à Monsieur l'admiral quà lheure il apela à
thémoin, et luy avoir dit, quant l'homme d'Orléans arrivast, que
jamays il ne consentirest la sortie dudit connestable, mondit Sᴿ le
Prince n'y entrast, et que ce moyen tyroit toute choses en longueur;
desirant tousiours avecques toutes seuretés, soit de son fils ou ce
que choysires, de pover parler à ceux d'Orléans qu'il aseure ranger
et manier de sorte que dedans dix jours il espère la paix; et au cas
qu'il falle se randre où il sera ordonné au tembs, qu'il sera tenu
incapable et indigne du nom qu'il porte, et permet à tous le tenir
pour méchant, et sa vie en abandon, le faisant mourir comme poltron,
pardonnant sa mort. Le tout que dessus a dit devant mondit Sᴿ
l'admiral. Vela, Madame, ce que j'ay peu tirer de ce petit homme.
Il n'y a rien de nouveo. La venue de Monsieur de Limoges nous
aprendra quelque chose, mesmes si avés parlé à Madame la Princesse.
Il demande fort à vous voyr si l'avyés agréable; il me semble que
ne seret maulvays l'ouyr parler, mais davant partie du conseil y
asseroit jugemant sur ces propos et asseurances et promesses, et
davant tous on y adviseroit, et chacun parleroit pour congnoystre
s'il y a tromperye. Quant à moy, Madame, je voy des langajes que
je n'avoys jamays entendues. J'espère vous en dire davantage. Se
n'est au serviteur an parler plus avant; en playne compagnye j'ose
dire mon opinion, vous assurant, Madame, que le ferai en ma
conscience pour l'honneur de Dieu et service de mon maistre, et
utilité et advantage de ce posvre et affligé reaulme; notre Seigᴿ
m'en doint la grace.

(*Archives de Condé.* Original autograph.)

XIII.

The Prince de Condé ' aux magnifiques Seigneurs Messieurs les Syndics et Seigneurs du Conseil de Genève.'

Orléans, 28 mars 1563.

Magnifiques Seigneurs, puisqu'il a pleu à nostre bon Dieu commancer à réduire les troubles et confusions dont si longtemps comme chacun sçait ce pouure Royaume a esté affligé pour le faict de la religion à une pacification et tranquillité, et qu'il semble, à voir l'acheminement des choses, que nous ne pouvons désormais attendre sinon une augmentation autant grande en l'avancement du règne de Jésus Christ par la pure prédication de son Évangile, comme les ennemys de sa vérité luy doient présomptueusement non-seulement la retarder ou empescher, ains plus tost la ruyner et abattre, et que pour cette raison Monsr de Besze a là-dessus prins argument, quoyque à mon regret, de se retirer de ce pays pour aller au vostre rendre en vostre endroict le devoir auquel sa vocation le tient obligé, Je ne l'ay voulu laisser partir sans l'accompagner de ceste lettre qui servira non pour témoigner les vertueux et louables offices qu'il a faicts en la poursuitte et défense d'une si saincte et juste querelle, d'aultant qu'ils sont si notoires et congneus que ce ne seroit que superfluitté de les déduire ou publier davantaige, mais pour premièrement vous remercier bien affectueusement de la faveur que j'ay receu de vous, me l'ayant laissé aussi longuement que luy-mesme a jugé sa présence estre requise, et à moy son bon conseil nécessaire à la conduicte et maniement d'une cause si importante, veu qu'elle regardoit à la gloire de ce grand Dieu et la conservation de l'auctorité de mon jeune roy, en quoy il a beaucoup servy à inciter les ungs et contenir les autres à l'exécution de leurs charges, et puis, me remestant sur sa suffisance à vous découvrir et rapporter particulièrement les occurrences et événemens tant de la guerre que de ceste paix, et du bien qui s'en peult espérer, vous asseurer, Magnifiques Seigneurs, que toutes les gratifications et honnestes démonstrations de la bonne volonté que m'avez en ce faict offertes, tiendront toute ma vie tel lieu en ma mémoire que s'offrant occasion pour user envers vous d'une digne recongnoissance, vous congnoistrez par effect de quelle affection je m'y emploieray, et que par ce moyen je suis certain vous ne regretterez point les plaisirs que m'avez impartis, ainsi que j'ay prié ledict Seigneur de Besze vous le faire entendre.

(*Archives de Genève.* Original.)

XIV.

Despatches and documents from the State Paper Office, London (French Papers), January 1 to July 24, 1563.

The Prince de Condé to Queen Elizabeth.

17 février 1563.

Madame, si la comisération des paouvres affligez pour la parolle de Dieu, si la recordacion des mesmes occasions passées ont aujourd'huy quelque lieu en vostre endroict, et si la continuacion de voz premières bonnes volontez à employer les moyens qu'il a pleu à ce grand Seigneur vous impartir, n'a aucunement altéré ou interrompu en mon endroict ce que desjà V. M. a tant et si vertueusement tesmoingné, il fault que maintenant je vous supplie considérer mon estat et condition, et ce que mon estat requiert à présent, qui est de vous supplier pour ma délivrance, laquelle n'important moins que la pleine liberté des consciences fidelles et chrestiennes, la conservacion de l'authorité, du bien et du service de mon roy et le soulagementz de toute la France, vous appelle et sollicite à vous encourager au secours de celluy qui, comme chef en ce royaume, vous supplie très-humblement, Madame, que, augmentant vostre affection, vous en hastez aussi l'effect, jugeant en cela combien les jours et les mois, et encore plus les années sont longs et insupportables. Aiant doncq esgard à ce que dessus, me confortant d'une bonne espérance de vostre bienveillance, je ne m'estendray plus avant en propoz, sinon prier le Créateur, Madame, conserver en longue prospérité V. M. saine et heureuse.

De la prison, le XVII février.

Vostre très-humble et très-obéissant serviteur,

Loys de Bourbon.

The Prince de Condé to Queen Elizabeth.

Orléans, 8 mars 1563.

Madame, tout ainsi que j'ay tousiours singulièrement desiré estre trouvé aussi véritable en mes effectz comme mes parolles en ont baillé la première asseurance, aussi desirant que mes actions rendissent ung clair et ouvert tesmoignaige de l'intérieur de mon cueur, je n'ay pas voulu oublier, incontinant que l'on m'a commancé à entamer quelque propoz d'entrer en une pacification des troubles esquelz la France est enveloppée pour le faict de la religion, de satisfaire à la promesse faicte de ma part à V. M. de sousdain vous en tenir advertye, qui est la principalle occasion de cette depesche ; par laquelle vous entendrez comme depuis la mort de feu Monsr de Guise, il a pleu à Dieu tellement disposer les cueurs des personnes de l'un et de l'autre costé, que, après avoir bien discouru, tantost sur la calamité qui afflige ce royaume, et tantost sur la commodité des remèdes, finallement la Royne, avecques la meilleure et plus saine partie des princes du sang, a advisé que M. le connestable et moy, qui estions tous deux prisonniers, nous entreverrions, affin que comme ceulx qui y avoient le plus de moyen, nous eussions à diligemment y vacquer et entendre, ce que cejourd'huy commençasmes, et n'y eut seulement qu'une visitation de passes et salutations, entremeslée de plainctes de veoir ainsi les François se précipiter d'eulx-mesmes à une piteuse ruyne.   Et pour autant que la captivité et prison de l'un et de l'autre ne pouvoit comporter de librement conduire une chose si importante à quelque bonne et heureuse fin, nous délibérasmes de supplier très-humblement la Royne d'estre contente que sur nostre foy, chacun de nous seroit mis en liberté, ce que S. M. nous a cejourd'huy accordé, et à moy particulièrement ung saulf conduict pour la seuretté de ce gentilhomme qui s'en va vers la vostre, laquelle je supplieray très-humblement, Madame, que suivant les vertueux offices de piété, dont si sainctement vous avez usé à l'endroit de ceulx qui taschent de conserver la pure religion, et que Dieu a tant honnorez que de les faire instrumens de la gloire de son filz Jésus-Christ, du nombre desquelz il vous a appelée au premier rang, maintenant vous faictes congnoistre tant au Roy, vostre bon frère, que à ceulx que vous avez daigné tant favoriser que de les recevoir en vostre bonne grâce, combien cette cause vous est chère et affectionnée, et que autre occasion ne vous a menée à nous favoriser que le seul zelle que vous portez à la protection des fidelles qui desirent la publicacion de la pureté de l'Évangille, selon que la protestation que V. M. en a si manifestement faicte le porte et déclaire ; vous avisant, Madame, que à mesures que nous entrerons au faict de ce négoce, je ne seray paresseux de continuer à vous faire entendre le plus souvent qu'il me sera possible, tant par mes lettres que parce que j'en communiqueray avecques vostre ambassadeur de par deça comme les choses passeront.

The Prince de Condé to Smith.

Orléans, 11 mars 1563.

Monsieur l'ambassadeur, j'ay esté fort ayse d'entendre par mon oncle, Monsieur d'Andelot, le moyen qu'il avoyt de vous tenir seurement adverty de l'occurrence des affaires et de l'estat de quoy les

choses passent pour la pacification de ces troubles, affin que, par ce
que je vous en manderay, ce vous soyt plus juste occasion de le faire
sçavoir au vray à la Royne vostre maistresse, et rendre capable S. M.
de laquelle franchise et sincérité je me veulx conduire en toutes mes
actions, et conséquemment rompre, s'il m'est possible, le cours des
faux bruicts que l'on pourroit semer au préjudice de ma situacion en
son endroict; qui me fera vous dire que, combien que auparavant la
blessure de feu Monsieur de Guyse, il y eut quelque propoz de nous
faire parler ensemble, Monsieur le connestable et moy, et regarder
s'il se pourroit trouver quelque remède expédient pour esteindre ce
turbulent feu de sédition, et faire respirer la France d'un repoz plus
désiré que espéré ne attendu ; touteffois les obstacles des négociations
passées avoient engendré telz soubzons et meffiances d'une part et
d'autre, que les seurettez de cette entreveue seullement se retrouvans
difficiles à accorder, rendoient l'accession de cest achemynement mal
aisé, voire impossible. Mais depuis qu'il eut plu à Dieu appeler le
feu seigneur de Guyse, duquel je ne veulx qu'en toute sobriété,
modestement parler, il sembla que toutes les difficultés et doubtes
eussent avecques sa vie prins fin ; de façon que la Royne reprenant
les premiers arretz de ses desseingz qui tendoient de parvenir à la
paix, y a si vivement proceddé, que, ayant ordonné que sur la foy de
l'un et de l'autre, nous nous entreverrions à l'Ille-aux-Bouviers,
joignant presque les murs de ceste ville, dimenche dernier cela fut
exécuté. Et de faict, après avoir devisé de prime face des choses
plus communes, nous entrasmes sur celles qui causoient ce voyage
et de ce qui se pouvoit faire pour contanter S. M. et restaurer les
ruynes et calamitez de ce royaulme, et dont le discours des propoz
seroit trop long à réciter, sinon pour conclusion nous arrestaasmes
que, pour plus librement y adviser, il estoit requis que moy d'ung
costé, et luy de l'autre, devyons conférer, moy avecques ceulx de
ceste ville, et luy à la Royne, de ce qui nous sembloit le plus
propre. Et ainsy nous départismes jusques au lendemain, où ladicte
dame vint au mesme lieu pour nous octroyer ceste licence, laquelle
obtenue, tellement a esté disputté par l'espace de deux jours : de ma
part, sur l'instance que je faisois pour l'observacion et entretenement
des edictz du Roy, mon seigneur, et principallement de celluy que
S. M. feist au moys de janvier cinq cens soixante ung (V. S.)
avecques une très-notable et insigne assemblée, pour le faict de la
religion ; et de celle de Monsieur le connestable, sur l'impossibilité
qu'il alléguoit de le pouvoir tollérer par les papistes, veu l'infrac-
tion que par violance en avoyt esté faicte ; que finablement S. M.
de son auctorité, nous envoya par escript ung mémoire, dont la

coppie est cy-enclose, pour sur icelluy respondre de ce qui se pouvoit davantage requérir ; à quoy, tant pour tesmoigner des effectz de nostre continuelle obéissance envers S. M. que pour ayder à la nécessité d'un temps si nubilleux (*nébuleux ?*), après avoir protesté ne vouloir en rien nous départir de la substance de la loy de mon roy, synon en tant qu'il estoit besoing de prévenir le péril qui mena-çoit sa couronne et son estat, je, par l'advis des seigneurs, gentilz-hommes, et aussi des gens de bien qui sont icy, en dressay ung autre à peu près pareil, duquel semblablement je vous envoye la coppie pour vous faire congnoistre que tout ainsi que je ressens les grandes obligacions dont je suys redevable envers la Royne, vostre bonne maistresse, m'ayant assisté de sa faveur en mes affaires et afflictions, aussy je ne veulx estre paresseux de la rendre participante du bien et consolation qui se prépare pour nous, premier que nous l'ayons receu ; vous priant, Monsieur l'ambassadeur, luy faire fidelle-ment entendre que l'inclination de mon naturelle est telle que mon cueur ne sçauroit comporter une ingratitude, comme le vice entre les plus énormes, qui m'est autant odieux et en horreur. Et quand Dieu permectra que j'aye les moyens en ce royaume de luy démon-strer par effect ce que je sens entyèrement beaucoup mieulx que je ne puis en apparence déclairer, alors S. M., s'il luy plaist, confessera qu'elle n'aura point regret d'avoyr obligé ung prince de sa bonne volunté, et de s'estre acquis ung tel serviteur.

P. S. Je vous prye, Monsieur l'ambassadeur, faites entendre à la Royne, vostre bonne maistresse, que comme je n'ay prins les armes que pour la gloire de Dieu et la conservacion des édictz du Roy, aussy ne m'en deppartiray-je point que je ne veroye son service premièrement estably, mon roy obéy, et ses subjectz en repoz et liberté de leurs consciences, au contantement de tous les princes chrestiens, et au soullagement des pauvres fidelles.

This and the preceding despatch have been inaccurately printed in Forbes's Collection. They are here republished on account of their special importance.

The Prince de Condé to Queen Elizabeth.

Orléans, 17 mars 1563.

Madame, je croy que vous aurez, de cette heure, receu la lettre que je vous ay dèrnièrement escripte, et par icelle entendu les pré-paratifz qui se dressoient pour la paciffication de ces troubles, et pource que ce commancement a esté fort vivement poursuyvy par la Royne, comme chose à quoy S. M. ne pouvoit assez tost à son gré voir une fin heureuse et plus desirée, je n'ay voullu faillir, suivant ma promesse, d'advertir incontinent la vostre, comme ayant esté pressé d'y vacquer, et ne m'estant honnestement licite de refuser à y entendre, ou retarder l'effect d'une tant saincte et nécessaire négociation, nous avons résolu sur le poinct de la religion le contenu aux articles que je vous ay envoyez, par le bénéffice desquelz la pure foy est sans viollance tellement enracinée en ce royaume, que si la malice des hommes ne s'oppose à la bonté de Dieu, nous espérons que en peu de temps, chacun verra l'accroissement du fruict qui en proviendra à son honneur et gloire et au repoz et seuretté des consciences et biens de tous les pauvres subjectz de la France.   Et desià, Madame, je vous puis bien asseurer que pour la jouissance d'un si grand bien, nous craignons plus tost avoir faulte de ministres pour le distribuer, que des lieux et endroictz pour le recevoir, mais d'aultant que ordinairement ce grand Dieu suscite des moissonneurs scelon que la moisson est grande, aussi nous nous asseurons tout sur sa providence, et ce qu'il sçaura bien pourveoir à tout.   Et combien que la principalle occasion qui nous a faict prendre les armes est maintenant levée, si est-ce que nous avons tousiours fait l'arrest de tout le négoce jusques à l'arrivée de Monsr l'amiral, ayant supplié la Royne ne trouver mauvais si, sans le consentement de luy et des seigneurs qui sont de sa compaignie, nous ne pouvons rien accepter ny conclure, auquel temps j'ay remys à parler ce que touche le bien de voz affaires particulières, n'ayant touteffois oublyé cependant d'en entamer et ouvrir quelque propoz à S. M., et principallement de l'obligation que je ressentois de la faveur et du secours que vous avez tant libérallement conféré pour la conservation de l'estat et auctorité du Roy son filz, vostre bon frère, qui n'est seullement que pour aplanir le chemyn, et rendre d'une part et d'autre les choses difficiles ains plus aysées et faciles, d'aultant que, ayant communiqué avec luy, qui entend très-bien ce qui sainement en cela se peult faire, tous ensemble, nous tenions la main en ce que la fidélité de nostre devoir le pourra permettre, de conseiller à S. M. ce qui se devra légitimement octroier, où de ma part je vous supplie très-humblement, Madame, d'estimer que je n'obmettray chose en quoy consciencieusement je me puisse employer, et qui se peult attendre d'un loyal subject à son Roy, et à vous, Madame, très-affectionné serviteur.

The Admiral of France to Queen Elizabeth.

Brou, 21 mars 1563.

Madame, j'ay cejourd'huy receu une lettre de Monsieur le prince de Condé, par laquelle il m'advertit comment toutes choses sont concluttes et arrestées, pour la pacificacion des troubles de ce royaume, synon qu'il reste à prendre une résolution sur ce qui touche vostre faict, puys aussy de l'authorité qu'il aura, et quant est du contenu aulx articles de ce traicté, il ne m'eschet vous en dire aultre chose, Madame, synon qu'ilz sont (à peu près) suyvant ceulx desquels je vous ay envoyé une copie par le sieur de Chastellus. Au surplus, sur ceste occasion, je n'ay voulu faillir avecques la lettre que mon dict S^r le Prince vous escript, de vous faire aussy la présente, pour supplyer très-humblement Vostre Majesté de croire que quant on sera sur la délibération de ce que touche vostre faict, Madame, laquelle on me mande avoir esté remise et différée jusques à ce que je me trouve au conseil, où l'on advisera de ce point, je ne fauldray poinct de m'acquitter de mon debvoir, suyvant la promesse que j'ay faicte à Vostre dicte Majesté.

Myddlemore to Queen Elizabeth.

Orléans, March 30, 1563.

It maye please Your Ma^te, the admyrall arryved at this towne the XXIII^d of this present, leavinge his reystors in garisone fyve or VI leagues from the same. The morninge next after, I spake with the prince of Conde, and declaryd unto him as muche as was in my charge, by myne instructions, for the which he gave Your Ma^te his most humble thanks, sayinge that next after God Your M^te was the persone onlye that he dyd holde his lief of, and that, as he was most bownden, so he dyd most owe unto the same, the best service he coulde doo, reservynge only his dutye towards the Kyng his master, with manie other fayer and goodlye words tendinge to Your Ma^te great honor and praise, and to the declaration of the greatness of his, the prince's, bende towards youe, which being at an ende, he toke occasion, upon some wordes that I had sayd to him, to tell me howe muche the Queene mother seamyd to be for him and his partye at this daye, and that not longe before she had declaryd unto hime that the deathe of the duke of Guyse had no lesse redemyd hir out of prison than the same had sett him, the prince, at lybertye, and that as the prince beinge was captyve by him, so she, by the forces he had about the Kinge and hir, was no lesse his prisonner, and depryved of lybertye by him; and tolde me further that the sayd Quene mother gave him advice to have always about him in the court a good troupe of gentylmen, by meanes wherof he shulde be both in suertye and obeyed, as the Kynge and she dothe desyer he shulde. And as touchinge Your Ma^{tes} satisfaction, he sayd he had hitherto lefte the same unmovyd, avydinge the admirall's arrivall, without whom and whose advice he thought not good to deale with the Quene mother in yt, but nowe that the admyrall was come, they wolde not fayle, but forthwith go in hande with the same, and that in suche sort, as he trustyd, yt shulde be to the good contentation of Your Ma^{te}. The prince and the admyrall have bene twise with the Quene mother since my commynge hyther, where the admirall hath bene very earnest for a further and larger lybertye in the course of religion, and so hath obtaynyd that there shall be preachings within the townes in every balliage, wheras before yt was accordyd but in the suburbs of townes only, and that the gentylmen of the visconte and provoste of Parys shall have in theyr houses the same libertye of religion as ys accordyd elzwhere, so as the sayd admyrall doth nowe seame to lyke well inoughe that he shewyd by the waye to mislyke so muche, which was the harde articles of religion concludyd upon by the prince in his absence. The prince and admyrall wyll not be acknowledged unto me that they have as yet spoken or openyd Your Ma^{te} demands unto the Quene mother, otherwise then in generall tearmes, but I ame suer they have in cowncell togeather had great discourse of the same, and reasonyd at large of all the particularyties. . . . . . .

The XXVIth of this present, the prince of Conde declaryd unto me . . . that he wolde not suffer the peace concludyd here emongst them to be publyshyd, untill he hade made Your Ma^{te} prevy to yt, and so from thence came to requyre me to tell him the very demands of Your Ma^{te}, that he myght (as he wolde assueredlye, by the best meanes he coulde) satisfice Your Ma^{te} therin; which I dyd, accordinge to the instructions given me by myne old M^r sir Nicholas Throckmorton at Caen in Normandye the XV of marche. But before I came to declare the thre points wherupon Your M. demaunds doo specially stande, videlicet: to have Callis with the contrey adjacent renderyd presentlye unto you, accordinge as ys mentyonid in the treatye of Cambraye; that hostages for two yeres be geven to Your M., only to th'intent the peace maye be kept and obseryd untyll Calles and the other places of force therabouts ruynyd and demolyshyd at the taking therof and since, maye be reedifyed and fortifyed; that all such somes of moneye as Your M. had lent to the prince, the admyrall and his associates, or shulde hereafter lende, might be re-payed; I declaryd at good lengthe unto him what and howe muche Your M. had cause and in reason might demaunde, alledginge all particularytyes wherof there ys mention made in my sayd instruc-tions, and tolde him further that yf Your M. had to deale in these your demaunds with any other, what somever he were, then wyth him and the admyrall, you would not content yourselffe with any lesse satisfaction then the hole of that I had particularlye namyd to him; but for his sake and upon consideration of the good wyll Your M. thinketh he beareth you, you had streyghtenyd your demands to the uttermost, consistinge in the first III poynts before rehersyd by me. His answer was that he was marvelouse sorye to here Your M^{te} demands to be in that sort, and that yt was impossyble to have Callis renderyd before the tearme lymyted in the treatye; that the Quene mother wold never consent unto yt, and that he trustyd Your M. wolde stand to your protestation (which they doo always alledge against Your M. demands) and to that you had promisyd therin, which was that you came onlye to ayde and assiste the Kynge against suche as went about to usurpe upon him and to overthrow religion, and not for any particular proffitt or comodytye, wheras nowe in Your M. demaunds, sayinge youe wyll not depart with Havre-de-Grace untyll Calles be renderyd unto you, you shewe that neyther the Kyng's case, nor the cause of religion, hathe movyd you so to doo, but onlye to make your particular gayne and commodytye, which wyll be a great discredyt to Your M. honor and reputation, and a most great hynderance to the advancement of God's religion, and by these demands he sayeth Your M. doth undoo him, make him the most unfortunate prince that ever lyvyd, and utterly unable to doo you the service he desirethe; for yf yt wolde please Your M. to showe yourselff nowe accordinge to your protestation . . . you shuld not only gett great honor and reputacion in the worlde, but also bynd the Kynge, the Quene his mother (and by the meanes therof make him also able) to seake to gratifye Your M. in all that they coulde, and so might be wonne by the memory of suche a benefyt to render you Calles before the tyme lymytyd, yea, and soner per ad-venture then yt maye be imagyned, wheras to go this waye to worke, ys the waye to brynge him, the prince, into such disgrace and dishonor as that he shall never be able to shewe his heade, nor to stand Your M. in any stede, and the way also to make you never to have Calles renderyd. The lyke language hathe bene usyd to me in every poynte by the admyrall. . . .

The prince and admyrall tolde this daye that they wolde send

Mr de Bricquemault well instructyd to Your M. as well most
humbly to beseache you to have consideration of them, theyr honors
and estats, as also to declare unto you particularlye theyr requests,
desyers and opinions (which hitherto they wolde neither lett Your M.
ambassador, nor me othervise understand then in generall words)
trustynge Your M. wyll take beleave and embrace them, as
commynge from two suche as do think them most bownden to
Your M. and do desyer to do you most agreable service. The sayd
M. de Bricquemault ys the rather sent at this tyme, for that he hath
heretofore negotiatyd in these affayres, and also for that he ys well
knowen unto Your M. Hys speciall charge ys, as I canne learne,
to persuade Your M., yf he canne, by any meanes, to chawnge your
present demaunds for the present renderynge of Callis, and to faulte
into some other assuerance to have the same here after renderyd unto
you. . . .

The Emperour's ambassador presently in this court, maye, in my
simple judgment, serve Your M^{te} to some pourpose to the obtain-
inge of your demands, by pressynge earnestlye and stoutlie the
rendition of Metz, Toul and Verdun, but the same must be wrowght
from Your M. by the waye of Almagne, and so farr forth yt maye
please Your M. I maye speake my pore opinion, that I beleave at
this daye and in this tyme there ys nothinge that canne or wyll
prevayle more to have reason at these men's hands of that your
demawnde, then to shewe yourselffe stoute and in deliberation to do
yourselffe reason yf they wyll not.

The Spanishe humor ys now chayngyd and theyr good counten-
nances doo nowe shyne upon us, by the open shewe of theyr
ministers here, which ys to be taken no otherwise (as Your M. well
knoweth) but for a declaration of theyr mislykinge of this peace and
accorde; neverthelesse the same maye be wrestyd to serve Your M.
torne someways.

If Your M. wyl be pleasyd to take words in payment, ye shall
have inoughe, and these hope, I perceave, by words to wyne tyme
of you.

I do here, and please Your M., that the Quene mother and the
prince be secretly accordyd that he, the sayd prince, shall be
conestable, after the Kyng's commynge to his maiorytie, to th'intent he maye be styll in creditt and authorytie, and that al thoughe
the conestable that now ys doo lyve, yet he shall resigne the sayd
office of conestableship unto the prince of Conde, havinge nothwith-
standinge the name and fee therof durynge hys lyffe. I have also
bene tolde secretlye that the sayd prince wolde marvelouse gladlye

enter into a partyculer allyance with Your M^{te}, doubtynge greatlye
the enterprises of his ennymys here, but of those matters he hathe
as yet sayd nothinge to me.   The admyrall had before many
ennymies, and by this imputinge of the duke of Guise's death to his
occasion, the nomber ys marvelously encreasyd, and so he lyke to
be in marvelouse daynger of his person, unlesse God defend him
from theyr dayngerous practises.   The XXVIIth of this present, the
peace was proclamyd in the pallays at Parys, 'en la chambre dorrée,'
in the presence of all the parliament, the cardynall of Bourbon and
the duke of Montpensier being present and sent thyther by the
Kynge for that pourpose, but the dores of the sayd chamber were
fast shutt for feare of some mutyn by the people durynge the tyme
of the procleamynge of the same, since which tyme they dare not
otherwise publyshe yt, the populace there do so muche mislyk yt.

. . . . . .

Myddlemore to Cecil.

Orléans, March 30, 1563.

. . . Sir, these men seame greatlye to mislyke Hir M^{te} demande of
the renderyng of Calles, forthwith, and have cast out words to me
as thoughe Hir Ma^{te} were lyke inoughe to lose all, yf she pressyd to
comme by Calles in this sort and so hastelye, and that the other
partye havinge their force nowe in a readyness, they could not tell
what they wolde doo, when they shulde understand wherabouts the
Queene's Ma^{te} went, and what she dyd demande.   Myne answer was
that yf by force they sought to keape Hir Ma^{te} from hir right and
that dyd appertayne unto hir, she must defende both hir right and
hirselffe as she coulde, and that per adventure those that first toke
the matter in hand might honest repent them, mary in very dede,
yt shulde be another waye of recompense then Hir M^{te} dyd loke for
at theyr hands, wherunto the prince answerid that his sworde
would never cutt against the Quene's Ma^{te}.   Althoughe I knowe,
Sir, you shall receive from my L. ambassador at thys tyme th'effect
of all such talke as hathe bene betwixt the prince, the admyrall and
him, durynge his beinge here, yet I have thought mete to shew you
that howesomever you fynde the sayd prince and admyrall by my
sayd lord ambassador's letters, affectionyd to the Q. Ma^{te} demands,
I canne assuer Your Honor that at all tymes they have to me
declaryd the contrarye and shewid most apparentlye to mislyke
them.   And nowe, Sir, what somever they promesse by Monsr de
Bricquemault yf yt be not with dilygence and stoutenesse earnestlie

followwyd, yt wyll prove to nothinge, and this you must beleave, Sir,
that yf the prince inter ones into his governement and auctoritye,
and so be quyetlie settelyd therin, before Her M^{te} be consideryd in
hyr demandes as she dothe desyer, yt wyll afterwards be very harde
to bryng the sayd prince to doo Hir Ma^{te} any reason; and as for the
admyrall, I fynde him more mislyking with the Q. Ma^{te} demands
since his commynge to this towne then he was by the waye. . . . The
forces on the other syde be for the most dispercyd, at the least all
retyeryd from before Orleans, but the prince's forces be yet hole
and not dyschargyd.   There goeth a great garison of the other syde
to Calles, and very manye towards the contrey of Newhaven, as ys
nowe reportyd, and whatsoever many hope of this peace, the wisest
sort beleave yt wyll prove to a marvelouse confusion.   Lyons hath
refused to have any masse within the towne, all the faithfull in
Orleans have protestyd rather to leave the towne then to have masse
within yt.   Privat quarrels begynne alredy betwixt the gentylmen;
Theodore de Beze doth so muche mislyke theyr doinges here nowe
as that this daye he dothe retyer himselfe towards Geneva, and
telleth me all wyl benaught, and that he wyll comme no more here
untyll he se the worlde amendyd.

Sir Thomas Smith to Queen Elizabeth.

Blois, March 31, 1563.

That night (27th of *March*) I cam to Orleaunce, where I was verie
well enterteigned.   After sowp I cam to the prince's lodging, who
is now as governor of Orleans, and not that onely, but doth as I
perceave command all, as well in th'one campe as th'other, as
lieutenant generall to the ffrenche king, altho as yet that methincks
is not fullye established.   There, in a chamber, the prince, the
admirall and I, we three onely, sat as it were in counsell, the prince,
with a longue oracion, declaring how miche he was bound to Your
M^{te}, how that he doth owe his lief and all that he hath to Your
Highness, and what honor Your M^{te} hath gotten to have taken such
travaile, such costs and dangers for the word of God, and for
delivering this realme and the King's Majestie out of captivitie, and
the tyrannie of him who wold have destroied them all, with other
such pleasant words, as one who is in his tongue verie redy and
eloquent; at the last he cam to this that where as I desired
particularities, he differed yt untill th'admirall was com, who having
Sr Niclas Throckmorton with him, and having had, by diverse

messengers to and fro coming and goinge, conference with Your
M^{te}, could declare better how things hath proceded, and more
fresshelie then he could do, who, by reason of his emprisonment
could little understand how things did go, and what accord,
promises or agreaments was betwixt you two for Your Highness
contentacion.

Uppon that, th'admirall toke the tale and shewid how furst M^r
Middlemore came, and after Sir Nicolas Throckmorton, and how
ther had diverse letters and messages gone betwixt Your Ma^{te} and
him; Your Highness did still presse him to com to some honest
accord with the Q. mother, and shewid how necessarie and how
convenient it was at this tyme, and what charges it was to main-
teigne the warre, and that ye requirid but to be certefied of ther
doengs at all tymes, and he said that both the prince when he could,
and he at all tymes had certefied Your Ma^{te} from tyme to tyme of
the procedings and done nothing without Your Highness know-
ledge, and so had fulfilled all Your Ma^{tes} requestes, and that which
they had accordyd to and promissid to Your Highnesse.

This matter semed strange to me, and this manner of dealing and
talke as muche unlokid for; for to tell Your Ma^{te} the truth, I do
not like long ploges and small matter; wherfore I went rowndlie
to the matter, and shewyd them that I did understand all which
thei have said. . . . . . .

The next daie, which was sonday, the prince and th'admirall and
th'others went to the churche, where, after there order of praier
and sermon of Theodore Beze there was also the communion or
Cene celebrated, where the prince and all the rest of the gentlemen,
and all other ladies, and all other men and women, I thinke to the
nomber of V or VI^m, received at II tables, and as the preacher
sayd, it was the daye XII moneth that thei received at Meaulx to
conjoynge themself for the defence of the religion, and nowe yt is
when they shall sever themselfes eche to his house and countrey, to
suche libertie againe for the consciences and religion, as God had
given them of his great mercie, though not such nor so ample as per
advanture they wold wishe, yet suche as thei ought to give God
thancks for it.

That daie I dyned also with the prince, wheare th'admirall, M^r
d'Andelot, Mr Rochfoulcauld and me; where, the table and chairs
set, we, the said fyve, sat againe as in counnsell, they axing me yf I
had the writings there, I shewid them, and so I red furst and
explained my demaunds, standinge in those III points, religion, then
ranks and offices, and the third Calais. Then red I the furst and

second chapter of the treatye (of Cateau-Cambresis), wherin is the renderinge of Calais after VIII yeres, and after the XIIIth where yt is to be rendred immediately upon any attempt made upon Your Highnesse, your crowne or realme, which things beinge done, as I said, immediately after the treatie by the bearing of Your Highnes armes, by the poursuite at Rome, which shewid there extent, and by the sending of such force into Scotland, and the preparing and having in readynes of miche more, which declared there attempt to invade your realme, and to despoyle Your Ma^te of the crowne. The said treatie was broken, and the possession of Calais therfore imeadeately to Your Ma^te due.

There was some replieng that you weare th'armes of Fraunce. That is no invasion, said I, and your auncestors hath of longe tyme done so, but this new bearing of th'armes, and this new taking of the stile doth declare a new entente more then before; as when king (*Edward*) the third did furst declare his armes with th'armes of Fraunce and use the stile, he did full declare his intent and en-terprice to conquer it yf he could, and that great preparacion, doengs and words of many of the captaynes at that tyme in Scot-land, beside other evident indices, doth plainly shew the attempt. . . .

In the end th'admirall said to me: this is to be declared to the King, or to his hole counsell; we can not be judges here, and trea-ties be to be handlid of princes and emong princes. To that I sayd I did declare and shew this unto them, bicause I wold thei should not be ignoraunt of the Queene my sovereigne's right, and that thei might understand yf she moved warre, or deteined any other place untill that that which was his were restorid, she did not against conscience.

And, quoth I, yf you whom she takith for hir best freends, and of whom she hathe deservid no unkiendnes, do not let and hinder hir, she do not dowte but to recover hir right, as well as hir auncestors hath done hertofore, but I think there be som other paction, ac-corde or agreament more then not to hynder Hir Matie, and me thinks now that ye have your demaunds, and are at quiet, the rest also should be done, that Hir Matie be likewise satisfied. Then th'admirall was verie earnest with me, and axid how the Queene's Maties forces entrid into Newhaven, and upon what pretence, and that it was onely for the defence of religion, and for the suretie of them that weare of the religion, and that this, which I spake of, was not contenied in the Q. Maties protestacion.

To that I answerid in Newhaven, I, myself, was never, and ther-fore I know not how Your M. forces entrid, nor what pretence was made betwixt them that delivered it up and them that toke it, I know not. As for the protestacion I had it delivered to me, and I deleverid it myself to the Queene mother, and I thincke I was som cawse of the making of it, ffor having but a small wyt and memorie and litle frenche, and so many and diverse thinges told me, I desirid that I might have yt in writing, and so I had. But I thinck there was some Frenchman who made it; but, quoth I, as I do remember, and as I did take it, the protestacion contenieth in somme those III causes :

Th'one, the persecution for religion ; th'other the greatenes of the house of Guyse ; the third, that the Queene did feare by him, and his greatenes and malice to lose the fruit of the treatie of Cambresis, which was Calais.

Then th'admirall said he had your protestacion under the greate seale (wherat I do marvell), and so thei brought there books of the protestacion printed at Orleans ; I said they and that protestacion, which I delivered up, did not agree in diverse points, and even in that point it lackith and alterith ; ffor, where that which I delivered, hath : ' par où ils eussent nécessairement mis en péril la continuacion de la paix, suivante la treatie qu'est entre son bon frère et S. M. pour la priver des fruictes de celle contre son inten-cion ; ' and upon the margent therof it maked thus : ' la restitucion de la ville de Calais ; ' which declarith Your Ma^{te} entent fully to demaund Calais, and wherupon I have alwais fownded my demaundes, to be agreable to your protestacion.

That which was printed in Orleans, hath : ' par où ils eussent nécessairement mis en péril la continuation du traicté de la paix qui est entre son dict bon frère et Sa Majesté,' and nothing ells, with words more obscure and dowtefull. . . .

After this the prince began with an eloquent and copious oration to declare that Your Matie had now done such an acte as ye were worthie to be renownid for ever, and how that all the world doth nowe prayse and esteme you as a lady most excellent, and a princes who has taken upon you, and brought to passe such a thing for the glorie of God, for the benefit of the realme of Fraunce, for th'advauncement of true religion, for the delivery of a pore orphan prince from the power of a tyran, for saving of himself and so many noblemen, as no other prince was able to do, and that your fame should therfore be everlastinge. But yf ye should dysceyve this with a private matter of your owen, with a demaund of advantage, and under pretence of religion, seke your owen privat lucre and gayne, what dishonour yt should be unto Your Ma^{te}, and how evill the

papists, yea, and all other wold speake of you, and that Your Ma^te
hath said she sought nothing but the safegard of them of Fraunce,
th'advauncement of true religion, and setting forward of the
Gospell.

At this I must crave of Your Highnes pardon, yf, when thei
touchid your honor, I waxid somewhat hot. I answerid that, for
Your Highness honor, your dedes nor words did declare what ye
have done; how ye have neither sparid your men, your money, your
care, your perill, by embassade, by lendinge, by sendinge men of
warre, by adventuring, and the taking upon you of warre for ther
sakes, and put in hasard, yf nede had bene, or so had chauncid, the
displeasure of the greatest princes in all Europe; and ye have not
ceasid till they have had their willes, ther lives, lands and honors
savid; the religion, though no so fullie as you wold, yet so much
as thei are therwith contendid, propatid; and all this while till thei
had ther purpose, ye had not entermeadlid your owen private cause,
nor wold not that it should prejudicate ther commodities. . . .

Th'admirall said then that thei knew and did confesse how miche
they weare bound to Your Ma^te, ther lives, goods, honors, wief,
children, and all thei did owe unto you, but yf they should now
deliver Calais, or yf ye should now kepe still Newhaven, what an
infamye and slaunder it should be to them, not onely in this age,
but in cronicles for ever they should be infamid persons, and all the
world should speake evill of them; and that, as for Calais, we could
never get againe, yt was now impregnable, and Newhaven was so
chargeable and so costlie to kepe, and the comons and nobilitie of
England was so wearie of the warres now, that it was reportid to
him of one whom if he should name I wold think it true, that in
the trois estatz, he ment our parlament house, rather then they wold
for Calais sake be at suche charge as to kepe Newhaven thei wold
rather acquit and renounce ther right they had to Calais; but yf yt
were for the propagation of religion, they wold yet voluntary spend
of ther owne II millions of gold.

To this I replied that I knew no infamie could come to them,
more in rendring Calais according to the treatie, then to the rest
who rendrid Piedmont according to the treatie.

Yea, but the tyme is not yet comme, said he.

Yes, that it is, said I, for you take but the VIIth chapitre where
VIII yeres is determined, I, the XIIIth, where the condicyon is
expressid, which broken, Calais ys all readie due, as well as the
cities of Piedmont was due, and yt is all in one treatie, and all of
one like force: the VIII yeres terme, and the condicion enfringed.

But, where ye speake of Calais impregnable, and the chargeable keepinge of Newhaven, and the evill will of men toward yt, what you have hard, I can not tell; what I knowe, I dare saye; there is Vᶜ gentlemen, yea thousand in England, that, rather then the Queene's Maᵗᵉ should not have hir right, and be thus elydid, will follow the warre one XII moneth upon ther owen charges, without one penie cost to the Q. Maᵗᵉ, and I am one of them myself, who will make ye such warre as ye never had the like in Fraunce.

And what our marchaunts of London and other cities and all Kent will do to have Calais againe, and what all the rest of the nobles and commons, yf this were propowndid, wold conclud upon it, I am in no dowte. But, who so ever should saye those words or such like, as you report, eyther in the parlament, or owt, in good ernest, I dare saye he should lose his head for it, and well worthie, and the hole parlament wold, without long respit, condempne him to yt, ffor we take Calais to be our pathway into Flaunders, and the Low-Countrey, and the verie treatie of Cambray doth give you but *possessionem et detentionem* of yt for the yers and upon condicions, not the proprietye, yf you loke upon it well.

Then said he that sir Nicholas Throckmorton did shew him, that Your Maᵗᵉ was content to tarie for Calais the tyme lymyted in the treatie, and that Monsʳ de Bricqmor and diverse others, which had bene there with Your Maᵗᵉ, did affirme that Your Highnesse for the zeale of religion could be content, not onely when that were agreed here, to leave Newhaven, but rather then that should hinder to acquite Calais.

In this I answerid that what sir Nicholas Throckmorton had said, or what Your Maᵗᵉ had said to other there, I could not do with it; what Your Highnes had said to me, and what commission you had given me, willinglie nor wittinglie I neither had nor wold go from it, and I never did sith my furst coming fiend your Maᵗᵉ, but allwaies in one saing, and all at one pointe; that is that ye woold never recongnise that ye had your right or accownte, amitie, love or peace at their hands, till ye had Calais rendrid, being your due. Yt is possible, quoth I, that sir Nicholas might say to you, or the Q. Maᵗᵉ to som of your gentlemen, that she wold be content with the treatie, and in that matter no more do I, ffor ye see, I saie, and have provid unto you, and am at all tymes readie to prove that by the word of the treatie, Calais is to the Q. Maᵗᵉ at this present due, and hath bene ever sith that the attempt made in the tyme of king François the seconde, and ought to be rendrid to Hir Maᵗᵉ immediately.

Well, saith he, the Queene shall have hir demaund, she shall have Calais. Is it not possible she may be entreatid for a tyme, upon good assurance, to forbeare it, and to leave Newhaven? Yt shall be the ruyne of us all, and the discredite of the prince, and we shall be able to do no good, with such other words. (I was yet in my heate). What assurance, quoth I, can we have of Frenchemen, whom no promis, accord, treatie, seale nor other can hold, as all princes strangers, and all ther ministers all most do certifie? I se no assurance but the sword, and in the meane while to kepe that we have.

To this they made no answer, but one of them lokid upon another. After the prince began: Monsieur l'ambassadeur, we must nedes satisfie the Queene, and we must not, nor can not be unkiend; but if ther might be some waie fownd that she might have hir desier, and yet we be put to no suche extremitie, or rather impossibilitie, were yt not mich better?

Sir, quoth I, I wold gladlie here that, ffor now thancks be to allmightie God, you have allready, or be very toward to have that which doth satisfie you. Yf the Queene also, my mistress, might be satisfied, I wold cownte my self in heaven. Let us devise somwhat, said the prince, and as he was aboute to comme forth with som thing, th'admirall staied him and said: I se, Monsieur l'ambassadeur hath his commission, and past that, he will not go, nor agree to any other condicions.

Yet, said I, yf I do here them possible, I may saie som thing to them that should do no hurte, or par advanture tell some gesse of the Q. Matie miend upon them (for I was desirous to here ther devise).

The admirall answerid it was all one, for I wold but send to the Queene, and take hir answer, and so make it here, and aswell should it be at the furst to send a gentleman to negotiate with Your M. owenself; and so they said they wold send Monsr Brikmor the next daie with articles and condicions to know Your Highnes miend therin, and ones or twies I attempted them, for I wold faine have knowen when and how, and what they wold have done againe for Your Maties satisfaction to have shewid some pece of ther gratuitie towards you, but I could com by no particularities, but generall and faier words, whereof I see Frenchemen hath plentie enough and with them they went to paie all the world. . . .

Sir Thomas Smith to Queen Elizabeth.

(ᴇxᴛʀᴀᴄᴛ.)   Blois, April 1, 1563.

In my other letters, having at large declarid my negociacion touching my demands, I have thought good to write unto Your Ma^te the extrabordinarye matters, also when I cam to take my leave of the prince of Conde, after gentle and ordinarie words of salutation, he fell in talk with me of Myl^d Robert,[1] praising him verie muche, and shewing, the good affection which he bore towards him.

To whom I answerid againe with as much comendacion of my said lord, both for his personnage, his birth, his gentle and modest behaviour to all men, and other his vertues as I could, and yet not otherwise then my said lord doth deserve.

After that, he cam to Your Ma^te mariage, when and whom Your Highnesse should marie, and whither the Lords and Commons of your realme had not bene sutors unto you for to marie my said lord Robert.

To that I answerid that being absent, and here in France, of my owen knowledge I could saye nothinge, but by such advertizements as I had of my freends in England, the request was earnest, and with great affection to Your Highnesse to marie, but generally, not onely, not particularly of my said lord Robert, but not so muche as specifieng any qualitie of persone, stranger or English, greate prince or meaner personnage. . . . Of any such promise to Myl. Robert, I was not privie, and if Your Ma^te had made any suche, I do not se what should let Your Highness to performe it, nor that any subject of yours would repyne at it.

Yt is not unknown, saith he, that Hir Ma^te doth beare a greate affection unto him, and his vertues and qualities doth deserve no les, and he is one whom I am verie muche beholding unto ; but *par advanture*, Hir Ma^te beinge of a greate and roial cominge, will not abase hirself so miche to take one of hir subjectes, but yf Hir Highness mind were not to farre that way, we have here a goodlie prince, our king, a faier personage, gentle and wittie, and not alltogither abhorrent from the affection of the Gospell. Yf that Hir Ma^te could enclyne that way, she should have one of the greatest princes in Europa ; she would governe Fraunce and England ; she should cleane expell all papistrie, and set the Gospell so abrode that all christendomme should be faine to take it, and do so greate a good that hir name

---

[1] Cecil. [Qy. Robert *Dudley* ?]

should be immortall; with other such words utterid in great eloquence and affection, axing me wither I could be content to help that wais, or to learne by some by means wither Your Ma^te could enclyne any thing to here of it. To this I answerid that I could not tell what to saie, nor durst not meadle in such matters, this were to greate for my capacitie, and at the first blush, and to speak rudely and plainely, the mariage semith to me very unequall. Yf there age weare tornid, that the king here were of Your Ma^te's and Your Ma^te of his age, I wold think it a great deale more equall, and when he shall come to be of age, Your Ma^te shall by course of nature wax old, and so he shall not set by you, but rather by others yonger, and shall be more grief then pleasure to Your Highnes, as was betwixt queen Marie and king Philippe; that his men did call hir the King's grand mother; and to marie this great prince, I do not se what it doth but bring greate trouble, as that of king Philippe did to us. Againe I said our men of Englande are proude, and disdainfull of strangers, and might as evill abide that Frenchemen should be in England, as we see that you may abide that we should be here.

Ah! (saith he) there maye be lawes and articles made, that all the offices should be onely given to Englishmen; that none of your lawes and customes should be changed; that the furst begotten child, be he man or woman, should allevais remaine in England; that, of ther be two, the second to have England, and other such things wherby ye might be fully satisfyed, and this so greate a benefit be brought to all christendom: and what prince living weare able to resist theis II realmes thus joined togither? I wold replie no longer, but said their meaning was not evill towards us, when they offer the chief knot of love, which was mariage, but in that I could not meadle, either to allow or to desallow it; marie I wold furst thei wold offer us reason to let Your Ma^te have that which is yours, and then that done, to enter into what amitie, freendshippe, love or allegiance as God should further offer to both the realmes. I wold be no hinderer, but a furtherer to the best of my power; and so with other words of course in taking of leave and thanks for his courtesie interteignement I departid.[1] From him I went to th'admirall, likewise to take my leave of him, who had Monsieur d'Andelot and a great nomber of other lustie gentlemen in his lodging; and taking me on one side: we do miend, saith he, to-morow or the next daie, to send Monsieur Brickmort to the Queene's Ma^te, yf ye will wryte by him.

---

[1] This strange marriage project was revived at a later period, and led, in 1564 and 1565 to a direct negotiation between the two crowns.

I do dispatch a post myself (quoth I) so sone as I com at home, for I have receyvid even now a pacquet out of England, to the which I must answer. How be yt, I will send one lettre by him to the Quene's Majestie. Well, saith he, we do se yt is necessarie, and we be very desirous, and not we onely, but all here, to enter with your mistres in a more streight amitie and league for both the realmes. Yt is mete in dede (saith he) that furst we do you reason, and render you yours, and ye shall have it; for this league and amitie for your realme, and also this is, at this tyme, most necessarie: hath not the prince commonid with you of that matter? I do not know, quoth I, wherof ye do meane? He saith some thing to me of a mariage, and I to him declarid my douts as they cam sodenly into my head: of any thing els I hard not. Well saith he, I trust we shall have all cause to rejoyse, and the Queene your mistres shall have no occasion to thincke us unkind; Monsr Brickmor shall be dispatchid to-morrow, with articles and condicions which the Quenes Ma^te, I thincke, will allow and thincke reasonable.

Sir, quoth I, of that I wold be right glad, but in the mean while, you had nede look well aboute you, for I here no man that liketh the accord, neither papist, nor protestant, nor that thincketh it will last XXI daies; what you, who are the heads and rulers, do, I can not tell, but every man thinckith that it is but a traine and a deceipt to sever the one of you from another, and all you from this stronghold, and then thei will talke with you after an other sorte.

Well, saith he, for that matter we shall do well enough with the grace of God; thei be not in that power now as thei were, as we indede be not now in the sorte as we were when the Guise lived, who tyrannically did governe the King. He wold saie: it should be thus (for though the King's name was addid, it was not the King, but the Guise), and therfore then we wold saie: it shall not be so thus; but now yt is contrary: we can have but that which we can obteigne by entreatie at the King's hands. Yf we could have the money at Newhaven but one XIII daies soner, we wold have talkid with them after an other sorte, and wold not have bene contented with this accord. We wold have driven him from his assiege, and made him glad to have taken such condicions as we wold have offerid, and then we could have answerid the Queene's Ma^te and you for hir commands otherwyse then we do now, but I trust she will be content with our offers.

The Prince de Condé to Queen Elizabeth.

Orléans, 1er avril 1563.

Madame, ne doubtant poinct que ne receviez autant de plaisir et de contentement d'entendre l'heureux événement qu'il a pleu à Dieu envoyer, pour la cessation des troubles et divisions suscitez en ce roiaume pour le faict de la religion, veu la démonstracion d'amitié et bonne volunté que vous avez tousiours faicte envers le roy très-chrestien, Monseigneur vostre bon frère, et le desir que portez au bien et conservation de son estat, je suis certain que les calamitez et misères qui en sont procédées vous ont esté tristes et ennuyeuses. Je n'ai pas voulu faillir, suivant ce que j'ay tousiours promis et asseure à Vostre Majesté, incontinent que les choses ont esté résolues et arrestées, vous en tenir advertie, et pour cest effect dépescher le sieur de Briqmault, que Vostre Majesté congnoit, pour vous aller rendre raison de ce qui s'est passé et de mes autres nouvelles, avecques charge expresse de vous remercier très-humblement du bien, du secours et de la faveur que en une si grande querelle vous avez tant vertueusement départy à ceulx que vous avez congneu défendre et soutenir l'équité.

S'il vous plaist doncques, Madame, Vostre Majesté luy aiant presté bonne et attentive audiance pour escoutter ce qu'il vous dira de ma part, vous me ferez cest honneur que d'adjouster la mesme foy à ses propoz que vous feriez à ma propre parolle.

Myddlemore to Cecil.

(EXTRACT.)

April 14, 1563.

Sir, I doo perceave, by words the prince of Conde hath had to me at twoo several tymes, since my last letters, that there ys nothynge lesse ment then the renderinge of Callice to the Quene's Ma^{te} before the tyme in the treaty be expyred, for the X of this present he sayd unto me, that the Q. Ma^{te} do persever in that her *opiniastreté* (which was the tearme he gave yt) to seake the some on this sorte, and to saye that she wyll not leave Newhaven untill Callice be rendered, that yt wyll bothe make hir loste hir rights, and all the reste she hathe, or may have in this contrey, wheras yf she wold shewe hirselfe accordyng to hir protestation, and as she had donne in the realme of Scotland, she shulde, wyth a lyttle forbearynge have that she nowe requyreth, and make him able to be a worker at all tymes for yt; where to I was so bolde as to saye that Hir M^{te} in askyng hir right and that dyd apertayne unto hir, dyd not goo against hir protestation. . . . As to Hir M^{te} doings in Scotland, I sayd yt seamyd to me that she had more favorably dealt towards them of this nation, first for that these warres had coste Hir Ma^{te} another manner of some of money (besyde that she had lent him and his) then all the warre in Scotland had donne, and were without comparison more dangerous unto hir, and then because Hir Ma^{te} havynge so great meanes and occasion offeryd hir to make hirselfe ladye of all Normandye, ye, and to have in Picardye also what she had wolde, hathe at no tyme seasyd, nor taken any on towne, post or place therof, nor troubelyd or sufferyd to be spoyled any on subject of the Kynge, but only hath kepte the Havre, which by him and his consent, and by the contract betwext Hir Ma^{te} and hym, was delyveryd unto his hands. . . . Therupon I toke occasion to desier him to consyder howe muche the Q. Ma^{te} had donne for him, howe muche the same touchyd him in honor, what opinion the wole worlde wolde have of him, howe muche God's enemyes, Hir Ma^{te} and his, wolde make theyr profett of yt, with many other words. Wherunto he answeryd nothinge but that he was the most desyrous in the worlde to doo Hir Ma^{te} service, and to lett the same to understand how muche he felte himselfe bound unto hir, but that she toke awaye, by these her demaundes, all occasion from him to shewe himself accordinglye. He trustyd, at the reatourne of monsieur de Briquemault to here better newes from Hir Ma^{te}, and in so doinge he wolde, not only endevor himself by all the beste meanes he coulde to purchasse for Hir Ma^{te} that she now desirethe, but also travaill to make suche a league offensiffe and defensyffe betwixt the two realmes of England and Fraunce, that bothe the prince and subjectz therof should have great occasyon to rejoyce.

There ys none here, Sir, as I am well enformyd, that is more against the rendering of Callice into the Q. Ma^{te} handes then the king of Spayne and his ministers, and therfore to dissuade all that they canne therin, notwithstandinge the fayre shewe they make to us otherwyse.

Sir, the VIII of this present, the prince of Conde was establishyd in his estate of lieutenantship,[1] to have and use the same in as

---

[1] Myddlemore is mistaken, or else refers to some other office or honour. The Prince de Condé never was pro- claimed Lieutenant-Général of the Kingdom.

ample and large manner as his decessyd brother the kyng of Navarre had and dyd use, and the IX followinge the sayd prince toke his othe, in the presence of the Kynge, to do him faithfull and true service. It ys here greatlye fearyd of his friends, lesse he will become, with the tyme, another kinge of Navarre, and yf all reports be true (as I am suer some be) there ys alredye evill presumptions of yt. . . .

Myddlemore to Cecil.[1]

(**EXTRACT.**)   Amboise, April 19, 1563.

. . . I do fynd by the beste intelligence that I canne gett here *that these ar resolvid to make you warre,* therfore yt maye please you *to looke* about you, and yet I see no reason *in it,* nor howe they *can well do it,* no nor in dede *do not beleeve it; for all* such as be of the religion were never more discontentyd; never thought them-selffs in lesse suertye, nor were more lykly to growe into a broyle agayne; and as touchinge the late edict of the peace, there ys no papist towne in Fraunce that hathe or dothe as yet obey yt. Agayne such pryvatt quarrelz begynne to sprynge emongst the greatest here as that a man wolde beleave they *shuld first put order into theim,* and into the piteous state of this realme, *before they did take in hand any other matter, especially a thing of so great consequence* as this is. Neverthelesse, the greatest and best of this court do say it in gevinge oute the brute that the Q. Ma^te wyll begyn the warres upon theim, and which maketh me most to marvaile, the prince de Conde hath sayd in playne tearmes this daye to two of the chifest, nearest and honestest *about him,* that they *have resolvid* (puttynge himselfe in the nomber) *to make warre upon the Q. M.,* if *she do con-tynue* in her ' opiniastreté,' and will not leave the Havre ; wherunto was answeryd by them that he shoulde bothe *do and goo against that he had promysid Her Ma^te,* which considerynge howe muche and howe greatlye *she had done for him,* wolde be first a very displeasant thinge to God, and then a marvelouse *shame and dishonor* to him, with a great nomber of *other persuasions,* tendynge to dyvert him from the enterprisinge of *so unjust a quarrell ;* but fyndinge him, *for all they could say,* to contynue in evell opinion, they sayde unto him these wordes following : that in their consciences they fownde that the warres shoulde be wrongfully made, and upon an unjust quarrell, and therfore they coulde not, nor wolde not fynde them-

---

[1] The passages in italics are in cypher in the original.

selffs, nor serve in it, but leave him and all them that shulde take yt in hande to such issue as God shulde be pleased to send them, in retyerynge themselffs quyetly *home to theyr houses*, and in prayinge God to send them good successe that had the best right. The prynce mislyked suche *this language*, but they assueryd him that not only they wold do so, but also many other gentilmen. . . .
The prince hath said sondry tymes, and last of all to one M^r de *Bouchevannes*, a discret, wise and honest gentylman, that *if the visdame of Chartres had put into the contract betwixt the Q. Ma^{te} and him* any suche thinge *as that she might kepe the Haven, untill Callais wer rendrid unto her, that he shuld and wer to answer to it, and not he, for he had put what they wold into the said contract*. In the meane tyme, the confiscation of *the poore visdame's lyving is geven, and that sins* the conclusion of this peace.

Queen Elizabeth to Sir Thomas Smith.

April 22, 1563.

Trustie and well beloved, we grete you well. Although by your letters written to us the second of this moneth, we understode that Bricquemault was departed thence with message towards us, yet came he not hither before the XXVIth of the same, and coming with the french embassador, gave us letters from the prince and the admirall, only without any of the King, and said his charge was to gyve us thankes, which he did with many good woordes, and to make request that we wold be content to render Newhaven and to have the treaty for restitucion of Callice newly ratified, and hostages to be given at our choice, excepting the King's brethern and the princes, both of the blood royal and all other princes of byrth. This was the somme of the request, which as it was in dede lytle to be estemed, so did we lykely regard yt, and gave him, as we have good cause, the shorter and rounder answer. For we told him as to the thanks, although we had deserved as many or more, yet they might have been either written or sent by somme other messenger that had delt lesse with us for the prince then he had, and for the overture, we sawe no cause why to renew the treaty, but rather to deliver us that which by the treaty is due unto us, and we so concluded for that tyme. The next daye he sought to speke with us aparte, without the embassador, but yet we thought not mete so to commune with him, but that some of our conscile might be present, for that he had, at his beyng with th'admyrall in Normandy, reported certen things of our speche touching the matter of Callice, untruly, as the admirall himself told Sr Nicholas Trockmorton, and therein the visdame of Chartres and la Haye were sayd to be his witnesses, who do playnely deny it. And we gave him privately to understand that for this respect we wold not speke with him aparte, whereupon he seamed to be much perplexed, and perceaving the particularitie of our offence, did utterly deny wherewith he had been charged, and seemest so earnest therein as he required some tryall of his parte; but we, knowing how the matter. had passed, left of that particular matter, and hard him what he had furder to saye in the common cause; and therein we had little more then the day before, saying that he was told by the admirall, after he had departed from the courte, that the Quene mother had said to him, the admirall, that for more satisfaction and assurance of us, she wold be content that bondes were made to princes strangers for the observacion of the treaty and delivery of Callice: and finding no more matter of weight at his hande we made short work with him, and told him that our resolucion was that we liked none of these offers, and then he required us that we wold devise of some maner of waye of assurance for our contentacion, and we made plaine answer we knew of none better then to kepe that we had, untill we had that whereunto we had right. Many other things passed betwixt us, but the substance of the wholle was this before written, and now because he doth returne without our satisfaction, and wether he will make juste report or no of our answers, we wold that you should as sone as ye can speke with the prince, and the admirall, or either of them, declare breefly as we have writen, and that being doone, ye shall saye that we have comanded you to tell them that this manner of dealing with us, so contrary to there promissees, to there wrytyngs, there seales, there speeches, yea there privat letters, wherof we have good nomber, can not but move us to thynk our benefitts bestowed uppon them the worst that ever prince cold bestow, and that we thynck if the world shuld know how inwardly they have delt with us, for to furder ther enterprisees, there estymacyon shuld be greatly decayed through christendom, and you may saye that we now see howe, on some of ther parts, relligion served. but a collor to bryng themselves to authorite, and to ridd out of the waye such as stode before there eies to lett them. Ye may therfor conclude that if there promises be not better observed than of late they have bene, we shall be occasioned to notefy to the world what just cause we have to doo as we shall doo, for defence of our title and demands, and we dout not but God shall therin assist us, and confound the enterprisees of such as shall, ether by force, or by engynes agaynst honor and fayth, deale agaynst us, that have had so great compassion of theyr misery, and in this matter ye shall not lett to extend our offense for this ther ingratitude, as the case deserveth, and to lett them thynk that we will notefy to the world in whom the fault is. Our meaning is that you shall not alter your former charge in demanding of Callice, by force of the treaty, as hitherto ye have done whensoever ye shall deale with that King or the Quene his mother; and of your doings and other the procedings there mete to be advertised unto us, we wold you should diligently advertise us, and not to impeache there divises in any other kinde of overtures to be made unto us, more likely for our satisfaction then these have hitherto been, using the same nevertheless so as ye gyve them no occasion to thinck that you do allowe of any thing, but only of the restitution of Callise.

Myddlemore to Cecil.

May 3, 1563.

Right honourable, the second of may the count of Ryngrave cam to this court, the same beinge at Sainct Germayns. I do not certaynlye knowe what news he brought, nor the occasion of his comyng, but I am suer they were displeasant inoughe to the Queene mother, and as I canne learne, to this effect that the Quene's Ma^te had great forces in a readynesse to send over, and that the same shulde come oute of hande to Newhaven, that there was daily labourynge at the sayd Newhaven for the fortifyinge of yt a thre or fower thousand persons, and that his Allemains wold not sturre nor marche till ther wer paye of that is due unto them. The same night, the prynce of Conde caulyd me unto hym, and askyd me yf I had of late receavyd any letters out of England, and I answeryd: I had not hard from thence since Monsr de Bricquemault's goinge, at what tyme he enteryd into his old manner of discoursing with me, and tolde me that he understode from his ministers there that Her Ma^te was become his great ennemy, and woold him all the evil in the woorld. . . .

Then he said he wold offer the Queene mother his hed to satisfie Her Mageste with, the present rendringe of Callais, he knew she wold not do it, and therfore it wer but tyme lost to speke any more of it to her, for all Fraunce was not able to bring her willingly to it, and that he was not a littell sorye that Her Majestie's desire is so great to have it, and the Quene's mind here so contrarye to depart with it; for he dyd by all the beast meanes he coulde seake to keape them in peace and good amytye; but if Her M^{te} did persever in that her demande to have Callais presently rendred, or to kepe Newhaven until it wer rendred, it woold cause her to lose both Newhaven and all the right she canne pretend to Callays, for that Newhaven was not long gardable for us; all theyr forces wer in readiness, and in short tyme being ones before it, wold render it impossible for Englande to ayde or succour, and, sayd he, you know that all places that cannot be succored, being besieged, must be taken.

Sir, quoth I, I have herde it estiemed a place of greater force then you nowe make it, and I think those that be within it will not so easily quite it, neither yet the Quene's Majeste leave it unsuccoured when tyme shall requyre it, but if matters ones growe so farre, I can assure you, Sir, that Her M^{te} is resolved to spend half her realme but she will kepe it against all those that shall come before it.

At what tyme there cam one for him to cum to the Quene, and so he left me saying: we shall understand all when Monsr Bricquemault cometh.

Sir, I am tolde in great secrete, and therfore yt may pleas you to use it therafter, that, at this present, the prince of Conde hath written to the visdame of Chartres to persuade him by all the wayes that he can to do by the Quene's Ma^{te} as he hath done, that is to saye, to denye that ever he was consentying to the article in the contract that speaketh of Her Magesties keping of Newhaven untill Callays be rendred, which if they here coulde bring to pass, they think to make them moost profit of it. This is the Quene mother devise, and the visdame is promised great things to do it; for Monsr de la Haye, they think he will playe the good fellowe and will be easely ynough brought to it; and if the visdame only consent to this foule act, then the prince hath written to him to conveye himself out of Englande, hither by the best, secretest and spedyest meanes that he can, or if he cannot so do, they will then devise sum way or other to have him thence, and being her, he shall make open protestation, and sende it to the Quene's Majestie that he never knew of, nor was consentyng to the sayd article, and where he shall not receve and followe this godly advise of the prince he hath plainly written to him that he, for his part, will denye it utterly and charge him holy with all, wherby he shall for ever loose his lyving and countrey, and be reputed and estemed for a traitor all the dayes of his lyfe after, wheras yf he will doo this to content the Queene mother, ther was never man that shuld be

better welcom than he, nor more made of, and this is a matter of
greate consequence and so secretly practysed as that none but two
besyds the prince knowith of it.   The matter must be so handled as
that, neyther by word nor visage, eyther of them may fynde that
you know or suspect any suche thing untill suche tyme as you may
take knowledge therof som other waye.   In the meane tyme please
you have an eye to them, and that they be not sufferid to departe
from thence as yet.   He that hath discoverid this matter to me is
greate frend to the visdame, but more to Her Majestyes service, as
yt doth well appeere ; therfore yt may lik you so to use yt as that
may not tourne to hys prejudice in any sorte; he is of opinion that
the saide visdam will never be wonne to do a thing so much against
honor, and that yt is ynough he may discover this fowle practise to
the prince's, to Her Matie and you, or it be long ; to make you most
proffit of the said visdame, is to use him with fayre words and
gentle dealing, as I am given to understand.

Sir, I could be very glad, and I know yt wold serve well Her
Ma^{te} turne many wayes, that ther wer a declaration made and set
fourth in print, togyther with the contract betwext the Q. Majestie
and the prince of Conde for the justification of Her Ma^{te} doengs, and
to make knowen to all the world the greate and manifest wrong these
doo her, so as it might not prove prejudiciall to the admirall, who,
it is thought, will and must now for his owne suerty and well doing
shew himself frind towards Her Ma^{te}, wherof, for all that I see by
lyttle lykelyhode.   But untill the admirall be throughly decypherid,
the saide declaracion can not be effectually made, which will be
soone don after his comming to the courte.   In my letters of the
XXII of aprill, I wrote unto you of one Mr Robert Steward here,
a scottish gentleman, the same in effect which nowe I have wrytten
unto you.   Myn old M^{r} is well hable to tell you of the good parts
in him, and of his long good will towards the Quene's Ma^{te} service,
and my lord embassador now here can and hathe good cause to
wytnes of his good affection that waye, and for my parte, I must
sayé he hathe well shewed yt since myne arryvall in these parts.
He is desyrous, yf the prince doo change and suffer himself to be
wonne of his enemyes (wherof he hathe greate feare at this present),
to retyre himself into England, and therin regarde of Her Ma^{te}
greate favor towards the religion, and her good right in this quarrel
to doo Her Highnes the best and most faithfull service he cann, as
in the meane tyme, untill he see what in very deede will becom of
the saide prince, he will not faile to do in this countrey.

Sir Thomas Smith to Queen Elizabeth.

May 12, 1653.

It may pleas Your Ma^{te}. The IIII of this moneth Mr Killegrew arrived at Paris, with Your Highnes letters. The next day I cam to Poissy, and the VIth sending for audience, I had it appointid me the VIIth, but the sixth, not fiending myselfe well, the next day I was a greate deale more troublid with a catarre and a little fever, so that I was fayne to send myne excuse; and the saturday, fiending small amendement in myne health, and my most grief in my throte and my tongue, so that I could not well speake, understanding that Mr Bricquemault was, either allreadie come, or shortelye to arrive at the courte, and not knowing what ende my sicknes wold have, I thought best to send Mr Middlemore thither, with myne excuse to the prince, and full instructions to declare to him, according to Your M. letter, for th'admirall is not yet come, nor Monsr Dandilot, and diverse other which he looked for. . . .

And when he replied that yf ye weare thus dealte, which Your Ma^{te} should be compellid to manifest to the worlde, the whole which hath passed betwixt you, that all men might perceave how syncerely and entierly ye have gon with them, and how little they do regard againe their promisses, contracts, writings, seales and letters, etc.; he said for his parte he was contente that it should be published any thing that hath passed betwixt Your Ma^{te} and him, and for the keping Newhaven till Callice were rendrid he did never consent to it; thei had blancke signid and selid by him, wherin his ministers were forcid to consent to the putting in of that article: he himself did know or agree to none suche.

He said also that Your Ma^{te} did take greate pleasure to speake evill of him, so that yf one should continually bring you money into your hand, he should do Your Highnes no greater pleasure then to give you occasion to speak evill of him.

And when Mr Middlemore did saye he did not suppose that to be so, and could not thinck yt, he said, Monsr Bricquemault so told him. But in th'ende he praid Mr Middlemore to move me to write to Your Matie to have a better oppinion of him and that he was Your Highnes servaunt, and to entreate you to consider better of the matter, and to devise some gentill and good order, werby all theis matters might be appeasid without further troble, and he wold be therof most glad, and helpe to yt to the best of his power.

On sonday, feling myself somwhat better, and with extreme abstinence my ague gone, I did deliberate on monday to go to the

courte, ffor I did perceive that I was lokid for daylie, sith the furst
tyme I axid audience, and that of an other sorte, then I was at any
tyme yet. And I was also desyrous, bicause I had not bene there of
long tyme, to se the courte and to learne yf I could, by the speches
and ther countenances, now in this hote preparacion to Newhaven
and 'in this troblesom broiling and uncertaigne tyme emong themselves, something wherby to make some gesse. So, on monday,
altho it was yet some payne to me to speake, when I am to the courte,
being better enterteigned as before. The King, the Queene, the
duke d'Orleauns, and Madame Marguerite being there, and the
young prince of Navarre, and other there, the chamber full.

My mocion to the Queene was, that the naturall desier which I
had to have peace and quietnes betwixt the two realmes, wherof I
knew Hir Mageste and the cardinall of Ferrara, and all such as had
had to do with me, at hir commandement, were witnesses, was th'occasion of my desyringe of audience, also now at this tyme; and that
I had thought that Mr Bricquemault, goeng into England, should
have done som good, but as I have lernid now, it hath done little,
and as I se, it was not likely to do otherwise, for, furst the Quene
my mistresse hat great cause to thynck yt strange that my man and
he, both being dispachid at a tyme, which was aboute the second of
aprill, my man (by whome I sent advertizements what the prince
and we had negociated togither, and that the said Mr Bricquemaulte
was to come ymmediately) should be there three hole wekes before
he cam, and that he should come without the Queene or the King
hir sonne's commission or letter, which should have bene his chief
authoritie; and the third was that he especially being one of the
doers hertofore, and who knew what the Queene my mistress did
requier as touching hir right, should come now and offer other and
diverse things from ther promisses made heretofore, but according
as he went without aucthoritie, and upon such requeste, such (as I
understand) his answer was.

To the first, the Queene said in dede she knew of his goeng, but
he went, not as from the King, not hir, but from the prince and
admirall, to se what they could do, and therfore he had no letter
from hir.

And to the promis, whie, saith the Queene, what promis have
they made? Yt is they now that do call most upon me, and doth
most encourage me to go against Newhaven.

That is strange, quoth I, Madame, but if they do, there promis
shall appear when tyme is; and for the rest, not onely by them, but
Your Mate doth knowe and hath knowen at all tymes by me what

the Quene my mistress hir demands be, and that not onely by word of mouth from tyme to tyme but also in writing signid with my hand.

Well, saith she, he saith he went but to putt the Quene, your mistress, in remembrance of his protestacion and promis. To that I replied, that Your Mageste did not go from your protestacion, and for that protestacion which was printed in Orleans, Your Ma^{te} doth not take it for youres.

And then she said that in your protestacion, which I delivered hir at Rouen, yt was that when the King his sonne's subjectz weare at accord for religion, ye wold retire your forces and render Hable-de-Grace.

I said I did not take any such promis to be there, but yt was there that ye wold not usurpe nor appropriate any towne or citie of the Kinge unto you, no more you did not, nor did not claim Newhaven as youres, but ye kepe yt as a pledge or caucion till ye had right done you, of that which by the treatie is youres. . . .

In th'end I said : Madame, ye do se wheruppon we do stand, and what reason the Queene my mistress had to demand that which she doth demaund, and to pursue hir right as she doth, asking but to have reason done unto hir, and in my miend it weare better for Your Ma^{te} to call som wise and grave men, lernid and others, such as will indeferently and without being to muche affectionate judge of our reasons, and so inform yourself therof, then to go to it by force, for that will but provoke force againe, and bring *par adventure* many other inconveniences, which yet be not knowen, and hard it is to saie what will be th'ende of them.

To that she made answer she wold not come to force, she with hir good will, but this manner of doeng wold but protracte the tyme, and be to long.

This is the some of that which passid betwixt the Queene and me at that tyme, and this was the mannor without eyther storming words or any unkiend or angry countenances betwixt us ; methought I did perceive that she did not lyke amys that Bricquemault's message nor himself was no better acceptid, which thinge conjectinge before that she wolde do, I took it for myne entry into the speache and communication with the Queene ; methought the King all this while lokid heavelie and sadly upon the matter, or els as though he had bene half sick.

Streight from the Queene I went to the prince of Conde's chamber, who being occupied in the meane while, I was brought to the princesse's chamber, wheare, after salutacions accustomid to the princes, I began to declare unto hir that I hard that there was a rumor spred in the courte that the Queene my mistress should speak evill of the prince hir husband, and that she, the princess, should be persuadid that it was true, and that the Queene, my mistress should, not onely in words, but also in writing and by letters sent into this court of Fraunce, speak all the evill of the prince that might be.

For that matter, furst of writing, I did assure hir that this VII moneths, Your Ma^te did sent never a letter nto this courte that ever I could lerne, but to me, or by my meanes to be delivered; and in the letters to me, Your M. never made mencion of the prince, but honorable, as one whom Your M. did take for your good freend, which thing we have declarid, not onely in words, but in dedes, and for my part I neither did deliver nor know of delivraunce of any letter of Your Highnes to any person, sith the peace concludid at Orleans, and therfore she may well understand that that was but a devise of som who wold make strief and distore betwixt the prince hir husband and the Queene my mistres, to th'intent that she might lose suche a freend as the queene of England is, and the Queene my mistres all the benefitts and pleasurs which she hath shewid to the prince and his freends.

She made answer she had hard so, and so it was reportid and hir husband could tell more, but she took Your M^te to be a ladie of such honor and vertue that ye wold not take pleasure in any such thing, and that the prince hir husband was your servaunt, and bound unto Your M^te and wold be most sorie to gyve any cause that ye should write speak or think evill of him. Truth it is he could not do so much as he wold, but so sone as he were able, Your Highnes should se that he should be your devoute servaunt. Fayne wold I have pressid hir to have declared to whom that letter should be written, for it is reported that the Queene mother should show to the prince a letter written from Your M^te *to hir*, wherin ye speke many injurious wordes of the prince, and herof the princess hirself had complained to a certeigne ladye in the courte, but in no wise I could drive hir to particularise any otherwise to me then before. . . .

Thus as we were talking, the prince comith into the chamber, who furste made his excuse that he was at that tyme very miche busied, and therfore praid me to have him excused that he cam not streight to me, saieng that he was dispaching to th'admirall a thing which requireth very much haste, and then said he was sorie that I was sick, and that Mr Myddelmore had bene with him and shewid him from Your M^te for the which he was sory, and that he trustie Your

Ma^{te} should have no cause to conceive any evill opinion of him; when tyme and place wold suffer, he wold shew that he was your affectionate serviteur, with many such wordes. I said he should not marvell though Your M^{te} did thinck much to have now such affers made to you, by them whose hands and seales weare at the contrarie. Still he denied that contracte be his.

I said his hand and seale was there, and yf yt were not his, he must take it upon those whome he most trustid, *ffor th'admirall and a great many more was at it*, who now againe, even at the last coming downe, did ratifie and affirme the same.

Well, saith he, and *th'admirall* is to be touchid in it then, for I was then prisoner ye know. But, saith he, there is nether he nor I, but what we can do will do, but at this tyme I meddle not, nor do nothing no more then the leest in this chamber, seynge they have begone it without me; thei shall go through it if they will; I will not meddle. Thei wold have me to be ther chief in it, but I have plainly and flatly refused it.

I pray youe, Sir, quoth I, and will thei avance streight *to New-haven to beseage it?* I pray you, let me know that of you.

By my troth, saith he, I can not tell, I do assure you; for my parte, I wolde there weare som other way taken in the matter; you come new from the Queene, saith he, what doth she say?

I answerid that I did not perceive that she was so hastie, me thought rather she might be persuadid yf any bodie had authoritie with hir, *to let the matter be comonid of*, but she tellith me it is you that doth hasten hir to it.

I, saith he and smiled, doth she name me? Naie, quoth I, I will not saye she namid you, but she said, they whome hastings *the Q. M^{tie}* hath done most for, and whom she trustith most, and those of whome we take you to be the head.

And doth she so in dede, saith the prince; I must and will move hir an other way, ye may be suer, yf I could have any rule or aucthoritie with hir; ye se how and in what case we stand here now.

Mary, quoth I, me thincks ye stand in case where ye had more nede to make freends then to lose any, for I can not perceive that ye stand very suer for religion.

No, I do assure you, saith he.

And I pray you, said I, what doth *the Parisians?* They *were here yesterdaye*, do they agree to the peace and shew themself conform-able? I here say the promysse money a pace.

That matter is not a point yet, saith he, they be in such order yet that neither the Q. *mother* do thincke ourselves suer yf we should come thither, and ye se here what gard and force we are fayne to kepe about the King. Thei speak and talke such things of the *Quene mother* and me that ye wold wonder to here it.

Then I axid, how it chauncid that th'admirall comith not, being so lokid for.

He answerid that the Q. mother had sent for him, and wold have him here; but it was *the prince* that did let it and caused him so to linger, for I am afraid, saith he, that now emongst so many men of warre, which be here, some should *discharge a pistolet at him*, and I take *as much care of hym as of myself*.

That is verie well done, I said, and addid that *Madame de Guise, as it is said, doth pursue verye sore against him.*

He said yt was true.

Sir, quoth I, ye must take order for that.

He said he wold most gladlie do it.

Then, I said, you do remember when you, *th'admirall and Mons*
d'Andelot were togeather at Orleans, I said to you that yf good faith weare not ment, they wold go aboute III thinges. Th'one to have your *strenght of Orleans* from you, which is done; the next to divide you on sonder, which, if they could not otherwyse, they wold devide your case, as now it apperith they will do, *the admirall's* from yours in this of *Poltrot,* and yours from the rest in this of Newhaven; and thirdly make you show yourself unkiend to your freends, that ye should never loke for helpe at their hands; or els put some pike betwixt you and your freends, and so weaken you. And when thei have cleane devided you a sonder, and made you weak enough, then they will by one and one order you as thei list; all this working I se now, and you had nede take hed of it. I do understand by theis rumors which be spred abrod, and that you have complaynid of to the *master Midlemore that the* Q. M[to] should report evill of you, and that injurious letters should be written of you by the Q. M[tie], what is gone aboute on your syde; and yf I should beleve and wryte home, that yt was you and your sute, who were th'eggers on of the Queene here *to drive us out of Newhaven,* as it was told me even this day, were not this enough, thinck you, to set a pike betwixt the Q. M[tie] and you, and all youres on th'other side, and so to make hir to lose all hir benefitts and you to be estemyd the most ingrat men in the world. But I do know, quoth I, the Q. *mother* well enough, and I am partely acquainted with theis practizes. Uppon this, he did excuse himself, and shew that he was and would be your servaunt, and that he desired nothing more then ones to have occasion to se Your

Highnes, and for him, he wold most wish of God to se theis II great powers joynid in one (he ment England and Fraunce), that he might be Your Highnes servaunt doble wais, and that nothing did greve him so miche, as those evill reports, or that Your M^tie should conceive any evill opinion of him. And when I pressid som authors he wolde name none but *Monsr Bricquemault* that came from theme, whither it was eden (*sic*), which is most likely, or som other whome he ment I know not, nor can not gesse, but this was the somme of our communication; *the prince semed* to me in his talke drowly, heavie pensif, and to speake as one who had his head occupied, or not verie well pleasid, and as one that had no ast to talke. . . .

Myddlemore to Cecil.

Saint-Germain, May 17, 1563.

Sir, the admiral beinge, the XIth of this present, at Essone, a XIII leagues from Sainct-Germaines in his waye to come to this court, according to the comandement he had receavid from the Quene mother, the prince of Conde, by the order of the sayd Quene, and by the advyse of his (the admirall's) frynds, went and mett hym at the sayd Essone, whyther fyndynge the same so mete *for the Quene's Matie service,* I went in the trayne of the sayde prince, at what tyme was discovryd unto the admyrall the secrett menees and enterprises of hys ennymys in and without this court, and so great daynger founde in them towards him, as that all his frynds dyd advyse him not to come there, of which mynd also the sayd Queene mother shewyd hirselfe to be but *rather for feare of the admirall and to kepe him styll out of the courte then of any desyre she had to have him escape those daingers,* for yf the wisest sort here be not disceavyd, *she dothe carefullye entertaygne all practises as do, or maye tende to the ruyne of the sayd admirall*; and, as I canne learne, this that followeth was ment to be putt in execution by hys ennemys at this tyme against him. They had obtaynyd and gotten forth secretlye that they caule here a *prinse de corpz* against him, for the deathe of the duke of Guyse, which they did meane to have servyd upon him in this court immedyatlye after his commynge; having for that purpose wonne and corruptyd many of the court, but most of all the forces and gards about the same, and where he shuld have shewyd himselfe resistant, as they were desyerous he shulde, to have cutt him in pieces, as a most desobedyent and greavous offendor of the King's lawes, which enterpryse, in the opinion of most men, wolde never have bene taken n hande, without the connivance of the *greatest of this courte.* Thys

matter ys found so dayngerous for the admyrall as the accordinge to
the counseil and advice of hys frynds, and the pleasure of the Queene,
he doth for this tyme retyer himselfe home to his house of Chastillon,
where he ys lyke to remayne a good whyle before he be sent for, *yf
the Queene mother's opynion* maye be allowyd of. But, somwhat to
heame to content him, mary in dede to doo themselffs a pleasure
and to keape the sayd admyrall the rather from interprisinge of any
thinge against them, they have ordeynyd that his brother, Monsr
d'Andelot, shall be a courtier.

The XIIth of this moneth I dyd declare unto the admyrall, as so
given me *in commission from Her M^{tie}*, howe disagreable she had the
offers made by Monsr de Bricquemault ; how lyttell she lokid to have
from the prince and him offers so farre different from all theyr promisses, *contractz* and letters, and howe that Hir Ma^{te} had good cause
(yf they wold acquytt themselfes no otherwise of theyr promisses to
hir then they had done hytherto) both to thincke and saye that she
had bestowyd great benyfytts of most ingratefulle persons, and that
that manner of unthankfull dealynge was the waye to move Hir Ma^{te}
to doo that which, per adventure, he and others wolde be right sorye
for, er yt were longe after. *Th'admirall*, before he cam to touche
any part of that talke I had holden to him, begane to tell me, by
waye of bemonynge to me, of words Hir Ma^{te} shulde have of him.

Yt is, saith he, geven me to understand that the Quene, your
mistrys, hath sayd that I ame the falseste and dishonestest man that
lyveth, and that she wyll declare that our intent was not to esta-
blishe religion, but to distroye the Kynge, and make ourselfs
kings and rullers. These be matters, sayd he, that touche me very
nere, but greave me most of all that they shuld be spoken of them of
whom I never deservyd any suche language.

Myne answer was, that I dyd not lesse beleave but suche reaports
had bene made unto him, for that I dyd knowe that there were many
that did nothinge but devise and some suche false brutes to putt
division betwext Hir Ma^{te}, *him*, and the prince. But how unlikelye
yt was that such wordes shulde proceade from Hir Ma^{te}, I did make
him only judge. Mary, Sir, quoth I, yf Hir M^{te} shewe hirselfe
offendyd towards you, yt can not be denyed but she hath good cause
so to doo, considerynge the promises you have made hir, and howe
contrarye you doo nowe by hir.

Well, sayd he, as unto those matters, me thinketh Hir M^{te} hath no
cause to be offendyd, yf hir money be renderid to hir, and hir right,
and that she canne any waye pretend to Callice, be assuerid her ;
and as unto that, I protest before God and all his angells, yf myne

obligation were nothing towards hir as yt is most great, I wolde all that I might further hir right therin, for that I knowe and fynde in my conscience that it doth rightly appertayne unto hir, and what I have of late sayd for the keryinge of that treatye with hir, God and the Quene mother canne be my judges; and as I have alwayes bene of that mynde hitherto, and so declare yt francklye to all the worlde, so Hir Ma^te maye be assueryd I wyll never cesse to worke therin for hir to my uttermost; for any promisse made by me on any letter wryten by me to Hir Ma^te, wherin she hathe to shew that *she shulde kepe Newhaven untill Calles were rendrid unto her, I doo not thinck I ever made any, and wolde be gladde to see them, if Hir Ma^te have any suche letters of myne to shew.* Touching *the contract you speake of, I protest I never sawe it, untill my comming into Normandy, at what tyme Mr de Throckmorton shewid it me, but I had first ratifyed it, and yf I did think before that there had bene any more conteynid in it then the assurence only unto the Q. M^te of suche money, as she had and shulde lend unto us, and that ayd and succours, which she had and shuld give unto us in this cause, might not prove domeageable in this sorte to her right and interest to Calles,* God never doo me good! and to lett you understand more of that matter, and that you may thincke I had some reason *to beleve so, Mr de la Haye wrote to me to Orleans soone after the contract was made in England,* that, as touchinge the said contract, yt was promyssyd there unto him *it shuld be rendrid him, when he wolde.* And so sayd he wolde *sent it over to me,* for that they had playnely answeryd hym there *they coulde not serve themselfes by it,* nor yt coulde *serve them in my steade,* which *Mr de la Haye hathe here since confyrmid to be,* and wheras, sayethe he, Hir M^te dothe seame to accompte me an ungratefulle person, that do no better recorde me of hir benefitts bestowyd upon me; yf she did knowe howe greatly I esteame them, how much I honor and serve hir for them, and howe contrary that vice of ingratitude ys to me, she wolde not so easelye condenyme me, and so much yt shall lacke that ever I wyl be ungrate towards hir, as that I confesse I am most bounden to hir, and next after the King my master, there ys no prince nor princesse in the worlde unto whome I beare that respect of honor and service as I doo to Hir Ma^te, and so I praye you assuer hir, from me, and with all besiche hir, that *so as she have so good assurance as that,* she may be out of all doubts for *the rendition of Calles to her at the end of the tearme specified in the treaty,* that yt maye please hir to accept it without further *troubling* herself, *indangering her frends or attending issue of a doubtfull* warre, for, sayd he, lthonghe *Newhaven be very stronge yet she will lose it in the end yf they go to yt by force,* which I have and *do lett to my possible.* Lett Hir Ma^{te} nowe, said he, so devise *her counsell as that she may demande suche assurance in dede as that here after she may be out all doubts or suspicions of not rendring it; for God forbyd but she shuld have what is her right;* and by this waye, she shall not onlye *perfourme that she hathe promised in her protestation,* and have that neverthelesse she desyreth, but allso *wynne the harts of an infynite nomber of poore Christians,* werby her *honour, reputacion and greatnes* shall marvelouslye *increase.* And when I semid much to *styck upon the contract, and recyted to him the words therin, he sayde yf the contract come to disputing,* yt ys of all others the worste and weakest *wapon the Q. M^{te} hath to defend herself,* yf you will well consyder of it; for, you knowe, *we can not gyve awaye that is none of oure, nor the King can lose his right by any promise we have made;* and (sayd he) *ther is* mannye other reasons *to be allegyd,* which I am suer the Q. M^{te} and her counsell understand well inoughe and therfore I trust wyll procede accordynglye. . . . . . .

Sir, I had forgotten to wryte to you of that that passyd betwixte the *Queene mother and Mr de Bricquemault after his coming from* England, which was with eyvill contentment, and so *speakith therafter of the Q. Ma^{te}, you, and others. The eight of this monethe he sayde to the Q.* mother that *yf she had gyvin him any commission* to have dealt further with Hir Ma^{de} in those matters then his simple legation, he beleavyd he coulde have made such an offer to hir as she shulde have acceptyd yt, and yet *Calles shuld not have bene rendrid untill the tyme lymytid in the treaty.*

So the Quene asked him what offer that was. He sayde: to gyve her presentlie suche assurance *that she might know and beleve you did meane to render Calles to her in deede, at the end of the tearme,* and so to graunt *her in hostage, eyther your sonne, the duke of Anjou, or the prince of Navarre and the duke of Guyse, to remayne ther untill suche tyme as tearme wear expyyred. Wher* at the *Queene laughed.*

Whye, said he, Madame, what care you *whom or how many you gyve in hostage, yf you meane in dede to keape the treaty, and render her Calles. Mary, yf you do not meane to kepe the treaty your husband made with the queene of England for the restitucion of Calles.*

I wolde not weshe you there *to gyve such hostages, no,* sayd she, *je m'en garderay bien.*

But in the meane tyme, sayd *Bricquemault,* what canne *the quene of England do, ye see, yf you refuse to gyve her sufficient assurance for the rendring of Calles, then to kepe still Newhaven in her hand?*

And I will, sayd he, assuer Your Ma^{te} of on thinge, that yf you seke yt by force, you wyll have your hands full, for she hath made great preparacion for you, and ys reasolvyd to defend yt to the uttermost.

Well, sayd *she, Bricquemault*, yt is not longe of you that all things be not well compounded ; *go your waye, and rest you at your house*, and in the meane tyme *nous ne perdrons point le temps.*

Sir, I doo the rather advertise you herof to the ende you may se *howe these are bent to observe the treaty, and how lyttell it is ment that the Q. Ma⁶ shuld ever have Oalles renderid her*, yf they might once gett Newhaven out of her hands without *very good assurance.* . . .

Smith to Cecil.

May 19, 1563.

Sir, the XVIIIth of this monethe, bicause I had sent (as I wrote before) to the prince, Mr de la Hay and Mr Steward cam to accompany me to the courte, at St Germaynes, in the which the King, the Queene and the chauncellor being at Paris, there was not left but the prince, Monsr d'Andelot and such as be of that trayne and sute. That daie I dyned wyth the prince, and before dinner, I had some talke both wyth the prince and the princesse. The occasion of my goeing to him, I said, was to understand yf I might now after my last communication before the Queene and the counsell what way thei wold take, either to go to Newhaven with force, and so we should have warre out of hand, or by gentle meanes thei wold do right and reason to the Queene my sovereigne mistress, and so bring all to a good accorde, which is most necessarie at this tyme, and most profitable to both realmes, and if thei did tend to accord, as me thought the Queene mother by hir talk betwixt hir and me did rather enclyne, then of the good zeale and love I did beare to the prince, I had a desier to come hyther to put them in mynd that it were better for the said prince and those of the religion to have the honor of yt, then th'other faction, so that it might be said that it was they that had brought the realme of Fraunce into quiet and order, and th'other into all this troble and disorder.

Long communication and verie eloquent and full the prince had (as I assure you he hath words at will) to this purpose, and they ment suerly by force, and that no hold is so strong to resist the power of a hole realme, yf not in one monethe, in II or III or in XII moneths, it wold be wonne, and that if the Queen's Majeste wold nedes stand upon Calais to be rendrid incontinent, he knew no remedie, and that he spake to me now as an Englishman, not as a Frencheman, for th'affection which he dothe beare to the Q. M. and not to make us afraid, etc.

To this I annswerid as I could, in somme : we had no feare of ther force ; we lokid for it, now ever sith we were there this VII moneths, and my comming thither now was not to pray them to leave of, but let them hardelie (if thei thinck to have honor of it) make the attempt ; but as I did saie before ; yf thei did encline rather to accord, that he and his faction should rather take that honor then ever parte eny part of it to the papists. This manner of communication did passe before dynner, as we weare walking togither in the park at St Germaynes, and when we were com in, with other talk and annswereth we had as touching the Quene's protestacion in printe and under seale ; th'end was the princesse breaking the talke by pressing him to prayers, all that our talke passed without any resolucion, as me thought.

At after dynner the prince and I, begynnyng agayne and beinge set besyde a bay-wyndow, there cam in M^r d'Andilot, who cam and sat with us, and the prince callid Mr Grammont, who stode by, there the prince to Monsr d'Andilot declarid my good affection to him and all those of that religion, and my desier which I had to have a good order and wais taken for the peace.

But, saith he, I can not get of Monsr l'ambassadeur that the Queene will be content with any thing, but furst to have Calais rendrid immediately, and that can not be, or els she will kepe Newhaven, and ye know what force and power is toward it, and ye know what daunger is like to come of it, if it should be lost.

Uppon this, Monsr d'Andilot beganne with a long discourse (he is not uneloquent, nor unredye of his tonge) touching the Q. M. protestacion in printe, and that under seale, touching th' honor she should get in, showing hirself to have kept hir furst promesse and designe, and onely to have come for religion ; and that the contracts made for Newhaven were but blank signid with protestacions before made ; they were ment onely for money ; that that article of Newhaven was extortid of them by force ; that subjects could not give away, nor by end the townes of ther prince, that now uppon this accord and peace, they can but aide there king to recover his owen, and what daunger and troble that should be to the Q. M. Herin also the prince addid that the Q. M., he was suer, wold not helpe herself with those contracts, for, even that contracting with the King's subjects was a forfeiture of our right of Calais.

Uppon this manner of talke ye may be suer I was somwhat

heatid and began furst to declare my zeale to religion, and how that in England I am well enough knowen in those matters from the beginning, not onely to be a follower, but to have at all changes of religion to the new and evangelicall, to have bene a speciall doer and setter forwarde, etc. ; and therfore as I am affectionate that wais to helpe forward the Gospell, not onely in our owen realme, but in all places, so I am the bolder to speak, and seing ther ys none here but of the religion, I will franckely and freely speake my myend.

Monseigneur le Prince, quoth I, and Monsieur d'Andilot, yf this matter come to a peace and accord without force, then there is no more a do; all particular doeings shall be shit up with silence and coverid with the mantell of love and amitie. But, yf it breake out into warre, then the Queene, my mistres, shall be contreynid as the mannor is now, to set out hir appologie or defence, wherin she shall declare furst hir right to Calais, and how it is hirs by treatie, the condicion fulfillid on hir side, and broken by king Fraunch the second, and so by forfeite oures immediately by the same treatie, which, as M^r le chauncellor, at my last being before the counsell, did passe over (as I am suer you do remember) Monsieur le Prince, marie you Monsr d'Andilot, was asleepe all the while.

So I was in dede, saith he, I could not holde up my heade.—But, quoth I, as he passed it over lightly, so nother he, nor no man living is able to aunswer yt, and I thinck verely he thincketh in his conscience it can not be answerid. . . .

Then belyke ye ment to mocke and to deceeve your freends, and to make them fooles, but yf we or our counsell have that note to be fooles in our bargaines, I know the note of ingratitude, and an other note as dishonorable as that, all the world will give you for yt.

With that the prince callid Mr de la Hay. Howe saye you? saith he, Monsr l'ambassadeur saith that if we come to Newhaven, the Queene will set out in printe all those matters of our billes and contracts for Newhaven, and that that article was not put in by force.—Monseigneur, saith he, God forbid it should come to that, ffor the love of God, seke some other waie; let us not put that good Queene to that extremitie; we be utterly undone then, and dishonorid for ever.—Monsieur le Prince, quoth I, yf there were a papist here to here me, I wold not for X^m crownes have said so miche, no, nor the Queene, nor the Cardinall could never, with all ther traine and crafte make me confesse that there was any contracte, as ye might well perceive that both by my doengs and my saiengs, and here answers, the last daie at the counsell, and yet I have the copie of it, and what names and signes there be at yt. But, Monsieur le Prince, I said, where ye said that the Queene wold not show theis contracts, for then she should lose hir right to Calais, ye know well enough what she should do; but if it come to force and the warre be openid, then we have Newhaven; and yf we take all Normandie and Calais, and all Picardie also to it, if we can get them, thei are oures. . . .

Now that we have come to save your lieves, your goodes, your estates, your honours, and ye have all that ye can desier, ye have made your peace and agreament, shall we loke to have you against us when we demaund but our owen right? Yf there had bene no covenaunt nor agreament, yf there had bene no benefite, yf we had put ourself in no daunger (as now ye know we put ourselves for your sake in daunger of warre with king Philippe, with the pope, and with all the confederatz against you), but, I sais, yf we had put ourselves in none of this daunger, yet methinks you for religion's sake, and for conscience, wold have helpid us to our right without striefe or warre.

And now, methinks, ye saye ye will and must come against us; I wold be loth to se that daie; yf ye will nedes have warre, send the Guisards, I meane the papists against us, and yf thei be not well received, yf thei get not dishonour enough, let us beare the blame; and if thei be handlid as thei should be of us, you shall have th'advantage; thei shall be the weaker and you the stronger, but yf warre do ensue, and you do come against us, I tell you what will follow.

Furst, th'opening to all the worlde of the hole procedings betwixt the Q. M^{te} and you, the evill opinion of unkiendnes that the Queene, my mistres, shall conceive at you; this league and amitie which is begone for religion, and for th'aide and strenght of you, shall eande in discord and debate, and in hatrid and evill talks of th'one against th'other; and what thing can the papists desier more? What greater pleasure can thei take then to se that? And this must be the utter ruyne of you, and the weakening of all this league for the Gospell; all the world shall laugh us to skorne, and not without a cause.

Mon oncle, saith the prince to d'Andilot, M. l'ambassadeur was not so hote against us before dynner, when he and I were alone.

To me he said: M^r l'ambassadeur, we did agree better when we were but we two; we know and do se all this to be true that ye saye, and we do beleve that all ye saie comith of a good love and affection that ye beare to religion and us; I pray you, tell us your advice, what ye wold have us do to satisfie the Q. your mistres; yf it were to spend my life, I wold do it, and I am bounde thereto.

I answerid: ye have commytted two greate errors alreadie, amend you those. I still speak frankly, quoth I, it is my nature, I can do noue other, furst I may saie to you as he said: *Vincere scis, Hannibal, victoria uti nescis*; when ye were a greate deale stronger than your enemies, and might have commandid and given lawes, at the furst making of the peace, ye wold nedes submit yourselves, and take lawes at there hands, even so miche and so little as they wold give you, which was a marvelous great faulte, a discouraging to your freends, an encouraging of your enemies, which hath made them hitherto triumphe over you at ther pleasure. An other was in sending to the Q. M^te my mistress, furst to send one with so slender a commission, not so miche as a letter of credite from the King or the Queene. Yf the Q. my mistress wold have condiscendid to the offers, what authoritie had he to ratifie them, and how miche the nerer had the Q. M^te bene?—In dede, saith he, he had none but my letters and th' admirall, and that was no authoritie to ratifie and affirme.

Whien then, quoth I, belyke ye did but to attempte Hir Majeste what she wold saie to it; they saie: *Non tentabis Dominum Deum tuum.* God loveth not to be temptid; no more do great princes neather. Then th'offers weare so slender and of so small force, and so farre from Hir Highness expectacion; the Q. M^te, as she is of greate spirite and understandinge, and by and by can feele what valor and weight things be, that be movid to Hir M^te, so is she also of greate courage, and hir father, king Henry th'eight doughter, and will not sticke to saie hir miend plainly as I am suer Mr Bricquemault can beare witnes, and partely by Mr Middlemore and me ye have understood, and yet I am suer she settith more by you, Monsieur le Prince, then all the rest of the princes in Fraunce, and wold be loth now to linck in, or on any benefite or kiendness to any other faction, or to loose all those benefitte loves and amities that she hath shewid to you, what so ever tales and reports be made unto you by them that wold break this league and amitie if they could, by which league hitherto all ther designes hath bene overthrown. Now, shall I tell you what I wolde have you do; I have hard what you and mareschall Montmorency did in the cownsell the last daie as I was gone, and I did rejoise of it not a little. Yt was done honorably, courageously and friendly, and in dede ye could do no les, for if you beginne one ones to shrinck from an other, ye know what will follow. Yf ye be stowte and holde your strenghte and whie shall ye not do the same now? Yf it had bene that the connestable or the duke of Guise that had had so miche hold as ye have now, he wold have said to the Queene mother: we must not fall out with the queene of England, nor we can not. She must have reason; she demandith but hir owen; let us consider hir right. Yt is not worth the making warre for it; ye se what they do to king Philippe without stoppe or stay, what lately to the duke of Savoye, and, if there be any thing to be gotten at the queene of England's hands, take it upon you, that you will do it.

No other man shall medle with it, and if she shall have reason at any man's hands, let ir have it at yours, so it will be most thankfull, and if ye might se this courage in you, and that ye went to it on this sorte; not as fearing and dowtinge and instructing and craving at yours enemies hands that which thei should do at youres, then wold I be glad to joigne with you with my letters, to entreat, if nede were, and to amend all this unkiend talk, and to make the Queene have such an opinion of you as I wold wish she should ever have, and for this cawse have I staid my curror till I had spoken with you, that I might give Hir M^{te} occasion to conceive better of you then she began of late to do.

With this the prince stode up, and Monsieur Dandilot, and cam nerer togither; for as we sat, I was betwixt them. And, saith the prince, uncle, I told you Monsr l'ambassadeur and I should agree better, but it must be so belike when we meete, we must every tyme have furst a crashe of chiding, but in th'end we parte frends.

And staieng a little, saith Monsr Dandilot, yt shall be well done to consider this that Monsr l'ambassadeur saith, me thincks he hath said well.

And the prince: ye have reason, saith he, Monsieur l'ambassadeur hath put things unto my head now; we had nede thinck of them; I will send one to the Queene very straight, and you and I will debate of theis matters how to ordre them yf Monsr l'ambassadeur could put us in som comfort that the Queen wold relent.

I assure you, quoth I, I have no commission for that, nor to saie so miche as I do, but my zeale onely that I have to religion and desire that th'amitie, love and league might be still betwixt the Queene my mistress and you, and the rest here for the conservacion of religion makith me to saie this, and even seke occasion to wryte som good thing to the Queene of you, Mons. le Prince, and upon this I staie my curror.

Ah! saith the prince, that I might se the tyme that Mylord Robert might com hither, to se the league and treaty sworne, and

I might for the same matter go into England to se that Queene, whom I do so love and honor, and to whome I am so miche bownd. But, he told me that he with whom he talkid with before dynner so long cam to him from the conestable, who had not visited him of long tyme, but now, saith he, we be great freends, and things, I trust, shall do better then ye thincke for, saith he to me; but you will now go home, and we will dispatche to the Queene, Monsr Dandilot and I, but I pray you, staie your curror till you here from me.

And so he willede Monsr de la Hay and Mr Steward to conduct me to my horse.

Smith to Cecil.

(EXTRACTS.)   May 22, 1563.

Sir, the communication I had with the prince and Monsr Dandilot, I do perceave hath taken some effect, for the prince dispaching immediatly to the Queene, the same night about midnight there cam annswer to him againe in post, that he should speake with the Queene at Paris. The prince and Mons. Dandilot went the next day, but not to Parys, but to Madry, which is an house of the King's hard by, where the Quene and thei had long conference. Thei retornid the same night to St-Germaynes, which was the XVIIIth, and at tenne of the cloke at night, Mr Middlemore cam from the prince to me, requiring me to staie my curror, which I should send into England, till I had word from him, belik the matter went not altogither as they wold, for the next daie, the XXth at night, he sent Mr. Middlemore to me, praienge me yet to staie my curror. . . .

The protestants may thinck yf the force should come to New-haven, then furst the Queene's Ma^{te} wold to maintein hir doengs and honor utter that which thei wold not gladlie here, and if thei come against us, their untruth, dissimulacion and unkiendness should be knowen to all the world.

Yf they do not come against us, yet there unkiendnes in making ther peace without us, and the little either aucthoritie, wisedom in conducting there affaires to redound so to ther dishonor, must nedes be an example and discredit to themselves for ever. . . .

The prince of Conde, as thei saie here, swymeth betwixt two waters, nother the *Catholiks* nor the *Protestants* doth well love him. To saie the troth, I can not tell of which of the two *he* is more hatid, by such wordes as I here of them both; and *then* plaieth the parte that Machiavelli (as I remember) saith the pope or *la Chiesa* doth in Italie and was wont to do emong the christian princes; *tener gli desuniti*, for ells his power wold be nothing, or, as one that is in a tottering bote leanes upon the higher and stronger side, and ever flowith that, and yet by meanes, plucketh up the lower and weaker side; to make yt contervaile th'other.

By cause *the prince of Conde* trustith nether th'one nor th'other, but as little or lesse then they trust *him*. . . .

This day, the XXIIth of may, M[r] d'Alluy, one of the secretaris of comandements, was dispachid from the court into England, with condicions to be offerid to the Quene's Ma[te]. He goeth by the way of Chantilly to the Conestable's house, where the prince hath requyred that he might stay the night. The Quene mother will have him go, because he is an indifferent man, as she saith. The prince wold have had som greater personnage, and of more authoritie and of his faction, and as I understand, Mons[r] de la Haye shall come shortly, or the busshop of Aixe. What manner of condicions shall be offerid as yet I knowe not. Yesterday ther was XII canons, besyde other peces, pouder, and shot, wheate and tymber, sent downe by water from Paris to Newhaven ward. They gesse it shall be at Caudebeck about the XIIth or XVIIth of june. . . .

The Prince de Condé to Cecil.

31 mai 1563.

Monsieur le secrétaire, puisque par le passé vous avez tant et si ouvertement faict paroistre le zelle et affection que vous portez à l'honneur de Dieu et à la conservation et défense en général de son Église, et à moy une particulière bonne volunté (ainsi que par les lettres de Monsr de la Haye, conseiller du Roy Monseigneur, et maistre de requestes de son hostel, estant par delà, et depuis son retour, par sa bouche, j'ay peu entendre), je ne me puis persuader que une tant bonne amitié procédant d'une si saincte occasion et logée dans ung cerveau si solide et constant puisse jamais estre esbranlée, ne souffrir altération par quelque faulx rapport que l'on s'efforce vous faire, ny que mes ennemys sceussent artificieusement semer. Car, estant nourry, comme vous l'estes, de si longue main au maniement des grandes affaires, vous n'ignorez poinct combien les grans sont subjectz à une infinité de calumnies; par quoy, de ma part, je ne trouve poinct estrange, d'aultant que Dieu m'a appelé et faict naistre en ce rang, s'il ne m'a voulu exempter de ceste condicion; mais il me desplait grandement que telles impostures parviennent aux oreilles de ceux dont je recongnois avoir reçeu beaucoup de

plaisirs, comme de la Royne vostre maistresse. Touteffois, combien
que la vérité ait ceste puissance, par la vivacité de ses rayons, de
pénétrer avecques le temps l'obscurité des plus espesses mensonges,
si n'ay-je peu avoir cette patience d'en attendre l'événement, ains
estant adverty de la sinistre oppinion que l'on essaye d'imprimer de
moy en la fantasie de ladicte dame, deschiffrant mes actions et
déportemens au grand désadvantage de ma réputation, je n'ay
voullu faillir de redespescher soudain iceluy Sr de la Haye vers
S. M., et l'accompaigner de la présente, par laquelle je vous priray,
Monsieur le secrétaire, que s'il vous reste encores quelque scintille
de cette première amitié vers moy, vous le démonstrez en cest
endroict, affin que ledit Sr de la Haye, faisant entendre à ladite
dame la pureté de mon cueur, et le meilleur de mes intentions, vous
luy assistiez tellement de vostre crédit et faveur envers elle que, de
son consentement, il m'en rapporte le gré et la satisfaction que j'en
attendz et desire ; et, pour ce que pour y parvenir il s'en va très-
bien instruict de toutes choses, lesquelles je luy ay prié vous discourir par le mesme, je ne vous en feray icy autre ne plus ample
discours. . . .

Myddlemore to Cecil.

Forest of Vincennes, June 19, 1563.

Sir, the *inconstancy* and *miserablenes of this prince of Conde is so
great, havinge bothe forgotten Godd and his owne honor, as that he
hath sufferyd himselffe to be wonne by the Q. mother to go against Hir
Ma^{te} at Newhaven, and for the present is the person that, above all
others, as taken in hande to persuade them of the religion to fynd this
his going thither good, just and lawfull, and that doth most solycit the
said of the religion to serve in these warrs against Her Ma^{te}. The
sevententh of this moneth he had this talk openly that the Q. mother
wolde have him to go to Newhaven, and that he wold go thither, and
that therfore all his shold prepare themselfes for that voyage, meaning
to make it out of hand*, declarynge unto them that were ther *the Q.
Ma^{te} had sent word hither to them* that she had neyther for the cause
of religion, for respect of any persone, neither for ayding the King,
nor for other ende, taken and kept Newhaven in this sort, but to be
revengyd of this realme of the injuryes and wrongs the same had
donne to her, and since the takyng of Calles, and to do hirselfe
reason of the sayd Calles, which was hir right, dyd appertayne unto
hir, and which she wold have before she left the other. So, as *he
sayeth, that this beinge true, as yt ys most true, that Hir Ma^{te} hath*

*sent such word hyther, there is no protestant in Fraunce but may, with
a good and safe conscience, go employ himself in these warres against
hir. Sir, this reaport runneth marvelously through this courte, and
althoughe yt may easilye appere to them that be wyllynge to wage yt,
a matter for the most parte of more mallice then trothe,* yet, *I assure
you, Sir, it tourneth many gentlemen in this courte,* and such as I
wolde have *beleved could not so lyghtly have bene reamoved.* The
Q. mother, *the prince of Conde and the conestable, confederats in this
poynct,* and he, *the prince, specially desiering nowe to have every man
to shew himself as wycked as he, have sent for the admyrall and M^r
d'Andelot, his brother, to come to the court,* out of hand, takyng order
that all *theyre ennemyes shall dislodge and retyre* themselfes, *to bringe
them there thither* ; where beinge ones arryvyd, *they think to prevaile
so much with them* as to wynne *them to like and take in hand* the said
enterprise. How *necessary it is that some declaration come from thence,
with all spede, to putt men out of these doubtes, and to kepe an infinite
nombre from offending by false persuasion,* yt may lyke you to
consyder.

All such *other* noblemen as be in this court, and that have governments shall be sent to resyde in them. Sir, as I have, in these my
letters, truly and sincerely as I can, and as the uncertenty of the
tyme will permit me, advertised you of ther intents and preparations
for war here, so havinge occasion presentyd me at the making up of
this letter, *I cannot but shewe you that I am advertised since the
writing of the premysses, from thre or foure of good credit that for all
these braggs, these here do meane to come to peace with Hir Matie, but
will not shew the same as yet, hoping by bravery and approching to
Newhaven to come by peace, the better cheape, and specially by bringing
the prince of Conde thither, and doth advise them never to take the
matter in, have to procede by way of force, assuering them that yf they
do attempt it by force, they shall lose both their laboures and honors, bring
themselfes and ther nation in contempt; pluck a forrayne warre upon
ther heades, in the tyme of the King's minoritye, which takyng evyle
successe, may cost them all ther heades in tyme to come, with many
other great reasons, but that he is of opinion and dothe wishe that the
end of these differences be sought and procedinge in by waye of composition, which, he beleaveth, shall not be rejected of Her Ma^{te}, so as
reasonable offers be made hir, and suche assuerances of hir right to*
Callice, as she may take and think to be sufficient. . . .

Myddlemore to Cecil.

(EXTRACT.)   Paris, June 29, 1563.

APP.
XIV.

Right honorable, beinge at Pont d'Oyse, VII leagues from Parys, in the prince's trayne, to followe him in this journey of Normandye, accordyng to that I wrote to you in my letters of the XXVIth of the last; the said prince, hearyng of my beinge there, sent for me, and desyerid me (after a longe protestation that he dyd yt only for the advauncement of Hir M[te] service) to retyer myselffe, and to tarye with my Lord ambassador for a tyme, sayinge that me so followinge of him, would render hym so suspectyd to the Quene mother (who had alredye somewhat touchyd him for me) and to the house of Guyse, which dyd desyer no better occasyon, as that he shuld in no sort be able to doo Hir Ma[tie] that good service that he desyeryd to doo.

Sir, quoth I, you knowe well inoughe that the Q[ne] M[te], my mistres, dyd send me hyther of pourpose to tary and remayne by you, to th'intent Hir M[te] might have the more often and more commodyouslye of your good newes, and you, Sir, also of hers; and therfore, Sir, thar ys to be done one of these two things, eyther that, accordyng to the charge commytted to me, I be sufferyd to followe you, or elz that yt maye please you to gyve me leave to retyer myselffe towards the Quene's M[te], my mistres.

At what tyme, he sayd that he wold never consent to my goinge awaye in any such sort, but prayed me to be consentyd to tarye for some dais with Hir M[te] ambassador, where, he sayd, I shuld not be idle nor, as he termyd yt, inutile, for he wold from tyme to tyme send me such newes as shuld be at the court, and trustyd before yt were longe to have occasion to employe me in some good and gratefull message to Hir Ma[te]. I replied that since yt was hys pleasure not to have me to followe him, that I had no commission to tarye here any longer, and therfor I dyd ones agayne beseche him to gyve me leave to retyer myselffe home to Hir Ma[te], and that he wold for my discharge gyve me hys letters to the same, wherin he myght, yf yt so pleasyd him, wrytt the reasons and occasions that movyd him thus to retourne me towards Hir Ma[te].

But notwithstandinge thus my pressing of him, which I dyd of pourpose the better to decypher hys and theyr meanyngs towards Hir Ma[te], he wolde in no sort gyve me leave to goo me waye, but, in the end, he gave me his letter to my L. ambassador, and wyllyd me in anye wise to tary with him, untyll I hard from him agayne;

which, by cause I have no order from Hir Ma^{te} and you, Sir, not knowinge howe my leavinge the prince and this contreye in this manner myght be lykyd, I have hytherto obeyed to the prince's reaquest and so doo remayne with my L. ambassador.

It maye therfore please you, by the next, to signifie unto me Hir Ma^{te} good pleasure and yours, howe hereaften I shall have to governe myselffe. . . .

Queen Elizabeth to Sir Thomas Smith.

July 5, 1563.

Trustie and right well beloved, we grete you well. We have perused both your common and private letters, and herd Thom. Dannett at lenght, and allowe your diligence and circumspections in your wholl procedings, *but of the matter* that caused Dannetts jorney, we find no such successe as we ment. It seemeth that others have more to do there than the *prince*, but yet non can be so mete to deale in our causes *as he or the admirall*, and therfore we have thought mete to send answer to the princes letter, as you shall perceave by the copy herewith sent, wherby to gyve you occasion to enter furder in the matter. It should much content us, you know, to recover Callice presently, *but if nether cost nor treaty can procure it, than it is wisdome to be contented* with that which may stand with our honour and suerty. We *never used* such kind of speche as we wold never deliver Newhaven except we might have Callice presently, but the phrase of our speche hath ben except we had *reason* rendred us for Callice, so as the one or the other may be answerable for our honour.

Our letter to the prince shall gyve you occasion to prosequute that which shall seme mete for our purpose, and though we prescribe you to deale with him and the admirall, yet, if occasion be given up to deale with the *constable* or any other whom ye shall thinck not unmet for the purpose, ye may use that discretion which we know you have to cause your speche to appeare to come of yourself.

We could be content for the love of peace, and for the advancement of the matter of religion in France, to render *Newhaven,* so as we may be answerid our money lent as it hathe ben promised, and our charges sustayned, and *such assurances made to us* for to have Callice *at th'end of the III yeres or soner,* as may be thought by commissioners to be named on both parts, sufficient and honorable.

.   .   .   .

Yf you see cause, ye may also deale plainly with the prince, that where the world is lett to understand that we do kepe Newhaven without any colour, if he and his frends do not better acquite our good will towards them, we must nedes, lett it be also understand abrode, what covenanty we have of the prince, the admirall and other the nobilytie associated with them under their hands and seales to the contrary, and what other great and strange offers were made to us of more importance then Newhaven is, which hitherto we have kept in silence, because we wold not harme them as long as any spark remayned to hope of gratitude in him or them. . . .

You may also saye that, for proofe of our indifferent dealing, we wold not refuse to referr the same to be herd at good lenght by any soverain prince christian and specially by king Philip although he be brother in lawe to the french king, for what more can be required than to be content *only with good assurance* for that which the French themselves do not deny but we shall have, and therfore seing the wholle difficulty will rest upon the *maner of the assurance*, why should they, yf they desire peace and meane sincerely stick *at any kind of assurance*, but if (because they meane otherwise), they will not yeld to *good assurance*, why should we procede any other way than to kepe that gage which we have; and beside many other great reasons to move us to be very exquisite and precise in seking assurance, none is better than that the French themselves make the kings deeds in his mynorytye to be of small moment, if they be not assisted or fortified with some other helpes. The other is the great cause given by them of diffidence that they meane not the delivery of Callice by force of treaty or compact, insomuch we know it hath ben reported by their owne ministers here, yf they doute whither it be so ment. The motions moved by you to the prince and la Haye *doth not miscontent us, nether dothe* those conteyned in the prince's letters *with some addicions*, which, by commissionners are to be devised for furder suerty, and therein no mention is made of repayment of our money and our charges; we write the largelier unto you, because ye may now at this tyme so fully procede, as we may knowe whereupon to rest, for we se the matters are even come to the full, and can receave no more delays.

Sir Thomas Smith to Queen Elizabeth.

July 3, 1563.

Mr Middlemore being rejected from the prince of Conde, and sent with a letter of the XXVII of junii to tarie with me for a tyme, for the prince said yf he should tarie with him, he shoulde make him to be suspectid, I sent him, because he should not be idle, with a letter from me, to the *admirall* and certaine instructions to like effecte, as I and Mr Dannett should have said to the admirall, yf he had bene at the court. He toke myne advertizments in mervelous good parte, thincks himself mich bound to Your Ma^te, lamentith the imbesilitie and pussillanimitie of *the prince of Conde*, and thinkith reasonable those offers and condicions, and all good assurances; and iff thei should be refused *of the French*, that they should be in great wrong, and shew themself not to meane uprightly. He said he wold dispatch out of hand *Bricquemault* in poste to the court *to stir the prince of Conde* more, and to work what as is possible, and is marvelous sorie that *he is forbidden to com* to the courte, who if he weare there, he thought the matter should not go thus. *Bricquemault* I know, is gone thither for him, for on tewisday the VIth of this moneth he came by Paris to have spoken with *Delahay*, who was then removid. *Delahay and* I have bene ones or twies together; I compleined as well to him as to *th'admirall* of the prince of Conde's letters, which I sent Your Ma^te by *master Dannet*, how slenderly yt was made, having no thing but frerely harengues in yt. I fiend *Delahay* marvelous willing that all should be well, but he is sicke, and I thincke *the prince of Conde his* evill handling of this matter is some cause of his sicknes. . . .

Sir Thomas Smith to the Prince de Condé.

Rouen, 23 juillet 1563.

Monsieur, incontinant que mon courrier fust arrivé en la cours d'Angleterre, il fust sur le champ aussi despesché avec peu de motz, et la Royne, ma souveraine, vous remercie bien fort de la peine qu'avez prins pour accorder ces différentz d'entre les deux princes, et pour ce que la commission, pour estre escriptes et sellé demandera par adventure le traict d'un jour ou deux, la Royne l'a voulu retourner incontinant et me certifier de cela, et pour ce, je vous prie, Monseigneur, faictes tant qu'il me soit donné logis en quelque lieu près de la court, et pour celuy ou ceulx qui seront envoié avec moy en ceste commission, lesquelz j'attends de jour en jour. Je sçay bien qu'il n'y aura nul empeschement, sinon de la mer, laquelle a empesché mon coureur ung jour par la calme, et si vous semble bon, veu que aux principaulx poinctz nous sommes d'accord, et qu'est certainement délibéré d'avoir paix, de quoy je vous assure de la part de ma souveraine sur mon honneur et foye, et ne refuseray le serment s'il m'est requis : il m'est advis que c'est ung œuvré digne de crestien, de faire abstinence de guerre, tant d'ung costé que de l'autre, cependant qu'on besongne de mettre en perfection cest accord et traicté, pour saulver les vies de beaucoup d'hommes qui ont meis par adventure honeur en danger. Et s il vous plaist faire tant envers la Royne, qu'elle commande ceste abstinence, estre sur de vostre costé, j'escripray à Monsieur de Waric, et j'entreprendray qu'elle sera entretenue et avisé.

The Prince de Condé to Sir T. Smith.

Fécamp, 24 juillet 1563.

Monsieur l'ambassadeur, j'ay receu la lettre que vous m'avez escripte, pour respondre à laquelle, je vous diray que l'ayant communiquée à la Royne et faict entendre le meilleur que j'ay pensé de vostre intention, S. M. est sy contente d'entendre à toutes bonnes condicions, qu'elle a advisé de vous ordonner ung logis, où facillement on pourra discourir de toutes choses, le succès desquelles je prie à Dieu qu'il soit tel que les deux Majestez soient satisfaictes, leurs peuples en repos, et touttes occasions de mal puissent prendre fin. Vous verrez par la responce que S. M. vous faict la délibéracion de son intention et bon plaisir.

XV.

Unpublished letters of the Prince de Condé, written in the interval between the first and second civil war (1563 to 1567).

A Monsr de Humières,[1] Cher de l'Ordre du Roy Monseigneur.

Amboise, 12 avril 1562 (for 1563, old style).

Monsr de Humières, par la publication de lédict qu'il a plu au Roy Monseignr faire sur la pacification des troubles de ce royme, vous auries peu scavoir comme Sa Maiesté veult et entend que doresnavant chacun se maintienne et comporte affin d'obvier aux malheurs dont nous avons par le passé esté assés et trop travaillés.

---

[1] Jacques, Sire de Humières, Marquis d'Encre, &c., Governor of Péronne, Montdidier, and Roye. In 1567 he was made captain of fifty men-at-arms, and Lieutenant-Général of Picardie in 1568. He was a fiery Catholic; in 1576 he formed 'the League,' in opposition to the establishment of the second Prince de Condé in Picardie.

Et pour ce qu'il est bien requis que vous et les autres gouvern^{rs} des villes et places de mon gouvernement soiiés advertis des particularités de l'intention de Sa Magesté, lesquelles il m'a faict cest honneur me déclairer, oultre ce que je les ay envoyées par escript à Monsr de Senarpont po^r les vous communiquer, j'ay bien voulu encore vo^s f^e cette recharge par le s^r du Breuil, p^{nt} porteur, et par luy vous dire que puisque maintenant nous voions ce grand feu presque estainct et amorty, chacun en son regard, et principallement ceulx qui ont les charges du peuple en main, doibt bien regarder de retrancher le chemyn aux occasions qui le pourroient rallumer ; ains suivant le bon plaisir et intention de sad. Majesté soutenir les ungs et les autres en tous office et devoir premièrement d'obéissance envers elle et puis d'unyon et concorde entre eulx, les laissant vivre en liberté de conscience, ainsi quil le^r est préfix et ordonné, sans qu'ils soient po^r cest effect aucunement molesties ne recherchies. Faisant en sorte que ceulx qui po^r le faict de la religion ou po^r loccasion des guerres passées pourroient estre détenus, arrestés ou emprisonnés en quelque manière que ce soit ès lieux où vostre pouvoir sestend, soient incontinant relachiés et mis à pure et pleine delivrance. Veu que sad^e Maiesté expressément le déclaire par son édict, ainsi que led. s^r du Breuil vous dira plus amplement de ma part.

Original ; autograph signature and endorsement. (*British Museum*, Egerton Collection.)

To M. de Humières, &c.

La Fère, 15 avril 1564.

Monsr d'Humyères, je sçay pour certain qu'il y a grand nombre de personnes de Roye, le Plessier, Guermigny, Crapaumesnil et autres lieux circonvoisins qui sont de la religion refformée, et qui desirent en toute douceur vivre en l'exercice d'icelle ; mais ilz craignent que, par le moyen de plus^{rs} personnes de contraire opinion, vous ne soiez solicité de les empescher, et, pour ceste cause, se sont retirez vers moy, tant pour sçavoir mon intention sur cela, que pour me suplier vous en escrire : et considérant que ce seroit chose pernicieuse et dommageable à la conscience de tant d'hommes de vivre sans religion, je leur ay, pour ceste raison, permis et acordé que ès terres qui m'appartiennent hors la ville de Roye et ses faulxbourgs ils puissent, en toute honneste liberté, exercer le ministère de lad. religion, sans aucun empeschement, et mesmes aler à Cany, si bon leur semble, à la charge de se contenir en telle modestie les uns envers les autres qu'il n'advienne aucun tumulte. Parquoy je vous prie, Monsr

d'Humières, tenir la main à ce que lesd. habitans puissent paisiblement et sans contredit aler et venir ès lieux où se fera led. exercice
hors lad. ville de Roye, et mander, pour cest effect, à vostre lieutenant et gens du Roy dud. lieu qu'ilz prennent garde qu'aucune
sédition n'advienne. A quoy je m'asseure que sçaurez bien et pru-
demment pourveoir et contenir par ce moyen les subjetz de Sa Ma^te,
en paix et transquilité.

To the Prince de Portien.[1]

Condé, 6 mai 1564.

Mon nepveu, le desir que j'ay d'entendre de voz nouvelles me faict
vous escrire ceste lettre, et par icelle vous supplier (si vostre commodité se présente) venir veoir et consoller vostre bon parent et
amy, qui est fort ennuyé de l'extrême maladye qu'a eue sa femme,
avec voz levriers et aussy voz chevaulx et armes, s'il est possible ; et
vous prometz que je vous montreray icy une aultant belle carrière
que sauriez veoir. Mes chevaulx et armes arriveront aujourd'hui en
ce lieu ; espérons que si vous venez nous aurons moiens de nous
resjouyr, si Dieu plaist.

To M. de Humières, &c.

La Fère, 12 juin 1565.

Monsr de Humyères, ce mot de lettre ne sera sinon pour vous advertir de la résolution que j'ay prinse de visiter les places de mon
gouvernement, et pour cest effect partir jeudy ou vendredy de ce
lieu pour tenir le chemin d'Amyens, où je serois bien aise d'estre
accompagné de mes bons amys. A ceste cause, je vous prie tellement disposer voz affaires que vous me puissiez venir trouver à
Corbie ; espérant vous fère là entendre le surplus de mes nouvelles,
je ne vous en diray d'avantage fors après m'estre de bon cueur
recommandé à vous.

To M. de Humières, &c.

Conty, 19 juillet 1565.

Monsr de Humyères, j'ay entendu que vous avez envoié yci ung
homme exprès pour sçavoir quand j'arriverois à Péronne ; je vous

---

[1] This person has been already mentioned. The letters addressed to him
by Condé, to hasten the departure of
the reîtres, are not here inserted, having
been, as was said above, printed both
in the *Mémoires de Condé*, and in the
Additions of Le Laboureur to the *Mémoires de Castelnau*.

avise que aiant, depuis deux jours, receu lettres du Roy, par lesquelles il me mande de l'aller trouver en diligence, je me délibère
aussi de haster mon chemyn, partant tantost de ce lieu pour estre
demain à Maignelay, puis passer par ma maison du Plessier, et m'en
aller chez moy, pour donner ordre à préparer mon voiage, afin de
satisfaire au bon plaisir de Sa Majesté, estant bien marry que je n'ay
peu suivre le cours de ma délibération ; mais vous sçavez qu'il se
fault accommoder selon la disposition du temps, et les occurrances
des affaires.

Originals ; autograph signatures and endorsement. (*Bibliothèque impériale*, Mss.
Mémoires du règne du roy Charles IX, 8696 and 8705.)

A M. de Mathignon,[1] *Chevalier de l'Ordre et Lieutenant-Général pour
le Roy Monseigneur en l'absence de M. de Bouillon au Gouvernement de Normandye.*

Vendôme, 10 novembre 1565.

Mr de Matignon, ceulx de léglise réformée d'Alençon se sont
retirez par devers moy en ce lieu pour me faire entendre la peine où
à pnt il se retrouvent à faulte de navoir la continuation de lexercice
de religion qui leur a este concédé par le Roy Monseigneur comme
ils souloient auparavant que vous eussiez interdict Me Pierre Merlin,
leur ministre, soubz prétexte quon luy a voulu imposer davoir
presche en un vergier ès faulxbourgs de la ville, davoir receu à la
Cène aulcuns personnages qui ne sont du bailliage et davoir pris à
femme une damoiselle qui estoit nonnain en labbaie du Pré. . . .
Et sçachant d'aultre part que Sa Majesté leur a octroié ltres patentes,
tant pour remectre ledt Merlin en son ministère, que por le laisser
paisiblement converser avecques sa femme legitime, lesquelles, à ce
que lon ma adverty, vous avés retenues en vos mains. Je vous ay
bien voulu escrire ceste lre pour en premier lieu vous dire que
naiant ces povres gens en rien contrevenu aux ordonnances et
plaisir de Sa Maiesté, il n'est pas raisonnable qu'ils soient ainsi
privés du bénéfice de leur religion, qui est, je vous asseure, le plus
ferme lien que l'on sçauroit choisir por contenir le peuple en toute
obéissance et devoir envers son prince, et puis à ceste occasion vous
prier, etc.

Original; autograph signature and endorsement. (*British Museum*, Egerton Coll.)

[1] Jacques de Goyon, Sire de Matignon, &c. He held the post of Lieutenant-Général of Normandie, from
1562 to 1585, when he exchanged it for
that of Guyenne. He was made a
Marshal of France in 1579. He always
belonged to the Royalist party, and
fought against the League as well as
against the Huguenots. He died at his
château of Lesparre, in 1597, at the age
of seventy-one.

To M. de Humières, &c.

Anisy, 14 février 1567.

APP.
XV.

Monsr de Humières, pource que j'ay entendu qu'en ces quartiers de delà il y a plusieurs levreteux et gentz à qui tel mestier n'appartient, et n'attendant que l'heure de la venue de Sa Majesté en ce pays, selon l'advis qu'elle en pourra prendre, desirant luy reserver, à tout le moins, ce plaisir et à ceulx à qui cest exercice est destiné, je vous prye tenir la main que ce qui est particulier à aucuns ne soit rendu commun à tous, comme j'entends qu'il a esté depuys quelque temps, et est encores à présent; et m'asseurant que d'autant aussi qu'en vostre privé cela vous peult toucher, vous y donnerez ordre, je ne vous en feray plus longue lettre.

To M. de Humières, &c.

Anisy, 1er avril 1567.

Monsr de Humières, vous avez puis naguères assés clairement peu entendre les causes et considérations qui ont meu le Roy Monseigneur de décerner l'édict portant inhibitions et défenses à tous estrangiers de se retirer en quelques lieux et endroictz que ce soit de son roïaume, et à ses subjectz de les y recevoir, loger ny recéler,[1] non en intention d'enfraindre l'honneste liberté et franchise permise par les traictés à noz voisins et amys de fréquenter, habiter, aller et retourner les uns avec les autres, tant pour le trafficq de marchandises que pour autres conversations louables et accoustumées de païs à autre et d'amy à amy, mais pour certaines grandes raisons non moins nécessaires et importantes que l'occurence des affaires et du temps sembloit la requérir, et combien que, suivant le contenu d'yceluy vous vous soiez mis en devoir, comme j'estime, de le faire publier, exécuter et observer, néantmoins, Sa Majesté aïant eu advertissement, ainsi qu'elle m'a faicte cest honneur de me l'escrire, que veu ce qui est advenu depuis peu de jours à Vallentiannes et au Casteau Cambrésis, et la fraïeur que cela a mis au Païs bas, y en a qui délibèrent de se sauver et réfugier par deçà, ce qu'elle vouldroit moins permectre que auparavant, elle m'a commandé expressément de l'empescher et y donner ordre: c'est la cause pourquoy je me suis avisé de vous en faire ceste dépesche, vous priant, incontinent icelle receue, que vous aiez à songneusement tenir la main preste et l'œil ouvert pour faire exécuter sur ce son bon plaisir et intention, faisant

[1] To hinder Flemish immigrations into France.

(afin que nul en prétende cause d'ignorance) derechef publier iceluy édict, et y faire selon la confiance que j'ay de vostre dextérité et bon entendement.

Original; autograph signature and endorsement. (*Bibliothèque impériale*, Mss. Mémoires du règne du roy Charles IX, 8696.)

XVI.

Selections from the correspondence of M. de Gordes, Lieutenant-Général in Dauphiné.   (From the *Archives de Condé*.)

(May 1563 to July 1567.)

The *Archives de Condé* contain a series of documents of great importance to the historian of France during the reigns of the last two Valois; namely, the collection of letters addressed to M. de Gordes, Lieutenant-Général in Dauphiné, between 1562 and 1576. These valuable original papers are contained in twenty-seven portfolios, entitled *Guerre civile en Dauphiné*. As we have drawn from this source some valuable information and various new facts, we have here reprinted either *in extenso* or partially the letters from which we have borrowed, and which relate to the period included between the first and second religious wars. In order that the character and nature of this correspondence may be properly understood, it may be useful to add here a few words of explanation as to the part which the recipient of these despatches played, and the situation which he filled.

The government of Dauphiné had been given, in 1562, to Charles de Bourbon, Prince de la Roche-sur-Yon. As this prince did not reside in his province, he was represented there, according to custom, by a nobleman of the country, who really exercised all the power. In 1564, the Lieutenant-Général thus delegated was Laurent de Maugiron, an ardent Catholic, excessively devoted to the Lorraine faction, and a very fierce persecutor of the Huguenots. In the course of that year, the Court sojourned for two months in Dauphiné, and the Queen-Mother was beset by the complaints of the Protestants. Catherine was at this juncture on the point of throwing herself into the party of the advanced Catholics, and the mysterious but very significant interview at Bayonne was soon to be the consummation of the King's great progress. Meanwhile the Queen still held the balance uncertainly, and, with the assent of the titular governor, she agreed to supersede Maugiron. The King had scarcely re-entered Provence, when, by a decree signed at Aix, he nominated the Baron de Gordes 'his Lieutenant-Général for the Government of Dauphiné, in the absence of his cousin the Prince de la Roche-sur-Yon.' (September 1564.)

Bertrand Raymbaud de Simiane, fifth of his name, Baron de Caseneuve and de Gordes, a member of one of the most illustrious families in Dauphiné, was born on the eighteenth of October, 1513. He had served with distinction under Bayard in Italy and in Champagne, under Brissac in Piedmont; and had been a Chevalier de l'ordre since 1561. Being closely connected with the Châtillons, he seemed early inclined to the Reformed views, which had gained many adherents in the province, and which two of his brothers openly professed. Still he never renounced the Catholic communion, and kept himself very much in the same line with the Montmorencies; in a word, he was already what at a later period came to be called a 'politique.'

It may be imagined that this appointment was not very agreeable to the friends of Maugiron, and to those who wished to see the power in the hands of a violent enemy to the Huguenots. Every device therefore was tried to ruin the new Lieutenant-Général at Court, or to destroy his authority in the province; but he foiled these intrigues with much ability and determination. When, on the death of the Prince de la Roche-sur-Yon in 1565, the title of Governor of Dauphiné fell to the Duc de Montpensier, who was much more earnest than his brother in matters of religion, De Gordes was compelled to give way a little in deference to the views of his new chief, and to show himself rather less tolerant towards the Protestants. He thus incurred ill-will from an opposite quarter, and found himself a mark for the attacks of both the extreme factions, yet still without fundamentally deviating from the path of moderation and fairness which he had marked out for himself. He had won the affection and esteem of all who were not blinded by passion; and thus was always kept well informed of the state of affairs. Accordingly, in the summer of 1567, he vainly warned the Court that the Huguenots were about to take up arms a second time. The majority of the *Parlement* of Grenoble, under the direction of Truchon, their first president, supported him steadily, and were especially associated with him in an occurrence very honourable to his memory. It was by means of the active support of the *Parlement*, that De Gordes was enabled to evade the sanguinary orders which had been sent him from Paris in August 1572, and to save his province from a share in the Massacre of Saint-Bartholomew.

While showing himself just and tolerant towards the Protestants, he prosecuted the war against them with energy when it was his duty to look upon them as rebels. This was no easy task. The Huguenots of Dauphiné were under three successive leaders of remarkable military capacity, Des Adrets, Montbrun, and Lesdiguières. The first of these was the best commander; but he was a man of brutal selfishness, without any dignity of character or consistent principles of action; the second was inferior in capacity, but fierce, resolute even to obstinacy, and most splendidly daring in his achievements; the third, whose qualities were less dazzling, but better balanced, was most singularly favoured by fortune. In the middle of the first civil war, Des Adrets, finding himself excluded from the first rank of the Protestant leaders, went over to the Catholic camp; and no one quite comprehended for whom or with whom he acted. De Gordes had nothing at all to do with him; but he was often brought into collision with Montbrun, and at last had the honour of defeating and capturing that great soldier in 1576; he refused, however, to sit upon his trial, or to take any part in the proceedings which ended in his execution. He was carrying on the conflict with Lesdiguières, with more perseverance than success, when his life came to a close. He fell a victim to his devotion to duty; he was lying ill at Grenoble when the news arrived of an attempt about to be made on the part of the Huguenots of Provence and the Vivarais to attack Valence; he set out immediately; but grew rapidly worse, and breathed his last at Montélimart, on the twenty-first of February, 1578.

We are not here writing the biography of De Gordes—a task which would be worth undertaking; for indeed it is disgraceful that while a butcher like Des Adrets has found a historian, no one should have told the life of a man whose position was at least of equal importance, who evinced very high capacity of every kind, and who ever maintained, in most trying times, the character of a good Christian and a good citizen.[1]

The only purpose of this brief sketch is to give the reader what may be called the key-note of the correspondence from which the following letters are extracts. It will be understood that in addition to official letters of the king, communications from public functionaries, and memorials from the gentlemen of Dauphiné, as

[1] *Vir antiqui moris et qui summam aequitatem his in turbis semper adhibuerat.* (Thuanus.) The omission on which we have remarked above has just (1859) been supplied. M. Taulier has published a memoir of Baron de Gordes. (Grenoble, 1859.)

well as information forwarded by the governors of neighbouring
provinces, these portfolios contain a great number of private letters,
of despatches sent from the Court or elsewhere by confidential
agents, or by friends in both camps, and it will be evident on which
side lay the secret sympathies, and what were the habitual tendencies,
of the Baron de Gordes.

D'Andelot to M. de Gordes.

Chastillon, 27 mai 1563.

. . . Je me tiendray pour quelques moys en ce lieu ou à Tanlay,
estant depuis ung jour retourné de St-Germain-en-Laye, à cause du
séjour que le Roy doibt faire à Paris plus qu'il ne pensoit et que je
nespérois, et aussy que je trouvois ce lieu incommode pour ma
fiebvre et peu seur.   Monsieur le Prince faisoit son compte de partir
dudit St-Germain le jour mesmes que j'en ai deslogé ou le lendemain
pour aller faire ung voyage en sa maison. . . . Je ne puis au reste
vous escrire pour le présent autre chose de nouveau de ce que jay
peu apprendre durant ce peu de temps que jay esté à la cour, sinon
ce que vous en a pu dire Monsʳ de Soubize.   .   .   .

The Admiral de Chastillon to M. de Gordes.

Chastillon, 23 septembre 1564.

. . . Quant à mes nouvelles, il y a sept ou huict jours que je
suys de retour de Vallery, où jestoys allé veoir Monsieur le prince de
Condé.   .   .   .

(*Autographe.*) Monsieur de Gordes je vous pry faire estat de moy
comme lun de vos meilleurs et anciens amys, et penses que ceulx la
ne sont pas des pires.

De Losse [1] to M. de Gordes.

Lyon, 27 janvier 1564 (1565).

. . . Ils disent questant Monsieur le cardinal arrivé à la rue
Sainct-Denys dans la ville près l'église St-Innocent, Monsieur le

---

[1] Jean de Beaulieu, Seigneur de
Losse, a Knight of the Order, Field-
Marshal, and Captain of the Scottish
Company of the Royal Body-guards.
He has been already mentioned in a
note (App. VI. p. 277).   He was at that
time commanding in Lyonnais; his ap-
pointment to this is dated, according to
Pinard (*Chronologie militaire,* vi. 11),
March 1, 1565. It appears from the
following letter that he had taken the
command as early as the month of
January.   He held it till August of
that year.

mareschal de Montmorency vint de quelques uns bien accompagne et dict-on que le comte . . . . . de mesme bien tost après luy. Sadressant ledit seigneur mar^{al} à Monsieur le cardinal, luy dist que le Roy nentendoit poinct que lon portast les armes dans Paris et quelques autres parolles eurent ensemble, sur quoy aucuns courent aux armes, de manière que mondit S^r cardinal descendist à pied et se gecta dans une maison et y poussa devant luy Monsieur de Guyse. Lon ma bien asseuré davantage que ung varlet de la maison où ils se refonçoient, fermant la porte, eut ung coup de harquebuzade en travers du bras. Somme il y en eut trois ou quatre tuez. Lun desquelz estoit audit comte de . . . . . Vez là ce que je vous en sçaurois dire. Si nest que Monsieur dAumale y arriva demye heure après ce faict, lesquelz frères et nepveu sen alèrent tous loger ensemble à lhostel de Cluny et le lendemain ilz partirent à Meudon.

Crussol [1] *to M. de Gordes.*

Toulouse, 4 février 1565.

. . . . Cest que la royne d'Espagne se doibt trouver à Bayonne le XVe davril, et nous partirons bientost dicy pour aller à Bourdeaux et de là la trouver. Cejourdhuy sont arrivées nouvelles de la mort de

[1] Antoine de Crussol, Comte de Crussol and de Tonnerre (in right of his wife, Louise de Clermont), Vicomte d'Uzès, Baron de Lévis, &c., a servant of the Queen-Mother, and, like her, very vacillating. It was he who had been sent to Nérac in August 1560 to persuade the King of Navarre and the Prince de Condé to appear at Court. On the tenth of December, 1561, he had been nominated Commander in Dauphiné, Languedoc, and Provence, and had arrived at his post in the following January. At first he showed himself favourably inclined towards the Huguenots, and became more and more closely attached to them, till at last, in November 1562, he accepted from the Protestants of Languedoc the title of 'chief and guardian of the country during the minority of the king.' After throwing some difficulties in the way of the execution of the edict of peace, in March 1563, he gradually returned to the Catholic side, and completed the change of his principles, upon a hint from the Queen-Mother, in August 1564. On the day he wrote the following letter, he was at Toulouse, in attendance on the King, who had arrived there the day before to hold a Bed of Justice. Charles IX. left Languedoc in April, and proceeded to Bordeaux, thence to Mont-de-Marsan, where he created Antoine de Crussol Duc d'Uzès. His further services to the Royal and Catholic cause were rewarded by his being named 'Pair de France' in 1572. He died childless on the fifteenth of August, 1573, leaving his title and his estates to his brother Jacques de Crussol, better known under the name of D'Acier, as one of the bravest of the Huguenot leaders. Another brother, Beaudiné, also a Huguenot, had been killed in the Massacre of St. Bartholomew. (Dom Vaissette, *Histoire générale du Languedoc.*)

M. d'Estampes que je ne tiens touttefois asseurées. J'estime que vous
estes bien informé de ce qui sest passé à Paris entre le card^{al} de
Lorraine et Monsieur de Montmorency, par quoy je ne vous diray
seullement que Monsieur ladmiral depuis y est venu, qui a esté fort
bien veu de tous, mesme de la court du clergé et de la Sorbonne, qui
le sont allé visiter et offert infiny service, sy bien qu'il en est le plus
satisfaict, et les autres de luy, qu'il est possible. Ce que jestime
nimportera peu à la réunion. La desfiance des deux parties que
lung avoit de l'autre amortie, lon a voullu abbreuver ycy le Roy et
Monsieur le Prince [1] de quelque remuement prochain qui se brassoit
en Daulphiné, mais jestime que vous y avez l'œil. . . . .

Pasquier [2] to M. de Gordes.

Toulouse, 9 février 1565.

. . . . Par Monsr le Secret^e Guyon, vous avez peu entendre toutes
nouvelles de ceste court, nestant survenu aucune chose de nouveau
depuys, si ce n'est l'asseurance de l'entreveue de la Royne et de la
royne d'Espaigne, sa fille, qui se doibt fère à Bayonne le deuxiesme
d'apvril prochain, où ladite royne d'Espaigne doibt venir. Je me
doubte bien que se ne sera à jour nommé, car vous savez les céré-
monyes espagnolles. Il s'en faict de grands préparatifz d'un cousté
et d'aultre. Et mesmes que la Royne veult que sa compagnye soyt
bien équippée et en grande triunphe. L'on a voullu dire ses jours
passés que le Roy ne yroit poinct. Toutesfoys l'on tient que cy. La
court ne partira de ceste ville qu'environ le huict^{me} du moys qui
vient pour s'en aller à Agen, et dellà l'on prendra le chemyn de
Bayonne sans passer à Bourdeaux qu'au retour. Je croy que vous
aurez sceu ce qui est advenu à Paris tant à Monsieur le cardinal de
Lorrayne venant audit Paris que quelque doubte en quoy sont
entrez ceulz dudit Paris pour l'arrivée que feit là Monsieur l'admiral.
Mais, Dieu mercy, toutes choses sont réduictes en bon estat. Bien
vous diray que ceste court en a esté troublée quatre ou cinq jours.
Le Roy a despeché le chevalier de Seure devers Messrs de Paris

---

[1] The Prince de la Roche-sur-Yon,
governor of the province.

[2] Aleman Pasquier, Seigneur de Pasquier, Knight of the Order, a great
friend of Maugiron, and one of the
principal managers of all the intrigues
set on foot in Dauphiné against De
Gordes by the ultra-Catholic faction.
He had great influence among the noble

families of Grésivaudan. The breach
between the Lieutenant-Governor and
Pasquier was not openly made till some
months after this; and was occasioned
by a domiciliary visit made under orders
from De Gordes, by an officer of justice,
at the house of Pasquier, in search of
concealed arms. (Chorier, *Histoire du
Dauphiné*.)

pour cest effect. Je vous diray aussi que le Roy et la Royne et toute ceste compagnie font fort bonne chère et ne se y parle poinct de peste : se ne sont que festins, triunphes et pasetemps. Le Roy ira disner dimanche prochain à la maison de ville, où l'on faict de grands préparatifz pour luy donné du plaisir. Je croy que vous avez sceu la mort de Monsieur d'Estampes. Son gouvernement a esté donné à Monsr de Marteigues, et sa compagnye supprimée, pour l'importunité des poursuyvans, que je croy que Monsieur de Vennes,[1] votre frère, vous a faict entendre, lequel n'a dormy cependant que les choses ont esté en estat de poursuytte, comme ont faict le semblable les aultres de vous amys.

Crussol to M. de Gordes.

Toulouse, 10–13 mars 1565.

Monsieur, trouvant ceste commodité de vous escrire, je n'ay voullu la perdre encores qu'il ne s'offre rien de nouveau et que ie sache que Monsr vostre frère qui est ycy vous tient de tout ce qui y passe bien adverty. Mais c'est pour tousiours vous continuer en la volunté de me faire part de voz nouvelles. Nous partirons lundy prochain pour prendre le chemin de Bourdeaux par Assier où le Roy a voullu passer. Après Pasques nous prendrons le chemin de Bayonne. Lon a despesché les affaires de Languedoc que bien que mal. L'on veult renouveler ycy la persuasion quen vostre cartier l'on se remue, tant il y a des gens qui se playsent à faire courir ce bruit. Mais je m'asseure que vous estes tant aymé en ce pays là et sy vigilant à vostre charge, que s'il en estoit quelque chose ce ne seroit sans que vous le sceussiez et en donnissiez advertissement de deçà, qui me faict croyre que du tout il n'y en a rien. J'escris à Monsieur de Gap,[2] mon frère, touchant son evesché. Je vous prye luy faire tenir la lettre. S'il s'offre chose deçà cy après qui le mérite, je ne fauldray par toutes les commoditez de vous en départir.

(*Autographe.*) Surtout, je vous prie, allés tous les jours à la messe, et jeusnés le caresme, affin quon ne die que vous estes huguenot, car lon dit desjà partout que vous estes assez homme de bien et assez abille pour lestre. Donnez-vous-en bien guarde.

Le voyage dAssier a esté rompu, celuy de Bourdeaux quelque peu deffect.

---

[1] Gaspard de Simiane, seventh brother of Bertrand, Seigneur d'Évènes, d'Olioules, and de Sainte-Nazaire, Knight of the Order of the King in 1576, Gentleman of the Chamber in Ordinary in 1598 ; subscribed the test in 1603.

[2] Gabriel de Clermont, brother of the Comtesse de Crussol, Bishop of Gap from 1527 to 1572.

D'Andelot to M. de Gordes.

Tanlay, 23 avril 1565.

. . . . Je ne me délibère poinct partir encores d'icy, si ce n'est que j'aille avec Monsieur le cardinal de Chastillon et Monsr l'amyral, mes frères, jusques à Orléans, rencontrer Monsieur le prince de Condé, qui s'en va à la court, et lequel nous a mandé qu'il avoit volunté de nous voir tous trois là avant que passer plus avant. Je fust desià party n'eust esté qu'il a eu cinq ou six accès de fièvre tierce qui ont ung peu retardé son partement, mais ce sera pour incontinent après ces Pasques. Nous lui pourrons faire compaignye jusques à Vandosme, où est la royne de Navarre. Ce voyage faict, je délibère me retirer icy pour n'en partir de quelque temps, si autre occasion ne survient. . . .

Ce que je vous puis dire au reste, c'est qu'il y a tousjours quelques espritz mal composez qui ne cherchent que occasion de troubler la paix de ce roiaulme, comme vous pouvez voir par la coppie de la lettre cy-enclose, l'original de laquelle est en bonne main. Vous jugerez par le discours d'icelle l'occasion que chacun a de prendre garde à soy. . . .

(*Autographe.*) Je ne sçay si je dois espérer de vous pouvoir veoir quelque jour céans. Mais si jamais je vous y tiens je vous monstreré assez d'allées pour vous altérer et donner envie, avant que les avoir toutes achevées, de boire ung aussy grant trait que cestuy duquel vous feis gagner pour ung escu en Almagne, et si vous feray veoir que j'ay bien remué du mesnages et à quoy je suis enchores bien empesché.

J'escris à Monsr de Saint-Aulban[1] que, s'il vous veoit, vous lui ferez part de la lettre de Monsr d'Aumalle.

Hector Maniquet [2] to M. de Gordes.

Paris, pénultième d'avril 1565.

. . . . Ceste venue (*de la reine d'Espagne à Bayonne*), comme j'ay entendu, ne peult estre plus tost que le vingt-cinquiesme de may,

---

[1] On Captain Saint-Auban see the King's letter dated June 28, 1566 (p. 381).

[2] Hector Maniquet du Fayet was Maître d'Hôtel to Charles IX., as his father had been. He was sent as an envoy to the Protestant princes of Germany, to explain away to them the Massacre of Saint Bartholomew. Another transaction proves, says Chorier, 'that he had the honour to enjoy the confidence of his King.' When Marie Touchet found herself to be pregnant, and Charles IX., who was recently married, did not wish the condition of his mistress to be noticed by

car Monsieur le comte d'Aiguemont,[1] qui partist hier en poste de ceste ville, venant d'Espaigne et s'en allant en Flandres, le dist ainsy à Mons^{gur} le mareschal de Montmorancy, lequel feist loger ledit sieur conte d'Aiguemont en l'hostel neuf de Montmorancy. L'on bruict icy que les actions de la relligion ne sont moings préparées du costé de la Flandres au remuement des armes qu'elles ont esté en France. Toute ceste ville est si bien régie et commendée par la prudence de mondit sieur le mareschal, qu'il n'est nouvelle d'aulcuns troubles ny émotions. Passant par le Vendomoys, où la royne de Navarre est, il y avoyt quelque apparence de deffiance les ungs des aultres entre ceulx qui tiennent le party des deux religions. Monsieur de (la Curée?), qui en estoyt gouverneur, fust tué y a jà quelque temps, dont se sont ensuiviez jà quelques exécutions, que ladite dame royne de Navarre a faict faire par auctorité de justice. Il y en a plusieurs de prisonnierz qui ne sont guières bien asseurez de leurs vyes.

De Losse to M. de Gordes.

Lyon, 12 mai 1565.

. . . . Depuis trois jours le filz de Monsieur de Chamberg, qui est gouverneur de Rocroy en Champagne, a escrit à son père de ceste ville de Rains en hors du 5ᵉ de ce mois, et lui mande qu'il arriva avec Monsieur de St-Paul audit Rains le soir avant la date de sa lettre, auquel lieu Monsieur d'Aumale se doibt trouver ce jour mesme, et aussi Messieurs les princes de Condé et cardinal de Lorraine, et dict qu'ilz tiennent pour certain que c'est pour arester le mariage de mondict sieur le Prince avec la fille de feu Monsieur de Guise. Quant à autres nouvelles, j'ai bien eu ces jours lettres de la court; mais il ne se parle que de la venue de la royne d'Espagne, et cuide quils seront bientoust trestous à Bayonne. . . .

Lyon, 19 may 1565.

. . . . Je vous avois escrit que Monseig^r le Prince se debvoit rendre à Reims. Il ne si est pas trouvé. On pense que cest à raison de la maladie quil a eue. Lon ma asseuré à ce matin quil estoit à Paris. Je receuz hier lettres de Monsieur de Tavanes, par lesquelles

---

his bride, he chose Maniquet as a fitting person to be entrusted with the charge of the fair lady. That faithful servant took Marie Touchet to his own house, a hundred and thirty leagues away from the Court; and the Duc d'Angoulême was born at Le Fayet, on the twenty-eighth of April, 1573.

[1] Lamoral, Comte d'Egmont, a nobleman of Flanders, who was beheaded at Brussels, by order of the Duke of Alva, June 8, 1568.

il me mande que Monsr dAndelot est parti ces jours icy de ce pays de Bourgogne. Et a mené avec luy environ de deux cens chevaulx que bons que mauvais. Jai pensé quil sen va trouver mondict seign^r le Prince et la Royne à Reims, que toute ceste compagnie s'en va trouver le Roy. . . .

X. . . . to M. de Gordes.

Toulouse, 13 juin 1565.

. . . Lon tient pour chose asseurée que le Roy a faict une assotiation avec Messeigneurs les princes et chevalliers de son ordre de vivre sellon léglise catholique romaine, et de ne prendre les armes pour quelque parti que ce soit sans le sceu et exprès commandement de Sa Majesté, et que tous la signeront, et les refusantz déclarez atainz du crisme de lèse-magesté, et par édit at déclaré que nul proucès criminel peult nestre faict à aulcun chevallier de son dit ordre que par le Roy mesme appellé et avec luy tel nombre daultres chevalliers de son dit ordre que luy plaira. Interdisant à tous aultres juges et courtz toute juridiction et connoissance. Ce fust le 24e may, et disent que le mesme jour signa les articles du consille, mais nest chose asseurée. . . .

Le Vicomte de Cadenet [1] to M. de Gordes.

Paris, 14 juin 1565.

Monsieur, ce qui me garde de vous escripre si souvent comme je desirerois, c'est qu'il n'y a pacquet qu'il ne soit vollé et crochetté, et de signer des nouvelles d'importance pour les exposer à la volle, je ne treuve que je le puisse ou que je le doibve faire. Et de les mander par chifres, oultre ce que elles sont deffendues par les ordonnances du Roy, il n'y en a point entre vous et moy. Comme sçavés semblablement, le Roy n'est point icy, et par concéquent il ne peult venyr nouvelles du costé de deçà, s'il ce n'est ce qui est d'importance, que je puis sçavoir par le moyen de Monseigneur le mareschal,[2] chose comme dict est que je ne vouldrois fier à la poste, s'il ce n'est à ung homme congnu. Des nouvelles du Palais, je sçay bien que vous n'en voulés point, n'estant que des inventions que les hommes forgent suyvent leurs passions. Mais, pour vous parler en

---

[1] Antoine, Baron d'Oraison, Vicomte de Cadenet, a Provençal, and lieutenant of the gendarmes of the Connétable De Montmorency. He became a Knight of the Order, and a captain of fifty men-at-arms.

[2] François de Montmorency, governor of L'Ile de France.

termes généraulx, je vous advise que nous avons heu à Paris le duc de Parme et le conte d'Aiguemont venant d'Espaigne pour s'en aller en Flandres. Monsieur le mareschal les a fort festoyés et logé à l'hostel neuf de Montmorency. Ils s'en sont allez fort satisfaictz dudict seigneur. Semblablement nous avons heu Monsieur le prince de Condé, qui a esté à Paris, faysant estat de s'en aller à la court; si est-ce qu'il a esté contremandé pour s'en retourner à son gouvernement, et tous les gouverneurs des villes et places de la frontière ont reçeu commendement de eulx en aller à leur charge. Mondict seigneur le Prince a esté à Paris six ou sept jours, estant entièrement relié avec Monsieur le cardinal de Lorrayne, ayant maintefois conféré avec luy, dont ceulx de la religion prétendue réformée a une grande jalozie et semble que beaucoup, comme l'on dict, se sont distrait ou pour le moings rabatu quelque chose de la voulenté qu'ils avoyent de luy faire service. Monsieur le mareschal luy a rendu tout l'honneur qui luy a esté possible, ayant esté au debvant de luy accompaigné de huict ou neuf cens chevaulx, et si en avoyt renvoyé plus de cinq cens, comme n'ayant plus qu'il ne luy estoit nécessaire pour s'opposer aux préthendus desseins de ses ennemys, que l'on pensoit avoyr quelque entreprinse soubz la faveur dudict seigneur Prince, lequel toutesfoys a faict assez de remonstrance d'amytié à l'endroict dudict seigneur mareschal, estant si gentil prince qu'il ne favorisera jamais que la raison et le repos des subjects du Roy. Du cousté de deçà, à l'absence de Ça Maïgesté, Monsieur l'admiral avoit une estrange trouppe d'aultre part, en sorte que tous les villaiges ses voisins cy estoint farcis. Monsieur d'Andelot a esté à Paris, ayant conféré beaucoup avec mondict seigneur le Prince, lequel faict démonstration de vouloir entretenyr inviolablement l'amitié d'entre lui et Messeigneurs de Chastillon. Cependant nous sommes venuz en ce lieu l'Isle-Adam, où je me suys faict le plus grand veneur de France, ayant encores hyer prins deulx cerfz à force. . . .

Nouvelles données par Hector Maniquet, le 1er août 1565.

Les nouvelles que nous avons de deçà sont que à l'occasion de quelques secrettes entreprises et eslévations d'armes qui se faisoient en ceste ville (*Paris*), comme l'on murmuroit, Monsieur le mareschal de Montmorancy y est venu en dilligence faire pourveoir de par advis de Messrs de la court de parlement. L'édict de paciffication a esté de nouveau publié par ceste ville a cry publicq. A quoy Monsieur le prevost de Paris a assisté bien accompaigné de harquebouziers et aultres archers, en sorte que cella s'est faict sans esmeulte. Aussi a esté défendu le port des armes.   Le tout sur peine de la hart.

Par lettres escriptes de la court, du 21ᵉ du mois passé, l'on disoit que le Roy seroit à Nerat le cinq^{me} de cestuy-cy, approchant de deçà pour venir à Blois faire sesiour et passer une partie de son yvert.

A la vérité les séditions grandes advenues en la ville de Tours et Amboise et audict Blois, et les esmeultes d'Orléans avecq la suspition de l'entreprinse en ceste ville, crient et appellent de faire approcher Sa Magesté, à raison do quoi l'on tient le voiage de Bretaigne fort doubteux, et non toutesfois rompu.

Mondict S^r le mareschal est mandé pour aller trouver le Roy. Monsieur de Mèru son frère demeure gouverneur en son absence.

Les remuements de Lorraine sont très-grands, ayant Monseigneur le cardinal faict amas de gens de guerre, jusques à sept ou huict mil hommes, et de douze pièces de batterie.   A tout cella Monsieur d'Aumalle commande.   L'intention de cecy est de prendre trois places, qui sont des deppendances de l'évesché de Metz, et néant-moins villes impérialles, en l'obéissance toutesfois de la Magesté du Roy, dont le cappitaine Sarceddo s'estoit emparé, soubz prétexte d'une sauvegarde de l'Empereur obtenue par mondict S^r le cardinal, laquelle il voulloit faire publier ès dictes trois places, à quoi ledict Sr Sarceddo n'auroit voulu satisfaire ne obéir.

Truchon[1] *to M. de Gordes.*

La Palice, Noël 1565.

. . . (*Le Roi est arrivé samedi à Moulins,*) et n'est-on en assurance de long séiour à cause de la famine qui suit la court de près, de quelque part qu'elle voise.   Monseigneur le connestable et Monsieur ladmiral sont attendus à Moulins, et estoient dès hier leurs fourriers arrivez à Bourges.

. . . Monseigneur le cardinal de Lorraine sen vient aussy à la

---

[1] First president of the Parlement at Grenoble, a post he had held since 1549. He was a magistrate of the school of the De Thous, an honourable man and a good citizen. 'His close unity with De Gordes,' says Chorier, 'secured for a long time that of Dauphiné.' We find him constantly employed in the work of conciliation among the southern provinces of France. It was his eloquence which, in 1572, carried with it the Parlement of Grenoble, and determined the resolve of that assembly to co-operate with De Gordes in preventing the Massacre of St. Bartholomew from being carried out in Dauphiné.   He died in October 1578.

court, accompaigné comme je pense de Monseigneur le duc de
Nemours.   Mais Monseigneur le duc Daumale n'y vient pour ce
coup, et a esté réglée à Monsieur ladmiral la trouppe qui le doit accompaigner.   Partie des financiers sont despeschés. . . . On vouloit
seulement par la vérification de leurs estats entendre le fonds des
finances et la charge du dommaine, ce qu'on pouvoit sçavoir à beaucoup meilleur marché. . . .

Gayette, 2 janvier 1566.

(*En route pour Moulins, où l'on ne parlera d'affaires qu'après les
Rois.*)   Monseigneur le connestable et Monsieur l'admiral arrivèrent
lundy.   Monseigneur le prince de Condé et Monsieur Dandelot y
estoient jà auparavant. . . .

Moulins, 5 janvier 1566.

(*D'Andelot n'est pas en cette cour, mais en sa maison,*) et dict-
on qu'on l'a voulu tuer et faict espier à ces fins : je ne le sçay encore
au vray ; cella viendroit mal à propos, parce qu'on est sur le poinct
de traicter quelque réconciliation entre les maisons de Guise et de
Chastillon, qui seroit ung grand bien pour la paix et union de tout ce
royaulme.   Nous ne sçavons encore pourquoy nous sommes icy : la
Royne nous a dict que nous l'entendrions par la bouche de Monseigneur le chancelier, qu'on attend à demain, et Monseigneur le cardinal de Lorraine à mercredy, ensemble Messeigneurs de Guise, de
Nemours et d'Ellebeuf, avec Madame de Guise. . . .

Aucuns disent qu'on nous parlera en ceste assemblée, non-seulement du règlement de la justice, mais de la réconciliation de ces
deux maisons, de l'appanage de Messeigneurs les frères du Roy, des
moyens de rachepter le dommaine aliéné, et du règlement des
finances. . . . Vos povés estre asseurés que estes en fort bonne et
digne reputation entre les grans, mesme de la Royne, et de Monseigneur nostre gouverneur, lequel me la dict de sa bouche ; je mets
en ce ranc Messeigneurs les connestable et mareschaulx de Vieilleville
et de Bordillon, qui sont tous bien vostres. . . .

Depuis ma lettre escrite, Monsieur le mareschal de Bourdillon ma
dict que un laquais et ung homme de peu d'apparence ont esté con-
stituez prisonniers pour le faict de Monsieur d'Andelot, cest-à-dire
dune embuscade de cent cinquante hommes, quon dict avoir esté
descouverte, mais que, pour mieulx esclaircir la vérité, avoit esté
ordonné que ce laquais et laultre seroient amenez en ceste ville.   On
vous pourra escrire que cejourdhuy, veille des Roys, sur lissue du
disner du Roy, y a eu quelques parolles assez haultes entre la Royne
et M. le connestable, présens plusieurs gentilzhommes.   Cella a

quelque apparence de vérité, et touttefoys nest rien. Mais icy et ailleurs faulx bruit va par la ville et par les champs plus viste qu'en poste, *viresque acquirit eundo.* M. le mareschal de Bourdillon sen va au-devant de M. le cardinal de Lorraine, entre aultres choses pour luy faire ou à ses gens poser les armes, comme à ceulx de M. ladmiral, cest-à-dire à leurs gardes. La Royne a bon zelle et bonne espérance à ung bon accord. On est fort après la casserie, mais la compaignie qui vous a esté donnée ne sera de ce nombre.

Montjay to M. de Gordes.

Moulins, 17 janvier (1566).

. . . Quant à laccord que veult faire la Reine de la maison de Guise et Montmorency et Chastillon, qui n'est point sans grande espérance de faire quelque chose de bon, touteffois jay peur que cela aille ung petit en longueur. Car le cardinal de Lorrène et Madame de Guise disent en vouloir prendre conseil de leurs amys, et pour ce faire ont dépêché aujourdhuy à Ferrare et Lorrène. Monsr de Guise ny ses oncles despée n'ont encores comparu. On les a mandé comme on a faict Monsr le mareschal de Montmorency. Dieu leur donne la grâce à tous de faire ung bon accord! Pourveu qu'il n'y ait fourreure ! . . .

De Brianson[1] to M. de Gordes.

Moulins, 18 janvier 1566.

. . . Lon avoit donné à entendre à Monsieur de Monpensier et presque à tous les grands de la cour que vous estiez de la relligion. . . . Monsieur le cardinal de Bourbon me dit que lon avoit parlé de mettre vostre compagnie au rosle de la cassation, mais que la Royne en avoit tellement pris la parolle que despuys chascun en a eu la bouche close. . . .

Moulins, 21 janvier 1566.

Monseign^r, depuis mes lettres du 18e, j'ay parlé à Monsieur ladmiral, lequel j'ay trouvé desià bien informé de vos affaires et tant

---

[1] This was an old family of Dauphiné. Chorier mentions a Briançon who was a great favourite of De Gordes, and subsequently says that Briançon, first consul at Grenoble, was the delegate of the noblesse of Grésivaudan to the States of 1576. Allard (*Nobiliaire du Dauphiné*) mentions a Pierre de Briançon, Sieur de Saint-Ange, who distinguished himself in the religious wars. Perhaps all these three passages refer to the writer of this letter, who was a regular correspondent of De Gordes.

affectionné à vous y ayder quil nest besoing luy faire grandes solli-
citations. Il est vray que mesmes par son conseil je suis contrainct
de me cacher quand je luy parle, pour la crainte de Monsieur de
Montpensier, comme je vous diray plus privément quand je seray
de par delà; jay aussi parlé à Monsieur le chancellier, [1] lequel
trouve merveilleusement mauvais les procédures que lon a faict
contre vous, jusques à m'avoir dict tout hault qu'il ne veult aultres
preuves de vostre vertu, ayant cogneu par expérience qu'en ce
reigne les gens de bien sont seullement calomniés. Il a lavé la teste
dune estrange lessive à Bucher Pierre, [2] luy ayant donné tant du fol
par la teste, que depuis il n'a osé comparoir par-devant luy et n'a
aultre recours qu'à mondict seigneur de Montpensier, duquel encores
il ne se pourroit beaucoup promectre, tant il est cogneu en ceste
court, si les affections de la religion ne lui estoient en ayde. Il est
presque tous les jours en conseil avec Monsieur de Paquiers au logis
de mondict seigneur, qui me faict pencer quils se prétendent pré-
valloir de luy. . . .

Truchon to M. de Gordes.

(No date.)

Hier sur les quattre heures du soir arrivèrent Messeigneurs les
cardinal de Lorraine et duc de Nemours, et furent au-devant deulx
Messeigneurs les prince de Condé et son filz, duc de Montpensier
et prince Daulphin, son filz, duc de Longueville, et plusieurs
aultres. Monseigneur le cardinal de Bourbon receut mondict
seigneur le cardinal de Lorraine à l'entrée de la chambre du
Roy, lequel se leva en sa chairre, sans touteffois s'advancer. Et
après fut baisé par la Royne, qui aussy se leva de sa chairre.
Cependant Madame de Guise, par une aultre porte, entra en la
chambre de la Royne, qui est joignant à celle du Roy, et semblablement salua Leurs Majestez. Monseigneur de Guise n'est venu.
Touteffois on dict qu'il viendra. Mais cependant on commencera à
accorder la musique, sy faire se peut, et à mon advis que dans trois
ou quattre jours on mettra bien advant les fers au feu, et vous
escriray ce que jen pourray apprendre et don je verray le papier et
l'ancre estre capables. J'avois oublié à vous dire que lesdicts
seigneurs cardinal de Lorraine et Monseigneur le connestable, qui
estoit en la chambre du Roy, s'entre-saluèrent et caressèrent avec
bon visaige. . . .

---

[1] Michel de l'Hôpital.
[2] Pierre Bucher, Procureur-Général
of the Parlement of Grenoble, a partisan
of Maugiron and Pasquier, and a steadfast opponent of De Gordes and Truchon.

Moulins, 15 février 1566.

. . . Monseigneur de Guyse arriva hier, et furent au-devant de luy Messeigneurs le prince de Condé et cardinaulx de Lorraine et de Guise. Mouseigneur le mareschal de Montmorency nest encore arrivé. . . .

Montluc, Bishop of Valence, to M. de Gordes.

Toulouse, 20 juin 1566.

Monsieur, j'ay receu la lettre que vous m'avés escript de Laval du 5⁰ du passé, de laquelle je vous mercie. Je suis icy à combatre tous les jours des gens qui sont plus folz et plus fantasticz que n'est Bucher Pierre, car il recognoist en sa conscience qu'il est fol. Et ceux-cy sont cent foys le jour en colère de ce qu'ilz sont trop sages, et vous puis bien asseurer, Monsieur, que sans moy ceste ville estoyt sur le poinct d'estre saccagée, mais, Dieu mercy, il n'y a point eu de mal, de quoy le Roy m'en a sceu fort bon gré et m'en donne la louenge par lettres qu'il m'en a escript. Je ne feray pas long séiour en ce pais, et espère d'arriver à la court à la fin du moys d'aoust.

Monsieur, il y a eu de la folie à Pamyés, où les huguenaudz ont tué beaucop des catholiques, et le demeurant chassé hors de la ville, et tout est venu pour une dance. A Foix les catholiques ont faict le semblable.

The Admiral to M. de Gordes.

Saint-Maur, 24 juin 1566.

Mons. de Gordes, je vous eusse plus tost faict responce à la lettre que vous mavez dernièrement escripte, si je me fusse trouvé à propoz quant lon vous a dépesché où quil est allé quelques-ungs par delà, ce que je n'ay peu faire de tant que jestoys à Paris. Il y a plusieurs particularitez que je vous vouldroys bien faire sçavoir, mais nous sommes en ung temps quil ne fait pas bon escripre. Je vous diray seullement quil y a quinze jours quil y eut une alarme en ceste court, à cause de quelque compaignye de gens que lon disoit estre assemblée à Paris par Monsieur Dandelot, mon frère, et moy, dont il y eut des mareschaulx commys pour sen enquérir et informer. Et croy quilz ne trouveront pas ce que lon eust bien voulu. Je ne doubte point que vous nen eussiez esté bien adverty. Je faictz mon comte de séjourner encore quelque temps en ceste court, mais je ne vous puys encore asseurer combien ce sera, car je me gouverneray selon ce que je verray et au doigd et l'œil. Je vous prieray au demeurant, Monsʳ de Gordes, de faire entièrement estat de moy comme de lun de voz meilleurs et plus seurs amys.

The King to M. de Gordes.

Saint-Maur, 28 juin 1566.

Monsr de Gordes, j'ay esté adverty que aucuns de la religion prétendue refformée, de costé de vostre gouvernement, brassent quelque secrette menée d'entreprinse sur Avignon et les villes du Contat. Ayant mesmement le capp^ne Sainct-Aulban tenu certain langaige fort aprochant de cela en la ville d'Orenge, après s'estre desparty d'une assemblée de ministres qui fut faicte à Nyons, disant entre autres choses que l'on eust encores ung peu de patience et que bientost l'on verroit beau jeu pour eulx. Au moyen de quoy j'ai advisé de vous faire la présente, pour vous faire entendre ce que dessus, à ce que vous ayez l'œil ouvert à descouvrir telles secrettes entreprinses pour les rompre et empescher de tout vostre pouvoir, estant chose si contraire à mes edictz, vouloir et jntention.

Guyon to M. de Gordes.

Paris, 7 juillet 1566.

Monsieur le prince de Condé a esté en cette court, et s'en retourne à Vallery, ne pouvant laisser seulle Madame la Princesse, qui est fort grosse. . . .

[This and several other letters are filled with details of the journey to Court of M. and Madame de Lorraine, the troubles in Flanders, the march of the Spanish reinforcements, the measures being carried out in Picardie, the postponement of the King's projected journey, the mutual recriminations of Catholics and Protestants, &c.]

X. . . . de Simiane to his brother M. de Gordes.

Paris, 26 j. 1566.

. . . . Il ne se parle que de guerre. Le Roi a mandé les princes et seigneurs. On attend quelque bonne résolution.

Truchon to M. de Gordes.

Saint-Germain, 30 juin 1567.

Je partys de Paris le jeudy 19e de ce mois et vous escrivy à mon département. Je vins ledict jour coucher à Montfort, et le lendemain je fus à Sainct-Léger, où le Roy estoit arrivé le mardy 17e. Le vendredy, environ trois heures après midy, Monsr de Thevalles partit dudict Sainct-Léger en poste pour aller querir les six mil

Souisses; le dimanche ensuivant, qui fut le 22ᵉ, le Roy partit de Sainct-Léger, et alla coucher à Beyne, d'où il départit le lundy matin, et vint disner en ce lieu où je suis présentement arrivé, ayant prins le repos de cinq ou six jours avec mes frère et sœur. Depuis mon arrivée j'ai entendu que, sur l'advertissement que le Roy avoit eu que, du costé de Luxembourg, on avoit levé quarante enseignes de gens de pied et trois mil chevaulx, Sa Maiesté a dépesché Monsieur d'Andelot pour aller à Attigny sur la frontière de Champaigne, accompaigné de cinq mil hommes de pied, où tireront aussy ces six mil Souisses et deux cents hommes d'armes, mais on ne dict encore soubs quel chef; et combien qu'on peut penser que ces quarante enseignes et trois mil chevaulx ne soient levés que pour favoriser l'armée d'Espaigne allant en Flandres, toutesfois on a advisé estre le plus seur de tenir la frontière de Champaigne en seureté, et ledict Sʳ d'Andelot est party ce matin pour aller à Paris faire sonner le tabourin pour remplir ses bandes, dont quelqu'unes ne seront sans jalousie. Monseigneur le connestable se trouva ici incontinant après l'arrivée du Roy, accompaigné de Messieurs les mareschaulx, ses enfans, bien unis, et y estoit aussy ledict sieur Dandelot. Quant à Monsieur l'admiral, il est en sa maison. Monseigneur le prince de Condé doit, comme l'on dict, bientost venir. Lesdicts sieurs maréchaulx frères, depuis estre arrivez en ceste court, ont par deux fois esté ensemble à la chasse et retournez ensemble, de sorte que tous ceulx qui les ayment louent Dieu de ceste union fraternelle, et ce bon vieillard en semble rajeuny. La Royne est partie ce matin à quatre heures pour aller à Paris, mais c'est pour revenir au giste ; l'un dict que c'est pour aller veoir le bastiment des Tuilleries, l'aultre dict que c'est pour emprunter de l'argent, les aultres que c'est pour quelque mystère qu'on n'entend pas. Sy est-ce qu'elle est accompaignée des principaulx financiers, c'est-à-dire de Monsieur le Mareschal de Gonnor et de Messieurs de Morvillier, de Limoges et de l'Aubespine, lesquelz quattre partirent dès hier, et Monsieur de Valence les a suivis cejourdhuy matin. Cella est quelque conjecture apparente qu'on parlera des finances. . . .

De Sault [1] to M. de Gordes.

Savigny, 30 juin 1567.

Monsieur, j'ay esté fort ayse d'avoir trouvé ceste commodité du chanoyne de Pionsin, qui s'en va de par deçà pour vous faire en-

---

[1] François d'Agoult, de Montauban et de Montlaur, Comte de Sault, a nobleman of Provence and a very active Huguenot. He was killed in the battle of Saint-Denis.

tendre de nos nouvelles, qui sont fort bonnes, grâces à Dieu, et aussi de celles de ce quartier, qui sont qu'ayant le Roy entendu que du costé de Flandres se fait grand préparatif d'armes, artillerie, munitions, et autres choses nécessaires pour la guerre, cela l'a fait entrer en quelque jalouzie de pourvoir aux frontières de son royaume de ce costé-là. Et pour cest effect a ordonné d'y envoyer quelques compagnies d'hommes d'armes, et d'envoyer Monsieur d'Andelot là au long de la frontière avec pouvoir de faire la reveue de ses compagnies d'infanterie, jusques au nombre de deux cens hommes pour chacune. Ce qui fait ainsi esmouvoir Sa Majesté, c'est que toutes choses en Flandres sont paciffiées et réduictes souz l'obéissance du roy d'Espaigne comme il desiroit, tellement qu'on ne peult autrement juger desdits préparatifs, sinon que ce soit pour nous venir troubler en ce royaume. J'ay esté ces jours passez à Vallery, au. baptesme de Monsieur le prince de Condé (qui m'y avoit convyé), et a esté porté ledit enfant par Monsieur l'admiral au nom du Roy, s'estant trouvé audit lieu de Vallery Monsieur le cardinal de Chastillon, Messrs d'Andelot, de la Rochefoucault, de Janlys, et plusieurs autres S^{rs} et gentilzhommes, tellement que la compagnie estoit fort honnorable et fut bien festoyée dudit S^r prince, et récréée de plusieurs honnestes passetemps. Depuis Sa Majesté a envoyé querir ledit S^r prince, affin qu'il s'en vienne à la court (comme elle a aussi fait Messrs de Guyse) pour regarder par ensemble ce qu'il est besoing de faire pour le regard de ces préparatifs et autres entreprises que l'on doute que ledit roy d'Espaigne a en ce royaume, tellement qu'on ne peut encores sçavoir comme se résouldront toutes ces menées. Il est bien vray qu'encores que nous n'ayons point besoing de guerre, si est ce que toutes ces choses nous purroient bien causer quelque meilleure union entre les uns et les autres que nous n'avons de présent. Au reste, Monsieur, je m'en suis venu en ce lieu de Savigny (il y a jà sept ou huict jours) pour donner quelque ordre aux affaires que j'y ay, et espère en partir demain pour m'en aller retrouver la court, d'où je vous feray entendre quelquefoys de mes nouvelles.

Guyon to M. de Gordes.

Saint-Germain-en-Laye, 3 juillet 1567.

. . . Arrivant icy Monsieur le connestable, et regardant Leurs Majestés aux affaires qui se présentent, il leur persuada bailler *cœur* (?) aux compaignies estant soubz la charge de Monsr d'Andelot son nepveu, ce qui fust résolu et dépesché pour cest effaict, tellement qu'on faict estat il commandera à six mil hommes de pied, lesquels se doibvent rendre à Atigny près Reims, où pareillement se joindront les Suisses et douze cens hommes d'armes, pour le tout former un camp et s'emploier la part qu'on en auroyt besoin. . . . Ores que lestat dudict S^r d'Andelot et l'affection grande qu'il a au service de son roy l'ayent appelé a ceste nouvelle *cœurs* (?), si est-ce que plusieurs en ont murmuré. Or ce présent ordre dressé par Leurs Majestés, plus pour tenyr en seuretés ce roiaulme que pour autres effaicts, a donné occasion à plusieurs de dire comme ils font que nous sommes à la guerre, mais pour tout cella l'on n'eust jamais plus de desir de conserver la paix que nous avons, si bien qu'elle ne sera rompue de ce cousté. . . . Ces jours passés Madame la princesse de Portian[1] a esté à sa premyère messe, puysqu'elle est veufve, au grand contentement de plusieurs et très-grand regret de beaucoup d'autres. . . . Cejourd'huy est arrivé Monsieur le prince de Condé et hyer Monsr d'Aulmalle. L'on a mandé Monsr le cardinal de Lorreyne. Vous ne sauriez croyre de combien est descheu Monsr le connestable en ceste dernière malladye, si bien qu'il semble vieilliz plus qu'il n'a faict durant six ans. . . . Il se parle fort du mariage de Monsr de Guise avec Mad^e la princesse de Portian. . . .

Truchon to M. de Gordes.

Saint-Germain, 4 juillet 1567.

Je vous escrivy lundy par un homme de pied, et mardy par la voye de la poste. Mercredy fut tenu conseil, où Monsieur présidoit, et y estoient Messeigneurs les cardinaulx de Bourbon et de Chastillon, duc d'Aumale, connestable et chancellier de France, mareschal de Montmorency, les sieurs evesques d'Orléans, de Valence et de Limoges, et les sieurs de Lansac, de Carnavalet et de la Cazedieu. Et fut résolu le faict des Souisses, quilz seroient entretenus, et rapporta Monseigneur le connestable que l'intention du Roy et de la Royne estoit qu'on n'y touchast, ni semblablement aux viséneschal et vibailly de robe courte, et fut lors bien entendu que cest entretenement estoit prins du retranchement des vingt archers, en y adjoustant neuf vingts livres tous les mois, ce qu'estoit besoin de remonstrer. Mais j'espiay bien l'occasion de n'estre absent cependant qu'on jouyait ce jeu. Hier fut tenu ung aultre conseil des gens des finances, où fut leue la paroolle du pais, et y furent faictz

---

[1] Catherine de Clèves, Comtesse d'Eu, widow of Antoine de Croy, Prince de Porcien, one of the leading Huguenot chiefs, a relation and a friend of the Prince de Condé. He died in 1564; and six years afterwards, despite the express injunctions of her husband, she married Henri, Duc de Guise.

tant de retranchemens et radiatures de fraiz et vacations, que j'ay grande peur que par cy-après on aura bien à faire de trouver des commis du pais, sinon que s'en trouvent quelques-uns de l'humeur des anciens preudhommes romains, qui faisoient les affaires publicques à leur despens. . . .

Monseigneur le prince de Condé arriva hier en ceste court. J'ai cejourd'huy veu le Roy, qui tenoit la teste de mondict seigneur le Prince à la main gauche, et celle de Monseigneur le cardinal de Bourbon à la main droicte, et par jeu les vouloit faire heurter leurs frons ensemble. Monseigneur d'Aumale caressoit Madame la connestable, et Madame la mareschale de Montmorency y adsistant, Monseigneur le mareschal faisant et recevant chère réciproque à l'endroict de mondict seigneur d'Aumale. Monseigneur le cardinal de Chastillon n'en estoit loing. Somme tous sans distinction me sembloient sy d'accord que je souhaitte ne veoir jamais plus grande division en France. Cella est ung bel exemple pour beaucoup de gens de moindre qualité, qui tiennent leur cœur, et se regardent par-dessus l'épaule, et prennent plaisir à entretenir querelles. On ne sait encore quant on délogera d'icy, combien que les laboureurs des champs ayent jà faict présenter deux requestes au Roy pour se retirer et sa suite à Paris jusques à ce que la récolte soit faicte. Car, pour vous dire la vérité, la plupart des gens de court font en France comme les soldatz des cinq compagnies en Daulphiné, je ne diray pas à la barbe de Leurs Majestés, parce que l'une est femme, et celle qui est masculine n'en a encores poinct, mais si est-ce que cella advient presque tous les jours aux villaiges mesmes où elles logent.

Guyon to M. de Gordes.

Saint-Germain-en-Laye, 11 juillet 1567.

. . . . Lon a sceu le passaige du duc d'Albe et de sa trouppe, quon dict estre de six mille espaignolz et quinze cens femmes. Monsieur le prince de Condé est party ce matin pour sen retourner à sa maison; plusieurs murmurent quil a heu ung grand mescontentement, ce que je laisse à ceulx qui en savent plus que moy. Tant y a je ne pense estre à reprendre quand après mille personnes je dys quil est party fort triste et fasché. Monsr l'admiral arrivera demayn icy, estant mandé pour le faict de sa charge. Monsieur d'Andelot a accompaigné ledict Sr prince jusques à Paris pour revenir avec son frère. . . .

13 juillet 1567.

LL. MM. partirent hier de St-Germain, dinèrent aux Tuileries et couchèrent à St-Maur. . . . Monsieur ladmiral arriva ce matin à St-Germain, qui receust for bonne chère du Roy. Monsieur le prince de Condé ne séjourna qu'un jour en ceste ville : je ne sçauroys vous rendre certain des propos ny *raisons* (?) quil a heus sen aller si soudain et mal content. . . .

XVII.

The Prince de Condé to I·abelle de Limeuil.

(Three letters extracted from the Minutes of Evidence taken against the aforesaid Isabelle. May to August, 1564.)

Sebastien de l'Aubespine, Bishop of Limoges, had been charged, in conjunction with Jean de Morvilliers, Bishop of Orleans, with the duty of taking informations against Isabelle de Limeuil, maid of honour to the Queen-Mother, who had been arrested at Dijon at the end of May 1564. In the body of this work have been related the motives of this arrest, and the leading particulars of Isabelle's captivity (pp. 208–211, 214). When the examination had proved fruitless, and the captivity of the fair prisoner had come to an end, the Bishop of Limoges still preserved the report of the interrogatories and depositions, as well as the letters which had been intercepted, and the other documents relating to the affair. The whole of these papers were formerly deposited, and doubtless are still, in the Château de Villebon, among the papers of Sebastien de l'Aubespine ; and were there discovered by M. Louis Pàris,[1] who has been kind enough to furnish us with copies. As in touching, with all due discretion, upon the gallantries of the Prince de Condé, we have been able to bring to light actual facts and to dispel the cloud of conjectures and contradictory statements in which the case had been involved to the present day, we purpose to vindicate the accuracy of our narrative by printing the original papers which have furnished its basis. But at the last moment we have been compelled by want of space to forego the purpose of inserting here the whole of the

---

[1] The clever and brilliant editor of Maucroix, M. Louis Pàris, has already drawn from the papers of M. de l'Aubespine a curious volume, which · has appeared in the *Collection des Documents inédits sur l'Histoire de France*, under the title of *Négociations, etc., relatives au règne de François II.*

documents : we confine ourselves to placing before the reader three letters addressed by the Prince de Condé to Isabelle de Limeuil, which appear to us to be an amusing specimen of his amatory style.

The first two must have been written shortly after her arrest, when her fate was yet doubtful. They were intercepted and put into the hands of the Bishop of Limoges, as was also the third, which seems to have been written some time after the other two.

Hellas ! mon ceur, que vous puis-je dire austre chose, synon que suys plus mort que vif, voiant que suys privé de vous servyr, ne sachant où vous estes, et vous voiant partir [*pâtir*?] et ne savoyr comment je vous pourrés secouryr. Monsieur du Fresne me mande prou souvant que luy etcryvés de voz nouvelles,[1] mes moy je n'an puys savoyr où vous estes menée. Je m'étonne fort, puys cavés le moien d'écryre à quelque ungs, que ne puys recevoyr de mesme de vos lestre, car vous savés quy n'y a home au monde quy tant sait faché de vos pènes que moy et qui vous sait tant oblygé que vous suys, ny quy de plus grande gaieté de ceur sait plus ressollu de asardé sa vye pour vous fére ung bon servyse que moy quy vous et ceur et servyteur esclave.

Je vous anvoye une de mes robes de nuyt qui m'a servy et à vous avecque moy, supliant de crère que plustost je vous soueste vostre ceur que vostre robe, car je vous ferés plus de servyse qu'une marte ; au moins, mon ceur, faistes-moy connestre cavés autant d'anvye de me concerver an vostre bone grace, ettant cative come an liberté, car vous savés que acoutumé n'avoyr compagnon, mes d'estre seul et preumyer, je m'asurre que n'avés perdue la bone opinyon cavyés de moy, mes au contraire quelle vous et plustot ocquemantée : reste an m'anploier et me donner le moien de vous aler mestre hors de la facherye où estes destenue, car y fault que j'é de vous les moiens, car j'é des yeux quy ne font que pleurer et ne voie goute, et des forces quy n'ont point de mouvemant, n'etant de vous commandée. Je lerés fère à vostre bon geugement pour anploier seus que sorés bien connestre quy on le myllieur moien de vous fère servyce : mes cants li vousloyr ètre fidelle, je suys le preumyer.—Je me contanterés de vous dire que j'é nostre fils antre mes mains, sint et galliar, et bien pour vivre, lequel vous et moy ne seryons, cant nous vou-

---

[1] It has been observed above (p. 211) that the Prince de Condé was somewhat jealous of Du Fresne, one of the Secretaries of State, and not without reason, it would appear. This jealousy discloses itself several times in the following letters.

dryons, désavoué, se que ne voudré fère. Je resu deux de vos
lestres par lesquesles vous me le reconmandés : n'an n'eyés peur, car
jens né le soint pareil que desirés que j'ée. Il let tropt an moy
pour l'abandoner de se quy et en ma puyssance.—Il let vray quil
avet été lessé cheu une pauvre feme quy l'a fait couché su la pallie
six nuys, come braque : que j'é trouvé fort étrange. Mes sy o
commansement seus à quy y n'apartené l'on ballié come ung petit
chien, je lé prys come père pour le noury an prince : il le mérite,
car sait la plus belle créature que jamays home vit.

Voylla ce que vous puys dire, sinon que sy bientost je ne vous
voys, j'émerés autant moury que de vivre sans ceur. Croiés pour
sertin que ne vous emys jamais tant, ny tant vostre que vous, ny sy
pret à le vous fère parrestre. Vous baisant les piés et mains,
atantdant myeus ; mes je pance, cant vous verai, que d'esse je
perdré la parolle, car je desire autant ou plus sela que mon salut.
Ellas ! mon ceur, ne m'abandonés point. [*Here is a monogram.*]
Ses chivres mouront ansemble.

The monogram is on the back of the letter.

Hélas ! mon ceur, que vous puisge mandé, synon que voz pènes
me rande le plus afligé jenstilhome du monde, vous voiant soufryr
tant de facherye et grande pasion, que je ne sé sy je suys mort ou
vif. Mes cant je pance à l'amour que vous porte et porterés pour
jamays, je me reconnés lors an vie pour vous fère ung bon et pront
service, qui sera le remersimant des grandes obligasions an coy je
vous suys demeuré redevable et serviteur esclave, ressentant an moy
vos annuys quy prosède de mon aucasion : sella me rant tryste plus
que sy moy mesme ettet captif an votre plase. Y a il une plus
meschante prysont en France, ny plus lanmantable que la miene,
quy ne me pryve seullement de ma liberté, mes de mon ceur et
contantement, me partysant tellemant mes esprysts que je desire plus
tost la mort soudène quene vie longe, facheuse, come et aujourdhuy
la myène, étant de vous apesant, et ne pouvant savoyr de voz
nouvelles ny le lieu asurré de votre demeurre, pour vous y aler fère
perrestre que l'estrème amour que vous doys et porte et telle quelle
ne counoyt ny estime que votre bone grace et veue, et de vous voyr
an lieu où vous et moy puyssions vivre et mourryr ensemble. Et à
saite heurre-là je pourès dire estre, an dépit de movesse fortune, bien
heureus, et ne seret ; car je ne vois que par voz ieux et ne sans que
par vos sanst:mans. L'afecsion et si fort anrasinée dedans nos ceurs,
quelle ne se peult par persones mortelles se départir, mes bien

socquemantera telle, sy se peut, se que plus né créable.—Je vous
asurre que nostre fils est une belle et forte corde pour nous randre
pour jamays bien atachés ansemble.

Je lerés mes trystes conplaintes pour vous dire lesse qué resu de
voyr et antendre l'amytié que me portés et que desiré me continué,
me faisant, par vos lestres, antandre que l'amour ocquemante et non
se dyminue. Vous avés raison de m'estimer vérytable, et crère que
ne fodré de vous tenyr foy et parolle et la fydelle proumesse que vous
et faistes, car je veus que me creyés, mon ceur, que veus conmbatre
pour vostre liberté, plustost que ne vous fasse connoystre que patissés
pour ung prynce quy vous reconnoys pour sont name et sa vye.

J'ay resu ung estrème plaisir, cant j'é veu se que m'avés mandé,
qu'estes résollue de ne voyr ny soufryr parlé home à vous, que moy,
ou venant de ma par, ne lestres de home quy vive. Saiste ressollusion
m'a tant cotanté et satyfait, que sy suyvés, come je m'asurre, se
chemain vous randra la heurreuse feme du monde. Car je vous
asurre, mon ceur, quy m'annuyrès bien grandemant que l'on pût
prendre seur voz ascions seuget de dire : à quy et sait anfant ? come
sy deus y avet passé : quy seret autant à dire, cant tennés deus à
une mesme faveur ; se que vous en dis, n'et pour le croere, car
je n'an n'é point d'ocasion, come je vous le ferés perestre, mes
que me croyés, car je vous ferés une preuve sy vous éme ou non,
dans peu de jours. Puys quant somes sy avant, mon ceur, y faut
du tout levé le masque, car tout le monde saist se qui an net ; y n'et
plus que question de fère partout perrestre nostre estrème et fidelle
anmour, et que saiste seulle cosse vous on fait plus m'émé que vous-
mesme, et par là vous serés honnorée et estimée de tous, cant leurs
montrés par vos effaits, tant an petite chose que grande, que ne
vouslés ouy parlé ny antandre nouvelles de home que de seluy cavés
plus émé que se qu'estimés plus cher que vous-mesmes. Et de par,
je ferés confesse que jorés fait le semblable. Vous avés jà antandu,
à se que m'a dit Dupont et le Basque, que l'on parle à la cour de
quelceun par icy ; vous y pancerés dofusqué se fauxs bruyt par
votre bon geugemant ; et pas n'an feré plus de conte, ne retenant
ryen plus de se quy vien de sa par. Car vous regardés plus grant
contantemant de mon conte que de la siene.—Y ne fault point
cantryés an sermant aveque moy pour me fère crère quy let myen,
votre filz, car je n'an né non plus doute que de seus de ma feme.
Mais faistes que d'ostre n'an puys antrer an doute, et pancés que
s'y le voiés, que diryés bien cavecque raysont yl let mon fils et le
vostre, car à sont vissage les deux nostres se reconnesse. Je vous
suplie doncque, mon ceur, m'émer et jamays ne m'abandoner, come

m'avés proumys, et cant vous vous resouvyendrés du lien je m'asurre que me tiendrés proumesse.

Je vous ranvoye mon Basque pour vous asurrer que ne vous lèrai guerre an la pène où vous estes, et que vous an méterés bientost dehors.—Je vous anvoie une robe de nuyt fourré pour vous servyr. Je voudrés estre auprès de vous an sa plasse, car je ne pance estre si hinutille que je ne pansisse vous fère plus de servyce quelle. Vous prandrés doncque de bone par mon afecsion, puysque ne vous an puys sytot que desire vous an montré les effais ; car se seret à saiste heurre, sy jens navés le moiens quy répondisse à la vous-lonté.

Nostre fils se porte bien et se fait fort bien nourry, et et antre mes mains, quy et ma seulle consollasion, étant de vous etlongnyé, quy met ung bon gage pour me randre asuré pour jamays me tiendrés en votre bone grace, quy é la chose que j'estime le plus, et plus sans foys que je né jamays fait. Ellas ! mon ceur, il fault que vous die les moiens que je prans pour me désannuyé, sait cant seul je pense à la fasont et èse que j'orés, mes que vous revoye. Mes j'é ferme opinyon que de moy la parolle se départira, du grant contantemant que prandrés de voyr mon espérance avoir ganyé sur mon dessespoyr ; car yl m'et avis que sytot camour m'eut randu votre pryssonnyé et m'eut attaché sous votre obeysansse, y me print pour me fère le plus heureus home du monde, espuys me met an ésil, me pryvant de mon ceur. Se met avis jà plus de myll ans : quy sera fin, par vous baiser les piés et mains aussytot que saiste lestre y touchera, et vous feré une requeste quy sera fort courte, m'asurant que me l'acorderés : sé qui vous plaisse, mon ceur, faistes de moy se que voudrés et commandrés ce quy vous pléra, car sans respect je vous y obéyrés d'ausy grande afecsion, come j'espère que ses chifre demeureront ferme ansemble, pour sine et marque que noz ceurs le sont ynséparablement. [*Here the monogram.*] Fin à la mort.

The above monogram is on the back.

———

Mon ceur, jé se matin, par mon Basque, resu de vous deus lestres quy m'ont fort resgouy de pancés qu'estes sy ressollue de prandre pasiance ; reste à vous dire que devés prandre asurrance de moy quy ne vous lérés jamays, et me couteras la vyc, ou je vous metrés hors de pène, mes que me veulliés crère : et vous suplie que vous mo donnyés moien que je vous puysse voyr, à selle fin d'avysser ensemble se quy faut que je fasse pour votre servyce, sait sy faut vous oter par force ou par anmytié et faveur, car je n'y veus ryen etpargnyé ;

et sy vous trouvyés bon fère une lestre à la Rène fort pitoiable, luy confaisant l'avoyr ofancé, et quy luy plaise vous pardonné, et quelle se veuillie contanter des annuys grans que vous portés, sans vousloyr permestre que vos annemys se serve de vous come de trofée, et de vous fère ètre de vos parans pour jamays délessée et la plus malheureuse feme du monde, veu que sela n'y peut de ryen servy, et à vous sy prégudissiable.

Je vous anvoie Dupont et ung apoticaire pour vous servyr ; et ung jentilhomme sers nostre filz pour le fère porter an sa maisont, là où y seras ausy bien traité cantfans que jée, que ne sans avoyr jamays porté tant d'afecsion que je luy porte, car je l'avousré, et sera de mon bien partisipant. Jé une estréme anvie de le voyr, se que ferés, Dieu aidant, et vous preumyerremant, que j'adorre et onnorre plus que jamays. Ganyé la viellie quy vous garde, et me faistes souvent savoyr où vous estes, pour vous voyr, et ne permectez comme du monde vous voie que moy et les miens, car par là vous ferés connestre que ne voulés jamays émé que moy, à quy vous ètes lésée allé ; et pour cosse je dis sesy, car je ferés pour vous se que ne pancés pas. Adieu, mon ceur : ne m'abandonés poinct, et seyés asurée que veus vivre et moury avecque vous ; et se chifre [*Here the monogram*] ne se séparera jamays. Fin à la mort.

The monogram is on the back.

XVIII.

The Cardinal de Chastillon to the Bishop of Aqs.

(EXTRACT.)

Condé, 4 juillet 1564.

. . . . Je vous ay bien voulu advertir par ce secrétaire que M. le Prince envoye à la court pour les affaires de Mad^e la mareschalle de St-André. Comme ledit seigneur a pris lad^e dame en sa protection, laquelle dame, pour user de mesme honnesteté et recongnoissance, aujourd'huy luy a donné la terre de Vallery et les autres de deçà qui lui sont échues par la mort de sa fille, ensemble a fait héritiers universels luy et ses enfants de tous les autres biens que les loix et coustumes des pays [*lui* ?] donnent ès autres provinces où lad^e fille avoit du bien, à quelques charges et conditions fort advantageuses pour luy, qui est un party qui ne se trouve pas tous les jours.

Je vous diray, aussi quant à la disposition de Mad^e la Princesse, qu'elle va diminuant de forces à veue d'œil, qui me garde de partir encore d'icy, ne faisant qu'attendre l'heure bien souvent que Dieu la veuille appeler à soy, pour les grandes et estranges douleurs qu'elle souffre, qui la rend et ceulx qui l'aiment si affligés que vous pouvez penser.

(Original. Noailles Collection ; Gaignères, 919. *Bibliothèque impériale*.)

XIX.

H. H. B. . . to X. . .

On the relations of Condé with Isabelle de Limeuil after his wife's death, the various projects of a second marriage for him, his relations with the Protestants and the Catholics, &c.

March 15, 1565.

. . . . Il Re finalmente scrive quà che li siano mandati l'informationi del caso avvenuto in Parigi frà 'l cardinale di Lorena et Mamoransi, a che proposito non si sa ; ben si pensa che per dare parole a casa di Ghisa et a catolici et per non disperare il cardinale. Non ve ne pur uno quà, ne ugonoto, ne catolico, che pensi doversi fare giustitia. Ho visto lettere di Madama di Chelle,[1] ne le quali mostra gran speranza de amicitia fra suo fratello et il cardinale. L'amico et jo stimiamo non potersi fare fondamento alcuno sopra le parole, ne sopra le attioni d'un huomo tanto leggiero come si mostra Condé, hora piu che mai passionato per la sua Limolia. Paroceli[2] è stato quà quatro o cinque giorni et ha secretamente predicato a suoi ugoniti. Langheto da lui ha inteso che, per cagione de la Limolia, è nata dis-

. . . . Finally the King writes here asking for the informations taken regarding the affair which took place in Paris between the Cardinal de Lorraine and Montmorency ; for what purpose is not known ; but it is thought to be in order to appease the House of Güise and the Catholics, and to prevent the Cardinal from becoming desperate. No one here, Huguenot or Catholic, imagines that justice will be done. I have seen a letter of Madame de Chelles,[1] in which she appears to entertain great hope of friendship between her brother and the Cardinal. My friend and I think that nothing can be founded upon the words, or even the acts, of so light a man as Condé shows himself to be, who is now more than ever enamoured of his Limeuil. Pérocel[2] has been here four or five days, and has preached in private to

[1] Renée de Bourbon, sister of the Prince de Condé.
[2] Pérocel, a celebrated Protestant minister.

cordia fra Condé et Sciatiglione, dopo fra'l medesimo Condé et suoi seguaci, et di tal manera che Sciatiglione si è partito da lui, è venuto a Parigi, et se ne andato, chi dice a Sciatiglione, chi dice a una sua abbadia, et che i seguaci quasi tutti l'hanno abbandonato, et l'occasione essere stata tale che essendo stato scritto a Condé da Parigi una certa lettera nel fine de laquale era scritto essere venuta la damigella, Sciatiglione che stava sopra Condé mentre leggeva la lettera, vide quelle parole et imaginatosi quello ch'era, disse a Condé : Jo saprei dire che damigella è questa venuta a Parigi. Al che Condé rispose certe parole per lequali mostro non essergli stato caro il motto di Sciatiglione ; pur la cosa non andò molto avanti fra loro per alhora. Dopo gionta la Limolia dove haveva ordinato Condé che fosse conduta, et vistisi insieme, certi gentilhuomini ugonoti andorno a trovare Condé et cominciorno a monirlo et quasi che riprenderlo de l'amica. Onde Condé imaginatosi essere stato scoperto da Sciatiglione il suo secreto a coloro, et per opera sua essere venuti a riprenderlo, adirato disse contra di loro molte parole, tassandoli di spioni, poi soggionse che Sciatiglione gli haveva detto questo, et fattili venire a parlarli, et questo con tanto sdegno che venne a dire grand male di Sciatiglione et de tutta casa sua . . . . et biasmandoli d'arroganza, di presontione,

his Huguenots. Languet learned from him that dissension has arisen on the subject of La Limeuil, between Condé and Châtillon, and subsequently between the same Condé and his followers, in such a manner that Châtillon has parted from him, has come to Paris, and has retired, some say to Châtillon, others to an abbey which belongs to him, and that his (Condé's) followers have almost all deserted him, the occasion being this, that a certain letter was written to Condé from Paris, at the close of which was written, 'The young lady is come.' Châtillon, who was standing over Condé as he read the letter, saw these words, and guessing what they meant, said to Condé, 'I can tell what young lady it is that has arrived in Paris.' To which Condé replied in certain words which showed that Châtillon's saying this was not agreeable to him ; and there the matter rested for the time being. After La Limeuil had arrived at the place to which Condé had ordered her to be conducted, and they had been seen in company, certain Huguenot gentlemen went and found Condé, and began to admonish and, so to speak, to reprove him on the subject of his mistress. Whereupon Condé, imagining that his secret had been discovered to them by Châtillon, and that it was at his instigation they were come to reprove him, grew angry, and said

et che volessero non solamente paregiarsi a principi, non essendo altro che piccioli gentilhuomini, ma ardissero ancora d'oltraggiarli, et ch'esso non era per comportare piu queste cose. Per queste o simili parole et forse peggiori Sciatiglione si è partito da Condé. Il medesimo hanno fatto la maggior parte de gl'ugonoti, di modo che si trova quasi solo. Jo per accertarmi meglio de la verità ho narrato tutto questo a un ugonoto amico mio per sapere da lui s'era vero, m'ha risposto sospirando esserci ancor di peggio, perche a lui era stato detto da gentilhuomini che solevano seguire il medesimo Condé.

many things against them, designating them spies, and then adding that Châtillon had told them this, and had sent them to talk to him; and this with such indignation that he went on to say much evil of Châtillon and of his whole house . . . . and accusing them of arrogance, of presumption, and of not only wishing to put themselves on a level with princes, when they were nothing but gentlemen of humble rank, but even more, of daring to insult him; adding that it was not in his nature to endure this any longer. By these and suchlike words, and even worse, it came about that Châtillon separated himself from Condé. The greater part of the Huguenots have done likewise, so that he finds himself now almost alone. I, with a view to more certain information of the truth of all this, have repeated it to a Huguenot friend, to ascertain from him whether it be true; and he answered with a sigh that it was even worse; for he had learned what follows from gentlemen who were accustomed to follow the aforesaid Condé.

Che per opera de Nal[1] la Limolia era stata conduta a Condé a fine di fare di lui quello che gia fece del fratello per mezo di Roet, del che dubitandosi Sciatiglione, i ministri et i gentilhuomini di Condé fecero fra loro consiglio per trovare rimedio a

It was Nal,[1] by whose contrivance La Limeuil was brought to Condé, with a view to his becoming what his brother had already become by means of La Rouet. Suspecting this, Châtillon, the ministers, and the gentlemen of Condé's party took

---

[1] Catherine de Médicis (?).

tanto male, et risolvettero tre cose, l'una che i ministri li parlassero galiardamente, rimostrandoli il pericolo et infamia propria et il scandalo commune a tutta la relligione per esserne lui capo, et persuadendoli, se non si poteva contenere, a pigliar moglie; l'altro rimedio, se questo primo non giovava, fu, che i primi gentilhuomini de la relligione et suoi particolari di commune concordia andassero a trovarlo, et fatteli le medesime rimostranze, li facessero intendere che se non appartava da se la Limolia, lo lasciarebbero solo, et in effetto, se negava di farlo, che lo lasciassero. Il terzo remedio fu, quando i dui primi non giovassero, che la Limolia si dovesse scomunicare, anatematizare et dare in potere di Satanasso. Et così i ministri prima essere andati a parlargli, et dopo loro i gentilhuomini, ma gl'uni et gl'altri in vanno, perche a ministri rispose in somma, che non poteva contenire, ne facilmente poteva pigliare moglie, per esser difficile trovare persona eguale a se, de la medesima relligione, et impossibile trovar la d'altra relligione. A gentilhuomini poi rispose di manera che furno sforciati lasciarlo, onde la relligione si trova in gran travaglio ne sa che piu si fare, perche dubbita di fare peggio se scomunica la Limolia, per essere Condé di natura così effeminato che gran pericolo è che in lui possa piu la Limolia che la relligione.

counsel together to find a remedy for so great an evil, and resolved upon three courses: first, that the ministers should speak out roundly to him, pointing out the personal danger and disgrace of the affair, and the scandal common to the whole [reformed] religion, since he was its chief, and persuading him, if he could not keep continent, to take a wife. The second remedy, if this first did not succeed, was, for the principal gentlemen of the [reformed] religion, and his intimate friends, in common accord, to wait upon him, and make to him the same remonstrances, giving him to understand that if he did not separate himself from La Limeuil, they would leave him alone, and in fact, if he refused to do so, they would leave him. The third remedy was, when the first two had not succeeded, that La Limeuil should be excommunicated, anathematized, and delivered into the power of Satan. And so the ministers first went to confer with him, and after them the gentlemen, but both the one and the other in vain; for to the ministers he replied in brief, that he could not keep continent, and could not easily take a wife, since it was difficult to find a person equal to himself, of the same religion, and impossible to find one of another religion. To the gentlemen afterwards he replied in such a manner that they were forced to leave him, whence the [party of] the religion finds itself in great trouble, and does not know what further to do, since it is afraid of doing worse by excommunicating La Limeuil, Condé being of a nature so inclined to women that there is great danger lest La Limeuil should have more power over him than the religion.

Et perche, dissi jo, non li trovate voi una moglie ? È possibile ch'in Francia non si trova donna ne donzella che lo satisfaccia ? Non, disse l'ugonoto, de la nostra relligione, perche non gli ne alcuna in Francia pare a lui. Trovate ne una fuora di Francia, soggionsi jo, se ce ne. Questo si tratta hora, rispose l'altro. Et chi è ? dissi jo. A questo non volva egli rispondere, ma jo l'astrinsi tanto che venne a dirmi essere la figliuola del palatino Elettore. Jo, per intendere piu oltre, fingendo essermi cosa nuova questa, dissi : Bel disegno è questo et di gran giovamento al stabilimento de la relligione, ma mi pare difficile à riuscire : il principe è povero, mal sano, carico d'anni et di figliuoli a quali tocca tutto quel poco che si trova havere il principe, si che a grand pena il Palatino vorra dargli la figliuola. Oltra di questo il principe ha non pur bisogno di moglie, ma d'una gran dote ancora, laquale non sogliono dare i principi d'Alemagna mai, et molto meno quando sono pregati. A questo non seppe che rispondersi l'ugonoto, anzi confessò es-

'And why,' said I, 'do you not find him a wife ? Is it possible that there is not to be found in France a lady or a demoiselle who will satisfy him ?' 'Not,' said the Huguenot, 'of our religion, for there is none in France of equal rank with him.' 'Find one then out of France,' subjoined I, 'if there is one.' 'That is now being considered,' replied the other. 'And who is it ?' said I. To this he would not reply, but I pressed him so hard that he told me at last it was the daughter of the Elector Palatine. I, in order to learn more about it, pretended it was a new thing to me, and said, 'This is a good scheme, and one which will be of great service for the establishment of the religion, but it appears to me difficult to bring it about. The Prince is poor, in bad health, burdened with years and with children to whom will come what little the Prince may be found to possess, so that there will be great difficulty in the way of the Palatine's being willing to give him his daughter. Besides this, the Prince not only wants a wife, but a

sere negotio difficile; nondimeno soggionse poi che le difficoltà cessarebbero in gran parte con l'ajuto che darebbe la relligione al principe, et che Monsr l'amirale et molt' altri s'affaticavano et travagliavano in questo.

great dowry, which the princes of Germany are never wont to give, and much less when they are begged so to do.' To this the Huguenot did not know what to answer, but confessed that it was a difficult business; nevertheless he added that the difficulties would in great measure cease, from the assistance which the [party of the] religion would give to the Prince, and that M. l'Amiral and many others were exerting themselves and labouring in the affair.

Da questo discorso, gionto con quello ch'jo le scrissi a dì passati de la Limolia, puo V.S. conoscere in che opinione sia Nal cosi appresso de catolici come de gl'ugonoti. I catolici dicono che, per impedire il matrimonio di Condé con la nepote del cardinale di Lorena, si serve del mezo de la Limolia. Gl' ugonoti dicono che per il costei mezo vuole inescare Condé et farlo tornare papista, come fu fatto di Vandomo impazzito per li amori di Roet; jo non m'accordo col parere di questi, ne di quelli, anzi penso, se pur ha parte nel negotio de la Limolia, che sia per volere fare tutto suo Condé, et che non dipenda d'alcun altro che da lei, per potersene servire a suo piacere, per ugonoto, per papista, et se bisogno sera per arista. Come che sia, quest' occasione non si doverebbe perdere da catolici di fare suo Condé. Doverebbe il cardinale di Borbone riscaldarsi per ricuperare il fra-

From this discourse, joined to what I have written within the last few days about La Limeuil, V.S. [your Lordship?] may know what opinion is held of Nal both by Catholics and Huguenots. The Catholics say that to hinder the marriage of Condé with the niece of the Cardinal de Lorraine, she is making use of La Limeuil. The Huguenots say that she is trying by the same means to entice Condé, and make him turn Papist, as were used with Vendôme when he was infatuated for love of La Rouet. I agree in opinion neither with the one nor the other, but I think that if she has anything to do with the affair of La Limeuil, it is from a wish to make Condé entirely her own, that he may depend upon no one else but her, that she may use him at her pleasure, whether as Huguenot, as Papist, or, if need be, as Arist [Arian?]. However this may

tello et tirarlo fuora de le mani degli ugonoti et del diavolo. Doverebbe il cardinale di Lorena stringere la pratica del parentado, doverebbe la Regina astringerlo con lettere, con preghieri, con favori, con dinari, et con honori a venire alla corte per non dare tempo et commodita agl' ugonoti di placarlo et farlo piu che mai suo; il che senza dubbio sera se non vi si provede, per che non puo Condé stare in piedi senza l'appoggio de catolici o de ugonoti; onde, se i catolici non lo sostengono, è necessario che vadi non solamente a cascare, ma a gettarsi nelle braccie degl' ugonoti. Hora che sia in dubbio, è facil cosa spingerlo non meno a l'una che a l'altra parte. Non voglio jo negare che la Limolia non possa in lui molto mentre è . . . . seco, ma se si facesse venire in corte, se gli offerisce una moglie bella, ricca et honorata, come la sorella di Monsr di Ghisa, se gli si promettessero honori, se gli si facessero favori, se vi s'aggiongessero i prieghi del fratello, le persuasioni d'huomini intendenti, credo per certo che si guadagnarebbe et diverebbe catolico. Certa cosa è che gl' ugonoti ne stanno in gran paura, et tanta che pensando ch' egli debbia essere tosto papista dicono mille mali di lui. Una sola difficoltà pare che si è in questo negotio, et che non debbia piacere a Nal la concordia di Condé et d'il cardinale. Quelli ch' hora regnano, et che, se 'l car-

be, the Catholics ought not to lose this opportunity of making Condé their own. The Cardinal de Bourbon ought to recover his warmth to regain his brother, and draw him out of the hands of the Huguenots and the devil. The Cardinal de Lorraine ought to draw closer the bonds of relationship; the Queen ought to press him by letters, by entreaties, by favours, by money, and by honours, to come to Court, so as not to give the Huguenots time and opportunity to pacify him, and to make him more than ever their own; which will happen without doubt, if care be not taken, since Condé cannot stand on his own footing, without the support either of the Catholics or of the Huguenots; whence it follows that if the Catholics do not sustain him, he must necessarily go and not only fall, but throw himself, into the arms of the Huguenots. Just now that he is in doubt, it is easy to drive him, as readily to the one side as to the other. I do not mean to deny that La Limeuil can do much with him while he is . . . . with her; but if he were made to come to Court, and were offered a wife beautiful, rich, and honoured, such as the sister of M. de Guise, if honours were promised him, if favours were bestowed upon him, if to these were joined the prayers of his brother, and the persuasions of sensible men, I believe for certain that he would be won,

dinale et Condé sarano in corte, non potrano regnare, sono quelli che a Nal mettono la paura ch' hanno di se stessi. A questa difficoltà potrebbe per aventura rimediare Mil[1] assicurando Nal di aiutarla con l'autorità et bisognando con la forza a tenere il luogo che tiene.

and would become a Catholic. It is certain that the Huguenots stand in great fear, so much so, that thinking he will soon be a Papist, they say a thousand things evil of him. One sole difficulty there appears to be in this affair; it is that concord between Condé and the Cardinal cannot be agreeable to Nal. Those who are now in power, and who, if the Cardinal and Condé were at Court, could not be in power, are such as infect Nal with the fear which they have for themselves. This difficulty might perhaps be remedied by Mil[1] assuring Nal of the aid of his authority, and, if need be, of his force, to enable her to keep the place which she holds.

(*Archives de France.* Simancas, B. 19, 158/288.)

XX.

(*The Prince de Condé*) '*à Monsr de Morvilliers, Conseiller du Roy Monseigneur en son privé conseil.*'

Condé, 17 mai 1568.

Monsr de Morvilliers, Madame la Mareschalle de St André a ung affaire au conseil, duquel vous avez ouy parler et sceu mieulx le mérite à mon advis que je ne le vous pourrois icy discourir; seulement je prendray occasion là-dessus de vous prier en amy d'avoir en telle recommandation son bon droict jugé desjà par deux cours de parlement, et esgard aux menées qui se feront pour révoquer et casser tout cela, que à tout le moins, s'il est question d'ordonner des juges sur ce que sa partie adverse prétend le pétitoire n'avoir encores esté jugé, que ce soient ceulx dud. Tholouze, d'autant que jà le procès y est tout instruict, et jà une fois ce pétitoire esté renvoyé,

---

[1] The King of Spain (?).

et de penser quelle raison ny espérance de pouvoir avoir jamais seine justice il y auroit si chacun jour on venoit ainsi à casser et révoquer les premiers arrestz de cours souveraines et évocations du conseil, ne vous en faisant pas moins d'instance que si c'estoit pour mes plus propres affaires, et vous m'obligerez grandement, pour m'en revancher où j'en auray jamais le moien.

(Original ; autograph signature and address. *Bibliothèque impériale*, Mss. Colbert. 24 V°. Pièce 151.)

XXI.

Sir H. Norreys, English Ambassador, to Cecil.

(EXTRACT.)

Paris, August 23, 1567.

I have, right honorable, acordinge to your letters of the xv[th] of june, incorragid the protestants, what I maye and intend so to doo; what ther request unto Your Honor was, I truste you kepe in mynde. This I must advertise you of, that you are the only man in whom they imposed ther greatest trust ther, and saye that they thinck you not only zealous by yourselfe, but also that you have an ernest desier that God's worde shuld florishe throughe out the worlde, so that hadd it not bin by your helpe therin, religion hadd bine as colde in Inglande as it is in other places, the number of God's enemys flowing ther as they doo. Sir, the attempt that is to be made ageinst them is like to be sodein, and how sone unknowin ; wherfor I humbly crave at your hands only that as sone as you may they may receyve some comfortable newis touchinge ther demaunde, wherby you shall not only miche conforte them, but also bringe soche honor therby to Hir Majesty, being the shute anker of the pore afflicted for God's worde, but also souche creaditt to yourselve, as cannot be deuized greater. . . .

The same to Queen Elizabeth.

August 29, 1567.

. . . The prince of Conde not becinge so evill frended in courte, but that he understandethe from tyme to tyme of theyr doengs, wrote a letter of late, as I have hearde, to the Q. mother, to this effecte, that were he had notice that the Kinge have waged certaine Suisses and mynded to disadnulle and revoke th'edict of pacificacion, he coulde hope for no better frute therof then an intente to ruine religion, with the unjuste persecution of a nomber of the King's good and loyall subjects, the daunger and inconvenience whereof Her M^{ty} might well ynoughe concyder by the late troubles; whereunto the Queene returned answer by letters, assuringe him by the faythe of a princesse *et d'une femme de bien,* for so she tearmed it, that so long as she might any waies prevayle with the Kinge, her sonne, he should never breake the sayd edicte, and therof required him to assure himselfe, and if he coulde come to the courte, he shoulde be as welcome as his owne harte coulde devise; if not, to passe the tyme without any suspect or jelousie, protesting that there was nothing ment that tended to his indempnitie, what so ever was bruted abrode or conceyved to the contrary, as he should perceyve by the sequele erst it were long; and, as for the Suisses that were levied, they are to defend the frontiers for the King's better suertie and to garde the same in case the spanishe forces passing into Flaunders woulde attempt the surprise of any peece within the frenche dominions. . . .

(*State Paper Office.* French Papers)

XXII.

Letters from the King (Charles IX.) to M. de Gordes.

Meaux et Paris, 28 septembre 1567.

Monsieur de Gordes, la présente dépesche sera pour vous advertir d'une malheureuse conspiration et entreprinse, que aucuns de mes subietz ont dressée de présent contre moy et mon estat; sestans eslevez en armes et assemblez en plusieurs lieux et endroictz de mon royaume, et s'estans saisiz d'aucunes de mes villes, et mesmement de celle de Montereau-Fautyonne, de sorte que continuent en tels et si malheureux depportemens, et est tout certain que en plusieurs et divers endroitz de mon royaume, où ilz n'ont pas faute de moyens et intelligence, ce feu courra incontinent, et s'essayeront den faire de mesmes. Et d'autant que j'ay assez congneu par expérience durant les derniers troubles combien la prinse de beaucoup de mes bonnes villes m'a apporté de domaige. A ceste cause, et pour évicter que à ceste seconde foys le mesmes n'advienne, je vous prie bien fort, mon cousin, que incontinant la présente receue vous donnez ordre et pourvoyez au mieulx qu'il vous sera possible à la seureté et conservation des places de vostre gouvernement, et de sorte qu'il n'en puisse advenir aulcun inconvénient, leur faisant pour cest effect reprendre les armes et faire garde aux portes de leurs dictes villes et au demourant, affin de rompre tout à ung coup tous les dessusdicts desseings, et que je puisse, comme la raison le veult, estre le plus fort partout, je vous écris, Monsr de Gordes, que au mesme instant vous faciez, par tous les lieux et endroicts de vostre gouvernement, assembler les arrière-bans et tous mes bons et loyaulz subjectz, gentilshommes et autres, pour vous assister et estre auprès de vous, affin de rompre, avec iceulx et telles autres forces que vous pourrez mectre ensemble de ma gendarmerye, estant de présent en garnison en vostre gouvernement, tous ceulx que vous sçaurez et entendrez s'estre armez et eslevez de leur auctorité, et sans avoir eu commandement de moy ou de vous de ce faire, et qui seront participans de ladicte conspiration et entreprinse.　Pourvoyant par vous tant à la conservation des dictes villes que à celle de la campaigne, de sorte que vous en demeuriez le maistre, et que je puisse partout vostre dict gouvernement estre recogneu et obéy comme je doibz et que je m'asseure vous sçaurez très-bien faire. Qui me gardera vous en dire autre chose, priant Dieu, Monsr de Gordes, quil vous aict en sa saincte et digne garde.　Escript à Meaulx, le 28e jour de septembre 1567.

Monsr de Gordes, depuis vous avoir faict escrire la présente, et comme je la voullois signer, j'ay esté adverty que ceulx qui se sont eslevez marchoient droict à moy pour me venir enfermer dans Meaulx, où avecques moy estoient logez mes Suisses.　Ce que voyant, je me suis résolu de monter à cheval et emmener avecques moy lesdicts Suisses, pour me mectre dans ceste ville de Paris, chose qui m'a si bien et heureusement succédé que, Dieu mercy, je y suis de présent, comme aussi sont lesdicts Suisses, lesquels aussi ilz ont essayé d'entamer et les combattre; mais ils s'en sont si mal trouvez qu'ils n'en ont rapporté que la honte, dont je vous ai bien voullu advertir, afin que si, suivant leur coustume, ils faisoient courir leurs bruictz accoustumés d'y avoir eu quelque advantage, vous puissiez certiffier à tous mes bons et loyaulx subgectz qu'il n'en est riens.　C'est de Paris, le 28e jour de septembre 1567.

CHARLES.

ROBERTET.

8 octobre 1567.

Monsieur de Gordes, encores que j'estime que, suivant le premier advis que je vous ay donné depuis huict jours des nouveaux remuemens de ceulx de la nouvelle religion, vous aurez donné si bon

commencement à pourveoir à la seureté et conservation de mon
obéyssance des villes et pays de vostre gouvernement, que vous
aurez prévenu l'exécution des desseings et entreprinses de ceulx qui
sen sont peu vouloir emparer, et que, pour les maintenir en madicte
obéissance, vous aurez fait telle assemblée de forces qu'il n'en
pourra advenir aucun inconvénient; si est-ce que, continuant de
plus en plus lesdicts remuemens, et ne voyant aulcun moyen de les
paciffier, j'ay bien voullu vous en advertir derechef, à ce que vous
regardés par tous moyens possibles à mectre lesdictes villes de vostre
gouvernement en si bon estat et seureté que j'en puisse demeurer
en repos, advertissant tous mes bons et loyaulx subgetz de monstrer
par effect en ceste occasion combien ilz me sont affectionnez et desirent la conservation de ma personne et de mon estat. Pour ce
que en meilleure saison et plus nécessaire que ceste-cy ne me
sçauroient-ilz jamais tesmoignage donner du bon zelle et affection
qu'ilz ont de me faire service, faisant par vous lever le plus de
forces que vous pourrez pour vous ayder et assister à ce que dessus
tant de gens de cheval que de pied, et mesmes les arrière-bans et
légionnaires du pays, en sorte que vous puissiez garder que personne
ne s'esmeuve et face la moindre chose que ce soit préjudiciable à mes
affaires, tellement que la force demeure tousjours de mon costé; et
là où vous en sentirez aucuns qui branlent seulement pour venir
secourir et ayder à ceulx-cy de la nouvelle religion, vous les empes-
cherez de bousger par tous moyens possibles, et, si vous congnoissez
quilz soyent oppiniastres à vouloir venir et partir, vous les taillerez
et ferez mectre en pièces sans en espargner un seul; car tant plus
de mortz moings d'ennemys.

P.S. du duplicata de la lettre du 28 septembre,
daté du 9 octobre 1567.

Monsieur de Gordes, je vous avois faict par deux fois les des-
pesches cy-dessus, lesquelles, à ce que j'ay entendu, ont esté perdues,
et depuis ce temps-là ceulx qui se sont eslevez contre moy se sont
tenuz quelques jours à Claies et ès environs, et après sont venuz
loger à St-Denis, ayant bruslé quelques molins à vent des faulxbourgs dudict St-Denis et St-Martin. Ils assemblent leurs forces,
et moy les myennes, auxquelles les leurs ne seront pour y respondre,
comme j'espère, moiennant l'aide de Dieu et celle de mes bons et
loyaulx subgectz, qui ne me deffauldront en cest affaire.

Paris, 11 novembre 1567.

APP.
XXII.

Monsieur de Gordes, la présente dépesche sera pour vous avertir comme, aiant hier matin fait sortir hors de ceste ville les forces que j'ay depuis six semaines en çà mises ensemble, je les fis marcher contre mes ennemys qui estoient à S\t-Denys, les quelz se metans de leur costé en bataille, assez près toutesfoys de leurs logis dudict S\t-Denys, S\t-Ouyn, et Haubervillers, les nostres, après les avoir salués de quelques vollées d'artillerye pour les attacquer, les contraignirent enfin sur les quatre heures du seoyr de venir aux mains, où Dieu me favorisa tant que, après ung grant combat qui dura près de deux heures, la victoire demoura de mon costé, les ayant mis en routte et deffaitz, estans demourez sur place plusieurs des leurs tuéz, et ung bon nombre de prisonniers amenez en ceste ville sans perte de mon costé que de bien peu de gens. Il est vray que le malheur est tombé sur mon compère Monsieur le conestable, lequel, combatant vigoureusement et extrêmement bien avec sa trouppe, fut grandement blessé en deux ou trois endroitz. Mais à la fin, par sa vertu et de mes autres bons serviteurs, le camp où se donna la bataille m'est demouré, y aiant cousché ceste nuict mes gens de pied. Nous ne sçavons point encores quelz chefs des leurs sont demourez sur la place, mais aujourd'huy l'on se recongnoistra, et, s'il reste quelque chose à faire, on n'y oubliera riens, faisant cependant avancer de toutes pars mes forces. Desquelles bonnes nouvelles je vous prie faire part à tous mes bons serviteurs de delà, et en faire louer et rendre grâce à Dieu.

Paris, 14 novembre 1567.

Monsieur de Gordes, depuys vous avoyr donné advis de l'heureux succez et gaing de la bataille que Dieu me donna lundy dernier contre le prince de Condé et ceulx de sa suytte, je vous veulx bien advertir de ce qui est depuys succédé, qui est en somme que, voyant ledict prince et ceulx de sa dicte trouppe la grande perte qu'ils avoyent faicte en ceste rencontre d'un bien grand nombre de gentilz-hommes des plus apparans des leurs, et la retraicte que ce mesme jour fut faicte par plusieurs de son party hors son camp et armée, et quant et quant ayant ledict prince et eulx esté advertys comme cejourd'huy je me délibérois de leur aller présenter une seconde bataille, il est advenu que hier au soyr sur les sept heures telle peur et alarme se mist en leur armée, qu'ilz sont deslogez et partis tous ceste nuyt dernière dudict Sainct-Denis, en telle haste et confusion que telle retraicte et deslogement si souldain ne se peult myeulx appeler que une bonne fuytte, et, pource qu'ilz ont encores quelques forces estendues en divers lieux, estimant qu'ilz se veullent aller joindre à eulx, je suis maintenant résolu de les suyvre avec mon armée quelque part quilz aillent, pour avec une aultre seconde victoyre mettre fin à ceste guerre. De quoy je vous ay bien voulu advertir, affin de vous faire part ordinairement de tout ce qui me succèdera en ceste guerre et que le faciez entendre à mes bons serviteurs de delà.

Paris, 17 novembre 1567.

Mon cousin, je vous veulx bien faire entendre comme, après qu'il a pleu à Dieu d'appeler à soy mon cousin le duc de Montmorency, per et connestable de France, j'ay faict et estably pour chef de mes armes et pour mon lieutenant général, représentant ma personne par tous mes royaume et pays, mon frère le duc d'Anjou et de Bourbonnois, sçaichant très-bien que, pour le zelle et grande affection que naturellement il me porte et au bien de mes dicts royaume et subgectz, il se saura très-dignement acquiter de telle charge, à mon contentement et satisfaction, au bien et soullaigement de mes dicts subgectz. De quoy estant par moy adverty, je vous prye, mon cousin, que doresnavant, quant il se passera quelque affaire en vostre gouvernement qui concernera le faict des armes, vous vueillez, oultre ce que vous m'escriprez et à la Royne Madame ma mère, en donner aussy particullièrement advis à mon dict frère, qui vous fera souvent entendre mon intention sur toutes choses. Et de ce que dessus vous advertirez les cappitaines des places et aultres aiant charge de gens de guerre en vostre gouvernement, affin que ung chacun saiche et entende à qui, pour le faict desdictes armes, ilz auront maintenant à s'adresser.

(*Archives de Condé.*)

XXIII.

[Documents relating to the negotiations in December 1567.[1]]

The Prince de Condé ' à Monseigneur ' (the Duc d'Anjou).

Bray-sur-Seine, 7 décembre 1567.

Monseigneur, par le premier mémoire qu'il vous a pleu envoier à Madame la marquise, ma belle-mère,[2] pour me faire voir, et par la dernière lettre que pareillement il vous a pleu luy escripre, qu'elle

---

[1] These documents are twenty-one in number. The first is dated December 1st. Those here printed are either written by the Prince de Condé, or present some feature of special interest.

[2] Jacqueline de Rohan, marquise de Rothelin.

m'a aussi faict voir, j'ai trouvé voz intentions telles que, pour y obéir et satisfaire, il me semble, Monseigneur, que le meilleur sera, suivant led. mémoire, que les deux armées demeurent fermes et arrestées où elles sont de présent, sans qu'elles puissent attenter ou entreprendre par armes ou autrement l'un sur l'autre, en quelque façon que ce soit, pendant l'abstinence et suspension des armes, laquelle commancera (puisque tel est vostre bon plaisir) lundi au matin, et finira jeudy à mesme heure ; qui sera, ce faisant, ung moien pour faciliter les choses et couper chemin à tous deffiances et jalouxies. Et la présente, Monseigneur, servira de l'assurance qu'il vous plaist requérir de moy.

The Prince de Condé to the Duc d'Anjou.

S. L. 17 décembre 1567.[1]

Monseigneur, ceste compaignie, aiant veu les articles signez de la main du Roy Monseigneur, que le Sr de Combault a apportez de vostre part sur la pacification de ces troubles, a esté d'avis, et moy avecques elle, de dépescher le Sr de Théligny[2] vers Sa Majesté, pour la suplier très-humblement qu'il luy plaise déléguer quelque nombre de gens de bien, d'expérience, et amateurs de paix, lesquelz, avecques Messrs les cardinal de Chastillon, conte de la Rochefoucault et de Bouchavennes, puissent conférer ensemble sur les poinctz qui requièrent interprétation et esclaircissement ; qui sera, par ce moien, gaigner le temps qui pourroit couller en allées et venues, afin que, aiant, sur le tout pris une bonne résolution, toute la France soit désormais soullagée d'un repos perpétuel, et le bien de ceste couronne demeure asseuré, qui est le seul but auquel nous avons toujours visé et prétendu.

Monseigneur, je mestois oublié de vous supplier très-humblement de faire bailler aud. Sr de Téligny ung sauf-conduict ; ce que, s'il vous plaist, Monseigneur, vous ferez afin qu'en toute seuretté, il puisse, si vous le trouvez bon, aller et venir sans dangier ny inconvénient, puisque c'est pour une si saincte occasion.

The Prince de Condé to the Queen-Mother.

Camp de Saint-Martin, 17 décembre 1567.

Madame, affin de satisfaire à l'invitation (?) de Voz Mates, et effectuer les bons commancemens d'une paciffication et tranquilité en

---

[1] The next letter shows that this was written from Saint-Martin.

[2] The instructions from the Prince de Condé to Téligny are dated from the camp near Épernay, December 16.

ce royaume, non moins desirée de nous que grandement nécessaire à ung chacun, après avoir bien considéré le mémoire (?) que le Sr de Combault a apporté, et icelluy communiqué aux principaulx de ceste armée, nous avons tous ensemble advisé de despescher le Sr de Théligny, présent porteur, vers vous, pour supplier très-humblement vosd. Ma^{tez} qu'il vous plaise depputer quelques bons et advisez personnaiges amateurs de paix, lesquelz, avecques Mes^{rs} les cardinal de Chastillon, conte de la Rochefoucault et de Bouchavennes, qui ont esté nommez de ceste part, puissent parachever et esclaircir ce que sur icelle pourroit tumber en difficulté, et se trouver la part qu'il vous plaira ordonner ; qui sera, en ce faisant, Madame, establir une parfaicte réconciliation et union parmy voz subjetz, et la seureté de cest estat, ainsi que plus amplemant la suffisance dud. Sr de Théligny vous sçaura très-bien discourir.

The Admiral de Chatillon to the Duc d'Anjou.

Notre-Dame-de-l'Espine, 21 décembre 1567.

Monseigneur, le sieur de Chimiervan, que vous dépeschastes hier devers Monsieur le prince de Condé, passa là où j'estois, lequel me dist de vostre part que vous entendiez qu'en attendant le retour de Monsieur de Telligny, auquel vous aviez donné congé d'aller trouver le Roy, que vostre armée ne passast point de là la rivière de Marne, et qu'il ne se feist nul acte d'hostilité. Toutesfoys, contre cela sont venuz quelquesungs de vostre armée ceste nuict donner à ung logis auquel il y avoit quelques gens de cheval logez de ceste avant-garde. Chose que je ne puys penser, Monseigneur, que vous entendiez ; et pourtant vous supliray-je très-humblement de m'en vouloir faire raison, et vous pouvant asseurer que, quant il se fust présenté toutes les plus belles occasions du monde, je n'eusse souffert que l'on eust rien entrepris contre la parolle qui m'avoit esté donnée de vostre part, comme j'ay donné charge à ce gentilhomme présent porteur vous faire entendre, et lequel pourtant je vous supplieray très-humblement, de vouloir escouter et croire.

The Prince de Condé to the Duc d'Anjou.

Apremont, 27 décembre 1567.

Monseigneur, aïant veu la dépesche qu'il a pleu à Leurs Ma^{tez} me faire par le Sr de Combault, ensemble le sauf-conduict envoié par Monsr le cardinal de Chastillon et ceulx qui le doivent accompagner en ceste négociation, limité jusques au nombre de vingt chevaulx seullement, j'ay bien ozé prandre la hardiesse de vous envoier ce gentilhomme, présent porteur, pour vous remonstrer très-humblement que la qualité de mond. S^r le cardinal, qui n'a acoustumé de marcher par païs avecques si peu de train, ny son eage ne permectent pas maintenant de commencer mesmement, attendu l'incommodité des logis par les champs et en ceste saison, sans y comprandre les S^{rs} qui l'accompagneront; vous suppliant, à ceste cause, Monseigneur, aussi très-humblement, qu'il vous plaise luy voulloir envoier de vostre part ung aultre sauf-conduict, par lequel il puisse s'acheminer avecques lad. compagnie jusques au nombre de cent chevaulx, qui est le moins à quoy ilz doivent estre réduictz, et pour plus grande authorisation de ceste charge vostre bon plaisir pareillement soit députer quelque gentilhomme ou personnaige d'honneur et de réputation qui les vienne recevoir vers Bar-le-Duc pour les vous conduire, si le trouvez bon, ou à tout le moins vers leursd. Majestez; ainsi, Monseigneur, que de toutes ces choses led. porteur vous fera très-humblement requête de ma part.

(*Bibliothèque impériale.* Colbert, 24 V°.)

XXIV.

Letters from the Prince de Condé to the King on the Peace of Chartres.[1]

Bonneval, 30 mars 1568.

Sire, il seroit impossible à moy et à toute ceste compaignie de pouvoir assés très-humblement remercier Vostre Majesté de la grâce et faveur qu'il vous a pleu faire à nous et à tout ce roïaume, en octroïant ung si grand bénéfice comme celuy de la paix, laquelle, nous espérons, Sire, moiennant la faveur et assistence de Dieu, apportera autant de plaisir et d'utilité au bien de vostre estat et de voz subjectz comme les malheurs de la guerre ont causé d'ennuiz et de calamitez. Et combien que ceste espérance nous doive rendre ung grand contentement, si estimerois-je ce contentement fort petit sans celle qui me promet d'avoir encores une fois en ma vie ce bien de vous pouvoir faire en quelque endroict ung très-humble service et qui vous soit agréable; n'aïant voulu faillir, Sire, pour aucunement satisfaire à mon devoir, incontinent dépescher le Sr de Boucart, présent porteur, vers Vostre Majesté, à cest effect, l'aïant prié vous

---

[1] Each of these letters to the King was accompanied by one to the Queen-Mother, repeating the same sentiments in nearly similar terms.

faire par mesme moïen les très-humbles remonstrances que j'ay pensé
estre nécessaires pour plus facilement effectuer vostre bonne intention, estant certain que si la bonté de Vostre Majesté daigne l'escouter, elle prendra de bonne part sa très-humble suplication, pour
y pourvoir selon vostre bon plaisir.

(*Bibliothèque impériale.* Colbert, 24 V⁸.)

Orléans, 5 avril 1568.

Sire, le retour de Messieurs le cardinal de Chastillon, conte de la
Rochefoucault et de Bouchaveines, par lesquels j'ai entendu le
favorable accueil que de votre bonté et grâce il vous a pleu leur
faire, aiant eu cest honneur de baiser les mains de Vostre Majesté
avecques un bon visage, m'a tellement faict participer à la joye et
contentement qu'ils en ont rapporté, que j'estimerois me faire trop
grand tort si j'oubliois de vous en faire par ceste lettre ung très-
humble remerciement, attendant que moi-mesme puisse, comme ilz
ont faict, joyr de pareille félicité et faveur.   Ne voulant au demeurant faillir à vous dire, Sire, comme, suivant vostre commandement,
aussitost qu'ilz ont esté arrivez, nous avons commencé, en la présence
du Sʳ de Verdun, à vacquer au faict des reistres, tant pour le regard
de ce qui leur sera deu, que pour haster leur partement, aiant cependant mandé Monsʳ le duc Casimir et ses collonelz pour avecques
eulx faire ung arrest final.   En quoy, Sire, nous travaillerons
avecques tel devoir et diligence, qu'il ne sera rien omis de ce qui
regardera le bien de vostre service, remettant sur la dépesche que
vous faict ledict sieur de Verdun à vous témoigner de quel pied
nous y marchons, comme je m'asseure qu'il ne fauldra de vous en
escrire à la vérité ce que desja il en a peu congnoistre.   J'espère,
puisque iceluy Sʳ duc Cazimir est icy, lequel y arriva hier au soir,
que cejourd'huy nous avancerons beaucoup ce négoce, duquel je
desire infiniment voir l'issue, et eulx en chemin de leur retour, afin
de lever de toutes partz toutes occasions de défiances, et seurement
joyr du bénéfice de la paix qu'il vous a pleu nous octroier, et de
laquelle je suis certain que Vostre Majesté desire l'exécution, et
toutes violences et excès cesser.   Sur ce propos d'excès, Sire,
la juste occasion que le Sʳ d'Esternay a de se complaindre et
douloir des torts que Foissy lui a faitz, aiant contre le droict de la
tresve que Vostre Majesté avoit donnée, au mespris de vostre exprès
commandement et de celui de Monseigneur vostre frère, faict brusler
sa maison de Lamothe, et commis tant d'exécrables indignitez que
les barbares ne sçauroient pis faire.   Et non content de ce, depuis la
paix publiée, il y est retourné pour parachever ce qui restoit à

ruiner, tenant, comme il a eu advertissement, ses serviteurs assiégez. Ce sont crimes, Sire, qui sont si insupportables, qu'il est bien besoing, tant pour la gravité du faict que pour la nécessité de l'exemple, en faire faire une prompte punition. Qui me faict suplier très-humblement Vostre Majesté, Sire, d'y vouloir mettre la main, à celle fin que, la justice en estant faicte, ung chacun congnoisse que vous ne voulez tollérer telz maléfices, ains conserver indifféremment tous vos subjectz soubz vostre protection avecques l'observation de vos édictz, qui sera ung acte digne d'une roialle grandeur.

Sire, depuis ma lettre escripte, j'ai esté averty qu'il y a en ce lieu encores environ quatre cents marcs d'argent en roiaulx et sizailles prestz à mectre le coing; ce qui a esté différé à cause de vostre édict. Et pour ce, Sire, que cela pourroit bien servir à satisfaire aux debtes, s'il vous plaist, Sire, vous en envoirez vostre permission, et Monsr de Verdun y prendra garde.

(*Archives of the département du Nord.*)

Orléans, 7 avril 1568.

Sire, aïant cejourd'huy arresté le tout avec Monsieur le duc Jehan Casimir, j'ay bien voullu vous dépescher le Sr de Bouchavennes, présent porteur, pour vous faire entendre bien au long les poinctz qui s'y sont traictez, et demain que le tout sera bien mis au net et par ordre, je ne fauldray vous renvoier soudain le Sr de Verdun, lequel aussi portera à Vostre Ma^{té} les nouvelles du partement des reistres, qui sera demain, et comme j'ay faict sortir des villes de Bloys et de Baugency les gens de guerre que je y avois, dont voz officiers aujourd'huy en font telle garde que bon leur semble, et dépesche les gentilshommes vers la Rochelle, Auxerre et autres villes, pour en faire de mesme, ainsy que plus amplement vous récitera ced. porteur, que je supplie très-humblement voulloir croire comme moy-mesmes; au demeurant, je supplieray très-humblement Vostre Ma^{té} que luy plaise me faire tant d'honneur et de faveur que mes petitz enfans puissent joyr du bénéfice de l'édict, comme voz autres subjectz, et que je les puisse veoir en ma maison, où j'espère m'y en aller.

(*Bibliothèque impériale.* Colbert, 24 V^e.)

Orléans, 9 avril 1568.

Sire, Vostre Majesté entendra par le Sr de Verdun, intendant de vos finances, présent porteur, ce qui a esté arresté avec les reistres et la peine que nous avons eue de les faire condescendre à raison, pour estre gens de difficile convention et fort malaisez à contenter. Comme des autres particularitez il vous sçaura plus amplement bien rendre compte. En quoy nous n'avons omis à y faire tout le bon mesnagement qu'il a esté possible pour le bien de vostre service, comme aussi je ne manqueray jamais en toute autre chose, lorsque j'auray cest honneur d'y estre emploié. Tant y a, Sire, que finalement nous en sommes venuz à bout, et deslogent cejourd'huy pour s'acheminer à leur retour. Cela faict, nous avons advisé mander partout de faire retirer les forces qui estoient aux garnisons, afin de rendre les villes en leur premier trafficq et libre commerce, ce qui est de ceste heure exécuté ; tellement que Monsr l'admiral et tous les seigneurs qui sont icy avecques moy, partons demain pour nos en aller en nos maisons, laissant ceste ville, au mesme repos et bonne union, en la garde des habitans qu'elle estoit auparavant les troubles. Maintenant je vous suplieray très-humblement, Sire, veu que de nostre part il a esté entièrement satisfaict à tout ce que nous avons pensé estre nécessaire pour affectuer l'exécution de vostre édict, qu'il vous plaise commander que mes enfans me soient renvoiez, à celle fin que je les puisse nourrir et eslever pour vous faire quelque jour le très-humble et fidelle service auquel ilz sont dédiés et consacrés, estant certain que Dieu leur fera et à moy la grâce qu'ils ne dégénèreront de la dévotion et prompte obéissance du père. Aussi, pour cest effect, Vostre Majesté, s'il luy plaist, ne me refusera en une si juste requeste.

(*Archives of the département du Nord.*)

END OF THE FIRST VOLUME.

LONDON: PRINTED BY
SPOTTISWOODE AND CO., NEW-STREET SQUARE
AND PARLIAMENT STREET